A COLORFUL PASSION

"Do not go," she whispered, her voice husky. She strung kisses along his jaw. "Do not. I need you."

She claimed his lips with a kiss both soft and lush, and he was lost in the maelstrom of need. He pulled her against him, surrounded her with arms and thighs, and slanted his head to deepen the kiss. Leila accepted it all, her body begging for more.

Heat lightning sparked around them, brilliant in red and blue and yellow.

Heat lightning? Inside? Red and blue? Jack opened his eyes, stilling at the sparkle of colors dancing about them.

Djinn emotions show as colors in the air.

Djinn emotions.

His gaze fastened on the turquoise tablet at Leila's neck. A turquoise tablet like the one all djinn wore as a symbol of their magic.

She was a djinni! It wasn't attraction he felt for her, it was a bloody spell!

KATHLEEN NANCE

Enchantment

LOVE SPELL NEW YORK CITY

LOVE SPELL®

September 2002

Published by

Dorchester Publishing Co., Inc.
276 Fifth Avenue
New York, NY 10001

ISBN 0-505-52484-8

The name "Love Spell" and its logo are trademarks of Dorchester Publishing Co., Inc.

Printed in the United States of America.

Visit us on the web at www.dorchesterpub.com.

Enchantment

Chapter One

Two years, twenty-nine days, three hours, and fourteen minutes after he faced the horrifying truth that magic existed, biomedical engineer Jack Montgomery finally found a way to negate it.

In his deserted lab, Jack held up the intricate chain forged from titanium and copper wires, and the sweet, familiar thrill of discovery, of a problem solved, coursed through him. A rainbow-faceted crystal gleamed from the center of the metal network, and attached to the crystal was a switch, a tiny, powerful battery and a computer chip. Energy flow, that was the key. Disrupt the flow of energy and the magic would fail.

At least, that was the theory. The computer simulations worked to perfection, but he hadn't had an opportunity to do an actual field test.

"Dr. Montgomery? Are you still here?" Maggie, the

cleaning woman, poked her head into the lab. A rubber band pulled her graying red hair off her scrubbed, shiny face.

"Yeah, Maggie, I've got a project at critical." Hastily he slipped the chain around his neck and tucked it beneath his collar. He'd done the research on his own time, used his own financial resources, but if it got out he'd been researching *magic* . . . A shudder coursed through him. The resulting ridicule would ruin his professional career and taint all his other work.

Maggie pushed in a cart loaded with mop, broom, and cleaning supplies. "You work too much. I see you in here too many nights." She dumped the mop into a bucket of water, then began to swab the floor of the lab. "Gotta admit, though, it's nice to see someone live when I come in here. All them legs and hands give me the creeps."

"They're only models and prostheses, Maggie. Polymers and silicon and computer chips."

Maggie gave a snort. "Big words don't make 'em easier to mop beside. I know you folks do good work here—ain't the fact my man's walking about proof of it?—but I saw this movie once about a hand creeping around, strangling folks. I keep expecting one to get me right here." She clutched her throat.

He laughed, sticking his hands into the pockets of his jeans. "I promise, no malevolent limbs here."

Only ones that might one day give a child a chance to walk. Yet, to ease her mind, he waited with Maggie until she finished, then followed her out of the lab, turning off the lights and locking up behind him.

"Thanks, Dr. Montgomery."

"Any time."

Waving at him, she pushed her bucket and cart down the narrow hall to the pharmacology labs, while Jack took the stairs out of the Tulane Medical School building. Heat slammed against him with the subtlety of a brick. Though the hour was past ten, New Orleans had not cooled with sunset, and the humidity warred with heat to claim discomfort bragging rights in a record-hot May. Every night solemn-faced newscasters intoned the facts of daily heat index and inches of rainfall below average.

He retrieved his car from the lot, then headed to his small Uptown house. The engine gave a jerk, reminding him he hadn't taken it in for scheduled maintenance. The past two years, he'd had neither time nor finances for anything but necessities. Research didn't pay what private practice did, and his savings had been depleted by his secret research into magic.

The weight of the device pressed against his chest, and the tingling reminder reassured him.

The sacrifices were worth it. His sister, Isis, had married a genie—or djinni as he was told they preferred—and Jack could not forget his firsthand experiences with the power that Darius wielded. Minor annoyances, true, but Jack had been unable to stop the djinni's telepathic speech inside his skull, nor had he been able to avoid sharing private matters when the djinni used a Truthspeak spell. The whims of a worker of magic had controlled him, and for a scientist dedicated to logic, equations, and combating the ravages of nature and disease, it was a shattering experience.

Never again, he swore, would Jack Montgomery remain powerless in the face of such a threat.

Inside the house, he tossed his keys onto the hall table, then froze, seized by a strange, compelling restlessness. It whispered through him, faint and alluring, an invitation to prolong the night. Was it the aftermath of achieving a goal long sought? Eagerness to test his theories? Faint discontent with the silence and plainness of his rooms? Whatever, he only knew he couldn't stay inside, not tonight. He tugged off his tie, exchanged the button shirt for a plain white T-shirt and loafers for athletic shoes. After a moment's indecision he shrugged and left the device around his neck. Wouldn't hurt to get used to wearing it. He ran a comb through his blond hair—a trip to the barber had also been postponed—before heading to Brigand's, a tavern around the corner.

The bar's interior was familiar: dark and cool and overlaid with the hum of conversation and the flicker of televisions set to ESPN and whatever channels carried a sporting event. Tonight it was Stanley Cup hockey, Arabian League soccer, and figure skating. Nobody watched the figure skating.

Jack found an empty chair at the end of the polished wood bar.

"Evening, Dr. Montgomery," the bartender greeted him. "Haven't seen you in a while. What'll you have? A draft?"

"Sure. How's your daughter?"

"Her artificial leg's working good, and she's excited

about going to that camp you told us about." The bartender handed him beer in a chilled mug.

Jack took a long swallow, enjoying the cold and the faintly bitter taste. "A lot of my patients have been there; she'll have a good time."

"Can you believe this heat? Hope you're getting out of the city this summer."

"I have a race in Canada in August."

"Another one of them adventure races?" The bartender shook his head. "Sliding across ravines, climbing up mountains, tromping through jungles—can't say as I see the fun in that."

Jack didn't answer, unable to explain the thrill of the challenge and unwilling to discuss the need to master self and environment. He'd been reclusive and frail as a child. Now he recognized the symptoms of post-traumatic stress, but then he'd only recognized the fear. It had made him the victim of schoolyard bullies, until Beau, his twin, had badgered him into a tae kwon do class. The martial arts discipline had restored his confidence and his health.

Since then, he never took either one for granted.

While the bartender turned to another customer, Jack drank his beer, feeling weariness settle across him at last. He rotated on his stool to survey the room.

At once his gaze lit on the lone woman sitting in the corner. How had he missed seeing her when he'd come in?

Sultry. Alluring. Tempting. The adjectives chased through his mind, but none was adequate. Delicate cheeks, full lips, exotic eyes, and straight, black hair.

He couldn't tell how long, only that it reached well past her shoulders and shone like polished obsidian. The V of her ruby-colored dress revealed some very feminine curves.

She was as out of place here as a wizard at an AMA convention.

And she was looking straight at him.

When his gaze met hers, her lips tilted in invitation. He looked around, unable to believe the invitation was meant for him, but no other likely candidates emerged. When he glanced back, she smiled again with the barest hint of seduction and leaned back. Shadows created a mystery of her face, but her body was an open invitation.

Pure sin and sex in a stunning package.

The odd restlessness reappeared. It tugged his muscles, urged him to get off the chair, brought his nerves—and other body parts—to attention. He dragged in a deep breath, hoping for air, getting only heat.

He downed a slug of beer, resisting her. His plans included a quick drink, nothing more. He was tired— or had been until one minute ago—and he'd never gone in for the singles bar pick-up scene. Tonight, though, this woman tempted him to take a chance, to lose himself in the pleasures of uncomplicated sex.

Determined to maintain his control, Jack gave her a regretful smile and turned around, away from temptation.

*　*　*

He had turned his back on her! Leila gaped at Jack Montgomery before she remembered that a mouth hanging open was not attractive. She closed it with a snap. *What call had he for such arrogance?*

If only her power was stronger, the attraction spell would have worked.

But no, she was the weak one, the one who'd been forced, from necessity, to develop other talents in a world where individual skill with magic secured both rank and comfort.

She would have to think of something else; all the portents said this was a night of auspicious change. Maybe one of the other patrons of this establishment?

She glanced around, her insides shriveling at the thought. Like that man staring at her? He looked more like a troll than a human. With a practiced haughty glance, she dismissed him. She would give her chosen . . . donor a night of delights he would long remember. Was she not entitled to a little pleasure in the act as well?

None of these others appealed to her like Jack Montgomery had from the first moment she'd seen him in the picture Isis kept in her work room. She liked the light-colored hair, so different from that of most djinn, especially now that he had grown it longer. She liked the well-formed body, the strong nose, the serious mouth. From the picture, she had not realized he had a thin scar that ran from his brow to his jaw. It did not lessen his appeal.

But what she liked most were his eyes. They were blue, the deep blue of the precious wells on her home world of Kaf, and Leila thought she saw kindness hidden in them.

He had other attractions as well. Isis said her brother was a near genius who had earned p-h-d and m-d in record speed. Leila had no idea what p-h-d or m-d was, but she knew what genius was, and if she could not have a man of power, she would take one of intelligence.

Moreover, he looked virile.

He was a good choice. It would be Jack Montgomery and no other. Her stomach clenched in anticipation, and for the first time in many cycles, she felt the stirrings of true desire.

By Solomon's shield, if only the man would cooperate! Instead, he was downing the last of his brew, handing the tavern keeper his barter, and *leaving*. Jack glanced once in her direction, and Leila gave him her most enticing smile.

He paused, took a step toward her.

Surreptitiously she sprinkled a tiny amount of red powder on the candle at her table. The rich scents of frankincense and juniper eased through the room. Leila rose, murmuring the words needed to draw her chosen lover to her side. Every bit of her small store of power enticed him to depart with her. He took another step closer.

Until a man entered and clapped Jack on the back with a hearty thwap. Jack blinked and turned away again.

The spell was broken. At least on Jack Montgomery.

Not so with the troll eyeing her from the tall wooden table.

Jack greeted his adventure-racing teammate absently, still bemused by the scent that lingered in his memory, almost as if he could smell the perfume of the mysterious lady. So, too, did the sudden erotic images persist. He pictured her spreading her dark, silky hair over him. Touching him in ways that raised urgent needs. Smiling as he entered her.

He shook his head, trying to clear the arousal that sent blood rushing low and fast. When had he started to think in poetic words and pornographic images? The strange urge to join with her was dissipating when she slid from the room, silent and smooth.

"So, I hear Beau's thinking about a run for district attorney." His teammate's hearty comment intruded. "You going to campaign for him?"

"Beau's the speechmaker. Not me." Jack frowned when he noticed the hulk at the bar throw down a bill and leave after her.

"How you two can look so alike but act so different I never have figured out."

"Look, I gotta run. Talk to you later." Not bothering with an excuse to his friend, Jack abruptly followed the bully out.

His gut burned when he saw the man, his hand over the lady's mouth, crowding her into a shabby car. She wasn't making it easy for him, but her delicate strength was no match for brutish power.

"Let her go," Jack commanded, his voice clear in the thick night.

The brute scowled at him. "Who's gonna make me?"

"You've lost the element of surprise here, pal. The lady's clearly unwilling and she's no longer alone. You're talking more effort than it's worth now." As he spoke, he closed the distance between them, trying to see if the attacker kept a gun or knife handy. None visible, but that didn't mean there wasn't something concealed in his lumpy pockets. Always try calm intellect and reason first was Jack's motto, especially if the enemy was twitchy and maybe packing a weapon. Keep your enemy off balance.

"I say she'll be interested enough once I get started."

"Everyone in the bar saw what was happening when I came out. I'm sure they've called the police. Now, we can stand here and discuss the matter until they come, or you might take this opportunity to get the hell away from here." Jack lifted his brows, and, as if on cue, a distant siren wailed.

The would-be rapist took off at a run.

"Are you not going to chase him? Apprehend him for your protectors?" The woman's voice was soft, melodious, tremulous. She had a faint accent, a quaint inflection to her words.

"Despite recent actions to the contrary, lady, I'm not that stupid." Jack clenched his fist against a primitive desire to chase after the jerk and wipe his face on the sidewalk.

"But your protectors—"

"Protectors?" He'd bet that English wasn't her first language. "You mean the police? That was a bluff. Nobody paid any attention to my leaving."

"Oh." She drew the sound out, and Jack wasn't sure if she was disappointed or relieved. "My name is Leila, not Lady."

"Leila. It's a pretty name. I'm Jack."

He held out a hand to shake, but instead she clasped his hands between hers, then leaned forward and gave him delicate kisses, one on each cheek, one on the tips of his fingers. "Thank you."

She was soft and oh, so warm and trembling. "Are you all right?"

"I—" Her legs seemed unsteady, for she swayed against him. His arm came around her for support, and her perfume, exotic and spicy, wafted across him. Jack fought the instinctive arousal it stimulated. After that scare, the last thing she needed was another horny male.

"Let me take you back to the bar. You can sit, have a drink. The bartender may know that jerk and we'll call the police—"

"No." She gripped his hand. Her nails were perfect, glossy ovals. "I cannot go back there. Where he was. Is there someplace private and quiet? Where I can compose myself?"

"My home is around the corner, if you'd feel safer—"

"Your home would be fine."

As they walked the short distance, she leaned against

him, a silent request for his strength. She couldn't be aware of the way her breast pressed against his side, for when he tried to shift away, she only murmured an incoherent protest and settled closer. Yet he was well aware of the generous silk-covered contour rubbing against his bare arm.

Leila didn't wear a bra. Obvious by feel. Obvious by the gap in her gown.

Dragging his gaze upward, he cleared his throat and began a mental recitation of the periodic table of elements, from hydrogen to ununhexium. Leila hummed, or chanted, under her breath, strange words he couldn't understand and could barely hear. Her fingers toyed with the turquoise tablet she wore on a delicate gold chain. The world around him narrowed to only her voice, her scent, her touch. Blood raced from head to heart to groin, filling him with heat beyond heat indexes and drought.

Number twenty-six. Iron. Symbol Fe. Atomic weight of fifty-six. Number twenty-seven. Cobalt. Symbol Co. Atomic weight of fifty-nine.

Her hair brushed against his cheek, soft as a kitten's tail. Every step brought the massage of muscle and curves. Her breast still rested against his arm, and he saw the protruding nipple. *Touch me*, it seemed to call. His body stiffened in masculine counterpoint. *Taste me.* The elements faded away behind a confusing whirlwind of desire that caught him by surprise with its intensity and its demand for relief.

Jack was breathing hard, and sweat dampened his back by the time he gestured her into his home. He'd thought that rampant hormone surges had been left behind with acne and high school proms. Inside he didn't bother with a light, just gestured her to a chair while he backed toward the kitchen.

"I'll get you something to drink."

He had to get away from her before he embarrassed himself or frightened her.

Apparently, Leila had other plans. Instead of letting him go, she laced her arms behind his neck and reached on tiptoe to kiss him. "Do not go," she whispered, her voice husky. She strung kisses along his jaw. "Do not. I need you."

She claimed his lips with a kiss both soft and lush, and he was lost in the maelstrom of need. He pulled her against him, surrounded her with arms and thighs, and slanted his head to deepen the kiss. Leila accepted it all, her body begging for more.

Heat lightning sparked around them, brilliant in red and blue and yellow.

Heat lightning? Indoors? Red and blue? Jack opened his eyes, stilling at the sparkle of colors dancing about them.

Djinn emotions show as colors in the air. Isis had told him that once.

Djinn emotions.

His gaze fastened on the turquoise tablet at Leila's neck. A turquoise tablet akin to the one Darius wore, to the one all djinn wore as a symbol of their magic.

She was a djinni! It wasn't attraction, it was a bloody spell!

He jerked away from the kiss, though his body protested with a sharp pain. "Stop it," he rasped. "Dammit, stop that magic. I will not be your puppet."

"No-o-o-o," Leila moaned. "Not now!" She clutched his hand, her fingers digging into the flesh. "Come with me."

She was stronger than she looked. A whirlwind whipped about them, blinding him. He felt himself lifted, spun around as easily as Dorothy's house in the tornado.

She was transporting them to her world. To Kaf!

No! He fumbled at his neck. The chain. Dammit, it was stuck beneath his shirt.

The room faded from view. He felt himself sliding, though nothing of substance touched him.

There, he had it!

All that was familiar vanished.

He clutched at the chain and thumbed the switch. The battery powered on; metal vibrated and the crystal scorched his palm with electricity, but he held on to his lifeline. Noise filled his ears. The whoosh of a roller coaster. The whine of vibrations. Light sucked into his hand, rushing like the Mississippi at flood stage, then vanished, leaving only darkness, utter and absolute.

An explosion erupted from his palm. Brilliant lights of red and white blinded him, while a dizzying tumble stole all hearing, all sensation.

Jack had one final thought before unconsciousness overtook him.

The computer simulations had missed a few relevant possibilities.

Chapter Two

Leila sat up with a groan. Every part of her body ached, her limbs felt like they were made of mahogany, and something hard and sharp poked her bottom. A rock? She was sitting on a rock? She never sat on rocks. She was supposed to be in her home, sitting on pillows.

What had happened? Where in Solomon's name was she? She shoved back the strands of hair blown into her face—by the spirits, she must appear a mess—and looked around.

Wisps of smoke spiraled out between the cracks of the flat, black rock where she sat. Jagged, dark spires and towers of stone appeared in all directions, broken only by smoke, intermittent plateaus, and the occasional patch of stubborn, green plants. She breathed in the faint scent of scorched metal. Overhead the familiar yellow sun blazed, matching the dry heat coming from the earth below. Past midday on Kaf.

Kaf, yes, but not her serene, breeze-cooled garden. Instead, they'd ended up in the Tower Lands. No question about it. She'd been here once, for her final test before leaving school, and she'd hated every moment in the wild, desolate land. No djinn *chose* to travel to the Tower Lands. How had she ended up here?

Her *ma-at*, though weak, had always been well controlled. She'd taken pride in the fact that the incantations she did master were precise and perfect. What had happened? Her gaze ran around, searching for some sign, some answer. Something had gone wrong while she was transferring with Jack—

Jack! Had he been brought here, too? She shot to her feet, fear clutching her stomach. Where was he? Had he been injured? She had intended no harm. She breathed a sigh of relief when she heard his voice calling.

"Leila?"

"Over here."

Jack strode around a thick jut of gray rock. Smoke swirled around him like a mantle, obscuring his features, revealing only long legs, strong arms, and that intriguing blond hair. A gust of hot air blew the smoke away. He wasn't hurt, but he also was not happy, judging by the storm in his face. "Where are we?" he demanded tightly.

"The Tower Lands."

"In Kaf?"

"Yes." Disappointment sat heavy and sour in her

stomach, like a too-ripe fruit. So much for the mood of desire. So much for her plans. She took his arm in a gentle grip, biting her lip against the unpleasant but inevitable loss. "I'll transport you back—"

He shook off her hand. "No magic. I'll walk."

"You cannot walk back to Terra. Only transport."

His lips tightened as though he'd just swallowed a bitter lemon. "Then I'll find my sister, and Isis can take me back. Which direction is her home?"

"You desire to walk to the city? To Tepe-ma-adaktu? The way is treacherous. We use these lands as a physical trial to hone and focus our *ma-at*. It is not safe to stay here long."

"Which direction?"

Stubborn human. She glanced at the sun, at the shape of the rocks, at the distant horizon, trying to recall the single time she'd been here. "That way," she guessed.

Without another word, Jack set off in the direction she had pointed.

He was leaving her? Just walking away? Fine! He was so anxious to walk, let him. His foolishness would not be her discomfort. She pictured her comfortable home—the soft pillows, the sweet-scented flowers and herbs of her garden, the linen walls rippling in a gentle breeze—and muttered the words of transport.

Nothing happened. Stomach churning, she stood frozen on the hard rock. The transfer spell was a basic one; *every* djinni mastered it. Desperately she repeated the words, but her body remained stubbornly planted on this Solomon-forsaken rock.

Her breath came in sharp pants, while panic swelled like a puffer toad. She tried another spell, something even simpler, concentrating as she recited the words to strengthen the smoke from the fires below.

It did not billow. It still wisped.

All around her she saw Kaf. The rock, the fires, the plants, the small animals that found a home under forbidding conditions. She smelled the smoke, basked in the sun's warmth, heard the wind. She sensed it, but she didn't *feel* it. Didn't feel the connection that was a part of every djinni's soul, that flow of fire and air that became *ma-at*.

She clutched her chest, unable to believe the irrefutable truth. She was empty, alone.

Her throat closed around the fear and panic, and a scream rose from her hollow insides. She fought it down. Breath. Think. Breath. Think. The Chant of Centrality, to calm inner turmoil, scarcely kept the madness at bay.

One question repeated itself, over and over. What had happened to her *ma-at*?

Think, Leila, think.

Her mind raced backward. During transfer, there had been a foreign energy, which both sucked at her and repelled her. Strange flashes of light, too, which seared her hand where she held Jack. She looked at her palm, saw no remnants of burns, yet the light and pain had startled her, reminding her of the terrifying storm she'd encountered during her test, so she'd thought of the Tower Land at the moment of transfer.

18

That was how they'd ended up here instead of her home.

Leila pressed her fingers against the bridge of her nose. Strange flashes of light. An aura from Jack.

Eyes widening, she stared at the man stalking away from her. No, not a man. Only a powerful wizard could do what he'd done. She did not know that Terra had such skilled workers of *ma-at*, but there could be no other explanation.

Panic fled. Her vision blurred behind a wave of rage. Jack Montgomery had taken her *ma-at*.

"Foul fiend! Give it back."

Jack spun around at Leila's furious shout, then staggered back as she launched herself at him. Her small fists pounded at his chest.

"Give back my *ma-at*. Why take it? Did you need power in our world?"

"What the hell are you talking about?" He grabbed her fists before she actually hurt him and held her hands behind her back.

"You took my *ma-at*." She twisted, her body brushing against him, her red robe swirling about her, her eyes flashing.

"Your what?" Jack focused on her words. The fact that the touch of her body still retained the power to excite him, that his mind insisted she was the most intriguing woman he'd met in a long time, had no relevance in the equation.

"My *ma-at*. You call it magic. Let go of me." She kicked him in the shins.

"Ouch." When she started to aim another kick higher, Jack let her go and moved out of reach. "I didn't take your magic."

"Do not lie, human."

Jack sucked in a breath, his anger returning at the reminder of where he was and who had stranded him there. "Right. I'm human, and you're a genie."

"Djinni," she hissed.

"Whatever. I don't have the slightest idea what you're talking about. Just stay away from me." He flung out his hand in a dismissive gesture.

She started at his vehement motion, her hands flinging up to protect herself. Her slippers lost traction on the rock, and she stumbled backward.

His heart froze in his throat. Behind her lay a long, steep slope of hard, unforgiving rock. He lunged forward, an adrenaline surge lending him power, and grabbed her. For uncounted seconds, they teetered; then he pulled back, taking her away from the precipice.

She landed flush against him. Of their own volition, his arms wrapped around her and held her close, while he waited for his heart and lungs to quiet. Once again, he noticed the delicate curve of her waist, the contours of her breast. The exotic scent he'd associated with her was gone. In its place was a scent like fresh clover.

And she was trembling. He patted her shoulder, awkwardly trying to soothe her.

Instead, she pulled away from his efforts. Eyes downcast, she fussed with her robe, seeming to gather her composure about her as she straightened the folds of cloth. Only when she was satisfied with the arrangement did she speak.

"You stopped my fall. Why?"

"You would have been injured."

"But I angered you."

To his surprise, she sounded scared. Of him. "I'm not going to hurt you."

"You already have. I did not respect your power, wizard; it will not happen again." She raised her head to look at him. Her dark eyes were luminous with unshed tears; then a single drop spilled over and rolled down her flawless skin. The fresh clover sent of her was stronger, tantalizing.

He no longer knew what to expect, what was illusion and what was foreign reality. "Are you working another spell?" he asked harshly.

"You know I cannot." The tears flowed harder, but she ignored them. He wasn't surprised to discover she was one of those rare women who cried with quiet beauty. "With all you command, why did you need my skills? Can you not give them back?"

"I didn't take your magic, Leila. I don't want it. Yours or anyone's."

She stared at him, aghast. "You do not want *ma-at*? Does it not work with your Terran magic, Wizard?"

"Wizard?"

"Is that not your talisman?" She pointed to the device of wire and crystal.

"My—?" He stopped. The crystal? He could feel its faint warm vibration, a tingling across his chest and up the back of the neck. Exactly what had it done?

21

He'd designed it to negate the effects of magic only on the holder, but had it instead taken her powers away from her? How? Did that unexpected effect work only while the device was on? If he turned it off or got far enough away from her, would her *ma-at* come back?

Leila's shoulders straightened. "I will comply."

Her sudden shift surprised him. "Comply? With what?"

"With whatever you would have me do for the return of my *ma-at*. What is your command, Wizard?"

Sudden, primitive answers flashed through him, raised from the demands of the id, unchecked by the trappings of civilization. He stared at her, unmoving, drawn in again by the exotic, erotic images she roused. The lore and the lure of having a genie to grant your every wish. The fulfilment promised by a seductive woman. The sweet demands of desire met in mutual need.

He saw the flare of her nostrils, the widening of her pupils the moment she identified, almost before he did, the source of his heat. He recognized the moment when calculation replaced her real fear.

"I have been told I am very good at the massage." She moved closer, her hips swaying as she circled behind him. Her fingers found a spot in the center of his back that Jack hadn't realized was tense until she rubbed it. Exquisite pleasure replaced tension.

Leila leaned closer, enveloping him in her heat and her clover scent, though the only place she touched him was at his back. "A powerful wizard like you can do anything," she said in a throaty whisper. "Even reverse what has been done. I would be grateful for the return of my powers."

Leila. Despite her claim of being without magic, she worked a spell on him. Her touch was too tempting, and testosterone replaced adrenaline. The sweat trickling down his back was not due only to the blazing sun and the desert heat.

He'd definitely spent too much time in the lab.

"So, you're willing to sleep with me if I'll give you what you want?" he asked bluntly, moving away from the tantalizing scent and touch of her. He crossed his arms and faced her.

Some emotion sparked in her eyes before the smooth, beautiful mask came down. "Is that what you desire?"

Jack got the distinct impression he'd hurt her feelings. Or annoyed her with his bald statement. His sister Isis claimed he needed to work on his tact and people skills, but, unlike Beau, his twin, Jack detested subterfuge and politics. He hadn't gotten where he was in life by ass-kissing or letting other people dictate his actions, but because he was damn good at what he did.

Suddenly he was tired of games. "Leila, I didn't intend to take your power, and no matter what you are willing to do, I can't give it back."

"You refuse to return a power you do not want?"

"I can't return it. I'm a biomedical engineer, not a wizard. When I get back to earth I'll figure out what happened. Until then, I'm going to walk to my sister's home and let her transport me back. You can come with me, if you want," he added, feeling a twinge of guilt again at her stricken look.

"*How could you?*" She didn't shout, didn't snarl, but her low voice was filled with horror and hatred. "You don't even want my *ma-at*, yet you take it from me. You dabble with forces, heedless of the results. You . . . human!"

He thrust away the pang of guilt at what he might have done. She'd been the aggressor in this whole mess. "Yes, I'm human. And you're djinn. You had no qualms about using some attraction spell to play with my emotions and get me into bed with you."

"I would have given you pleasure."

"Why? Was it just for laughs? To see the human dangling on your string?" The scar on his cheek burned in a thin line of fire, a reminder that he'd once been hopeless and powerless, and that he'd paid a grave price. A reminder that he'd never again allow that sick sensation of helplessness to rule him. "Was I just a lucky guy chosen at random?"

"No, I—" Her answer was drowned out by a rumble beneath his feet. The rocks shifted and an outrush of heat scalded his face.

Leila spun around, shouting a curse or an instruction in a language he didn't know.

"What?" he demanded.

"Run! The Tower Lands are displeased. We forgot the appeasement."

"What appeasement?"

Leila shoved at him. "Just run." She hitched up her robe and followed her own advice.

A plume of smoke burst through the rocks behind him. Needing no more incentive, he scrambled over the slick, black surface, following Leila. The footing grew more treacherous as eddying smoke obscured their vision. He glanced over his shoulder. A huge, pulsing cloud reached for the summit of the spires of rock. Like the geysers of Yellowstone, it charged the atmosphere, but with a dry heat instead of steam. And the air reeked of rotting vegetation, not sulfur. Heat shoved him from behind, singeing the back of his neck, and he concentrated on following Leila down a narrow, wandering path of flat rock.

Ashes floated down beside him. Ashes? The small flakes were gray, but no ash he'd ever seen glittered like these. He caught some in his palm, his rapid pace slowing as his curiosity rose. Nor did the flakes disintegrate when he rubbed his hand over them. He sneezed, drawing Leila's attention.

"Do not tarry!" Her shout was barely audible above the roar of the explosions spreading beneath their feet. "The rocks do realign and this Tower will no longer hold us."

As if to punctuate her words, the rock sheered off in front of them. Only a steep drop to an unseen bottom awaited them in that direction. He brushed off the ash and sought an alternate route.

"We need to go there." Leila pointed to a patch of green across a widening chasm. The violence around them—heaving rock, spewing smoke—seemed to cease at the fissure. "It is of another Tower, and we will be welcomed if we say the necessary appeasement when we touch it. Tell it, *'T'far dolient a'bakshemar. Mir jedaq fohilam de.'* It means, 'I do beseech thy tolerance. Allow me passage.' Do it as soon as your feet touch."

"What? Why?"

"Just do it. Can you jump far enough to span the chasm?"

He eyed the gap. "Easily. Can you?"

"I do not know. I have never tried without my *maat*."

"I'll go first, then." He took a short running start and easily leaped across the fissure. The rock shifted under his feet.

"The appeasement!" shouted Leila.

"I do beseech thy tolerance. Allow me passage," he muttered, feeling utterly ridiculous. Then again, every moment since he'd stepped on Kaf seemed like a trip to Wonderland.

The rock heaved beneath his feet, a violent lurch that sent him staggering. English wouldn't work, he realized; he had to say it in the language of Kaf. What were the words she'd said?

"T'far dolient a'bakshemar. Mir jedaq fohilam de."

The heaving rock quieted beneath his feet, still raised, as though poised before a final decision. Damn, he was glad he had an ear for languages. This was a place of magic, he could not forget. The rules he knew didn't apply here.

Leila took a few steps back, as Jack had done. Behind her, the wall of rock split in two and a cloud of smoke billowed from it, bringing the gagging scent of rot and a torrent of ash.

She wasn't going to make it.

"Leila, hurry!" He reached across the chasm, urging her forward.

She ran, jumped. Her toes caught the solid ground, her heels hung over the open break. She flung herself forward, assisted by Jack, and fell against him, tumbling them both to the ground. Immediately she rolled off him, and knelt.

"T'far dolient a'bakshemar. Mir jedaq fohilam de."

They both waited. The breath stopped in his lungs. The rock shook itself, then quieted. A finger of smoke rose, only to fade out into the yellow sky. The ash around them settled and disappeared.

The Tower allowed them to stay.

Jack rubbed the bridge of his nose. Definitely Wonderland.

Chapter Three

"How many hours until nightfall?"

Leila, busy frowning at a scrape on her toe, started at Jack's question. She looked at him blankly. "Hours?"

"How long do we have before the sun sets?"

She glanced around. "When the sky grows pink and the gecko disappears."

"Is that a long time?"

"I do not know what you consider a long time."

"But—oh, forget it." Jack resumed his pacing around the plateau.

She tried to ignore his restless energy by returning her attention to her toe. Her slippers had fallen into the chasm during the leap, so she had injured her skin when she landed on the other side. She dabbed at the injury with her finger, then winced at the small pain when her sweat touched the wound. How did one fix a scraped toe without *ma-at*? And when was the last time she'd had to worry about sweat?

"How far is it to Tepe-ma-adaktu? To my sister's home?" Jack once more interrupted her thoughts.

She shrugged. "We don't measure distances. We just transport."

"But you can't transport?" He ran his fingers across his talisman, and she heard a faint click.

"No." Her *ma-at* was gone. She could barely tolerate the truth of the words, much less give them the power of voice.

Her attention caught on her robe, and with dismay she noted the smudges on it. She didn't own many robes as beautiful as this one, and she couldn't afford to ruin it. She concentrated, hoping she'd retained some small bit of *ma-at*, but the robe stayed dirty. Futilely she wiped at the stain.

She had always felt so useless amongst the powerful djinn with only her face and figure as assets. All her life, to get what she needed, she had had to supplement her *ma-at* with seduction, manipulation, or her own labor, but she had never given up or accepted defeat by the limits her weakness imposed. There was, however, a vast distance between being unskilled in *ma-at* and being without it. Nothing she knew, nothing she could do, would bring back her *ma-at*. Nausea rose in her throat. What would she do? How would she survive?

"Are you sure the *ma-at* is still gone?" he persisted. "Try it again."

"Are you sure when your breath does not come?"

When her *ma-at* returned—and it must return, it must—she would feel it. She would feel the lightness of air and the heat of fire. Now, inside was only heaviness and emptiness and bereavement.

"*Ma-at* is our essence," she continued, glaring at him. "Our breath. It is a part of who we are. It weaves throughout our lives and enriches us. It cannot be severed without hurting us."

She recoiled at the flash of emotion that crossed the wizard's face. When would she learn to curb the part of her that rebelled at limits? Getting angry was a trip on a dead camel.

His voice came as low as the rumbling rocks. "Like blindness replacing eyesight? Or phantom pain in place of a severed limb?"

Horrified, she could scarcely draw breath against the pain. Blood pounded her chest. Was he capable of such cruelty? "Eyes? Limb? You would take those from me, too?"

"*No!* God, no, Leila. Never." He crouched beside her and cradled her hands with his. "Never."

Her frantic gaze raced across him, seeking the truth. Was it compassion she saw in his blue eyes?

"My work is about restoring what is lost. I was relating your loss to that, to something I knew. I won't hurt you."

"You already have," she whispered.

"Not again."

Silence enveloped them. His grip was comforting, and his vehement denial gave her a measure of reassurance. At last her heartbeat settled. In this, at least, she believed him.

He gave her hands one last squeeze before releasing them. "Our first priority should be to find food and water; then we should take advantage of the remaining daylight. These mountains will be treacherous to travel at night. Are you ready?"

She leaned back against the tree. Behind her terror, lethargy returned, sapping all energy and desire. "Go," she said.

He stood above her, his legs planted, one hand outstretched. "C'mon, Leila, time to get moving."

"I prefer not moving." Her *ma-at* would come back; it *had* to. She would wait here until it did; then she would leave this place and try to think no more of Jack Montgomery.

The wizard crouched down beside her. "You want me to leave?"

"Yes."

"But you plan to stay here?"

"Yes."

"Alone."

"Yes."

"Leila, you can't—"

"Go!"

Jack hesitated a moment, then gave a small nod of agreement. "If that's what you wish." He rose, then a moment later disappeared around a spire of rock.

With his departure, the air stilled. No breeze found its way through the small stand of trees, and the only sounds were the distant rumble of smoke and the crack of shifting rock. She had not realized how much vibrancy Jack Montgomery generated by his sheer presence.

She leaned against the bark of the tree, exhausted. Not even the woodsy scents of cedar and almond offered comfort. Only one fortunate circumstance stood out in this whole jumble of disasters. She was on her own world of Kaf. Djinn were sustained by their bonds to Kaf; those few who visited elsewhere must always return for renewal. In fact, only one djinni in all of history, Simon, now of Terra, had successfully exchanged the Kafian bonds of fire and air for the Terran bonds of earth and water. The few others who had tried it had perished. If she had been stranded on Terra, without the skill to return . . . A shudder ran down her spine at the thought.

As she sat, quiet brought no peace. Stillness did not lighten her worry. Isolation did not return her *ma-at*.

How was she to survive?

You will survive as you always have. By doing what must be done.

She stirred restlessly on the hard rock. Sitting without a cushion was uncomfortable. And inactivity, she found, was often boring.

Hunger bit into her, heralded by her stomach rumbling. She glared at the place where Jack had disappeared. The least he could have done was to find her something to eat. And begin a fire. A glass of honeyed tea would not be amiss either.

She ran a hand through her hair, knowing it had never been so tangled. And it had *adamana* ashes in it!

Solomon's sands, she must look a mess. So now she had not even that small pride. She swallowed down the lump in her throat, and her jaw tightened.

Jack Montgomery had much to answer for.

Beginning the painstaking process of removing the tangles with naught but her fingers, she discovered anger more satisfying than pity. Jack Montgomery. When he'd asked why she chose him, she'd started to tell him: his looks, his genius, his spirit.

Then the Towers had shifted.

Now she was glad she had not told him. He deserved no explanations. Because of him, inside her was a hollow echo of loss, an empty place where her *maat* should have been. A match for the aching knowledge that her secret dream was also fading.

Only one thing would she have kept from him, a secret she told no one.

She wanted a child.

Very few children were born to the djinn on Kaf, and her people found that for the best, since every child was raised and loved by the entire village. In this, too, though, she was different. She wanted a child born of her flesh. A child to love, to raise, to cherish. A child to nurture from infancy to adulthood. It had remained a dream of no substance, however.

Until Darius, their Protector, and Simon of Terra had both united with Terran women. Until both had, soon after, sired children. It was then that she had known: Only a human male could give her a child. She wanted none other than Jack Montgomery to sire that child.

A sigh escaped her. Unfortunately, despite everything, she could still envision only him as the father. By blessed Solomon, thoughts of him still had the power to stir her. Wasn't that a strange and unwanted turn of the spell?

For now, though, something else was more important. Something that overrode all. She wanted her *ma-at* back.

And she wanted the Terran wizard to regret his theft.

Which meant she had to find him.

When she did, though, there would be no more tears. Although she feared his power, she no longer feared he would harm her body, for twice he had saved her from injury. Though human, though unmoved to return her *ma-at*, he did not seem to draw his power from the sinister forces, and she did not believe he would deliberately harm her again.

A genius wizard would not be moved by tears, and seduction did not seem to work on him, although it was worth another try. Trouble was, Jack Montgomery did not seem to conform to any of her expectations.

Should she be surprised? He was, after all, human.

No matter; she would find a way. She ran her fingers once more through her hair, took a deep breath, and then straightened the turquoise tablet at her throat. Long ago she had learned to hide lack of skill behind assumed confidence, insecurity behind intrigue, needs behind commands.

Ah, but by the spirits, it was so hard to play the role. Too often she failed.

Her stomach grumbled again. First, though, she must find sustenance. She knelt and ran her hands through the sparse grass around her. Perhaps almonds had fallen from the tree. A shadow passed across her, a bird crossing the sun. She looked up, realized that midday was long gone.

She must find the wizard before sunset. Tonight only a few weak stars and a sliver of moon would dot the sky, while shadows reigned below. Suddenly, despite the heat, her hands felt cold. The dark—she had never liked it, and in three eves hence even the small illumination of the moon would be gone.

With Solomon's benevolence she would have her *ma-at* back before the Night of No Moon.

It took Jack only fifteen minutes of walking before he stopped, turned around, and headed back to Leila. Anxious as he was to find his sister, leave this world, and get back to his work, anxious as Leila was to have him gone, he simply couldn't leave her. If she was used to having magic do everything for her, then she'd be helpless.

He'd seen that look on her face, the same look he'd seen in his patients who'd lost a limb. Denial, shock, inertia. Losing her *ma-at* had to be as traumatic as losing a leg or arm. Maybe more so.

There must be dangers here. Could Leila defend herself? She hadn't even known what to do with a scraped toe. A bird's song gave him pause for a moment. It sounded harmless, but this was a world where rocks needed appeasement. He rubbed a hand across his gritty face, across the thin scar. God, he hated not knowing.

Nearby a small rodent grunted and tugged at a feathery plant until the ground gave up the single white root. The rodent locked jaws around it, glanced at Jack, then, with another grunt, sped off with its treasure. The greenery and root looked like a parsnip, but was it edible? He knelt, pulled out two more roots, and took them with him, back to Leila.

For a moment, he stood in the shadows, alone, and watched her. She was collecting nuts, almonds from the shape. She cracked one open with perfect white teeth and ate it eagerly. The polished seductress of earlier had faded. Her waist-length hair was still thick and lush, but the high gloss had faded to a subtle sheen with tiny dots of glitter from the ash. The red robe had a small tear at the hem, but it still fit her like liquid rubies. Jack sucked in a breath, amazed that she still had such an impact on him.

Before, an air of tantalizing mystery had surrounded her; now she seemed approachable. He shook off the bittersweet thought that some essential part of her was missing. Instead, he rustled his feet and cleared his throat, then came into the tiny clearing.

"Are these edible?" He held out the roots.

Leila's glance shot up, her eyes wide.

"Sorry, I didn't mean to startle you."

"I thought you'd left."

"I couldn't." He crouched beside her, his heart beating just a bit faster. "There's a small pond a short distance away. I see you've found some almonds. Are these roots edible raw?"

She glanced at the roots. "Yes. Although they're better cooked with spices."

"No spices, I'm afraid." He brushed the dirt off one root, handed it to her, and then took a bite of the other. "Tastes like parsnip." At her puzzled glance, he added, "Tuberous vegetables from my world."

Her face shuttered at the mention of Earth. "Why did you come back?"

"I thought we'd do better traveling together than apart. You have knowledge of this world—its dangers and customs."

"And what will you bring?"

"Defense. Protection. I'm bigger than you." He leaned forward. "I've spent a lot of time outdoors camping. Some of those skills may come in handy. We're bound to be more successful together than separate."

"On our return, will you give back my *ma-at*, Wizard?"

Jack sighed and rested a hand on the chain at his neck. The crystal was quiescent, unpowered by the electricity. He'd turned it off earlier, when he'd asked if her magic came back, wondering if the device had to be on for the effect to persist. Apparently not. Nor, it seemed, had his absence helped.

In his research, he'd read every book on magic he could find—and found most of them pure bunk. He'd also talked to purported practitioners—and found most of them pure bunk, too. The few that had sent a chill down his spine, however, had never addressed this. Obviously, he needed to learn more. "I'm not a wizard, and I don't know if I can give it back, but I'll try. I ask one thing. If your magic—"

"—*ma-at*. Use our word on Kaf."

Jack nodded. "If your *ma-at* does return, that you inform me of it. Don't spring it on me by doing some spell against me."

She didn't answer at first, her dark eyes searching his face. "This I will agree to, Jack Montgomery. We will travel together until we reach Tepe-ma-adaktu. You will seek a method to restore my *ma-at*. I shall tell you of its return."

"Shall we shake on it?" Jack held out his hand.

"Is that the custom in your land?"

"Yes."

"Djinn hold a bargain sacred and inviolate. Do humans also?"

"Not all, but I keep my promises."

"Then let us seal this bargain first by your custom."

Leila laid a hand in his. Her skin was softer than that of any woman he'd ever known—not even a finger callus from years of holding a pencil marred it. Yet beneath, her grip was firm. Jack shook her hand, reluctant to let go.

"Now we shall seal the bargain by djinn custom." She took his hands in hers and lifted them. She kissed the backs, first one, then the other; then still clasping his hands, she leaned forward and kissed each cheek. The kiss was so gentle, he should barely have felt it, but that small touch seared him. She sat back on her heels. "Your turn."

He repeated the gestures, a kiss on each hand, and a kiss on each cheek, and knew it wasn't nearly enough, yet was all there could be.

"The bargain is sealed, Jack Montgomery. May the ends be what your heart desires."

Jack was suddenly reminded of the stories his Aunt Tildy had read to him. Fairy tales and the *Arabian Nights* of Scheherazade. He hadn't enjoyed them, for it seemed that every time a human made a bargain with a magical creature, the human ended up regretting it.

Walking was about as much fun as the Twelve Trials of Passage. Leila stopped and leaned against a rock spire jutting beside the path. The surface—glossy as marble, cool as a night breeze—served only to remind her that she was neither cool nor glossy. Ahead of her stretched the endless expanse of tumbled black rocks, towering mountains, and ephemeral smoke.

Why had she ever agreed to this infernal bargain?

Wind whistled through the narrow valley where they trod. It flattened her robe about her and further tangled her hair. Though it was still light, the sun waned, and a night bird awoke, singing to the rising sliver of moon. She shivered—not from cold, but from the coming dark—and rubbed her hands together.

Jack, as if suddenly realizing she no longer followed him, came back to her. "We have to keep moving."

"I am not accustomed to walking."

"That's right. You flit from place to place."

"Djinn do not flit. We maintain our contact with the soul of Kaf. Must people on your world walk whenever they travel?"

Jack leaned one shoulder against the rock beside her and shook his head. "Mostly they take cars. Or planes, buses, and trains. Some people jog, though."

"What is jog?" So far, they had traveled in silence; the wizard, apparently, did not make idle conversation. For the moment, however, he seemed inclined to pause and speak, and she was eager to listen to his low voice. And to continue her rest.

"A light run. For exercise. Or pleasure."

"You *run*? For *pleasure*?" The idea was horrifying.

"It's a way to keep fit when most people have sedentary work."

"Keep fit?" She understood each word, but together they made no sense.

"In good physical condition. Muscles toned. Heart working strong. Lack of fat."

Her eyes ran across him. His muscles were toned. No fat rippled beneath the skin. Even his breath came with steady tempo. It was not fair that the human should look so well after walking. His hair had not tangled. His skin had no scratches.

Her nose wrinkled. He could use a little perfume, however. And maybe a gloss to the nails. She touched the side of his neck, feeling the smooth pulse of his heartbeat, and was gratified when it quickened at her touch. "You must do this jog, no?"

"Sometimes. I prefer more strenuous workouts."

"Djinn, too, believe in keep fit. One cannot do *ma-at* if the body or the mind is ill."

"How do you get your exercise?" His glance looked appreciative, although she guessed she could use a perfuming herself.

Exercise? Leila had to think a moment. Through the delights of sex. Through the practice of *ma-at*. Through the joys of her garden. All beyond her reach right now.

"Many ways," she said flatly, and her hand dropped. "Now I desire to stop walking, to have something to eat and water to drink, to find shelter."

Jack laughed. "Too bad you haven't got a magic lamp to rub and a genie to grant three wishes."

She reared back. "What a vile thing to say!"

"What? What's wrong?"

Oh, the wizard had perfected his look of bewildered innocence. "You know your cruelty."

"Because I said genie instead of djinni?"

"Only a bound djinni must grant wishes." She clenched her fist. "To be so bound is to be banished from all djinn society and concourse, marked by the unremovable copper bands at the wrist, until the servitude is at end." Words failed her at the horror of it. "All our legends—"

"Bah! What do *your* legends know? Do I look like I could live in a cramped lamp?"

"No. Look, I'm sorry, it was meant as a joke, and obviously it wasn't."

"Have you never asked your sister about the djinn?

41

Have you never spoken to her *zani*, Darius. Our Protector?"

Jack ran a hand over the back of his neck, uneasy at her accusations. To her, the genie of lore had been bound in a form of slavery. As a scientist, he was taught to gather information, to use every resource before reaching a conclusion.

Yet he'd deliberately avoided the one resource he should have consulted—his sister and her husband. Out of fear, he realized, his gut churning. Fear that, if they knew about his secret project, he'd be stopped before finishing his research.

And, maybe, fear that he'd learn more than he wanted?

Except fear was as unacceptable as helplessness, and ignorance was never the answer.

"Leila, I know you're tired." He changed the subject. They had enough problems without dredging up his past ones. "But it's getting dark. Night is coming. We need to find shelter before we stop. I was aiming for that spot over there." He pointed to another one of the occasional clumps of trees that had dotted their path, this one a short distance in front of them and on a plateau a few yards higher. "The vegetation might provide something softer than rock to sleep on and there's probably water nearby. Maybe food."

Leila made a face, but straightened. She said nothing, simply waited for him to start moving.

When they scrambled up the short slope, he surveyed the area. "No worse than the campsites on some of my rock-climbing trips." The ground was rel-

Enchantment

atively level, and a sheer cliff rose from two sides, adding protection from anything dangerous that might be wandering these lands. Fallen leaves and tufts of plants would make nice padding beneath to lie on. There was no well, but water trickled down the rock face. Food was still a question mark, but food was the least of his concerns.

He began piling leaves into a makeshift mattress, while Leila settled down onto a flat rock with a sigh. She sat, feet tucked beneath her robe, back straight and watched him work.

"Gather some twigs for a fire," he said at last, "while I make us a place to sleep."

Leila didn't stir, except to work her fingers through her hair.

"This would go faster if both of us worked at it, Princess," he added with a tint of annoyance.

"I am not a princess. Our King Taranushi has a daughter, but I am not she."

"Does she sit around and let people wait on her?"

"Her *ma-at* provides for her. Since you took mine, I believe you are responsible for my comfort."

How could she be so sexy one moment, so dauntless the next, and then such a pain in the butt? He didn't have the slightest clue. Not surprising, since he'd never had much of a clue about women, except perhaps his female coworkers in the lab, who seemed as driven as he. But Leila was more confusing than most.

He crossed his arms. "This is supposed to be a partnership, Princess, not a servant-master relationship."

"The raw fruits of that tree are edible." She waved

43

a hand in the air, pointing to first one tree, then another. "Those are pleasant to smell, but unpleasant to digest. There, I have done my part."

He gaped at her a moment, then burst out laughing. "Have it your way, Princess. If you're not used to walking, I imagine you are tired."

"I keep telling you, I am not a princess."

"It's not a title, it's a nickname." He finished the bedding, then collected twigs. In his pockets, he found a matchbook from Brigand's, and used one of the precious matches to start their fire. "Maybe I can catch the Kafian equivalent of a rabbit to roast."

Her lips curled. "I do not eat flesh."

"Are all your people vegetarian? Eat no meat," he explained when she raised questioning brows.

"Some will eat flesh. I do not."

"Then it's fruit for you." From the edible tree, he pulled off two green ovals that looked like mangos and tossed her one. "Here you go. What's this called?"

"Mango."

Jack tasted the pink-fleshed fruit, and found it was similar to the mango, although thinner skinned and juicier. Probably came from the same genetic source at one time. According to some folklore he'd read, the djinn were once part of Earth, celestial beings considered above man but lesser than the angels. They had fled to another dimensional world of their own, preferring to be masters over a less hospitable domain than to be beneath any, even the angels. Stood to reason they'd take some familiar plants with them, or would create them in the new land, and in translating, she would pick the word closest in meaning.

Which reminded him—"How do you know my language?"

"*Ma-at*," she answered briefly.

Of course. How else?

She looked up from her mango. "If I had my *ma-at*, I could give you *Fahrisa*, our language. I would touch you here"—she laid a finger against his temple—"and you would know it."

Let a djinni muck around in his brain? "No, thanks. I doubt it's quite that easy."

Her face darkened a moment, and her finger dropped. "Not always. Besides, I do not have my *ma-at*."

"Perhaps you could teach me as we go."

Her face shuttered. "I am not an Adept."

"But I'm a good student."

She hesitated, then looked over at him. "I make no promise as to the result."

"I don't expect one."

"Then—" she nodded. "*T'allet*. That means 'I accept.' It is used to seal a bargain."

"*T'allet*. I accept, too. See, you've already given your first lesson."

He was pleased to see some of the remoteness leave her. She gave him a smile, a small one, but the first genuinely warm one he'd seen from her. One without a hint of artifice. "Except," she said, "the way you pronounced it, you said, 'I argue.'"

He burst out laughing. "Good thing the rocks understood my appeasement today. Do you have a written language as well? Maybe it will help to see things written."

"Yes." She looked around, then took a charred stick from the fire and used it to scratch some symbols on a leaf. "Those are the two words."

He stared at the runic letters, something about them striking a familiar chord. He had seen them . . .

. . . on a tablet of Sumerian writing. During his research into magic he had studied countless texts of the ancients. Mostly he'd read translations, but he'd always gotten copies of the original scrolls and clay tablets to study. He had a gift for languages, spoke three fluently, and had picked up smatterings of several others in his travels. In the process of his research he'd gleaned a little of the ancient languages. *Fahrisa* wasn't the same, but obviously it derived from a similar root.

His finger traced the slashes of the letters. "*T'allet. T'alat.*"

"Yes." Leila stared at him, then leaned closer, all emotion leeched from her face. Her hand reached out, as though to touch the narrow lattice of wires in his device; then she drew back, fist closed. "Do you mock me? Asking for my help?"

"No. Why do you think I would?"

"Your talisman. It incorporates our symbols in the patterns of wire. Water. Earth. Protection." Without touching him, she pointed each one out. "As though you already knew."

"I don't, Leila." Mice feet ran down his spine, for the design of wires was no accident. He had constructed the network from a mix of metallurgic principles, ancient designs he'd discovered in his research, and optimal power to the crystal. "I still want you to teach me *Fahrisa*."

She drew back, her eyes dark and unreadable, and then turned away to stare at the darkness. "*T'allet*," she whispered, not looking at him.

They ate the remainder of the meal in silence, the brief hint of camaraderie lost.

Slowly he took in the world around him. Parts of it seemed achingly familiar: the rustle of wind, the hardness of the rock, even the taste of the fruit. Focus on these and he could imagine he was simply in the Rockies, or the Sierras, or even the Kalahari, or the remote edge of Taklimakan in Tibet. He had traveled to many strange places and still had much to see on Earth, yet all he had to do was look up in the sky and see utterly strange constellations to know this land was *foreign*.

He drew in a deep breath. Some of it he liked, he admitted. When free of smoke and ash, like now, the air was fresh, without a hint of pollution. The water they'd drunk had been refreshing, flavored of mint and faintly cool.

Yet every time he'd stepped on a new plateau and muttered the necessary appeasement, every time he glanced at his palm and saw the glittering residue of strange ash, he'd been reminded that his feet and wits and intellect could only take him so far.

To return home, he would need magic, and he didn't like that fact one bit.

He finished the last of his fruit and leaned over to rinse his hands in the trickle of water. "You said these lands are treacherous. We've come across reforming rock and indigestible fruit. What else might we come across?"

"This," Leila answered in a strangled voice.

Chapter Four

Jack spun around, heart lodged in his throat, to find Leila menaced by . . .

An oil slick?

Her wide-eyed gaze never left the strange phenomenon as it slithered forward, and he could see a faint trembling in her stiff arms.

"What is it?" he asked softly. The slick stopped, curled on itself. Turning to look at the source of his voice?

"A fire salamander," Leila whispered.

He squinted, unable to clearly focus on it. At the center of the green iridescent camouflage was something solid. As he stared, the shininess took on form. A flat snake? With tiny legs? It eyed the half-eaten fruit in Leila's hand.

Or maybe it was eyeing her hand.

"What does it do?" He inched closer.

"*Ma-at* of a rudimentary sort. Mostly it is venomous."

"Deadly?"

"If superior *ma-at* does not heal. A fire salamander is rare to see," Leila continued. "Perhaps it is curious why such large creatures as ourselves do not use a spell of discouragement. Without it, we become prey."

Breathing around the knot in his throat, he inched closer. Tension tightened his gut and muscles. He was considerably larger than Leila; his body could tolerate a larger dose of venom, if it came to that. Or maybe his human physiology would react differently. He clicked on the crystal.

All in all, he hoped he didn't have to find out.

The wires around his neck began to vibrate, reaching deep inside him. At the edge of his vision he could see the crystal glow a brilliant green.

The salamander stopped. The green sheen surrounding it thickened and brightened, concealing the body.

He tensed, waiting. The wires burned from his throat to his chest, and the hairs on the back of his neck stood electrified. Heat and power coursed through him. Slowly he reached down and plucked a stick from the fire.

"No!" hissed Leila. "Fire *attracts*—"

With a high-pitched whine, the salamander leaped forward.

Adrenaline spurted through his veins. Electricity flowed with it, from battery to crystal to heart to wrist. A whine—from the device, the salamander?—obliterated all sound, all thought but survival.

Suddenly the salamander changed direction. It streamed past his ear, dipped behind him. He twisted, blocking Leila's body, thrusting out the stick of fire. Jaws wide, the creature sped toward Leila's hand. A second later, mango fruit in its mouth, it disappeared into the thickening smoke of the Tower Lands, followed by the fading sound of Leila's terrorized scream.

Leila stared at the droplets of blood on her thumb. Her chest heaved with terror. With her *ma-at* gone, she could not heal herself.

"Your hand. Did it strike you? Damn, what I wouldn't give for a well-stocked first aid kit right now."

Jack's voice became a background to her fear. The fire salamander's bite was painful, she'd heard, with death at the end of an agonizing journey. Unless *ma-at* reversed the poison.

So why did her hand only sting? Was the stinging a prelude to much worse?

"Leila, give me your hand!"

Would the human wizard show compassion and aid her? Mutely she held out her hand.

His fingers were strong on hers as he took the edge of his shirt and swiftly wiped away the blood. Despite his haste, his touch was sure and gentle. He held her hand in his palm, peering intently at the wound, while he reached into his pocket and brought out a short wand. With a mere click, a blade appeared at the end.

He laid it against her thumb, the sharp tip a single point of pain.

She screeched and pulled away. "You cut me?"

Jack brought her hand back with a firm grip. "I'm going to excise the wound and suck out the venom. I've treated snake bites and scorpion stings in the wild, although I prefer a hospital and antivenom serum at my disposal." He gazed at her hand again. "What does the bite look like? Does the salamander have fangs or teeth or stingers?"

The sting was fading from her hand, bringing a measure of relief. Oh, how cruel to give hope. She tried to wrap her mind around what Jack was asking. "Fangs, I think."

He peered at her hand. "I don't see any puncture wounds."

"I did not cut myself."

She joined him in looking at her hand, bending her head close to his. So close she could feel the heat of his skin and the brush of his untidy hair. She did not see a puncture wound either, only a long, shallow scratch across the base of her thumb. Blood droplets welled from the break, and the bright red made her dizzy. She fought back nausea. She'd never seen her own blood in continuous flow. The few injuries she'd had—a jab from a thorn in her garden, a burn from the spell fires, a bruised wrist during her testings—she had healed at once.

"Does a salamander have claws or talons?" Jack's voice seemed distant, faint.

"What?" She could barely form the word.

"Claws or talons? Is there poison on them? Think, Leila."

Jack's command pulled her back, and she took a deep breath of the sweet air. Since the agonizing journey of death appeared to have been delayed, she drew her gaze from the blood and stared into the night-rising plumes of smoke, recalling what she knew of the fire salamander. "It has claws, but the venom is only in the bite. The *ma-at* it uses is of a rudimentary type, which paralyzes the chosen prey until it can strike. It is born of fire, and to fire it returns." She cast a sidelong glance toward the man at her side.

His lips twisted in chagrin as he collapsed the bladed wand and returned it to his pocket. "And I brandished a flaming stick at it."

" 'Twas not the best way to repel the creature," she agreed, surprised that he had admitted his error so readily.

His hand still cradled hers, and now his thumb brushed away the vestiges of blood. "It looks like the claws scratched you, but there was no venom."

"I would be writhing in pain, my hand swollen, had the salamander bitten."

For a brief moment, Jack's fingers tightened around hers; then he relaxed. "I don't know if you have things like infections here, but you should rinse your hand off, just in case the claws were dirty. At any rate, the cold water will stanch the bleeding."

"Can you not simply heal it, Wizard?"

"I'm not a wizard. I told you that," he said impatiently.

Not for a moment did she believe he was not a wizard. Had he not taken her *ma-at*? Had he not repelled the fire salamander after inciting it to leap?

"If your people do not call you Wizard, then by what title are you known?" she asked.

"A scientist. Dr. Montgomery. Most people call me Jack." Jack pushed to his feet. "C'mon."

Leila followed him to the trickle of water. In the waning light she could barely follow his actions as he rinsed her hand under the stream. More than saw, she felt the touch of him as his flesh rubbed across hers, the caress slick with water. The cold water and the hot touch did seem to take away the last bite of pain, and the bleeding did stop.

"Do you have a title?" he asked absently as he tended her.

So quickly faint pleasure turned sour. Most djinn children refined their skills by studying with a mentor; Leila had shored her small store of *ma-at* with knowledge gained from secretly studying all the printed lore available. Her favorites had been the ones that contained the beautifully crafted pictures of plants.

She had learned much about her world, but knowledge had not stopped the taunts and jokes of her more skilled classmates. Knowledge had not granted her a mentor or an apprenticeship or a title.

"I am known as just Leila." She jerked her hand from the water and pushed down the hurt she felt at his question. He did not know. "The blood has stopped."

"It looks clean." Jack pulled the wand out again and

used it to tear a strip of cloth from his white shirt.

"Why do you damage your garment, scientist?"

"You need a bandage, and I don't want to tear that beautiful dress of yours."

She smiled and smoothed the wrinkles with her un-injured hand, mindful that the gesture pulled the robe tight across her curves. "You like the robe? It is one of my favorites."

"Yeah, I like the robe," he muttered and tore his eyes away. "Now hold out your hand."

Leila obeyed, dipping her head so her hair brushed against him. He grew still for a heartbeat, and a faint thrill coursed through her. Was he perhaps not as un-responsive as she thought?

He used part of the cloth for a pad, which he pressed against her wound, then wrapped the remaining cloth around her hand, splitting the end to fasten it. When he finished, she held up her hand. In the growing dark, with only the sliver of a moon and the yellow flame of their fire, the white stood in sharp contrast to her skin.

Scientists wielded a cumbersome *ma-at*.

"Thank you for your kindness," was all she said.

Jack cleared his throat. "We should get some sleep, get up early. We'll have a longer time to walk tomor-row. You'll need to rest."

When she didn't answer, he splashed some water on his face and on the back of his neck, then lay down on the leafy bedding he'd assembled earlier. He turned his back to her and burrowed down in the leaves.

Leila sighed. She could use the aid of a few fragrant

55

oils and grooming tools right now. Lacking that, she'd follow his example.

She rinsed her face and hands, dropped some water on her hair to aid in finger-combing out the dust and tangles, splashed the dampness between her breasts. A clover plant grew in the cracks above the miniature waterfall. Carefully she plucked a single leaf, rubbed it over her fingers, and then chewed it. The oils would sweeten her touch and her breath.

When she finished, she turned to find Jack watching her. The night was dark; she could barely make out the outline of his body, yet she saw the flame of his eyes. They reflected the rainbow-hued needles of light that spread from the crystal of his talisman. Animals, wind, plants were all asleep. Only the Tower Lands themselves stood sentinel, the plumes of smoke wisping through their small campsite to touch her tongue with the taste of heat. All around her smelled of rock and fire and the eternity of Kaf.

She took a deep breath and knelt at his side. With her night-sharpened senses, she heard his sharp inhale, felt the fire of his skin against her knee. Despite the dark, her forefingers found the warm throbbing of his temples, and she began a delicate massage.

"What are you doing?" His question was harsh in the quiet night.

"Thanking you for helping me." She would stand in no one's debt, and thrice had he helped her.

He grabbed her wrists, not enough to hurt, just enough to still her hands. "You don't owe me a thing." His voice was harsh and grating.

"No?"

She spread her hands, planting them on either side of him. The motion brought her close to him, until the edges of her robe caught on his cheek. She heard him swallow, and he lifted one hand to stroke the length of her hair. "You have the most beautiful hair," he whispered. "Have you ever cut it?"

"No." She was glad she had taken the extra moments to cleanse her hair as well as her skin. His hand brushed against her shoulder, bringing her skin to tingling life. Beneath them, the rocks rumbled, then settled.

He ceased his caress. His hand dropped and he loosened her other wrist.

"No, Leila," he said. "Don't try to seduce me. I don't know why you think you need to, but you don't. Maybe djinn are easier with sex than humans. Or at least this human. But we've agreed. Together to my sister's, then we are worlds apart. That's all. Ever."

"You do not want me?"

He gave a humorless laugh. "I didn't say that. But I can control myself. I'm not going to act on my baser instincts."

She sat back on her heels. Pain at rejection joined her with the speed of an old friend and competed with sudden new fury. She chose the men she took to her bed, and, knowing that only the rare was valued, she had made herself rare. A treasure few possessed. No man, other than Darius, Protector of *Ma-at*, had so bluntly refused her. No other man had she desired with such rapid, unexpected fierceness. "Do you refuse my gift?"

He propped himself up on one elbow and let out a huff of air. "I know I need to work at this. Isis says my people skills are nonexistent. I'm sorry if I've hurt your feelings, but—"

"No explanations," she said bitterly. "Your desires are clear, Scientist. We are companions only for the needs of our journey." She stretched out on the leaves, putting her back to him, cutting off all further talk. She heard him settle back down and did not need to turn to know that his back too faced hers. They lay in silence, while she feigned the even breath of sleep and believed he did, too.

Despite her fatigue and sore feet, she remained awake, replaying each word, each action, trying to figure out why her plans had gone so badly awry. She had chosen this human male to give her a child, but she knew little of him, of Terra, or of his world's magic, which had taken her *ma-at*.

She had only been to Terra twice, and neither trip had ended well. Once, while she was a schoolgirl, her friend Xerxes had taken her. She had had fun with him, but oh, they had gotten into such trouble for the excursion and had been given the unpleasant task of refining divination crystals as penance. The second trip, to meet Jack, had landed her in her current troubles.

Perhaps there was more she should learn of Terra and this science magic.

And of the Scientist.

She thought back on their conversation, unable to fathom why he had rejected her. Sex was a natural part of the cycle and rhythm of Kaf, something to be enjoyed and celebrated. Was it not so with humans?

What did he mean, no "people skill"? Each word she understood, but the grouping had nuances that failed her. *I know I need to work at this.* His excuses rang through her.

Suddenly she smiled as she understood. Biting back the shout of discovery, she burrowed deeper into her bed of leaves.

"People skills" must be a human phrase for making love. He must have rejected her because he believed he had not the techniques and skills for the pillows.

Confidence blanketed her, bringing with it a contented sleep.

She would teach him the rare pleasures of a true, slow seduction.

And then she would leave him.

He was ten kinds of a fool. Jack lay in the night, watching for the first slivers of dawn. A beautiful, sultry woman had offered herself to him, and he'd turned her down. What kind of red-blooded male did that?

One who was cautious by nature, by training, and by experience. One who thought everything to death, according to a certain female member of his family. One who didn't believe in no-strings-attached offers. There was always a catch, always a downside, and he wanted to know what it was before he acted.

One who knew that the couple of condoms in his wallet

wouldn't be nearly enough if he even started kissing her.

Leila made him want to throw all caution and control and thought away. Made him want to feel and to make love to her until they were both mindless with need. To laugh. Even without her *ma-at* she wove a spell around him, as did this land with its vibrant air and sweet scents and clear water.

Which made it that much more important that he make decisions by intellect, not by impulse.

Jack rolled onto his back and stacked his hands beneath his head. Above him there was almost no moon, just a thin crescent, and virtually no stars. Though the air was fresh and clean, the blackness was nearly as unrelieved as the sealed closet.

Breathing grew difficult, as though suffocating weights sat on his chest, and the scar on his cheek burned. He took a deep breath, stretching the tightness about his lungs, thrusting back the fear, then rubbed a finger down the thin scar, easing out the pain. He'd lain many nights like this, but he still had not wholly conquered his dread of the darkness.

So he would think of other things.

The only other thing he could think of was Leila.

Apparently, she hadn't taken his rejection too much to heart, as she'd soon fallen into a deep sleep. So why had she come to him on Terra? In the silent shadows, he could not ignore the question.

As far as he knew, she didn't know him from Adam, and it certainly wasn't his dashing manners or handsome face that had swept her off her feet. Jack was under no illusions about his appeal. Being a doctor carried a certain respectability, and he could easily entertain a woman for an evening. He knew he was reasonably presentable looking—his identical twin, Beau, had assured him of that fact. In fact, Beau, a district attorney, had once confided his disgust that his political career was rising as much because he looked good on camera as because of his ninety-plus-percent conviction rate.

Although Jack had little trouble finding a date, or a bed partner, when he needed one, he also knew that he didn't have women flocking to him like Beau did. Partly because he had a tendency to forget about the dates when he got absorbed in his work. And because he never got the hang of remembering those niceties that women expected. Like flowers for their birthday. Or phone calls. One short-lived affair had ended when the woman had dubbed him an AMP—absentminded professor. Another had told him with well-meaning sincerity that he was clueless.

There had been a woman once, someone he'd thought seriously about marrying. They'd shared many of the same interests: she'd taught in the medical school, worked on genetic research in a lab down the hall, and had been the female member of his adventure-racing team. Sex was a pleasant pastime. Then she'd gotten the opportunity for a full professorship in California. He'd urged her to accept—it was a career-making proposition—and she had. With distance, they'd drifted apart, and she'd married someone else last year.

With a soft sigh, Leila rolled over in her sleep and her hand brushed against his shoulder, then rested against his arm. A wisp of a breeze carried to him the faint scent of clover mixed with exotic woman. He glanced at her, but she seemed firmly asleep and she made no further move.

He returned his attention to the sky—luckily, the blackness was not so complete now as dawn neared—and his question. Why had she come to him? What did she want?

Leila was a puzzle. He'd expected her to be pampered, soft, and useless.

She sighed again and snuggled closer, perhaps automatically seeking his heat, although the dawning air was starting to warm. Soft, she was definitely that, and likely pampered. But useless? No. She knew a great deal about her world, about the plants and animals that inhabited it. She had secrets, but didn't everyone?

Leila stirred, rubbing against him like a sleek cat, awakening his body to the scent and morning touch of her. Desire slammed into him with no subtlety and no warning. Blood thrumming, he bent over her and brushed back a soft tendril of hair. Even sleep looked beautiful on her. Silky hair, smooth skin without the imprints of leaves or rocks, lashes delicate against her cheeks, faint blue veins on her lids. He touched the corner of her eye, swallowing against a mouth dry with wanting. Slowly her eyes opened, at first sleepy, then clear and knowing. He held his breath, wondering what she would do. Would she touch him? He bent closer. Kiss him?

Wordlessly, she rolled away from him. She knelt beside their makeshift bed and placed her hands on the cool, slick rock. For a moment, she bowed her head and remained absolutely still.

"My *ma-at* has not returned," she whispered, then with sinuous grace rose to her feet. Without another glance, she disappeared behind a finger of rock. "I will be gone but a moment," she called. "The mango fruit are good to break our fast."

Chapter Five

"I'm tired, Scientist. May we stop?"

Jack groaned as Leila stopped walking, then lowered herself gracefully to a rock. Though she'd phrased her wish in the form of a pretty question, he knew they would not be going forward any time soon. If he insisted they keep going, she would simply ignore him.

Bowing to the inevitable—just as he'd given up trying to get her to call him Jack instead of Scientist; at least it was better than Wizard—he sat beside her while she brushed dirt off the soles of her feet. Damn, but she made even that look sexy. He stretched out his legs and rubbed his itchy nose.

Leila wasn't like any woman he'd ever traveled with. The female member of his racing team was as driven as he was, not letting fatigue, blisters, or wretchedness stand in the way of reaching the finish line, preferably in first place. Once, while camping with his almost-fiancée; they'd been surprised by an unexpected rain. No complaints there. She'd continued with him until night, when they efficiently set up camp together.

Leila, however, meandered.

She seemed in no hurry to reach any destination. She walked at no set pace, took frequent detours when something caught her interest, and was of the opinion that frequent rest stops were as necessary as fresh water. She hogged the mango fruits he'd picked. She hadn't hesitated to complain when she was uncomfortable or to make her displeasures known—silent endurance didn't seem to be her style.

Yet as they'd walked, he'd found that their relaxed pace bothered him less and less, as he lost himself in her easy rhythm.

Leila was an intriguing companion, if not an easy one. She told him about her world with a depth of understanding that surprised him and asked about his life with equal interest. She taught him words and phrases in *Fahrisa*. Her low, throaty laugh seemed a natural part of the untamed land.

She noticed details. Small things like a red insect she'd avoided stepping on and large things like a distant, lone tree she'd demanded they visit. The tree provided them with strips of bark to chew, which assuaged hunger pangs.

And she did it all with a simmering sensuality that seemed as innate as a blink or a swallow.

Leila began to massage her toes—there was that sexiness again.

"The Towers spew more *adamana* ashes," she observed as she unwrapped the bandage from her hand. "We cannot avoid them today."

"Unfortunately." A sneeze punctuated his answer.

"Hmmm, my hand seems to have healed." She held it out for him to see. Only a faint scratch marred the skin.

"So it has. You won't need the bandage. How are your feet?" He knew from experience how much damage the feet endured during a trek. She'd refused the offer of his shoes, probably wisely since his feet were so much bigger than hers.

"They grow tired." She held out one dainty foot. "Would you be generous, Scientist? A massage that I may continue?"

How could he refuse the invitation to touch her?

Her foot was small, without a single callus or blemish. The toenails were painted, each a different, glittery color. Shifting his attention from the rainbow, he inspected the skin, trying for clinical detachment. Trying and failing, as his fingers caressed the tips of her toes, brushing off the remnants of dirt and ash. He was relieved to see no cuts, no nidus for infection. He pressed against the ball of her foot, and she winced.

"Sorry."

"It is naught but a single spot of soreness."

"Probably bruised," he guessed, though there was no discoloration. He massaged again, more gently this time, and tried to keep focused on her foot, going no further than the ankle. Or maybe the knee. The thigh emerging from the folds of her robe. The . . .

He raised his gaze quickly to her face, while his fingers kept massaging the delicate bones and skin.

She was leaning against a slab of rock, her eyes closed, her face lifted to the sun. The turquoise tablet on its thin gold chain nestled in the hollow of her throat. Several mangoes were tucked into her robe. Their bulk caused the lapels to gape at the level of her breasts, revealing tantalizing glimpses of her smooth curves. Once, maybe twice, the gap widened just enough to show a flash of gold at the tips.

Don't even go there. Don't even think about it.

Hydrogen. Atomic number one.

Slowly her eyes opened, and she gave him a quizzical look. "Why do your eyes weep?"

He blinked his runny eyes. "Allergies."

He'd developed them suddenly as a child, at the same time he'd acquired the scar and an aversion to the dark, but he'd thought the years and numerous desensitization shots had gotten rid of them. Not so, apparently. He rubbed his itchy nose again. Here, the cause was unclear, so he wasn't sure what to avoid. There wasn't enough pollen in the air for that to be the culprit. Maybe he was allergic to the glittery ash that dusted his clothes and skin.

Her dark brows drew together. "Allergies? This is not a word that translates."

"My body is reacting to something in your world. Chemicals are released into my bloodstream and cause the reactions you see." Another sneeze.

"Why? What is the purpose of the unpleasantness?"

"Normally it's protective, helps us clear out foreign

substances. Sometimes, though, it gets out of whack."

"Whack?" Her toes curled against his fingers.

Stinging sweat dripped into his sore eyes as his temperature rose. "It goes wrong."

She frowned. "You are the Scientist. Can you not perform the rituals to realign the harmony of your body?"

"Our ritual is called Claritin. And I don't have any." He cupped her smooth heel and stroked down the Achilles tendon.

Leila gave a throaty purr. "Ah, you lack the necessary instruments. Perhaps if you tell me what you use, I can help you find them."

"I don't think this place will supply what I need." He forced himself to concentrate on the conversation, her voice, the mechanics of the massage, his itchy nose and eyes, instead of the curves of her body and the silk of her skin.

She glanced around at the barren rock where they sat and nodded. "The Tower Lands are said to be a place of deep *ma-at*, perhaps the most potent in all of Kaf. They are never said to be easy or hospitable, however. That is why they are a place of trial." She leaned forward and laid a hand on his thigh. Her fingers curled against the sensitive sciatic nerve.

Her soft touch sparked through him, short-circuiting thought and logic. She had touched him before during the day, not often but always unexpectedly, and each time the result was the same. Tiny moments of sheer mental chaos.

"When my *ma-at* returns," she continued softly, "I

can perform the Ritual of Harmony with you. It takes but a few special words, a candle of sun yellow, the resinous scent of galbanum, and standing naked in the dawn-rising wind."

Left in the wake of departing logic was an overload of need, fueled by quick, raw images: of himself and her together, of the wind brushing her long hair against him, of her touch curling elsewhere around him. Jack shot to his feet, dropping her foot, breaking the contact, denying the obsession, gathering back his control. "Are you rested? Feet better? We need to find a better site before nightfall."

"Yes, and I thank you, Scientist." She stood with sinuous grace. "Let us hope Solomon will be merciful and lead our footsteps to a place of respite."

Uncounted footsteps later, Jack decided that if Solomon was leading, then the deity wasn't in a generous mood.

He had lived through thirty-five humid summers in New Orleans. He had rock climbed and adventure raced in some of the most inhospitable climates on Earth. The Tower Lands of Kaf, he decided, ranked among the top ten for unpleasantness.

Not because of the stifling air or the jagged, slippery rock. Those were familiar and manageable challenges. The desolate landscape even had a stark beauty that he reluctantly admired.

It was the capriciousness of the land that he hated. Rising smoke plumes concealed their footing at odd and inopportune times. Hot, erratic breezes engulfed them in unpredictable odors ranging from the appealing to the rank. Solid rock formations shifted on a whim. Barriers sprang up where no barrier had existed. Plants grew where no vegetation should survive.

Unpredictable he could handle. Illogical bothered him.

And the area they now traversed was the most illogical to date.

The towering rocks had gradually changed from obsidian to crystalline, then thinned until they were no thicker than his wrist. He couldn't tell what kind of material they were made of. Silica, salt, mica, diamond? Likely something he'd never experienced.

Light danced through the prismatic structures, changing them to primary-hued spires and casting a brilliant white light intermingled with rainbows. That much light should have made the hot air almost unbearable, but if anything, it was slightly cooler here, as though the rising breeze came from a large body of water scented with myrtle and mint.

A distinct, formless uneasiness grew outward from his belly, while a sneeze gathered at the back of his throat. The sneeze he stifled. The uneasiness he could not.

Behind him, he heard Leila's footsteps slow. She'd been remarkably quiet since their last rest stop, yet she had stayed within touching distance. She hadn't reached out to him again, but he'd been acutely aware of the quiet fall of her surefooted steps and the clover scent of her. He turned to watch her, guessing she was tiring.

Enchantment

He found her gazing in rapt attention around her and paying no attention to her footing or route. A half-eaten mango dangled from her hand, while its juice coated her lips with a sweet dampness.

Jack cleared his dry throat, and she ignored him. The sneeze returned and escaped. It echoed around the needle-like spires of crystalline rock, then faded. But another sound grew as the clear stones began to vibrate. They emitted a melodic hum, which sounded as though the valley were filled with the chants of a thousand and one Tibetan monks.

"You have found it, Scientist," Leila breathed. "I thought it mere legend."

"Found what?"

"The *Kaliamahru*."

He sneezed again, and another harmonic tone rose. The pressure of a third sneeze grew, but he pressed his finger to his nose. Keep this up and he'd have an entire symphony.

"The choir of rock," Leila added, then gave him a puzzled look. "Few can find them. Fewer still entice their song. Yet you, a stranger, do both. How is this possible?"

"Maybe I've realigned the harmony in my body." His raspy voice gave the lie to that theory. "Do we need to go through this formation to get where we are going? Can we go around?"

"If it is here, then we must embrace it." She pointed to a small path that he hadn't noticed. "That is our route."

Jack would have preferred to avoid the whole maze.

71

Despite the harmony of the rock, he didn't like this. Didn't like it at all. The utter alienness of it made his stomach clench, warning him that, despite its beauty, this was not a friendly place. Yet Leila didn't hesitate. She walked into the *Kaliamahru*, and he followed her, the humming spires ringing in his ears.

Time and distance did not improve his opinion. There appeared to be a single route through the crystalline barrier, a route that urged them ever onward. Several times they hit seeming dead ends, only to turn around and find a small opening to one side. Jack could never decide if he'd missed seeing it or if it had just opened. Once, he tried to retrace their path out of the spired jungle, reversing the pattern of lefts and rights, but they never reached the edge. Instead, he suspected they were forced back along the path forward.

Where exactly was Wonderland leading them?

He stopped and glanced overhead, trying to judge their progress and direction by the sun. Impossible; the brilliance surrounding them blotted out the sky.

Besides, maybe here the sun didn't travel from east to west. Maybe it traveled in a circle, then dropped into a volcano top for the night. He checked his watch. Still stuck on 11:28 p.m. It could tell the time in six different countries, connect him to his e-mail, and direct him with a GPS, but not one of those features worked on Kaf. He glanced back at Leila, who had taken advantage of the pause to sit cross-legged in the path.

Jack sat beside her. She offered him a mango. He

took a bite—the flesh was warm from the contact with her skin, but still sweet and juicy—then handed it back. "We're being herded somewhere. Did you notice?"

"I had noticed the lack of choice in our route," Leila said around the mango.

"Doesn't that worry you?"

She shrugged. "Worry does no good. What other choice do we have but to go ahead? Besides, it is the will of the *Kaliamahru* and of Kaf."

He gritted his teeth, his jaw aching. He had always respected the awesome power of nature, but he had never personalized it, never defined it as good or bad. Now he could not rid himself of the gut-knotting notion that he was being led—being controlled—by the same land that required beseeching every time he turned around. He had thought he must guard against *ma-at* directed by a djinni. Not a land that suddenly felt . . . evil.

Oh, hell, was he turning as fanciful as a fairy tale? Clear pebbles littered the path. He sifted a handful through his fingers. Smooth and colorless, they left not a single mote of dirt or shard of crystal in their wake, yet his fingers turned blue from the contact. He watched the color slowly fade.

No, there had to be a *reason* they were being led, and he mistrusted any purpose that came from a living land of *ma-at*.

There was one thing he could do. He gripped the quiescent crystal lying on his chest. The device tempted him. Should he turn it on? He'd turned it off this morning, hoping to observe and learn about *ma-at* in safety, where no djinni wielded the powers. And he'd been curious whether Leila's *ma-at* would be restored.

If he turned it on now, though, and negated the *ma-at*, would all this disappear? Would the rock formation magically open? Or would their path vanish, sealing them in here?

Other than the strange path, so far the land had only sung beautiful chords. Until something specific forced his hand, he'd keep the crystal off, he decided. His ace in the hole, so to speak. For now, he would follow where the path led, and try to figure out what was happening.

Leila glanced overhead, then rubbed one hand along her arm. "When night falls, there will be little light from the moon. The Night of No Moon is but two days hence. We have some daylight left. I think it would be wise to continue."

"I think you're right." With any luck, they would be well and gone from here before the Night of No Moon. He rose, and she lifted her hand for assistance. He took it, her hand soft and delicate within his, and she followed him to her feet.

For a moment, he could not let go of her. Unease gave way to a different restlessness. Her robe was dusty, her feet dirty, and her hair blew about her, yet he could not deny her appeal. He'd never been drawn to sleek and polished, and as her veneer peeled away he found her attraction harder to resist.

One lock of dark hair caught on her cheek, and he

brushed it back, smoothing it behind her ear. Glittery ash dotted her chin. He rubbed a thumb across it, shifting the ash from her to himself. Her skin was as soft as thistledown. Lashes and brows as black as the Towers of Kaf framed her eyes, which, despite the pull of fatigue, still met his with the sheen of interest.

She was beautiful naturally, without the enhancements of *ma-at*. Beautiful outside. The few glimpses he'd had of the woman inside were inconclusive. Just as he knew little of this land, he knew too little about her.

A shadow fell across her face as a rare cloud covered the sun. She drew back and glanced overhead. "We should not tarry."

"I would prefer not to spend the night listening to rock lullabies," he agreed, and the moment of desire once again gave way to necessity.

The path here was wide enough that they could walk abreast, so he stayed at her side. "What do you know about the *Kaliamahru*?" he asked, partly because he wanted information, mostly because he wanted the music of her voice to counterpoint the eerie, soulless music of the rock.

"It is the choir of rock."

"Anything else?"

"It is a place of mystery, the origins shrouded in the beginnings of Kaf. I've known no one who found it, or seems to talk about it. It just . . . is."

"Could a djinni cast a spell on the *Kaliamahru*? Make it lead us somewhere?"

"For what reason?"

"I don't know. Boredom? Because it's there? The point is, could they?"

"It would take much power, much time, and much purpose." She shook her head. "I don't know."

Obviously he wasn't going to learn much more about the choir from her, and the landscape yielded few clues.

"Besides, there are much better things to do with one's time," she added.

He tilted his head, curious about her, about her society. "How do you spend your time, Leila? Do you have hobbies? Do djinn have jobs?"

"Jobs?" Leila sifted through her knowledge of his language, seeking the translation of the unfamiliar word. "There are needs of the body. Needs of the spirit. Needs of the mind. All must be met. Wind and fire sustain our souls. Do you not think the aroma of this wind appealing? Like cedar? I could almost believe I am at the grove by my home, should I but close my eyes."

"I mean, are there assigned tasks to do? Responsibilities?"

"Like the cactus must draw the water to its needles? Or the eagle catch the breeze to fly? Or the spider spin its web to eat? You remind me of the spider, you know." She tried to distract him, hoping he would not ask what *her* "job" was. She would not admit she had been given no title, no position of honor, no essential task.

It worked. "A *spider*? How?"

"A few djinn choose to ornament themselves with

beard or mustache. They create the adornment, full and thick or carefully styled."

"And this has what to do with me and the spider?"

She stroked his cheek, and the stubble of beard rasped against her palm. The scratchiness surprised her. "I have never seen an uncompleted beard before. Small hairs grow from your cheeks. A tiny bit longer than yesterday."

"And the spider?"

"These remind me of the sensitive hairs on a spider's legs. The hairs that inform the spider about the world around it. Are these sensitive for you?" She feathered a hand along his jaw and throat, avoiding the talisman.

"Not in the way you're talking about," he answered in a strangled voice. He gripped her wrist lightly, but firmly enough to stop her stroking. "Humans use a razor to cut the growth off each morning. If we don't, it grows in slowly, until we have the beard you mention."

He let go of her wrist, and she dropped her hand to her side. "It seems a tiresome, scruffy route to a beard."

"Sometimes slow is better—"

She gave him a wicked smile. "It is, isn't it?"

Jack scratched his chin. "—but in this case, I think you're right."

She laughed. Her Scientist surprised her ofttimes.

They walked in silence awhile; then the Scientist began again. "If someone was really good at growing things, would he grow the food for a village, while someone else weaves the cloth?"

"You ask more questions than any male I know."

"It's the Scientist's job to ask questions."

"Perhaps you should get your answers from a divination."

"That's not bloody likely. I'll stick to scientific method." He sounded more amused than annoyed. "So, about the jobs . . ."

She sighed, bowing to the inevitable. Jack was always full of persistent questions, which he kept asking in circular ways until he discovered the answer. It was simpler to answer him.

"We have tasks and responsibilities. Each to his abilities and interests."

"Is it physical work or is it all *ma-at*?"

"You cannot demand of the *ma-at* that all be done for you. The body and mind and spirit would grow weak, powerless."

"What might you do without *ma-at*?"

She thought for a moment. "You know, it is easier to transform than to create." Jack gave a noncommittal nod, and she continued. "Perhaps you like figs, so you choose to grow a fig tree in your garden. You tend and nurture it, giving it water and food and care. In return, it blesses you with the tender fruit to eat. One day, however, sweet as the fig may be, you crave a date. You may trade your fig for your neighbor's date, or you may transform the fig to a date."

"How does it work? Your *ma-at*?"

"There are rituals, incantations—"

"Window dressing. Focusing tools. No, I mean, how does it *work*?"

He asked how it worked, yet he dismissed the vital rituals? She stared at the Scientist, confused. He was so many contradictions. A powerful genius Scientist who could steal *ma-at*, yet knew so little of her world. He made mistakes, and then he laughed at himself. He invoked no incantations, but he banished the fire salamander. He asked her, a powerless djinni without *ma-at*, to perform the honored task of teacher.

She shook her head. "Work? It does not work. It . . . is."

"How do you draw the power?"

Irritation began to replace confusion. "I do not know." If she did, by Solomon, she would have drawn much more power long ago. She would have replenished what he'd taken.

Instead, her *ma-at* hovered just beyond her reach, like a sound too low to be heard or a sight too quick to be seen. Her feet still touched the soil of her home; Kaf still nourished her. She could sense that the power was there—the air still sparkled in unconscious reflection of her most intense emotions—but she could not grasp or use the elusive *ma-at*.

"How does it feel?" he persisted. "Electric? Cold? Spooky?"

His question reminded her of the empty hole she'd been trying to ignore. It reminded her of the dirt and the sweat and the sore feet and the scalding sun, none of which she could do anything about. It reminded her of helplessness and powerlessness.

"It feels missing."

"And you're afraid it won't come back," he said softly.

Jack Montgomery saw too much. "Do you not have fears, too, Scientist?"

He looked away from her. Then he sneezed, freeing her hands, and the *Kaliamahru* began to sing again.

"Those damn rocks," he muttered, and one more moment of intimacy was lost.

Privately she agreed with him about "those damn rocks." Finding *Kaliamahru* was supposed to be a rare privilege, but as with so many good things in this life, there were hidden costs. She discovered—Solomon forgive her for the blasphemy—that she disliked the song of the rock. It had not the perfect melody she'd expected. Some note, some tone of it grated against her ear.

Was it because of human Jack? Because she had not the *ma-at*? Neither was a pleasant thought.

"You said each djinni had tasks according to his talents," the Scientist persisted shortly after they resumed their trek. "What are your tasks, Leila?"

What should she tell him? She could not admit, not to a powerful scientist, not to a man whose appeal for her grew by each moment, how few her skills were. He spoke to her with admiration in his voice, and she did not want to lose that rare balm. She did not want him to look at her with pity or condescension. But what lie or evasion would satisfy a man who persisted in seeking the answers?

"My garden is renowned," she said at last. That much, at least, was true. "I . . ."

She broke off as they turned a corner and came to a halt. A large crystalline slab blocked the path.

"Over, around, or through," Jack murmured, staring at the obstacle. They both knew turning back was a futile option.

No *ma-at* doorway opened in the slab, so she guessed through was out. "There is a gap at the side. We might squeeze past."

He peered into the narrow opening. "I won't fit."

She eyed him with a sidelong glance, recognizing the truth of his words. His shoulders were broad and his body firm and large.

"You could try it," he suggested. "Go on alone."

"I do not think I will fit either." She shook her head. "Besides, I have made a bargain. We travel together."

"Then we have to figure how to get over it."

Leila stared at the crystal, unable to fathom a way to the top of the rock, which was higher than either of them. Yet she had no doubt that the *Kaliamahru* would allow them through, in some fashion. Perhaps they should wait to see what the fates would reveal.

The Scientist, however, did not seem content to wait for the fates. He ran his hands across the rock, momentarily distracting her. He had nice hands, she decided; they had felt very nice indeed on her feet.

He reached up, feeling higher along the rock, stretching with a powerful motion, and her body tightened at the sight. A beam of sun pierced the crystal, highlighting his strange light hair. Had it gotten paler

81

in the two days they'd traveled, as though the sun of Kaf took color from the strands? Along with his blue eyes, the fair hair gave him a foreign look, yet she found his very difference appealing.

"I think I've found a way across."

So singled-minded he was. Always pushing forward. "What is your way?"

"This slab isn't perfectly smooth; there are toeholds and handholds."

"Where? I see none."

"Right here." He took her hand and guided it to a small indentation in the rock. Yes, he had very nice hands indeed. "And here." He moved her hand up to another.

"There are not enough to climb with."

"There are. I've done some rock climbing. I can get to the top."

"You will leave me here?" When they reached the sands, she had feared he would find her more of a burden than a benefit. However, she had believed that in the Tower Lands she was of some use to him. Was he going to abandon her?

He laid a hand on her cheek, forcing her to look at him. "We have a bargain, don't we? Together?"

She nodded, unable to speak for the heat radiating from his touch, the relief that he would honor their bargain.

"I can climb up; then I'll reach down and haul you up."

Leila studied the rock a moment. So solid, so tall. Yet the Scientist assured her it could be climbed. She shook her head. "No. What if we come upon another rock and it is too big for you to reach down? I must be able to climb with you. You must teach me."

"I can't teach you all about rock climbing in a few minutes."

"I do not need to know all about it. I only need enough to get to the top."

Jack laughed. "All right. When you stick your chin out that way, I know you're determined. And in this case, you're right."

She wrapped the lower half of her robe about her hips, then pulled the ends between her legs and knotted them at her waist, leaving her legs free. "You will find I am a fast learner, Scientist."

"Oh, that I never doubted." Jack broke away from staring at her legs. "Now put your hand here. Curl your fingers, feel the break, grab the rock—that's right."

Straining, aching, her progress as slow as cold honey, Leila made her way toward the top. It was not far. As he'd said, he could have easily climbed alone, then hoisted her up. Yet Jack Montgomery never left her, never let her fall. With calm patience he taught her the basic skills she needed.

Blue painted her hands and cheeks and chest. The color came and faded, came and faded at each contact with the rock. She could feel the rock's vibration and the song's hum in her ear. So close, so much a part of her.

Her fingers burned from the effort, and her lungs heaved with the need for air. Sweat—by Solomon, how she hated sweat—ran down her back and stung her eyes. Her muscles quivered, unaccustomed to the effort. Still, she persevered, determined not to fail. She memorized each instruction he gave, each movement he made, learning what she needed.

Then she was at the top. No spectacular view greeted her, only the continuing spires of the *Kalia-mahru*. No welcoming wind caressed her to dry the unpleasant stickiness with a cool, mint freshness. No balms awaited to soothe her. All that faced her ahead was the problem of how to get down the other side.

Yet pride touched her, along with a touch of fear. She had *done* it. Without *ma-at*. When had she ever done anything without even a breath of *ma-at*?

Jack Montgomery stood beside her, blond and bristling, utterly foreign, infinitely desirable. His hands fisted at his waist while he studied the hind side of the rock. He looked strong, driven, focused, male.

"The ground below is higher on this side," he said. "I can slide down, then help you." He gave her a sidelong glance. "Unless you're going to insist on climbing down."

Her muscles protested at the mere thought. "The lesson is sufficient for now." She pressed her palms together and inclined her head. "Thank you for teaching me."

Jack shook his head. "You're different from anyone I've ever met," he said hoarsely. Then he turned and began to slide down the rock.

Leila watched him descend, irritated that he would burst her elation. Dismiss her thanks.

Different. How she hated that word. She didn't want to be different. She wanted to be part of something, of someone, wholly and without judgment.

Yet what did he mean about her differences? Admittedly, she had not been at her best these past hours, either in appearance or power, but she did not think she'd revealed her deficiencies. He knew she was without *ma-at*. Did he mean different because she was a djinni?

"Okay, your turn," he called from the bottom, oblivious to her annoyance.

She turned and began the feet-first slide down the rock. Grit prickled her hands as she slid, and her chest bruised against the hardness. A minute later, the Scientist gripped her waist and lowered her the remaining distance.

Feet on the ground, his tall strength behind her, she stood, trembling with fatigue and annoyance. She brushed blue, grimy hands against her robe. "How?" she asked, turning in his arms, enjoying the warmth and protection more than she wanted, for she knew how fleeting and illusory they were. "How am I different?"

He brushed her hair back; then his hand lingered, cupping her neck with strong fingers. His other hand was anchored at her waist. The small touches made her tingle, as though her powers had reawakened after a long sleep.

"You're so beautiful," he explained.

It pleased her to know that he thought her beautiful. Still, she could not suppress the small, irrational pang of disappointment that, like others, he chose her beauty to admire.

What did surprise her was that he thought her beautiful *now*. Though she had tried to keep herself cleaned and polished and sweet smelling, her efforts had not been entirely successful. A drop of sweat trickled between her breasts.

"Beautiful? When I sweat? When dirt coats my thumbs?"

"I like a woman who can sweat." He leaned forward and kissed the sheen of her forehead.

Heat blazed through her. The power of desire awoke, demanding its due.

Yet she could not give in to it. Not here, not like this without the familiar accoutrements of seduction. She wasn't ready, wasn't prepared.

Besides—he *liked* sweat? She had to understand this. Understand him. Was this why he first turned away from her in the tavern? Perhaps beauty was a rarity among human females. She had met but two, Isis and Zoe, and both were pleasant featured, but she would not have chosen *beautiful* as their description. "Do human females not have beauty?"

"Yes. Many do. I wasn't talking only about physical beauty."

"You do not like my appearance?" Maybe she didn't want to understand this.

"I like your appearance very much."

"So, you do think I am beautiful?"

"Yes."

"Humans do not prize beauty?"

"We do. Perhaps more than we should."

"But you do not?"

"I like it, I didn't mean that." He rubbed a hand against the back of his neck, loosening his grip, letting her go. "Hell, I'm making a muddle of this. You're beautiful, and yes, I like that about you. But it's more. You seem to have a zest for . . . knowledge. A curiosity. A vibrancy. That's rare. That's special." He pivoted, as if embarrassed by his words. "C'mon. You're right, we should make the most of the daylight."

Leila barely noticed the *Kaliamahru* as she followed him: Instead, his words echoed in her mind, as though repetition could strip them of their startling power.

You have a zest for knowledge. That's rare. That's special.

He liked her because of her *mind*?

By Solomon's toes, that would bear some thought.

Chapter Six

They trudged on as the shadows lengthened and the brilliant lights faded. The gleaming crystalline spires reminded Jack of a forest of white Glo-sticks. Or Hansel and Gretel being led by a line of white pebbles.

Except it wasn't a gingerbread house at the end; it was a green clearing. He halted at the edge, rubbed his bleary eyes, sneezed, and looked again, unable to believe in Eden amidst the harsh land.

"Oh, Solomon be praised," breathed Leila.

Perhaps Solomon *was* feeling benevolent today.

Or perhaps there was a serpent awaiting them.

The small clearing was covered with thick, soft grass, while sweet-smelling fruit trees dotted the outskirts. Feathery tufts of vegetables grew in one corner, and at the far edge, a waterfall tumbled from the rock walls into a large pool. Jack crossed to it. Lava-warmed or snow-fed icy? Sweet or brackish or poisoned? He hesitated a moment, then stuck the tip of his finger in the water.

"Is it warm?" asked Leila. "Oh, I want a bath."

"Yes, but I think you should—"

She wasn't listening. Instead, she stripped off her robe and walked into the pool. Jack stood as rooted as one of the fruit trees, his mouth dry. Only one part of him stirred.

Leila had a beautiful body. Curved and generous and soft. Her skin was golden all over, unmarred by a single wrinkle or blemish or tan line. She first splashed her face, arms, and shoulders, then lowered herself into the pond with a heartfelt sigh of pleasure. The surrounding water and the rocks were clear, yet the clarity concealed and shaded rather than revealed. Only when she lay on her back and stroked lazily through the water could he see that her breasts were gold-tipped and there was a tantalizing shadow lower.

He turned away, feeling like a twelve-year-old voyeur.

"Scientist," she called. "This water is a blessing. Do you not wish to bathe now?"

He had no trouble recognizing the subtle suggestion that he'd gotten ripe during the trip, and the prospect of getting clean was very appealing. "When you finish."

"You should find it pleasurable. We both would. It is like paradise."

This time, he recognized the subtle invitation, one he wasn't prepared to accept. "I'm sure I will."

"Why do you turn from me?"

"I'm giving you privacy."

"Because I have not the stones?"

She couldn't be using the word in the crude, human slang sense. "The stones?"

"The stone of privacy to light when I do not wish to accept company." She gave a low chuckle. "I rarely light my stones. Scientist, I will tell you if I require privacy. Now I do not."

He ran a hand around the band of wires at his neck. "I'll look for food," he managed, but when he tried to step away, her low voice stopped him.

"My nakedness bothers you?"

The woman was too good at reading him. "Humans don't get naked together unless they are very close. Or nudists."

He heard her splashing. "Djinn are raised without such restrictions. It does not bother me if you watch."

Leila might have no modesty, but his thirty-plus years of conditioning hadn't disappeared in two days.

"I should enjoying watching you," she added. "I would like to see your body. It appears very nice." The last words were almost a purr.

Oh, hell. Recount the Periodic Table? He couldn't even think beyond hydrogen. Desperately he sought another distraction. "I'll do a quick reconnoiter while there's still some light."

While they'd talked, the sun had disappeared behind the ledges of rock. In its wake remained a brilliant crimson that shaded the sky and the spires and sparkled atop the water. He skirted the edges of the clearing, unease growing as the red hue deepened and he found only a fence of trees.

Maybe it was the deepening twilight that concealed their route. Hoping he'd made a mistake, he searched further around the area where he thought they'd entered. Although the coming night camouflaged with shadows, he recognized the knobs on that rock and the clump of flowered bushes that had marked their entrance to the clearing.

Now, instead of a path, foliage formed an impenetrable barrier. The leaves wove a pattern as knotted as his stomach. He tried to squeeze through the trunks and spires, but even though the gap seemed large enough, he couldn't fit through. Bark, rock, limbs, and leaves grabbed at him, squeezing the air from his lungs. He gave up and circled the entire perimeter, looking fruitlessly for another exit, another small opening he may have missed.

Nothing.

His gut clenched. The tranquil clearing had become a prison. The path in, and out, had disappeared.

The glow from the spires faded, leaving only a single star and the sliver of moon as light. Had the night caused the trees to close, like sunflowers, or was it something more? Something magic? Something sinister?

As if to mock his fears, the rocks hummed in quiet counterpoint.

He picked his way back toward Leila. Between the waning moon and the overhead branches, his vision was nearly nonexistent. He tripped over a tree root and saved himself from a jarring fall by grabbing the trunk. The bark was warmer than he expected, as hot as body heat, and he jerked back, snagging the laced wires at his chest.

Carefully he untangled the device. The crystal hung heavy from its chain, a foreign talisman in this strange land. Jack fingered it, wondering again what would happen if he turned it on. Two things stopped him: the possibility that negating the *ma-at* might seal them in here, and the fear that while he might be free, Leila could remain trapped.

"Scientist?" Leila's voice broke through, delaying his decision. "Jack?" She didn't sound frantic, only worried—worried enough that she'd finally called him Jack.

"Coming," he called, following the sound of her voice.

It was lighter outside the concealing trees. His tension eased as he emerged into the open and saw Leila waiting at the edge of the pool, her robe once more on. Though it was past twilight, he could see enough to realize she'd brushed away the worst of the dust and smoothed the wrinkles from the robe.

The sweet scent of the fruit trees, the balmy heat of the night, the low hum of the rocks lulled and soothed, slowly erasing his worry. He raked a hand through his hair. Something, something wasn't right here. Shouldn't he be more upset about the barrier, bursting to tell Leila and figure a way out?

In her hands, Leila held roots and fruit. Her damp hair hung in a sleek curtain down her back, and she glanced around her with a quick, nervous motion. Then she spied him and gave a tiny sigh of relief. She moved closer, set down her food, and held out a hand. "I thought you'd gone."

He took her hand, fleetingly aware once again of its soft strength. Concerns evaporated under the tranquillity of the lush night. "I told you, we're in this together."

"But sometime you may not have a choice whether you leave or not."

He didn't have a reply for her. "You've been shopping, I see." He nodded to her collection of food.

"Shopping?" The confusion cleared from her face, and she gave her throaty laugh. "You are making a joke?"

"A feeble one, yes." Here in the clearing, with Leila at his side, the missing exit didn't seem so urgent. It should be, he thought, but it wasn't. They could talk about it later. He drew a finger across the silky tips of her hair. With such pleasant surroundings, with a beautiful, sexy woman by his side, why should he want to leave? "What's on the menu for tonight?"

"Turnip and beet and fig."

He hated beets. "No small edible rodents?"

Her horrorstruck look was answer enough.

"Another lame joke," he explained. He sat beside the stash of food, picked what he thought was the turnip, and bit into the crunchy vegetable. Not bad—in fact, very good, with a taste very different from the anemic sprayed and genetically engineered fruits and vegetables at home.

Leila picked up the fig. "You will bathe after the meal?"

Jack suppressed a chuckle, feeling more relaxed as he sat beside her. "Yes."

"Where did you go while I swam?"

Suddenly he remembered the barrier. Again that mixed sensation of knowing he should be doing something and wondering why he was so worried washed across him. "I walked the perimeter. Our route in has disappeared."

"Oh?"

She didn't sound surprised or upset. He wished the dark didn't prevent him from seeing her as well as he heard her. "Did you expect that?"

"No."

"Are you upset?"

"Will being upset open the route?"

Leila, he was discovering, could have a decidedly pragmatic bent. "Besides," she added, licking juice from her fingers, "we can do nothing tonight. It is too dark to see."

In that she was right. "But if the clearing's still closed come morning?" he murmured to himself, finishing his turnip and wondering why he persisted. Why was he so anxious about leaving?

"You will figure out what to do." Leila sounded supremely confident in his abilities.

He took a handful of figs and slowly chewed the sweet fruit. The air was as still as he'd ever experienced. No wind rustled the leaves, and no odors—pleasant or otherwise—stirred in the air. All the air carried was heat and oxygen. He'd been in isolated spots on earth—desert, mountain top, an island off the coast—But even in the most solitary there were sounds of nature. Not here. No birdsong, no creak of ice or snow, no lap of waves, no whistle of a breeze or chirp of a cricket. It was as though nature herself slept the sleep of the dead.

The only signs and sounds of life came from Leila, and as his wariness went to sleep, his senses awoke. He heard the delicate sigh of her breath, the crunch as she ate her beet, the rustle of her robe against the grass. Clover, fresh water, juice, her scents wafted over him. His mouth watered in anticipation.

"I do not like the dark," she said, looking up from her meal.

"Neither do I," he admitted.

"Did you ever get lost in a cave?"

"No. Did you?"

"It was an unpleasant experience. Have you always had the fear?"

"No." He bit back the urge to explain.

The dark, the silence, the stillness—all heightened his awareness further. Air brushed across his sensitive skin as she shifted closer to him. Her hip touched his. Heat shot through him, blotting out all but a thread of common sense.

"I'll take that bath now." Jack got to his feet.

"Have you eaten your fill, then?"

Not nearly. The unbidden thought, for it was not food he desired, resonated through him. "Enough," he answered.

"Do you wish privacy?"

Your body—it appears very nice. He laid a hand at the side of her neck. The silky fall of her hair caressed his hand, while beneath his palm he felt the flutter of her pulse. "Wait for me here, Leila."

"Yes."

He leaned over and kissed her. Slowly, sensually, expectantly. Blood rushed through him as he gently pulled away. "My bath first."

By this time, his eyes had made some accommodation to the meager light. He could see the trees and shrubs as shadows. He could catch the reflection of the moon in the clear water as he picked his way toward the pond.

At the water's edge, he didn't hesitate. Obviously, Leila's sensibilities wouldn't be offended if he stripped, and he wanted to be clean all over. He shed his clothes and placed his shoes beside the neat pile. One moment of debate; then he slipped the rope of wires over his head and tucked it beneath the clothes. The circuitry was shielded from the elements, but there was no sense in taking a chance.

The water was an ideal temperature. No shock of cold, not too warm, just a slight invigorating chill. He splashed water under his arms, scrubbed between his toes, ducked his head beneath the surface, and rubbed his scalp, cleaning as best he could without soap or washcloth. Lazily he turned onto his back and stroked through the water, and worry slipped further away from him. No wonder Leila had found such pleasure in the simple process of bathing.

Leila. He heard no sound from her.

Fear gripped him. Irrational fear, for what could harm her here? Nonetheless, he stood in the water, the surface lapping at his hips, and listened. All he heard was the drip of water off his shoulders into the pool. No breeze carried her scent or the sound of her movement. Had something happened to her?

"Leila?" he called.

"Here." Her voice came from the edge of the pool. Jack stroked to the side.

And found Leila holding his device. She looked ready to flee.

"Put that down!" His sharp command rang through the silence.

She dropped it at once, as though the wires, or his command, had shocked her. Immediately she backed away and pressed her palms together. "I'm sorry, Scientist. I merely thought to rinse your garments."

"Why did you take my talisman?" He strode from the water and flung his head back, shaking drops from his hair and out of his eyes.

"I didn't take it; I merely looked. Besides, I don't like it," she added.

"Why?" He retrieved the rope of wires and looped it around his neck.

He stood close enough to Leila to see her now, despite the dark. Her gaze scanned him, then lingered low. Though he'd looked at her as hungrily, her frank perusal still unsettled him, but he refused to cover himself. At least he didn't have any complaints on how he compared in that area. Her gaze swept up, and he thought her face softened, though it might have been a trick of the light.

"Your talisman feels . . . cold. Would you not wear it?" she asked faintly.

"I must." He fingered the patterns in the metal. How could Leila think it cold? Even when it was off, he seemed to feel the pulse of the vibrations and the warming heat.

Faint uneasiness returned. Faint and too amorphous to cause alarm. He shook his head, throwing off the feeling.

Her low sigh floated across the utter stillness. "If it is your will, Scientist, shall I rinse your clothes now?"

"I'll do it," he answered gruffly, surprised by her easy acquiescence. She was a contradiction—challenging one moment, plaintive the next. He could never tell what would ignite her temper, what would rouse her fears. "You don't have to wait on me, Leila. I can fend for myself."

Quickly he rinsed out his T-shirt and jeans. They'd be dry before morning. If Leila had no qualms about his sitting about in the buff, then he wouldn't either.

Brave words.

Foolish bravado.

When he turned, Leila was kneeling on the grass. She wasn't looking at him. Instead, her head was bowed slightly as she finger-combed her almost-dry hair.

His sex sprang to life, engorged, leaving him dizzy and incoherent and dry-mouthed. He drank in every detail of her. The gleam of her hair. The breast that peeked through the strands falling over her shoulder. The supple motion of her muscles as she tended to her toilette. And every detail hardened and tightened him. Naked in body, naked in reaction, there was no hiding that he desired her when she lifted her head to look at him.

She licked her lips with a delicate touch of her tongue, yet her gaze remained caught in his. She didn't even glance at his fierce erection. Instead, she straightened her back, then undid the knot at her waist and shrugged off her robe. The fabric settled in a pool around her, as crimson as the water had reflected the sunset.

Surrounding her he saw the sparks of emotion. Tiny filaments of red, blue, gold. She could no more hide her excitement than he could. Somehow that was reassuring. In a land where deceptions and magic ruled, this at least was real. Unvarnished, no illusion.

Irresistible. Logic, rationality, control—all disappeared behind the utterly overwhelming need for a brief interlude of sheer emotion.

Brief? Brief, yes, their time together would be brief, but tonight was an eternity.

"Scientist?" Leila's gaze broke from his and fastened on his abdomen. A blue aura deepened around her, and he saw a golden glow around her exposed nipples.

"Jack," he said hoarsely. "In these moments at least, call me Jack."

"Jack." Her voice held the rasp of need. She rose to her feet, sinuous and graceful, her gaze still heating his groin. "Will you turn from me this time?"

"I don't know if I could," he admitted.

"I have waited long for this moment." The prismatic colors around her darkened, as though a mirror of darker thoughts.

Why? Why did she want him so much? Questions unfurled at the back of his mind, questions he didn't want to acknowledge and that seemed unimportant right now.

Then she stretched, thrusting her breasts forward, and distracted him.

His palms itched to hold, his mouth ached to taste. He laid a hand between her breasts, feeling the beat of her heart. In this, she was not djinn, he was not human, they were only a man and a woman with mutual desire. He rubbed the back of his hand against the side of her breast, savoring her softness and roundness.

"Are you sure about this, Leila?" Whatever compelled him to ask that? This desire seemed so inevitable. This woman, who was so wrong for him, seemed so utterly right now. His fingers brushed against the turquoise tablet nestled between her breasts. Her only adornment. A reminder of the differences between them.

"It's only these moments between us," he persisted, driven by one tiny point of logic that asked: Was it too fast? Was it the enchantment of this place? "There can be nothing more."

"I know."

Leila knew he spoke the truth. But, oh, she wanted

this brief desire. This joining of flesh to flesh and, briefly, heart to heart. Not for revenge. Not for procreation. She wanted this union for herself. Moments of bliss with a man who saw past the weaknesses and admired, not the beauty, but the woman beneath.

So she settled for simplicity and answered only the question spoken.

"Yes, I'm sure." She stroked the length of him, the soft skin over engorged flesh. "Will you kiss me, Jack Montgomery?"

A low vibration sounded in the surrounding rocks, breaking the silence with a siren's call of need and enchantment. Thought, reason, doubt, plans, all vanished in a tempest of fiery craving.

His fingers tangled in her hair and his arm surrounded her shoulders. He pulled her flat against him, with a mastery that both startled and excited her. His lips lowered to hers.

Jack was not quite as inexperienced as she had thought.

The realization sparked through her, chased away by the rising wind of need. She kissed him back, passionately, expertly. Rainbow sparks exploded against her lids.

"That's better," he growled.

She tunneled her fingers through his hair as he tilted her head back, nudged aside her turquoise tablet, and kissed the sensitive spot at the base of her throat. A kaleidoscope of fire danced around them.

"Much better," he added.

She could find no voice but to moan as control fled. Jack's touches, his kisses, grew more frantic, as though he too had lost all sense and reason and skill. All that mattered was the touch of lips to eager skin, the brush of hair against chest and lower, the slide of caresses and the pressure of want building inside. He throbbed against her thigh.

Cool wind rose in the clearing, brushing leaves against them yet doing nothing to relieve the heat scorching between them. Waves lapped against the edge of the pool, driven by the breeze. Orange and sandalwood, cedar resin and jasmine attar, a potent bouquet surrounded them. She could almost taste the fragrant dates and figs.

She gripped his wrists, spreading his hands on either side of her as she lowered herself to her back. Soft grass tickled her back, and hard muscle pressed atop her. Her fingers wrapped around his talisman, shifting it from between them, and for once she didn't mind the metal or the crystal. It was warm, warm with his heat; through it, she felt him, vital and surging and powerful. Something sparked between her and her Scientist, something alive, something whole, something . . .

Her breath caught, and she stilled.

Her *ma-at*?

Was it her *ma-at*?

Jack Montgomery's kisses still rained over her. His hand still teased her lower, still excited her body's response.

Yet she held her breath, unable to give fully. Her mind, her soul, sought the elusive spark.

"Leila." His hand nudged her legs apart. She opened, granting him access.

There. She felt it. A connection to Kaf, thin and fragile as a spider's thread.

"Leila?" Jack also stilled, as if sensing that part of her attended elsewhere.

The thread grew thinner.

"No, do not stop," she begged, her hips lifting in invitation. She grasped, sought the thread, trying to gather it. Her fingers gripped his crystal; the other hand ground into his wrist. "Do not go."

"I'm not. What's . . . ? Leila?" He lifted his head, shifting his hips from her body.

She opened her eyes. Wind blew his hair across his forehead. The sweet scent of fruit overwhelmed her. Trees, bushes hemmed them in. "My *ma-at*—"

He was not looking at her. "My God, the clearing—"

The *ma-at*. She had to get the *ma-at* that surrounded them and invaded them.

"That tree!" His strangled shout rent the air.

Her fingers tangled around the wire and the crystal.

He reared back, jerking away from her. "No!" he shouted.

Slick with sweat, her grip loosened, and she felt something click, something give. Jack sprang to his feet.

White light exploded around them. Vibrant scents, cool air, refreshing waves faded as though pulled behind a thick veil. All sense of contentment and ease vanished. The connection with Kaf snapped, gone in an instant.

Her fragile *ma-at* disappeared once again, chased by her keening wail of loss.

Chapter Seven

The clearing! It was closing. Imprisoning them. Absorbing them. It was—

Gone. What the hell? Jack spun around, squinting to clear the spots of explosive light still dancing in his vision. The clearing had disappeared. All that remained of the false Eden were their clothes, the small pile of mangoes, a single fig tree, and a trickle of life-giving water seeping from the wall of rock. He stood on the barren shale, not soft grass, and beyond the edges of his vision was the indistinct glow of the *Kaliamahru*. The air smelled like scorched metal.

A headache clamped around his forehead, and he pressed the bridge of his nose, trying to make sense of a world that once again defied logic. He ached with unrelieved need, and his muscles felt as if he'd run a marathon. The activated crystal glowed silver and scarlet in the darkness, his single link to sanity in a life spiraling out of his control.

What the hell had just happened?

He strode over to the lone tree, grabbing his still-damp pants and stepping into them along the way, wincing as he zipped them over his softening erection. He'd looked up from making love to Leila into a scene drawn from his nightmares.

The clearing was closing in on them, and in the bark of the approaching trees were faces. Humanoid faces. So detailed were the features, they looked as if the trees had trapped the souls of imprisoned travelers.

A shudder passed down his spine as he hesitantly touched the bark of the tree. It was of neutral temperature, with no pattern or face in the rough bark. He ran his fingers over the ordinary bark, crumbled a small piece of it, and sniffed the normal woody scent. His heartbeat slowed to an even tempo, and the arid wind dried the sweat from his body. Just a tree.

Yet he hadn't imagined the clearing's movement, nor the faces. That was not the sort of thing a man imagined while making love with a beautiful woman.

His reluctance to leave, his unconcern about the closed barrier, his device being snagged by the trees, it all made sense now. The clearing had to be under some kind of mad spell. Another shudder ran across him. How narrowly had he missed becoming one of those faces in the trees? How narrowly had he missed being held in the eternal dark?

The glow of the crystal in his device caught his attention as the red faded from it. He remembered he'd reared back, and Leila, gripping his crystal, had accidentally turned on the device, he realized. It must have negated the *ma-at* in the clearing. *Ma-at* working on him, for he'd designed the device as personal protection.

He turned away from the tree. Trapped, caught, imprisoned. Old memories dragged at him, tried to pull him into the abyss, and the scar in his cheek burned. Instead, he sought out Leila.

She, at least, was real. She was still here, tying the belt of her robe with an angry jerk and hissing out words she had yet to teach him. He needed no translation, though; frustration bit at him, too. But the time, and the place, had been lost.

He raked a hand through his hair. Twice he'd started to make love to her, and both times he'd been under the influence of some spell. Was making love to Leila only part of the deadly lure? Was his desire only an illusion?

He watched her fluid, if angry, motions and the fire in her eyes as she glanced at him, and, that quickly, the embers of desire glowed again. He remembered his admiration for her tenacity during this trek and his pleasure at hearing her throaty laugh. None of those were fueled by magic. No, his emotions were the only real part of the illusion.

It was an unsettling thought, that his emotions could be trusted more than his senses or his logic. Especially when they were so intense. Intense desire, intense curiosity, and—*admit it, Montgomery*—intense fear. Those faces . . . He shrugged on his shirt, not wanting to remember, and strode over to Leila. When he tried to draw her into his arms, she jerked away, robe and hair swirling around her, and spat out something.

She had never looked so desirable. Or so foreign.

"I don't understand." Not her words, but he suddenly understood her anger. "I'm sorry; I shouldn't have jumped away like that. The clearing—did you see it?" He laid a hand on her shoulder, his fingers threading through her silky hair.

She batted his hand away, then glared at him, her fists clenched until her knuckles turned white. "You took it again."

"Took what?"

"My *ma-at*." She held up her hand, her thumb a scant distance from her finger. "This close. I touched it. I felt it. The clearing was rich with *ma-at*. It was coming back to me. Then"—she made a disgusted noise—"you destroyed it."

He fisted his hands on his hips. "That rich *ma-at* was evil, Leila."

"No! *Ma-at* is not evil."

"It was trying to absorb us. We'd never have gotten out of there."

She wasn't listening. "How could you? How could you? Oh, I wanted to believe that you did not know, or that you did not understand. Twice, however, can be no accident. The violence. The flare. It ripped the *ma-at* from me. It hurt."

"I'm sorry. But I would do it again. We were in danger."

"So you say. You *meant* to take it from me."

"I meant to repel the *ma-at* of the clearing. Not take yours." His fingers touched her wrist as he tried to give her some small measure of comfort.

She flung his hand away and glared at him. "Will you force me now? For it must be force if you are to touch me again."

"I'm not a rapist," he snapped back.

"What more revenge will you exact? Will you demand retribution for my anger?"

"What kind of a monster do you think I am, Leila?"

"I don't know." She stared at him, anger tinting her cheeks pink and glistening in her dark eyes. Absently she tucked her blowing hair behind her ear. "I don't know anymore," she repeated, her voice trailing off. "I do not understand you, Scientist."

"Well, that makes two of us. I don't understand you either." Frustrated, he raked a hand through his hair. "Leila, *you* are safe with me. Your *ma-at* . . . no promises. But if you'd just cool off and stop to think about it, talk about it, you'll admit everything about that clearing was *wrong*. Whatever force was there, it was not beneficent."

With a scornful look her only answer, she turned her back to him. "We have some hours of darkness left. I will sleep." A moment later, she was curled under the lone fig tree.

His fists clenched as he fought back opposing desires: either to kiss her until they were both mindless with need and uncaring of anything else, or to demand that she talk to him, understand his logic, and admit that the *ma-at* was wrong. Right now, he was leaning toward kissing, but even someone without people skills knew better than to approach her at this moment.

The air was cold, he suddenly realized. His skin tightened under the lowering temperatures now that the artifice of the clearing had vanished, and a chill invaded the night. "It will be warmer by the rock, Leila."

She didn't move. "Scientists," he heard her mutter, followed by a word that sounded like "root spawn."

Root spawn, he had a feeling, meant *slug*.

He sat down beside the rock, near Leila—not touching her but close enough to watch over and protect her. Luckily, the rock held remains of the day's heat. He found a few leaves and twigs, and, with the aid of one of his precious matches, he soon had a small fire going. It was a meager luxury in a night that was shaping up to be less than comfortable. No ground cover to provide padding. No sharing of body heat.

He poked at the fire with a stick, scraping the leaves and twigs closer together. With luck, there wasn't a fire salamander lurking nearby. As he stared at the dancing red and yellow and blue, as the heat scorched his face, he tried to sort out the images burned into his memory.

The topmost image was making love to Leila. He fought back the sudden rush of warmth and the remembered sensation of joy. Don't go down that road. Not now.

Then . . . the bushes and trees had brushed against his feet, his legs, his butt. Closing on him and Leila.

A vine had caught in his hair. His scalp tingled with the remembered sensation of pulling away from its grip. None of it touched Leila, only him. And carried with the foliage was . . . what?

Energy.

Power.

Ma-at. No other word seemed to work.

And with it? A sense of *wrongness* strong enough to cut through his desire.

He'd been positioning himself. Ready to lose himself in making love with Leila. Then he'd looked up, pulled away by that dark, cold sensation.

That moment had blazed through him, powered by all senses. The wild clover scent of Leila. The whispering of the leaves through the rising wind. The soft dampness of her skin. The pulsing blood. The difficulty breathing in the closing clearing. Fiery heat, outside and in.

The face.

He'd looked up and seen the almond tree so close, and within the bark he'd seen a face. An anguished face. With the tree branches waving as though a multitude of arms grabbed at him and for him, trying to trap him within the bark like that face was trapped.

And then he had felt it. The surge of power—not from the clearing, but from *himself*. From the crystal he wore and from his determined resistance to the *ma-at*. Like lightning it was transmitted through him and . . .

Bang.

Jack blinked, pulling back from the memory. He'd

been staring at the fire, he realized, and his eyeballs felt scorched.

Only the crystal had saved them. Absently he rubbed a hand across his chest. The crystal was warm to the touch, but not hot. A faint sensation of current, of power, emanated from it and resonated along his nerves and tendons. He stared ahead, although the sliver of moon didn't give enough light to see beyond the immediate area.

The violence of the reaction had surprised him. Although the radiance of the glowing crystal had dimmed now to the luster of an opal, immediately after the clearing had disappeared it had shone a brilliant red. When he'd chased away the fire salamander, there had been none of the explosiveness, none of the vibrancy he'd seen tonight. There'd been none of the wrenching dislocation that accompanied his first use on Earth.

What was different?

The *ma-at* of the salamander was rudimentary. The *ma-at* here had been strong. Leila had called it rich. So the more powerful the action, the more powerful the reaction. A basic law of physics.

The explanation was logical, comfortable. He leaned his head against the rock and closed his eyes, suddenly tired to his bones. As sleep crept closer, however, nagging thoughts flitted through his open mind.

Did he have it backwards? The more powerful the *reaction*—his reaction to the *ma-at*—the more powerful the action of the crystal?

Was it more than a passive shield? Was it something he directed and could control?

Was it his scientific magic?

Faint vibrations from the gleaming crystal passed through the chain of wires and into muscle and sinew, nerve and heart. The power lodged inside him.

The device had worked, and he would not turn it off again while he remained on Kaf. Yet he couldn't help worrying that worse was to come.

It would behoove him to study how best to use the crystal.

If Xerxes had not been chanting the Circles of the Adept, he would never have felt the strange ripple. It nipped through his concentration and disrupted the currents of pain coursing through him. The break jerked him from the powerful ritual, and in that moment of inattention one hundred sunsets of preparation and one hundred circles of continual ceremony were negated.

The power of *ma-at* and the power of sinister forces shot through him, separate, unraveling, not in the unity he craved. Bitter rage at the failure swept through him with the force of a desert sandstorm. Slowly he opened his eyes, mastering both the forces and the depth of his anger.

All that remained were pain and sweat and hunger—his constant companions during the journey. Utter fatigue pulled at his muscles and quivered through his nerves as he gazed out over this most remote portion of the land he claimed. Sand rippled under the wind, and the night cold wrapped him in frigid arms. The arid air stole moisture from his nose and eyes and skin.

Ignoring physical discomforts, Xerxes remained cross-legged before the divination circle, the fire as dry and scorching as his desert home. He touched the onyx tablet at his throat. What was it he had felt? There were sources of power on Kaf besides *ma-at*, and none did he consider unknown, unattainable, or unusable. Nothing, no knowledge, no force, was too tainted to use if it increased his power.

Yet he wanted more, wanted to find the final keys to ultimate power. He had collected old scrolls, old tablets, ancient legends, learned secrets to demand more of Kaf. But the last few embers of knowledge eluded him, lost in time or to other worlds.

Like the strange, foreign ripple. A mere aberration or a flicker of weakness within himself? Or was it a new source of power? If so, who wielded it?

Very carefully he eased into meditation, drew in the forces. Just a touch, enough to use and control, but not so much that they controlled him, for power was useless unless a djinni could wield it with utter precision.

His dark hair whipped around his face, but he didn't bother to smooth it away. He sought to see through the power, not through the eye. He held out both hands to the flames. Heat licked his skin, which had shriveled and mottled at the tips of his fingers.

The sun and desert wind and fires of divination and endless years had turned his skin dark, darker than most of the djinn. Yet despite the years and the ravages of nature and of corruption, elsewhere his skin stayed smooth. No wrinkles ringed his eyes, and his face was more youthful and appealing than that of a djinni of half his years.

Such was the benefit of power.

Such was the benefit of clarity of purpose.

Such was the benefit of ruthlessness.

Only his hands showed the poisonous touch of the sinister forces.

He chanted the rituals he had learned, pulled deeper the connection with Kaf and the connection with the other. The desert and her harsh joys disappeared. He reached his hand to the fire, allowing it to scorch the flesh, then sprinkled glittery dust on the fire. A pungent odor, both sweet and acrid, assailed his nose. He forced back the sneeze it prompted.

And then he felt it.

Faint. So faint that it disappeared almost as soon as he noticed it. Too fleeting to be traced, but now he knew it was no aberration and no weakness in himself.

The power was foreign, something he'd never experienced.

A power to learn about.

A power he would give anything to possess.

Leila awoke much warmer than when she'd gone to sleep. Jack lay at her back, his even breath soft against her neck and his hand resting at her hip. Sometime in the night they had gravitated together, drawn as inevitably as ore to lodestone.

Beneath her, the hard ground pressed uncomfortably against her hip, and her muscles ached with a continued fatigue that had become too familiar. She hated this "camping." Yet, for the moment, she did not move, trying to keep the comfort of warmth and connection and hold the memories at bay.

Forgetting was impossible. Inside her was the emptiness, all too poignant for the brief, yearning touch she'd had of her *ma-at*. She lifted the turquoise tablet she wore, and her fingers traced the familiar runes and patterns. The stone was warm from her skin, intact, and as vibrant a blue as it had ever been. At least she now had hope that her *ma-at* would return.

If she could stop the Scientist from taking it again.

Anger flowed back inside her, and she rolled away from him, denying the urge to stay and snuggle into his warmth. Instead, she rose to her feet, muttering at the pull of her muscles and the ache in her shoulder. He was to blame for this discomfort.

She stretched, easing out the stiffness as she lifted her hands and face to the sky. The cool mountain wind flattened her robe against her body and blew her hair across her face. Her toes curled against the rock where she stood, connecting her to the earth with an affinity she had always taken for granted.

A multitude of colors streaked the sky and heralded the arrival of the morning sun. With sunrise came the sirocco, that hot wind that rose and fell with the sun, although the air had yet to warm. They must be near the edge of the Tower Lands, approaching the deserts where villages and enclaves would lead them gradually toward Jack's goal: Tepe-ma-adaktu, the single large city of Kaf and the home of the King and the Protector. She felt a spurt of pleasure that her original choice of direction was correct. If she had chosen wrong and sent them across the breadth of the vast Tower Lands, they would have been lost for days beyond measure in the inhospitable mountains.

"You look like a pagan goddess." Jack's sleep-husky voice sounded from behind her.

She glanced over her shoulder, giving him no answer but a withering glare. Then her gaze caught on the landscape behind him, and her motions stopped.

The *Kaliamahru* had realigned.

She had not seen it last night, for it had been too dark. The crystal rocks were no longer a maze leading toward the deadly clearing. Instead they stood as randomly placed spires; a number of different paths meandered between them.

Jack shoved to his feet. "Does this place ever stay the same?" he muttered, circling as he, too, noticed the change of the land. A whirl of ash carried by the rising wind blew up his nose, and he sneezed, breaking the mood. Twice. Three times. The rocks sounded their harmony, but this time the sound was a pleasure. The deep chords soothed and cooled the racing blood.

"That is how the *Kaliamahru* should be," she whispered.

"You knew it was wrong?" He strode to her, planting himself in front of her. "Why didn't you say something?"

"I thought it was my lack of *ma-at*, or your being human, that displeased the choir."

117

"It was the spell."

"Oh, by Solomon, I do not want to believe in so monstrous a twisting of the *ma-at*."

"Leila, it happened. And your returning *ma-at* was part—"

"No," she spat. "*My ma-at* was not part of that perversion. I would know." Too angry to continue, she forestalled his response by pointing toward the mountains. "We near the borders of the Tower Lands. If we start soon, we should tread the sands of the desert before the sun sets."

"You're going to travel with me?"

"A djinni does not break a bargain," she challenged.

He gave her an even stare. "And neither do I. So let's get going."

By midday Leila was miserable. She hungered, she itched, and she ached. She wanted to stop and sleep, knew she could not. The land grew more inhospitable; the Tower Lands resented their intrusion. The bits of soil that supported plant growth had disappeared, leaving endless rock, which offered no food, no water, and no shelter from the keening wind. Only two things kept her going. One was the hope that this wicked terrain signaled the edge of the Towers.

The other was Jack. If he could keep going with that seemingly effortless stride, then so could she.

At least this day, he, too, sweated. And his *al-ar-gee* seemed worse.

So he did not talk much, leaving her only her thoughts as a distraction from the unpleasantness.

Walking gave one too much time to think, she decided.

Too much time to regret the loss of *ma-at* that prevented her from simply transferring to her refreshing garden.

Too much time to ponder the transformation of the *Kaliamahru* and reluctantly admit that Jack was right. The clearing had been spellbound. Who would so desecrate a place of reverence and pervert the power of *ma-at*, though, she could not imagine. And to what purpose? She must remember to tell the Protector when they reached the city.

Too much time to relive the moments of hot desire and soul-deep joy. Why had it felt so absolutely right to be with Jack? Why, despite her anger, did her gaze still linger on the play of his muscles as he walked, the confidence of his step, and the fair gleam of his hair? 'Twas not the enchantment of the clearing that caused the attraction between them.

Now, however, her body was too tired to support such thoughts. She could focus only on the soreness of her feet and legs, the dryness of her mouth, and the pit of hunger in her belly. Needing something to distract her from her wretchedness, she said at last, "Talk with me, Scientist."

He glanced back at her. "What about?"

"Something pleasant. Your family." She'd seen the pictures Isis kept and had thought it strange that so many shared the same blood. "And I will answer in *Fahrisa*, that you may continue your lessons." As she

119

tired, speaking in English became more difficult anyway.

"All right," he agreed readily. "You've met my sister. She's my half-sister actually—same father, different mothers. I have three brothers, one older, one younger, and one twin. Lots of aunts and uncles and cousins. My Aunt Tildy is the closest. She lives just up the street from me. She'd love to meet you."

"Why?"

"She's fascinated by magic. She'd talk your ear off. Do you know what a twin is?"

That they had shared a womb and shared suckle on their mother. Must that not mean they were two united by unbreakable bonds forged at birth? Was the spirit of life split between them? "Yes, but you are the first twin I have ever met."

They scrambled down an incline made slippery by a light coating of *adamana* ashes. When they reached level ground again, Leila said, "Tell me a story about this twin. About when you were children."

Jack hesitated, then said, "He kept high school from being a nightmare for me."

"How?" Too many of the words were beyond her ability to translate, but she was too tired to ask for clarification. Instead, she listened to the mesmerizing flow of words and the soothing rumble of his voice, getting the essence of his words, even if she didn't understand the total. It was a rare chance to learn about this enigmatic, confusing man.

"In elementary school, I was timid, and between allergies and asthma, I wasn't in the best of health." A shadow passed across his face, and for a moment he stroked the thin scar on his cheek. "Beau saved me from a daily pounding by the schoolyard bullies."

She had trouble reconciling the picture he painted with the man walking beside her. "What changed?"

"By high school, my health had improved, so Beau talked me into trying out for the ninth-grade football team. Turns out I had a flair for reading patterns and an accurate arm. Good skills for a quarterback. Beau was the wide receiver." He shook his head. "Some people believe identical twins have a psychic bond. That's nonsense, but, man, I knew his timing as well as my own. Worked in college, too." He chuckled again. "I always liked learning, but Beau made school fun, too."

In the brief time that she had known him, she had never seen Jack so relaxed, nor had she heard such affection in his voice. She swallowed against a tightness in her throat. When he spoke to her it was with irritation or desire. Thoughts of his brother relaxed him, she realized. So much love they must share.

She tried to think of an anecdote about school, something she could share, but so much of her training brought unpleasant memories. "When I was in school . . ." she began.

"There are djinn schools?"

"Of course." She rubbed her nose, brushing off itchy ashes. "I had a good friend—Xerxes was his name. Many rituals require stillness or solitude, but there is one, to celebrate the waters, that is invoked by two dancing. Together, we mastered it." It was one of the rare rituals that had come easily to her. Too easily, as it turned out, for their joined power had surprised her. She laughed, remembering. "We demonstrated to the Adept. Unfortunately, we had not learned sufficient control. We flooded the school. Such a sight it was, with mud and sand throughout, and it made for a very unpleasant penance when we had to clean it."

"A little *ma-at* is a dangerous thing."

With those few words he chased away the good feelings. "Do you mock me?" she demanded. "Mock my lack?"

"No," he said with a sigh. "We have an expression, 'A little learning is a dangerous thing.' I was paraphrasing."

"Oh." She thought about what he had said. "Do you consider me dangerous?"

"Yes." His brief glance before he returned his attention to their path was heated, and she had a feeling he referred to more than *ma-at*. "I think *ma-at* is dangerous, too."

There were dangers, but was that what he meant? "Why?"

"The first time I met Darius, my sister's husband—"

"*Zani*," she corrected. "She is his *zaniya*."

"*Zani*." Jack glanced over at her. "Do you know him well?"

"I know him." It was probably wisest not to mention that, cycles back, before Darius had met Isis, he had been Leila's lover. Or that some of her actions when she had met the Protector's chosen did not fill her with pride.

"The first time I met him, he did some kind of truth spell on me," Jack said.

She frowned. "So? He is the Protector of the *ma-at*. He wields it as he sees fit."

Jack waved a hand around at the harsh land. "*Ma-at* stranded me here, didn't it?"

"It was your Terran magic that did that."

"No, it was not," he said firmly. "I will not have anyone manipulating me like that, not again."

"You would take *ma-at* from anyone who opposes you?" She stared at him in disbelief, disliking her conclusions.

"I would stop anyone from controlling me, however I had to do it."

Jack Montgomery was the dangerous one, she realized with panic. Could he take the *ma-at* from whomever he chose, not just someone as weak as she? Would he?

The sun winked on the crystal resting against his chest, sending out beams of fiery rainbows. A brisk breeze raised the hairs of her skin, and she shivered, remembering his anger last night when she had touched the talisman. The alien mesh of wires held importance to him.

The talisman was important.

Suddenly her foot landed hard on the path, which was lower than she expected. In her inattention, she'd missed a depression. At once, a muscle in her leg spasmed to a hard knot.

"Ooooh." Her leg gave out under the pain, and she fell, landing on her rear. She clutched her calf.

"What is it?" At once, Jack knelt at her side.

Radiating pain kept her from answering. He brushed her hands away and rested her leg on his hard thigh. "Cramp," he said matter-of-factly, testing the calf. "Happens when you stretch the muscle too far."

"Just make it go away," she managed through clenched teeth.

His fingers might be blunt and unpolished, but their touch was skilled and the cramp eased. In its wake remained a deep ache in the muscle and in her heart. Gradually his strokes changed from firm massage to feathery caress. The rugged hands were as adept at one as the other, stroking down the length of her calf. Heat and need replaced pain and panic.

Sun glinted off the blond head bowed over her and off the metal chain at his neck. The muscles in his forearms moved with a lithe, rhythmic purpose. The fair hair and skin there fascinated her, so different from the smoothness she was used to.

Arcane rituals couched in symbolism and enigmatic verse were easier to understand than Jack Montgomery. He helped her, without a hint of condescension, then touched her with passion and care. He liked her thoughts, but he watched her body with the intense heat of a male with his newly claimed *zaniya*. Yet he stripped away her *ma-at* without remorse. No excuses of accident or confusion could explain the second time. Which was he: merciless or merciful?

She closed her eyes. The true battle was not in comprehending him; it was in understanding her own volatile, confusing reactions to him. How could she hate him for taking her *ma-at*, yet admire his genius? How could she believe him both dangerous and kind? How could she be angry at him in one breath, yet in the next desire him with such fierce need?

His soft strokes glided across her skin from knee to ankle, rousing and quickening her. She opened her eyes, and reached for him. Her fingers hovered above the thick strands of his soft hair and his temple. He looked up then, blue eyes blazing. She held still, breath bated. Would he go further? Did she want him to? He gripped her ankle tighter. Inside she grew fluid; her breath shortened. One quick tug and she would be across his lap, her thigh pressing against the growing bulge of his sex.

Instead, he gently lowered her foot back to the ground. "Is it better?" His voice was husky with a companion need to hers.

"Yes."

He pushed to his feet. The sun made a halo of his fair hair and glittered off the few *adamana* ashes fluttering in the air. The crystal at his chest glowed. His eyes, however, had cooled to the blue of a morning sky. He held out a hand, helping her up. Once upright, she took a careful step, then another.

"Can you walk?"

"I believe so."

"Then we should keep going."

Silence settled over them again as they made their way through the treacherous Towers. Once again, Leila was left with only her thoughts and her misery.

Chapter Eight

They reached the edge of the Tower Lands by early afternoon, and Jack paused at the base of the mountains. There had been no more singing rocks or trapped faces in the bark. There had been no more excuses to touch Leila or hold her. There was only a long hike on rough terrain, with the temperature growing steadily hotter and the wind stronger as they descended.

"Let's wait until nearer sunset to start," he suggested as Leila sat cross-legged next to the rock face. He settled beside her. He didn't relish facing the Kafian desert during the scorching day; night should be cooler.

She brushed her hair back from her face, then pulled two mangoes from her robe and handed him one. "Can we spend the night here? There will be little light to see by."

He glanced around. "No real shelter. No water, and this is the last of our food. We should push on."

She merely nodded, her eyes shutting as she nibbled her fruit.

Jack turned the mango around in his hands. It was looking a little the worse for wear, and he was getting heartily tired of only fruit to eat, but at the moment it was all he had. He took a bite. "Will there be a village or someplace we can get something to eat?"

She shrugged. "Djinn are quite mobile."

Meaning that a village moved around and the residents came and went. How surprising. He leaned against the cool rock. "Are there water sources on your deserts?"

"I have heard the area around the Tower Lands is barren, although I have not placed foot there. Everywhere else there are oases, with water in ponds or wells or brooks."

"How big an area is barren?"

She shrugged again, and he remembered that distance had no meaning in a land where instant transport was the preferred means of travel. As they sat, he heard her breath slow and he glanced over. Her eyes were closed, the dark lashes crescents against her pale cheeks. The half-eaten mango rolled out of her limp hand. Her chest rose and fell in a shallow rhythm. She had fallen asleep.

The edges of her robe blew in the light breeze, and he straightened the fabric, covering her legs. For a few moments, he watched her; it was rare to see her so still. Her beauty—fine skin, long hair, and soft curves—always stirred him, but it was her courage and challenge that intrigued him. She had burst into his cerebral life and filled it with pleasure, challenge, frustration, wonder, confusion, and desire.

He leaned against the sun-warmed rock. The crystal at his chest lay quiescent, but he could feel its power running through him. Content, he closed his eyes and let himself fall asleep as well.

Jack awoke with a start. He rubbed his eyes, and realized that several hours had passed, for it was nearing twilight. Beside him, Leila stirred awake. He rotated his shoulders, stretching stiff muscles.

A sliver of movement at the corner of his eye caught his attention, but when he looked, he saw nothing but dark rock glistening with ash and some scraggly vines. He wiped a hand over his itchy eyes—his crystal shield hadn't stopped whatever was causing his allergy so it must be a natural phenomenon, not magic—and looked again.

No change in the bare landscape.

Yet something was different. Something made his skin tighten with the sensation of being watched.

"Pink is not my favorite color," Leila commented.

He looked around. What had brought that on? Glittery ash, white and yellow sand, black rocks, scraggles of green. Not a dot of pink on the landscape.

"The sun will be down soon," she added. "Near the Night of No Moon, it heats the afternoon, then"—her hands gestured in a sweep—"streaks of pink and no more sun. I would prefer to lose the sun in purple.

Or red. Something bursting with life, especially before such blackness. Don't you think—" She turned to him; then a puzzled look crossed her face as she craned her neck to see around him.

"What is it?" When he looked around, the landscape behind him was unchanged.

Leila fingered the turquoise tablet at her neck. "I thought I saw movement at the edge of my eye."

"So did I, but it was gone when I looked." No heat or vibration stirred within the wires at his neck, so no *ma-at* acted against them.

A sound, the scratch of rock on rock so faint as to be almost inaudible, grated behind them. His gut clenched. What danger was it?

Leila leaned forward, bracing herself with a hand beside his. Pursing her lips, she made a delicate chirping noise.

"What—?"

"Shh or you'll scare it away." She repeated the chirping sound.

A rock crept forward. How, he couldn't understand, for he could see no legs, no muscles to pull it like a snake. It was an ugly rock, mottled gray, about three inches in diameter and with two side fissures that wheezed like a stony gill. He should be careful not to scare away a moving rock? He trusted that Leila knew what she was doing. The thing slid closer.

At last it stopped beside their two hands. The fissures quivered in indecision; then the rock moved on top of his hand.

"The *grucheek* has chosen you," Leila said with a hint of disappointment.

"This is a good thing?"

"They are said to be good luck."

He stared at the rock. "What does it do?"

She shrugged.

"Does it bite?"

"Not that any legend says."

"What does it eat?" *How* did it eat? Nothing he saw looked like a mouth.

"No one is quite sure. Turn over your hand."

He did as she suggested so the rock rested in his palm. No cute, fuzzy fur. No warm nose. No soothing Tribble trill. The thing was heavy and cold and ugly.

Somehow it slid closer to his wrist, where it stopped. A piece of the rock moved, and he thought he saw black spots, like two eyes, rotate upward. Maybe the creature, the *grucheek*, was inspecting the intricate network of wires at his throat. Or maybe those were two nostrils, and it was smelling him. Whatever, he appeared to pass muster, for a moment later it continued up his arm until it came to rest on his shoulder. Not so bad, he decided. What if it wasn't cute and furry? The rock had character.

"Okay, *grucheek*, welcome aboard."

Something tiny and sharp pulled at the fabric of his shirt, and then he felt a spot of wet warmth. "The thing peed on me," he said with disgust.

"Peed?"

"Urinated."

"Ah." Leila peered at his shoulder. "I think, rather, it has glued on you."

"Glued?" He shook his shoulder, but the thing held fast. "Oh, hell, you mean I have to go through life with this pet rock stuck to me?"

"Pet?"

"It's an animal you own and keep around the house for amusement and companionship."

"You would own another living creature?" Her voice held both horror and disgust.

"Actually, sometimes I think they own us," he answered, thinking of Asimov. His dad had bought the Labrador when Jack was five as protection against another kidnapping, but Asimov was too friendly, too unquestionably loving to make much of a watch dog. Instead, the Lab had comforted him during the night terrors. He'd been exactly what Jack needed at the time.

Asimov had died a quiet death of old age about the time Jack went off to college. He'd never had a pet since then, and until this moment, he had not thought about how much he had lost when he'd lost Asimov.

The grip of *grucheek* claws brought him back to the present of Kaf. "Pets aren't about ownership," he said at last. "They're about love."

"Ah." Leila ran a hand over the rock and tickled it under what might be a chin. "Well, it has chosen you, so I guess we may call it a pet."

Jack heard a low rumble from the creature, a sound like a distant avalanche or lava ready to explode, which he guessed was the *grucheek* equivalent of a purr. The

131

thing sidled along Jack's shoulder, closer to Leila. Apparently gluing didn't prevent it from moving when it chose. "I think it likes you, Leila."

"Really?" She seemed pleased by the idea and scratched the *grucheek* again. "You have chosen to glue to the Scientist, but sometimes, perhaps, you would like to ride with me?" A satisfied rumble was her answer, and Leila laughed in delight. "I believe it does like me."

Who wouldn't? Jack cleared his throat. "What should we call it?"

"We do not know what others of its species name it. We should not offend it by making one up."

Okay, so the purring rocks had names, language, and a tribe. "A title, then. Mister Rock?"

"Mistrock." Leila blended the words together, and her faint accent gave it a softer sound. "Does that meet with your approval, Mistrock?"

The answering rumble-purr was accepting. It appeared they'd added a pet to their entourage.

Jack glanced over the desert that faced them. The sirocco was dying, leaving a quiet, vast landscape ahead of them. The sun hung low in the sky, twilight soon to follow, and slightly cooler air surrounded them. They could make some miles before the dark took over, and with luck they would find a village where they could bed down.

He pushed to his feet. "Leila, Mistrock, are you ready to go?"

"Yes."

Rumble-purr.

Enchantment

A few minutes later, the transplanted human, the powerless djinni, and the sentient rock stepped from the forbidding Tower Lands onto one of the deserts of Kaf.

The desert was as quixotic as the Tower Lands, Jack soon discovered.

He had seen deserts on Earth and knew that their terrains were more varied than the common conception of a sandy wasteland. Rocks, mesas, caves, canyons, arroyos, mountains were all part of the harsh landscapes. Nor were the deserts barren. From beetles to lizards to bats, from scrub brush to saguaro cacti, from mice to camels to humans, life flourished and struggled in the harsh lands.

On Earth, however, different deserts sported different characteristics. The Kalahari in Southern Africa was largely sand dunes. The Sonoran in the American Southwest contained fertile patches from seasonal rains. On Kaf, however, the various elements—except camels and humans—coexisted in a jumbled juxtaposition of mismatched terrains.

Full night came too quickly. They had not gone as far as Jack wanted, nor had they found a place to wait out the night. He glanced around, trying to see by the light of a couple of anemic stars and a whisker of a moon. Leila shuffled behind him, though she made no complaint. Leila not complaining about discomfort worried him. If he was cold, tired, and gritty, she must be utterly miserable.

She began to hum, interrupting his thoughts with

133

Kathleen Nance

the unfamiliar tune. She had a melodic voice—he'd heard her sing to herself during their trek—but he'd never had Mistrock's grating rumble as accompaniment. He glanced over and lifted a brow.

"Do you think that is an oasis?" She pointed to a smudge off to the left.

"It could be." It had to be. They could go no further tonight. "Let's find out." Mistrock, riding on Jack's glued shoulder, rumbled agreement.

It was an oasis and they'd found it none too soon. He braced Leila the final steps as they staggered into the stand of trees and collapsed beside the small, central pool. He licked his dry lips; he hadn't allowed himself to acknowledge his thirst until now. "The water's opaque," he commented as he rolled to his knees and scooped up the water. Mistrock slid down his arm.

Leila crouched beside him and gulped water from her cupped hands. She turned to him, droplets clinging to her lips and chin. "But opaque is just as sweet as the clear."

"True." In silence, they drank their fill.

A breeze ran through the clearing, bringing a mint scent that cooled and refreshed, even as it faded away. He splashed water on the back of his neck. Mint again washed over him, then disappeared. The wires of his device vibrated with a faint charge, and the crystal glowed brighter. So *ma-at* lingered in this oasis, but nothing that acted directly against him.

Actually, he had detected very little *ma-at* on the journey. Occasionally when they crossed an outcropping of the obsidian rock, vapors spewed from the

134

cracks carrying the strange, glittery ash that set off his allergies. While they chanted the appeasements, he noticed a faint vibration in his device. The crystal stayed lit, but mostly quiet—no flashes of light, no pulse of energy. No explosions, ripping of reality, or wrenching disorientation.

Because no *ma-at* threatened him directly?

Or because his reactions remained calm?

He still didn't know. What had surprised him, though, was the sensation of power filling him that had grown through the day.

Thirst assuaged, he prowled around the edges of the oasis. Some of the parsnip vegetables grew here, and he pulled four. A tree tinkled with the sensual sound of a thousand bells, and a scrap of red silk fluttered from one limb—evidence of previous inhabitants now gone.

He brought the parsnips back to Leila, handed her two. "I found these."

"Thank you. At least it is a change from mango." She brushed off specks of dirt and took a healthy bite.

The tension in his neck and arms eased as he crunched his vegetable. This was not the false peace of the clearing. This was real. "We'll spend the rest of the night here. It's getting too dark to see safely."

"I was not moving."

Mistrock disappeared into the reeds that surrounded the pool, apparently agreeing with them. Meal done, Leila leaned against a tree and finger-combed her hair over her shoulder. Jack stretched out in the grass, his elbow bent and his head resting on his palm, while he watched her graceful moves. That familiar tightness in his groin, a constant companion whenever he was near enough to see her, or scent her, or touch her, reappeared.

Above them, the moon was a mere sliver and only two lone, pale stars remained. The draining light left the world so dark.

God, he hated the dark. Had hated it since he was five. Had hated it since a disgruntled employee of his father had kidnapped him and held him in a dark closet. Hurt him . . .

He fingered the scar, the skin burning with memory. The authorities, his family, had all said he'd been brave and strong to have convinced the man not to just hold him but to ask for a ransom. They said he'd been smart to send the clue that led them to him.

But he hadn't been. He hadn't been brave, or smart, or strong. He'd been scared and desperate before a man who held power over him. He'd cried, and he'd wet himself, and he'd begged the man to stop hurting him.

Never again. The crystal glowed into the night, surrounded by a white aura. Abruptly Jack lowered his hand from the scar.

Old memories. Old memories he refused to let have power over him. He drew in a deep breath, and the vibration inside him quieted.

"That's the problem with thoughts," Leila said, eyeing him closely.

When she didn't continue, he posed the expected question. "What's the problem?"

"Not talking and thinking."

He gave a laugh. "I know plenty of people like that. Who talk without thinking what they're saying."

"No, I mean people who think without talking."

"Oh." She meant him.

"Furrows appear here"—she ran a finger sideways across his brow, leaving a trail of fire at her touch—"when you puzzle over something, and I have learned, Scientist, that you do not hear in those moments. Nor do you speak."

"Oh," he repeated.

"Be careful of this furrow. When it appears, all your responses come from above, from thinking. None from here"—she touched his abdomen—"or from here." She touched his chest at the level of his heart and smiled.

What could he say? Especially when all he could think was that, after the disaster of last night, she had finally touched him again. Finally looked at him straight in the face, with interest, with pleasure. She dropped her hand, and then began to hum as she lay down. The tune was unfamiliar, more of a chant really, with an irregular rhythm that defied anticipation. Odd, but he enjoyed it.

As the night darkened, however, he was surprised to see a shining glow across the sky. Curiosity replaced the heat of arousal, and he sat up for a better look. "Does that look like the lights of a city or a town over there?"

She glanced where he pointed. "The people light the fires in preparation for the Night of No Moon tomorrow." A shudder ran across her, and she rubbed a hand along her arm.

He tried to judge the distance from the oasis to the glow, but the night was too dark. "We can't go now, but tomorrow we should head that way. They might have food to share."

"I would like some variety," she agreed as they settled down to sleep.

Leila, however, found sleep elusive. Her nap before setting out on the desert now served to make her unable to ignore the lumpy ground and her sore bones. At last she abandoned the effort and went over to the pool. It wasn't deep enough for a bath, but she took off her robe and splashed the minted water over her breasts, around her arms, and between her legs. She soaked her feet and leaned back, bracing herself on her arms as she let the night air dry her. The temperature was cool, tightening her skin and nipples, but she found the chill refreshing at the moment. Water had always been vital to her, not just because of the needs of the body to drink. Cool water invigorated her; warm water relaxed her. When she swam, she felt as if she could do anything.

At last a pleasant lethargy over took her, and elusive sleep finally crept closer. She slipped on her robe and returned to her makeshift pillows.

Jack was deep asleep, relaxed in his dreams. Pleasant ones, judging by his smile. Asleep, he was a different man from the Scientist who had stolen her *ma-at*.

Awake, there was a vitality about him that excited and sparkled until the air itself seemed to crackle with his power. Even when he was intensely focused—as he'd been focused on her when they almost made love—there was a restlessness about him that defied stillness.

Only now, in a sleep as focused as his thoughts, was he still.

Tentatively she reached out and touched his talisman with the tip of her finger. The intricate pattern of wires fascinated her; she traced the shape of many traditional runes embedded within it. The wires were smooth and shimmery and warm, as warm as the skin beneath, which surprised her, for the last time she had touched them they had felt cool. She laid her hand on his chest, right above the crystal. She felt the beat of his heart, the softness of his shirt, the dusting of wiry hairs on his chest, and the strength of muscle below. One by one her fingers curled around the latticework of wires that supported the crystal. Only the crystal seemed hard.

An acrid taste coated the inside of her mouth. The crystal vibrated against her skin and sent an unpleasant energy through her. It passed quickly, as though nothing in her impeded its progress, and then the taste disappeared. She pulled back her hand.

The talisman both fascinated and repelled her, so alien was it. The turquoise tablet she wore was a symbol of her djinn heritage, a notice of her passage into the full status of djinn adulthood. Rudimentary runes of protection were etched into the stone, and these had afforded her a small measure of protection against the worst rigors of the trek so far.

Kathleen Nance

But Jack's chain seemed far more than a symbol and a basic charm. She looked again at the clear, crystalline glow. She had seen it brighten to the intensity of a concentrated sunbeam and shift to red, or blue, or green, as though a prism turned within and reflected a different portion of the rainbow.

It had not always glowed with power. She sought back in her memories. At the very first, yes, then not. The glow had returned after the clearing had disappeared.

Again she replayed memories of their almost love-making, memories that were filled more with the scent and taste of the man sleeping beside her, with the excitement of true desire and the bittersweet touch of her *ma-at*, than any logic. She remembered grabbing the chain. Remembered a click.

Whoever heard of a talisman that turned on and off with a click?

But the crystal had glowed and the *Kaliamahru* had realigned and her *ma-at* had disappeared. She stared at the talisman, uneasy with her conclusions. Her earlier exchange with Jack came back.

I would stop anyone from controlling me, however I had to do it.

Jack Montgomery was dangerous; he could take the ma-at *from whomever he chose.*

The talisman was important.

The jumbled thoughts settled into a sure conviction. There was a way to protect herself and her people. There was a way to make him share the loss she felt.

He had taken her *ma-at*; she would take his talisman.

Her chest heaved as she drew in a hard breath. She must brave the dark and take his talisman to the distant village. There she could entrust someone to take it to the Protector along with her message. Then she would return to the oasis and to Jack's fury. They had made a bargain—they would remain together until Tepe-ma-adaktu—and she would abide by it.

The conclusion was undeniable. Still, she sat, unable to bring herself to move. The unshakable feeling that this was a very bad decision bore down on her.

Just do it.

Betray him.

For the people and the ma-at *you cherish.*

Do it. Before she lost her courage and before she thought too hard.

Carefully, so as not to wake him, she inched the chain up. Her hand slid along his chest, and she thought his breath caught. She froze, watching and listening.

No, she must have imagined it, for his breath came even and shallow.

The crystal had reached his chin. She leaned over him and grabbed the chain with both hands, opening it wider so she could slip it over his head. The dangling crystal banged against his nose. Again she froze, but he was sleeping with deep unconsciousness and did not stir.

At last she had the chain off. It lay on the ground, part of it still caught by the back of his head. She bit her lip against tears. Yet she knew what she must do. Drawing in a shuddering breath, she gently cradled his head in her arm and lifted it off the chain. She pulled the chain free, then lowered his head. Gripping the chain with one hand, she prepared to get to her feet.

Hands clamped around her wrists, stopping her with a hard grip. "Just where the hell do you think you're going?" Jack growled.

She turned to stone under his furious, blue-eyed glare. "You were faking!" she accused.

"Yeah. Fortunately, I'm a light sleeper. Especially when a beautiful woman doffs her robe and starts stroking my chest."

"Fortunately?" she repeated bitterly.

"For me. Not you."

His muscles tightened, and with an abrupt move, he rolled over. Before she knew what was happening, she found herself on her back, Jack straddling her hips, her fingers still clasping the talisman. Wordlessly he pried her numb fingers from the chain and slipped it around his neck; then he bent over and planted one hand on either side of her head.

She bucked up, desperately trying to free herself. *Flee!* her mind screamed. *Flee!* Even being powerless in a djinn village, even the dark of No Moon Eve, was better than the retribution of a Terran wizard. Oh, dear Solomon, would he enchant her with the copper bonds of servitude? She had never thought of that before. Frantically she twisted and shoved.

Her reaction must have surprised him, for she almost squirmed from beneath him.

"Stop it. Ouch! You little witch."

He grabbed her wrists and pinned her arms to the ground. The weight of his body held fast her hips and legs.

Surprise had been her only possible defense, for she was smaller and weaker than he. Now that was gone. When sanity returned, she stopped fighting. She must conserve her strength for the trials to come, though everything in her railed against the injustice.

None of her plans had gone right recently. Not her desire for a child, not her seduction, not this.

"I am not a witch."

"Closest thing to it." Jack leaned closer to her until she inhaled his breath and the masculine scent of him. His blue eyes still blazed. Everywhere he was hard: gaze, muscles, lower. "I repeat my question. What were you doing?"

She stared at him, defiant and silent. He knew what she'd been doing. It was obvious she'd been stealing his talisman. But she would show no fear. It was a rule she lived by. Never admit weakness. If you did, you were either pitied or derided.

He shook her arms. "Tell me."

"Curiosity." Old defenses were hard to put aside.

"I don't believe you."

"It's true. I have never seen wires enmeshed like that." A smattering of truth always helped with lies. "You can look at my turquoise tablet if you desire." Of course, that was a bluff. No djinni willingly surrendered his or her tablet for any reason. Was she surprised that Jack felt the same about his talisman?

"I don't believe you," he repeated flatly.

At least his initial fury seemed to have abated. Calm fatalism overtook her. He would do what he would do, and there was naught she could do to stop it. Still, she wiggled her arms, seeing if he would let her up. His grip tightened, and he glared at her.

"What caused you to try theft now?" he mused aloud as he studied her. "Why not before? Or later?"

She didn't think he expected her to answer.

"The village," he said a moment later. "It's the first time we've been near other djinn. You were going to take my device to the village." He tilted his head. "That raises the question of why. Were you going to sell it? Display it? Destroy it? Wear it?"

An involuntary shudder passed across her. His gaze fastened on the turquoise tablet. Or maybe on the gap at her neckline. Her traitorous skin flushed under his perusal.

"Your *ma-at*," he whispered. "Tit for tat. I take your *ma-at*, you take my talisman."

Leila gaped at him a moment, then snapped her mouth shut. How had he figured all that out so quickly?

Abruptly he loosened her arms, straightened, and rose to his feet. He tucked the crystal beneath his shirt. She scrambled upright, tasting the bitterness of defeat. He would not give her another chance. They stood, arms akimbo, testing one another.

She could think of nothing to say, nothing that

would heal the rift, however much she wanted to. Jack apparently couldn't either.

Mistrock, as if sensing that the worst of the storm had passed, emerged from the reeds with a rumbly chirp. It paused by her, until she bent down to pet it, then continued on to Jack. He picked it up and placed it on his shoulder, where it settled against his neck with a contented "grrr."

"I would have returned from the village," she told him, holding her gaze level.

Jack glanced out over the desert, then back at her. "So you still intend to keep our bargain?"

"Yes. Until our journey is complete or unless I am released from my word. We travel together until the city."

"Do you remember the rest of our bargain?"

"I will tell you of the return of my *ma-at* before I use it with you."

"And I will do all in my power to see your *ma-at* returned." He picked up a handful of sand, and let it trickle through his fingers. "This is your world, Leila, not mine. Unfortunately, I can't release you from the bargain, and I don't think you will release me. So, like it or not, we're together. I propose an amendment."

"What?" She waited, wary.

"I promise I will never knowingly take your *ma-at*. If that should happen again, it will be because of something out of my control."

"Will you extend that promise to all djinn?"

"This is between you and me, Leila. No one else."

"And what would I give in return?"

145

Kathleen Nance

"Your trust that I will keep our bargain. And your promise not to steal my talisman again."

She thought about his bargain. Because of her, the small measure of trust between them was shattered. She missed it, she found. Slowly she nodded. "I will promise not to take your talisman from you. The trust . . . I will work on that." She held out her hand to seal the bargain in the Terran manner.

"That's all I can ask." He shook her hand, then clasped her two hands in his. In djinn fashion, he kissed her fingers, then her cheeks. She repeated the gesture, lingering a moment with her cheek pressed against his. She drew in the clean scent of him and rubbed against the foreign bristle of his face. A yearning for more overtook her, and she squeezed her eyes against the pain of wanting.

They would have these days, this bargain, and then he would leave forever.

Slowly she drew back. "The bargain is sealed," she said, her voice thick with unshed tears.

"May it give you what your heart desires."

She didn't answer him. For she doubted very much that this bargain would bring her heart's desire.

Chapter Nine

The *Kaliamahru* had realigned. Xerxes circled the random spires, filled with a cold rage. Only a singular surge of power could accomplish this; that was what he had detected last night.

Now the spires were useless, pretty rocks that sang. He laid a hand on one, letting the *ma-at* flow through him. The spire shattered with a piercing whine. His fist clenched in satisfaction.

For cycles, since before Darius became Protector, Xerxes's spell on the choir of rock had endured. In his first searches for power, he had brought a few Terrans, ones who claimed to be workers of magic, to Kaf. He had studied them, extracted their secrets, and found them to be powerless braggarts. When he'd finished with them, for amusement he abandoned them to the maze of the *Kaliamahru*, and to the eternal captivity of the clearing.

Now someone had negated the enchantment; their souls had returned to Terra.

Only a powerful djinni could have done that.

But who? The Protector or the King? If either had found the clearing, there would have been much talk of it on Kaf. Darius, he believed, suspected someone was delving into the sinister forces, but suspicion was not proof. The Protector would wait to act until he knew for sure who it was, and then his judgment would be swift and stern. But Xerxes had been very careful to conceal his activities from both, to explore with patience and with stealth.

He glanced once more around the *Kaliamahru*, his rage becoming focused. Whoever had interfered would pay, with blood and sweat and pain.

Leila sat at the edge of the oasis, watching the rising sun glint off the few remaining *adamana* ashes. A faint haze from the Tower Lands settled on the desert in shimmering waves of heat. She nibbled on a parsnip, this morning's breakfast. Oh, what she wouldn't give for a honey cake and tea right now.

"Your desert is very colorful," Jack observed. He settled down a short distance away. "It was too dark to see last night, but there are vivid shades everywhere you look. Like there."

At first she didn't see what he pointed to; then she spied the long-legged purple insect crawling on the orange rocks at the base of an iridescent succulent. Jack sneezed, and the insect scurried back to the protection of the succulent thorns.

She glanced over at Jack. He'd slicked his hair back with water, but even wet it was as pale as sand beneath the desert sun. His bristles grew longer, and his nose was a faint red. He had never looked more appealing, or more distant. He was setting the limits for the remainder of their journey, she realized, and she accepted his decision. Their camaraderie was gone, and she missed it.

She sighed. She had done without many things she wanted, but this loss seemed much harder than the others. "Your al-ar-gee still bothers you?"

"A little," he answered, rubbing his nose. "I think it's from the ashes."

"I found some leaves that make a fragrant tea. When I sip the brew, I notice I breathe more easily. If you could start a fire, I would make you some."

"Thanks, but no, we need to get going."

She lifted a shoulder in acquiescence.

He did not rise, though. "You can't ignore those feet anymore. We need bandages, alcohol, and Neosporin, but I'll settle for soap, gauze, and footwear."

"You have footwear."

"I meant for you."

"You said we. Besides, I do not like footwear."

"Your feet are scratched and bruised. I don't want infection to set in."

She shrugged. "The runes in my tablet will prevent that." She hoped that was true.

"We'll travel faster if your feet don't hurt."

Ah, now there was the real crux of the matter, his reason for concern. "How will gauze help? Is not gauze something to wear when the days are most hot, or to drape around the pillows?"

"I was thinking along the lines of wrapping wounds."

She tilted her head, intrigued by the concept. "Really? Why?"

"To keep the dirt out."

"But gauze has holes in it."

"With enough layers it works, but it still lets air in."

"So air is an element of good and earth is an element of bad? Although our strength derives from air and fire, we do not divide them so. Each is special in its own way." She took another bite of parsnip, then looked at the vegetable with annoyance. Maybe she should have chosen the fig. Neither was the honey cake she craved, but at least she was not eating mango. After three days of mango, she would not care if it was another Night of No Moon before she tasted another.

Jack gave a snort of irritation. "Good elements, bad elements. That's not what I meant. I mean germ and infection . . ." He bit off the explanation when she raised a brow. "Never mind." He crouched down until he was at eye level with her. "Leila, we need to go to that village."

" 'Twill do us no good." She took another bite of parsnip, then set it aside. Not even to avoid waste could she take another bite. "Where are the figs?"

If Jack had suggested they go to the village for food, she'd be more enthusiastic about it. She'd never spent so many days eating such a boring diet. Camping and being powerless, she decided, were as unpleasant as the stench of the Mud River.

"Why would it do us no good?" He handed her a couple of figs from his pocket.

"What will we trade?"

"I don't suppose you have money on you."

"Money?" she asked, not understanding the word.

"So, no monetary system. I doubt American Express works either."

"American Express?"

"Don't leave home without it. Except they never planned on a world of magic."

"*Ma-at*," she corrected. Sometimes Jack put the strangest words together. Yet he seemed rational enough, so she decided this was some unusual Terran travel ritual. "If a djinni desires something his *ma-at* and effort do not provide, it is customary to trade or barter."

"What kinds of things do you trade?"

She gave him a sharp look. Did he know how she survived? By her wits? By her charm? By her ability to manipulate, an ability that seemed toothless against him?

No, the Scientist was blunt and direct. His questions meant exactly what they asked.

"I would exchange a song. Or a plant I had cultivated," she answered at last. "But these plants belong to this oasis. We cannot move them without their permission."

"Wouldn't want to do that," he said drily. He

looked at her then, a hardness on his face. "Do you want to sing for strangers?"

"No."

"Then you won't."

The underlying fierce note in his voice surprised her. What did she hear? Possessiveness?

She'd heard that note before, she realized, her heart and stomach doing a small twist. She had heard it in Darius's voice when he pursued Jack's sister, Isis. Jack's voice sounded like that of a male djinni who had found the woman who would be his *zaniya*.

After last night? Impossible. Jack was Terran, a human, and last night she had betrayed him and erased his passion for her. She must have misinterpreted.

Today they were not a man and woman who desired each other. They were travelers sharing a bargain and a journey. Her heart tightened in her chest. Or at least, he was.

She spread her robe. "I have nothing to trade. Thus going to the village is useless."

"Maybe I have something to trade." He held out his hand, and Mistrock glided from beneath a leaf to his palm. Jack set it on his shoulder.

She stared in disbelief. "You would trade Mistrock? Your pet?"

"What? No! I was thinking more along the lines of my pocketknife. Will it be sufficient barter?"

She remembered the blade he had used to bandage her hand after the fire salamander. "It should." Then she shook her head. "The village will be too dangerous. You are human."

"Why should that make a difference?"

"Many djinn do not like humans, and as the Night of No Moon approaches, their wariness will grow. They remember the tales of djinn bound to servitude and think of your kind as wicked and vile."

"We won't tell them I'm human. Any other reasons?"

"This is an unsettling day leading to a fearful night. It would be wisest to avoid them." She let out a huff of air. "Besides, I do not wish to approach the village as a powerless djinni. There will be too many questions, too much potential for mishap." Last night she would have gone because she'd had no choice. Today there was a choice.

He paused, and she thought she saw sympathy reflected in his face. "Leila, you need shoes and your feet need attention. You can wait here while I go. I'll trade my knife, get what we need, and leave."

Intractable male. The only thing worse than going together to the village would be for Jack to go alone. Leila sighed. "No, we go together. But you let me do the trading."

This walk through the desert to the djinn village should have been a relaxing pleasure. Jack enjoyed being outside. Camping, hiking, climbing, and racing were his escape from work, his method of stress relief.

It wasn't working. Not even Mistrock's grumbly purr helped.

The reason was walking beside him, her face lifted to the sun. Leila. A woman who didn't seem to have

153

an honest bone, or an uncalculated response, in her body. A woman for whom reality was a fluid concept. A woman who smelled like clover.

Her flowing gown highlighted her feminine curves, and her long hair blew across his forearm, as though she would trap him in silken bonds. His body tightened with an automatic response, and he knew that despite all the anger and doubts, he still wanted her with a depth of need that surprised him.

She accused him of thinking too much. Not here on Kaf, or with her. Thinking hadn't fueled his fury last night or prompted that impulsive olive branch in the form of a bargain. It wasn't his brain that had been claiming all the blood since he'd met her.

Unfortunately, trust was another matter. Trust, as Leila had said, wasn't something that could be promised. It had to be earned, and once shattered was difficult to repair.

He didn't trust her, and maybe he didn't need to, but he wanted to, he realized.

One small part of him questioned why he was trying so hard. Why trust and understanding seemed so important. Why not just get through the next days as quickly as possible? Minimum contact, minimum conflict, minimum risk.

Then he saw her draw in a deep breath as they approached the djinn settlement, and his brain stopped getting the blood supply.

Her steps slowed. "We should tell them you are doing the Circles of Cleansing," she said. "That will explain why you use no *ma-at*."

"What's a Circle of Cleansing?"

"Rituals that clear a djinni of all *ma-at*. They—"

A shout from the djinn encampment—it was too impermanent to be called a village or settlement—interrupted further explanations. They had been spotted. A man dressed in bright orange bloomers and shirt made an impatient gesture, motioning them to the left.

"There is a barrier of protection," she said. "They have opened it for us."

He hesitated. Maybe this hadn't been a good idea.

Leila laid a hand on his arm. "You asked me to trust you. Now I ask that you trust me, in this at least." She met him with a clear gaze. "I will not betray you to them."

It wasn't logic or thought that fueled his nod of agreement.

"Try not to say anything, and whatever you do, don't accept *anything* from them," she warned. "No gift, no food or drink, nothing."

Walking into the encampment was an experience both strange and familiar. He had visited a lot of odd places on Earth, and he felt now what he'd always felt: eagerness to experience new sights and tastes, caution that he didn't violate some local stricture, wariness at his reception.

One thing was different here, however: the evidence of *ma-at*.

Tents sat randomly about a central fire, but each domicile was as fluid as the land. He stared in amazement as panels of bright-colored silk or chiffon fluttered in the breeze, as thin walls constantly changed color, as sparkling ponds of water shifted in the central square around a roaring fire, as stones set before each home glowed, then faded. It wasn't noisy or very crowded; he saw only about a dozen men. But the hum of voices and the tinkling of bells and the snap of fires gave a life to the small gathering. The scent of smoke mingled with incense in an exotic mix.

Even without the evidence of his eyes, though, he would have known this was a place of *ma-at*. He felt the power as soon as he passed the barrier. The crystal vibrated, while mild heat spread across his chest.

The device responded to the atmosphere of *ma-at* but did not negate it. The *ma-at* continued in the encampment at large, he realized, because he had designed the protection only for the wearer. Until some power acted directly against him, the counterforces remained dormant.

Orange Pants called out to others of the djinn, whether in warning or greeting Jack couldn't be sure. A moment later they were surrounded by a cadre of wary, unwelcoming djinn.

Mistrock's low grate sounded in Jack's ear, like the warning growl of a dog spying danger.

He gave a mental curse, and the back of his neck tightened. He caught a few words, but his command of the language wasn't good enough to follow their rapid speech. In his travels he had often used a translator, but necessity never meant that he liked relying on someone else to speak for him. Here, Leila was his guide. Damn.

She had been the one reluctant to come. He was supposed to be leading her and protecting her. Not the other way around. He glanced over. How was she holding up?

Very well. His eyes narrowed as he took in details. She'd changed, in subtle but unmistakable ways.

She always carried herself with poise and grace, but now she held her head higher, her shoulders straighter, her jaw a little firmer. Her hips swayed in a delicate movement that set his blood racing. A faint smile played across her full lips. To look at her, he'd never have guessed the reluctance she'd shown to come here. She wore confidence wrapped about her like a shawl.

If he had not spent so much time with her these past days and seen her natural behavior, he might not have recognized the artifice. He'd bet not one of the men staring at them did, the act was so well done and seemed so much a part of her.

The woman he'd known was gone. In her place was a playful, confident seductress.

He ached—with a sudden desire to take her to bed and with a sudden realization that he didn't know her at all. Which was the real Leila? This seductress, the woman who tried to take his device, or the woman he'd been spending the past days with? Which was the artifice? Had she played a role with the human until she got back to her own kind, her own world?

A moment later the group was plying him with questions. He succinctly answered the few he understood, letting Leila do most of the talking and spin

157

her tale. Part of the group listened to her, while others eyed him with interest, sympathy, or disappointment. Suddenly she laughed, a sound as tinkling as the bells that lined several of the abodes, and glanced in his direction. He had a feeling there was more to this Circle of Cleansing than she'd had time to explain, and he wasn't faring well in whatever version she told. He shifted, restless energy setting his foot tapping; then he stepped forward, but a tiny movement of her hand held him back.

She lifted one foot to show the djinn, and he heard the sympathetic clucking. At least she seemed to be asking for what they needed.

He leaned one shoulder on a wall near him, settling in to wait. The wall was warm and supple, almost like living skin. There was a shimmer to it, like the lustrous skin of a pampered woman. As he leaned, the wall started to melt in the strangest sucking sensation he'd ever felt.

The lightning power of the crystal coursed through him. Warmth and vibration and a faint scent of scorched metal touched his senses; then the wall hardened and shoved him back. He jerked, recovered his balance, and stood upright. Mistrock gave a surprised yelp and tumbled from his shoulder. The *grucheek* scrambled away and disappeared behind a rock.

A glance around assured Jack no one had been watching. On the wall was a patch of gray amidst the luster, a patch in the exact shape of his shoulder and arm. As he watched, the pearly luster seeped in from the edges, until the patch disappeared. He touched a hand to the wall. Again there was the sensation of being sucked in, the crystal reaction, and then the rejection and a gray handprint on the wall until the luster overcame it again.

When he touched the wall, he realized, the *ma-at* allowed him passage until the device negated the effect. He glanced over at the group. Seeing they paid him no mind, he tentatively touched the wall again. This time he resisted his instinctive withdrawal after the wall hardened. He kept his hand against the cold, solid surface and watched the crystal.

Its light pulsed in a hypnotic pattern of colors. As he stared at it, the colors seemed to brighten, one lumen at a time. The change, if there was one, was barely discernible. He needed precise measurements to be sure he wasn't allowing suggestion to influence his conclusions.

From the edges of his vision he could see his spread fingers. A thin line of gray appeared around his hand. Had he widened the effect beyond the limits of his body? Did the *ma-at* respond to his continued contact? Or was he imagining the response?

His hand burned. He jerked it up, shaking and blowing on the flesh until the burning lessened, but when he examined his palm, it wasn't even reddened.

Experimenting, he touched the wall, and again resisted the inherent rejection. He focused on the crystal. Could he brighten it again by choice? Could he control the power and spread of the reaction? Sweat dripped into his watery eyes, and his vision blurred as he stared at the crystal. He drew the pulsing power deeper inside, then released it slowly, maintaining control. There. The colors had definitely brightened. He lifted his hand. The gray was misshapen at one finger, a sign that the power had spread beyond his person.

The rule of scientific method was to test every theory, reproduce the results. He reached for the wall.

"Scientist."

Leila's annoyed voice broke his concentration. He jerked his hand back and spun around. She stood a few feet away, her arms crossed, a smile plastered on her face. Behind her was an array of djinn, their loose, bright clothes catching the faint breezes that wafted across the desert. They were watching him in the same way they might view the village idiot. With pity, tolerance, and superiority.

After a single glance at the fading gray handprint, she came to his side. She said something he couldn't understand, then gazed expectantly at him as she whispered, "Just nod and give me your pocketknife."

Jack gave a short nod and reached into his pocket for the knife. "What—"

She broke his sentence off by a very simple means. She cradled his cheeks in her hands, rose on tiptoe, and kissed him.

Heat shot through him as clover and cinnamon teased him. His hands settled at the feminine curve of her waist, drawing her closer. Before he could complete the kiss, however, she pulled her lips from his. Only a scant measure away so he could still feel her warm breath.

"I'll be gone a few moments in that tent," she whispered breathlessly, pulling him from his erotic thoughts. "Remember: Say little; accept nothing."

"Why—"

"It is a long explanation. I shall tell you when we leave."

"Wait." He grabbed her wrist, refusing to let her go without assurance. "Will you be safe going to a tent with one of them? I don't like it, Leila. Let me come with you."

"Two of them actually, and I shall be perfectly safe." She grinned at him. "In fact, you may have more difficulties than I. But perhaps this will protect you." She touched her lips to his, then slid from his embrace and sauntered back to the crowd, her hips swinging. A moment later she disappeared into a tent with two young male djinn.

Jack frowned, not liking anything about this detour to the village. His fists tightened against the frustration of not knowing and the gnawing lack of control. She should have told him what she was doing. He shouldn't have insisted they come right away. They could have worked out a plan ahead of time.

A tug on his elbow dragged his attention away. Another male—were there no women in this place?—bowed. His loose red and yellow striped pants and matching shirt billowed in the breeze, as did his beard, two strands of braided black that reached his knees. The man invited him to sit by the fire.

Remembering Leila's admonition, Jack mumbled agreement, then gestured to the man to lead the way.

A moment later they were kneeling beside a roaring fire.

Fire hardly seemed a necessity on this hot day. Perhaps it was used for cooking, for he could see shish kabob skewers in the fire, although they didn't seem to hold anything. The man leaned over the fire, putting his beard at great risk, and grabbed one of the skewers. He held it out to Jack.

Electricity circuited through him, crystal to chest to fingers, toes, and skull, an easy flow that alerted him to the *ma-at* surrounding him.

The skewer wasn't empty. It held a square of meat, the outside crispy and studded with rosemary. Jack shook his head, resisting the sizzling sound and tempting aroma. The man selected another blank kabob, only suddenly this one wasn't empty either. It contained vegetables. Jack's mouth watered and his stomach rumbled, but he refused again.

Suddenly the man laughed and clapped his hands. The skewers disappeared. With a spate of congratulations, the man clapped Jack on the shoulder in a universal gesture of acceptance.

The hug he gave was definitely more than acceptance.

Other djinn joined them at the fire. All were men, he noticed, especially when one put a hand on his knee. Jack shifted away. Definitely he and Leila weren't staying here for the night.

Mistrock sidled out from beneath his shelter and repositioned himself on Jack's shoulder, gluing himself in place. One of the djinn noticed the little *grucheek* and peered closer, talking rapidly. It seemed he wanted to trade something for the pet rock. Jack didn't have to answer, however. Mistrock's irritated growl was all the answer needed.

Human and *grucheek* settled at the fire to wait. The tribe talked and Jack listened closely, recognizing some words, picking up more in context. Sometimes one of the djinn appeared to direct a question toward him, but remembering Leila's warning—and the warm hug from Stripes—he simply shook his head. Each negative response seemed to increase his approval rating with the tribe.

Instead of speech, he concentrated on the touches of *ma-at* that brushed against him. He didn't feel threatened, at least not by the *ma-at*, but nonetheless the power from the crystal interrupted it all. There were no voices in his mind, no color changes on his clothes; no plate of sliced meat suddenly appeared in his hands. The power that flowed through him became a natural counterforce. Not too much, no explosions or disruptions. Strange, but the more he used it, the more the force seemed not so much an external shield as an innate part of his internal chemistry.

Still, controlling it was tiring.

It seemed an eternity before Leila emerged. She wore a pair of moccasins, he noticed at once. She also looked tousled and mussed. One of the young men held out a skewer of food suspended between his palms. Leila leaned forward and tasted daintily of the roasted vegetables, then laughed at something the man said.

Jack gritted his teeth. Logic told him there was no reason for his sudden primitive urge to claim her. Especially in this group. Logic told him he had no right to possessiveness. Logic, however, didn't stop the raw need coursing through him. Dammit, she should have let him go with her.

Abruptly he pushed to his feet, giving the group at the fire a brief nod and a few polite words, and joined her. He draped a possessive arm across her shoulders, and the crystal at his chest took on a faint green hue.

The two companions gave him an amused look. *"Challest Leila d zaniya?"* one asked him.

Leila answered, then leaned over and kissed Jack at the corner of his mouth.

Heat again. Damn, he wished he knew what was going on.

"Ah," the companion said, as though she'd given an explanation he finally understood. Then he glanced upward.

The sun had passed its zenith and dipped toward afternoon. When the djinni looked back at him, the welcome had disappeared. Jack saw the encampment gathering in a tight knot, and despite the heated day, a chill seemed to go through the group. Stripes pointed to the barrier. "The night approaches."

At least that was what Jack thought he said. Leila nodded; then he felt the pressure of her hand on his butt. Time to leave. It was one order he had no problem following.

As they said good-bye and left the encampment, he simmered with questions, but caution kept him silent until they were long out of earshot. Then he pulled up and demanded, "Why did they turn unfriendly at the end?"

"Because the Night of No Moon approaches, and they wanted us well removed from them when the sun sets."

"Why?"

"They wanted no female there. During the day I was tolerated, but not tonight." She gave him an amused glance. "You are a man; they might have let you stay."

"Not bloody likely," he muttered.

"Well, they were concerned about your refusal of *ma-at*. You were right, Scientist."

"About what?"

"The footwear."

"Your feet aren't as sore?" Her comment momentarily distracted him.

"Not in the least. They are healed, and the slippers will keep them well." She pulled a pouch from inside her robe, opened it, handed him a slice of bread, and then started eating another piece. "Out of pity, they also gave me some food. You played your role very well, by the way."

"What exactly was my role?" he asked, remembering the expressions of pity and tolerance.

"Remember, I told them you did the Circles of Cleansing," she said brightly. "It was the perfect explanation, do you not think?"

"I might agree if I knew more what the Circles of Cleansing are."

"Ah, yes. Circles are a series of rituals and tests, each more difficult than the last. The Circles of the Adept intensify power and strength. The Circles of the Dark"—she shuddered—"no one does them."

"What are the Circles of Cleansing?"

"Mostly they've fallen into disuse. Some djinn, however, believe that to wield *ma-at* with more precision and strength you must first strip yourself of all power. Bring yourself back to the naked, primitive, powerless core. To the elemental self. The Circles of Cleansing do that. An essential part of the route is to use no *ma-at* for any purpose."

"That explains my lack of *ma-at*. What about my lack of language?"

She gave him a sidelong glance, full of mischief. "Djinn who practice the Circles of Cleansing do not hold the common opinions and they are considered . . . quaint. But they are tolerated. They do not harm others or the *ma-at*, so their eccentricity is accepted. I believed the explanation would also cover any oddities in your behavior."

Jack gave a short laugh and rubbed a hand along the back of his neck. If he ever started getting a swelled head, he'd just have to remember this day to bring him back to size. "So they considered me a village idiot."

"But a determined one. After all, you refused the food when your eyes said you were hungry."

"The food being—"

"—prepared by *ma-at*. Though they considered you struck by moonlight, they also admired your tenacity."

Jack laughed outright at the absurdity of it all. "And what was your role in all this?"

She glanced away, her fingers toying with the lapel of her robe. "They thought I was your *zaniya*. I could not tell them otherwise. What other woman would stay with a man who refused to use *ma-at* on the Night of No Moon?"

Zaniya. Wife. His sister had once told him the meaning was even stronger for the djinn. Few djinn formed lifelong bonds with a single partner, but those that did united in a days-long ritual that welded their souls. Then she'd flushed, and muttered that a *zani* usually displayed an annoying degree of possessiveness and protectiveness toward his mate.

Now Jack glanced over at Leila, who still avoided looking back. "What were you doing before you disappeared into the tent?"

"They had no supplies for healing, as I suspected. I was asking you for permission. Asking if it would break your Circles if they used *ma-at* to heal my feet and make my slippers."

"And I conveniently said go ahead. Was my pocketknife enough barter for all that?"

"No."

"What else did you give them?"

She looked at him then. "What do you think I used? My body?"

"No. In that group, they were more likely to want my body than yours. Besides, if they thought you were my *zaniya*, they'd know you'd never sleep with another man."

"Oh." It was a soft sigh of disappointment. "Not part of the role."

"Besides, I don't see you doing that, Leila."

She turned away, and her chin lifted. "Would it bother you if I did?"

"In the past? I won't judge you. Now, while we travel together?" He decided to be honest, even if he didn't understand his own reaction. "Yes. It would."

Again she gave a soft sigh, not disappointment this time, but she didn't say anything.

"So, what did you trade?" Then he shook his head. "Never mind. You don't have to tell me."

"A ritual," she answered. "I had read about it in an ancient text. I gave them the words and described the ceremony. They asked me to demonstrate, but I told them my connection to you during your time of the Circles prevented me from doing that."

His eyes narrowed. "What was the ritual for?"

That mischievous glance was back. "He wanted to meet a Terran."

Chapter Ten

"Tell me about the Night of No Moon."

Leila could not suppress the shudder that ran through her at Jack's question. How to explain the superstitious dread that permeated the days before the most frightening of times in the cycle?

"It is a night of no moon in the sky," she said at last.

He gave a faint laugh and assisted her across a boulder-strewn patch of desert. "I had guessed that much. The name gave it away."

She smiled at his small joke.

"On Earth, our moon waxes and wanes," he continued. "Grows bigger and smaller on a regular cycle, and we have days where it can't be seen. Is it like that?"

"We have that, too." She shook her head. "This is different and comes but once a cycle. It is a night of mystery when all light is sucked from Kaf. Not only no moon, but no stars. A night of utter blackness, and, according to legend, a night when the sinister forces can be released to wreak havoc."

"Sounds like a djinn version of our Halloween."

Leila shrugged, knowing nothing of Halloween. Her own fears of the dark had always made this a night of utter misery. But no djinn took the Night of No Moon lightly. Her people and their *ma-at* were sustained by the air and the fires of Kaf, and a night of darkness and cold was a dangerous thing.

"Do you have rituals or traditions for the night?" Jack persisted.

"We burn fires to give light and heat. We gather together to shield ourselves against the sinister forces. It is a time of song and dances, for joy is the antidote to fear."

She omitted the fact that it also tended to be a night of much lovemaking. On such a primitive, primal night, the heat of passion rose as the natural counterforce to the darkness.

None of that lessened her dread of the approaching night. Uneasily she glanced at the sky. They had not much longer before the sun set, and they needed to find shelter. Her hand was playing with the edge of her robe, she realized, and she forced herself to stop. *Look confident, feel confident.*

This time the chant did not work.

In the distance, lightning bolted from cloud to cloud. They were too far away to hear the accompanying thunder, but the brilliance was unmistakable. She rubbed a hand along her arm. A storm brewed.

All around her, she saw no sign of habitation. Except for the single encampment, there had been none since they'd stepped onto the desert. No flutter of a tent, no gleam of a celebration fire, no sound of voice or drum, no incense. No djinn to share a fire and a tale of past Nights.

A shudder ran through her, but she took a deep breath, trying to force back the fear. Over time, she had learned the power of simply not appearing afraid. She had learned the power of a woman. She had been forced to learn the power of manipulation. In the darkness, though, all that confidence dissipated, as fragile as mist in the morning sun.

Involuntarily she shifted closer to Jack. His body heat warmed her, and the familiar masculine scent of him gave her courage. She hated this weakness and fear, but in truth she was fervently glad she was not alone.

This Night she would not be alone. She would have the Scientist at her side. The dark did not seem so frightening with Jack to share it.

"We need to find shelter." Jack pointed toward the lightning, his sudden comment echoing her thoughts. "That storm's moving pretty fast. We should try to get to those hills. That way we won't be the tallest thing around. And there might be a cave."

"A cave sounds quite inviting right now." She tried to keep the quaver from her voice, but her fear was audible. Even Mistrock's grate was more irritating than soothing.

Jack took her hand. "We will get through this night."

How? And what would the morning look like? The Night of No Moon was more than darkness. It was evil unbound, sinister forces unchained. She could not dismiss her dread; it was worse than she'd ever experienced on this Night. Something was going to happen. Something was going to change. She feared the darkness.

She feared even more what would be let loose tonight.

The Night of No Moon—a perfect time for his task. Xerxes rose from the woman's bed—her name eluded him at the moment—and patted her silky hair, then stroked her throat. For a moment his fingers closed around the smooth column. What would it be like to block the air? To separate her from her breath? The thought was both terrifying and mesmerizing.

He had never experienced killing—the djinn strictures against it were very strong, and he had no desire to draw the attention of the King or the Protector. Not yet. Besides, he was not a barbarian. His realm was the power of *ma-at*, not crude physical force. But he wondered.

She rolled over, her skin sliding with perfumed sweetness over his rough palm, and she gave him a sensual smile. She did not look at his hand, he noticed with displeasure.

The illusion on it had faded, displaced by increased poisons in his hands. With a quick chant, he laid the image of smooth skin over the revealing wrinkles of his hands. It would not do for his hands to give him away.

"Would you like more?" The woman's voice was drowsy and sated.

He would. More knowledge. More power. That she could not give him. Still, the woman had been eager. She had pleased him tonight; she would be rewarded. He loosened his grip and fastened his robe about him.

"Later." He rubbed his hands together, and a gown as sheer as white smoke draped across her. She cooed her thanks even as the sweet scent of cinnamon drifted into the room on a faint pink mist. A moment later she fell back to sleep.

Xerxes put his fingertips on her lids. "May your dreams be pleasant." He could just as easily have given her dreams of terror or dreams of despair. "Dream of a creative way to express your devotion."

Moments later he was at the wasteland that surrounded his home. He shed his robe and sat cross-legged before the divination fire.

The Night of No Moon. A dangerous night to travel. The perfect night to search.

As the curve of the sun disappeared beneath the horizon, they found shelter. On first glance, it appeared to be a mere indentation in the rock, but as Jack peered further, he realized it went much deeper.

"Are there any predators in this area?" he asked, thinking of Earth tales of bears in caves.

"Larger beasts do not like it here, and I see no scorpions." Leila sat down in the cave, as close to the edge as possible. She gave a single glance at the inky interior, shivered, and turned her back to it.

Mistrock slid off Jack's shoulder and with an excited series of grumbles skittered into the cave interior. Soon the *grucheek* was lost in the darkness.

"Mistrock," she called. "Come back. Oh, Jack, we have to find it."

He peered into the cave, seeing nothing, hearing only the echo of Mistrock's contented rumble. "It'll be okay. It came from rocks, remember, and it seemed pretty anxious to go."

"I guess you're right." She gave one last glance behind her. "The *grucheek* are most independent."

"And ours has a penchant for exploring, it seems."

Overhead, streaks of lightning etched the sky as the storm finally reached them. The last of the light from the sun faded to pink, then to yellow, gray, nothing.

Utter black reigned. Jagged lightning split the sky like a flashbulb, and he blinked. The light, so bright and brief, was more blinding than illuminating. It must be heat lightning, for no cooling rain fell.

He stared out, straining to see, feeling the unwanted clutch of panic. Since the kidnapping, he'd never been without at least one source of light—stars or a flashlight or the thin glow of a bathroom night-light.

His fists clenched as he fought the weakness he hated.

"Scientist, can you light a fire?" Leila's soft question came through the night and pierced his rising panic.

He shook his head, then realized she couldn't see

him. "No. I have my matches. The leaves will catch fire, but I didn't see any kindling or wood. We have nothing to sustain it."

"Will you sit with me, then?"

He could not give in to fear and panic. She, too, feared the dark and would need his strength. Jack pulled in a long breath, his fingers rubbing against the wire mesh of his device. "Talk to me so I can find you."

Instead of talking, Leila hummed the tune she'd hummed last night. He heard not only the humming, but the catch of her breath each time the lightning flashed, and the rustle of her robe as she shifted on the hard rock. He followed the sounds, realizing, even as he did, that he didn't need sound to find Leila. Instinctively he knew exactly where she sat. Her clover scent, her female heat identified her to more primitive instincts than sight or hearing.

When he sat beside her, she at once leaned against him, as though she, too, did not need sight on this night. As though more elemental forces brought them together.

He wrapped his arm around her shoulder and pulled her flush against him. The press of feminine curves sent blood coursing through him. He buried his face in the soft curtain of her hair.

"Clover," he said. "You always smell of clover."

" 'Tis better than dust."

"It's a scent as beautiful as the woman who wears it."

"You can't see me."

"I have never needed sight to see your beauty."

Jack didn't know where the words came from within him. He never used even remotely flowery phrases, never thought in terms of poetry. But in this so foreign land they seemed natural.

He felt Leila touch his face with a stroke as light as a dragonfly. She traced his eyebrow and the contour of his cheek and the sensitive ridge of his lips. "I cannot see you, yet my mind sees you as clearly as if this were cloudless midday."

Her touch burned through him, destroying any questions or doubts. Primitive need, hot and pulsing, pounded in him.

"I know." With unerring accuracy, his hand found her side, his fingers caressing the silk of her robe, his palm against the side of her breast. When she didn't pull away, he used his thumb to stroke the lush curve.

Leila shivered against him. Was it fear or excitement or cold that made her tremble? The darkness hid the subtle clues of body language. He rubbed his hand along her arm, warming, soothing fear, stoking excitement.

"Are you cold?" he asked.

Her hair brushed against his cheek as she shook her head. "Not now."

"Afraid?"

"Some. Yes."

He kissed the top of her head and wrapped his other arm around her. "Does this help?"

"Yes."

"Then why do you still tremble, Leila?"

"You know."

"I need to hear it. I need to know that whatever happens tonight is not due to fear or solace or appeasement or mere proximity."

She gave a throaty laugh, one without a hint of the fear that had affected her so far. "You use too many big words, Jack." Her hand cupped his neck, and her thumb traced his cheekbone. The simple touch washed him with a wave of heat that made his breath catch. "Let me show you why I tremble."

She kissed him.

He'd never been kissed like that. Wholly, with abandon, as though she had no thought but that single kiss. Leila pressed against him until not a molecule of air could slip between them. Her fingertips met at his nape, and she pressed the sensitive nerves in his neck while her tongue pressed against his lips, then slipped into his mouth. Deep, wet, sensuous, the kiss ignited a sweet fire.

His hands slid from her back to her sides, curving against the rounded sides of her breasts. "What are your words for this, Leila? For breast and caress?"

"*Dol. Shaliana.*"

"And this?" He rubbed the nipples to tight buds.

"*L-ange avial,*" she whispered.

"This? And this?" He slipped beneath her robe to ring her navel with his thumb, while his finger caressed her lower bud.

As he explored, she breathed the words, teaching him the words of loving. Everywhere he touched was soft and curved and sensual and perfect.

She grasped his shoulders. "Oh, Jack, *mir dol shal-ian.*"

Only the thin silk of her robe denied him complete access. With the side of his hand he shoved away that barrier and cupped her breast as she demanded.

He had no trouble following her commands, for he ached to feel her, skin to skin. Her breast was generous in his hand—round, satin, smooth, hot. The scent and the heat of her surrounded him with sensuousness. Satin demands gave way to silky heat.

He could see nothing. No moon. No stars. No yellow street lamps or blue cathode glows from the television or green LCD displays from a computer screen. Around him was utter blackness without a pinprick of light to disclose what hid behind the ebony curtain. Even the strobe lightning did not illuminate, and the booming thunder covered up all sound but their two voices. Hot, rainless air crackled with power, and the scent of electricity surrounded them.

None of it was as strong, or as compelling, as the scent of clover and the feel of satin.

The only things that existed tonight were him and her and the desire between them. Tonight they needed no sight.

"Be still. Let me move," she whispered. "Let me show you."

This time she touched him low, giving him more words, more sensations. He followed her lead, too bemused by clover and silk and damp woman to do anything else. She cupped him and licked the side of his neck. Her teeth scraped very gently against his nipples, while her fingers touched him intimately. Sheer eroticism shot through him as bright as the lighting bolts above.

Heat in the cave. Cold air outside. Blood racing through his veins. Muscles quivering with forced stillness. Stiff jeans, stiff groin. Leila's incredible softness. Despite flashes of lightning, the glow of crystal, and the rainbow sparkle of djinn emotions, he could only touch, scent, and taste, not see. The contrasts intensified sensation and desire.

He could no longer stay still. Could no longer let her control the loving. With a growl, he gripped the back of her head, holding her to him as he stretched out in the cave. Strewn leaves and a thin layer of moss cushioned his back. Enough for his comfort, but not for Leila to lie on. She gasped at the sudden shift, then sprawled atop him with a satisfied purr.

His fingers tunneled through the mass of her hair, anchoring her to him, keeping her in place while he sought her lips. They were soft, and she tasted sweet, like the mangoes and figs of her diet, like honey and clover. He reached between them and undid the knot at her waist. A moment later he had her belt undone and he brushed the silken robe off her shoulders. He pulled her closer. His arms were surrounded by silk. Silk fabric on top. Silk skin beneath. Straddling him, she sat up, and he shifted his touch to her thighs. Ah, silk here, too. A moment later he heard the whish of fabric, and only the silk of her skin remained. She was naked.

Darkness was no barrier to imagination. His mind's

eye saw her as he had seen her at the pool. The golden tips of her nipples. The indentation of her waist. The curve of her hip. The rainbow of colors painted on her nails.

"You have on too many clothes." She plucked at his shirt, sliding the hem along his chest. With his senses heightened in the dark, the touch jolted him. His pounding heart skipped a beat, a brief, short-circuit arrhythmia.

He sat up, Leila straddling his lap, and tugged his shirt off with one motion. The crystal resting on his chest glowed a pure white, but beyond an inch the light was absorbed by the blackness. He turned the device to hang at his side. Then he gathered her close, his arms wrapping tightly around her.

His mouth devoured hers, while her hands consumed him with her frantic touch. Fingers tunneled through the hairs of his chest, traced the line that led to his groin, fumbled with the unfamiliar, unseen mechanism of snap and zipper. His cock, engorged and hot, pressed against his jeans, begging for release, begging for a different confinement inside her.

"Let me," he groaned as he reached down and unbuttoned and unzipped. She slid off his lap, even as she remained anchored to him with a deep kiss of tongue and teeth. He shoved off jeans and briefs in a single motion, and he sprang free. He rolled to his back, Leila following, and their hands flew across each other, stroking and teasing. Never letting the contact between them break.

Then she was gone.

The smell of clover and the musky scent of her arousal, the sparks of her desire, flashing and sparkling, told him she was still there. But where? He heard her rapid breath, but it surrounded him, everywhere and nowhere.

"Leila?"

Then he felt her. Oh, God, he felt her. Just her lips. Surrounding him low. Taking him deep in her mouth. Teasing him with a flick of her tongue. Only that single touch, only that single sensation, which consumed him with a fresh blaze of desire.

"No, I don't want to come in your mouth," he gasped, crudely, roughly.

"Not this time," she agreed, lifting her lips from him.

With a quick motion, he grasped her waist and twisted her, seating her atop him. She shifted, positioning herself, and then he was inside her.

She was slick and welcoming, hot and close, gripping and pulsing. His hands slid up the inside of her damp thighs, pushing them wider, as his hips surged upward until he penetrated as deep as he could.

Leila moaned in pleasure. Her hips moved as he stroked. He sat up and pulled her breast into his mouth, sucking on it as she set their joined pace with the rhythm of her hips. It wasn't suave or controlled. It was primal and primitive and wild.

Sparks. Rainbows. White crystal and whiter lightning.

Clover. Musk. Electricity. Desire.

Sweat. Slick heat.

Thunder. Rasp. Groan.

Sensations bombarded him.

The orgasm slammed into him as he exploded inside her. Leila pulsed around him, taking all he gave in her release. Her lungs gasped as she sought air.

Lightning shot through the cave, brilliant and blinding. Thunder echoed. Color exploded, a brilliant fireworks of crystal sparks as they came together, joined and flew across two worlds, and then released.

Slowly, slowly, the tension eased from him, and he felt Leila drape across him, as boneless and fluid as a blanket. He wrapped his arms around her and held her close. When he placed a gentle kiss on her temple, she gave a soft sigh of contentment.

He was too exhausted to move or even to pull out of her. His eyes drifted shut, even as he heard Leila's breathing slow and deepen.

He realized one thing as sleep overcame him. Never again would he fear the dark. For now, the memories were not of a kidnapper or pain. From now on, the dark would mean Leila.

Chapter Eleven

She had been wrong; the Scientist needed no guidance in the ways of a man and a woman. Leila woke from her sleep feeling the pleasurable ache of muscles used for something much better than *camping*. The glow of repeated satisfaction settled across her, bringing with it a peaceful contentment. Twice this night they had come together; twice she had found rare pleasure.

She opened her eyes and for a moment, in the absolute darkness, could not tell the difference between open and shut. Yet the instinctive panic at the blackness did not come this time. Tonight, surrounded by Jack's arms and his strength, she had conquered the fear. Now pleasure existed where once had resided blind terror.

Jack. He lay naked beside her, one arm thrown loosely over her hip, as though even in sleep he desired to keep her close. It was a rare sensation to feel so treasured. She drew in the masculine scent of him, even as the chilled air sent a shiver down her arms. The Night of No Moon had grown cold, but she'd never felt warmer. She burrowed closer, burying her face in the crook of his neck.

His hand tightened around her hip, and then his lips moved against her neck. She felt him stir against her, and, that quickly, he stoked the desire simmering inside her.

He stroked. She caressed. He kissed. She nibbled. They made love without sight, without words. Only the exquisite sensation of touch, the sound of breathing, and the spiraling excitement marked the passing moments.

His callused palm slid along her thigh. He had a working hand, different from that of a polished, smooth djinni, and his stroking set her skin aglow with the slight abrasiveness she had come to crave. She ran her fingers across his cheek. Here, too, was the rougher texture of Jack as his light-colored beard slowly filled in. Short bristles here, while the shaggy-cut hair atop his head was thick silk. She traced the line of hair down his chest to his groin. Here the blond hair was curlier and coarser, but still thick.

Her explorations were rewarded with his groan of arousal. She traced the curve of his ear, the skin behind his ear, the nape of his neck, then kissed the sensitive spot where his neck and shoulders met. She stroked him there with her tongue. Slowly, oh so slowly. She savored his taste, the freshness of water and the sweetness of fruit.

His fingers found the underside of her breast and the sensitive nipple, while his other hand massaged her bottom. His sex pulsed against her belly, and she was filled with joy and want.

She caressed him, no particle of skin missed, and he returned each stroke. The bone at the top of the chest, the curve of elbow and hip and thigh. Behind the knee. The upper lip. The lower lip. Between fingers and across toes. Contrasts. Pliant skin over unyielding muscle. Deep kisses and ranging hands. Heated sex and cool air.

She learned him intimately. Yet she knew him no deeper than the skin she stroked, she realized, while he had slipped beneath her defenses, which were unfortified by *ma-at* or artifice. And he stayed to enjoy.

This time he seemed keener on pleasing her than on reaching his own satisfaction. His hands and tongue caressed and demanded with an intimate exploration that brought her to the brink; then he banked the fires with soothing murmurs and cooling breaths over her sweat-dampened skin. Again and again, she, who had always needed to be the one in control of her sexuality, lay helpless and panting beneath his bewitching touch. Even when she found release, with an ecstatic, drawn-out moan, he did not stop. Again he urged her on—stroke and soothe, excite and temper, release. And again, until she believed more pleasure was impossible.

Then she discovered she was wrong. He entered her, swift and slick and demanding. She yielded. He stroked, fast and furious and without finesse.

She didn't want finesse. She wanted raw, primal energy. She drew him to her, past all boundaries. Colors exploded around them, the unleashed emotions so bright and beautiful that she had to close her eyes against their brilliance. She raced across uncharted towers to the precipice, Jack with her.

Together. One. She clung to him in her release as he pulled her tight. Then he came inside her, hot and wet and vital.

Time ceased. Fear, doubt, and trouble vanished. All that remained was one exquisite moment of unforgettable bliss.

But, moments end, and bliss is fleeting. Gradually his arms loosened and her fingers relaxed. Sweat dried in the chill of the night. She thought she saw a graying of the darkness, but she was too tired and content to move.

Sleep had almost overtaken her when, beside her, Jack began to tremble. Was he cold? She tightened her arms protectively around him and was surprised when a warm chuckle sounded in her ear. He wasn't chilled; he was laughing!

"What is it?" Her voice sounded rusty, dry.

"You were worried about Mistrock? It's back, growling in my ear. If rocks can growl, that is. I thought it was a distant landslide."

Concern washed over her. "Is it all right? Is the *grucheek* angry?"

Jack brushed back her hair. Even in the dark, he seemed to know unerringly where she was and what she needed. "Heck if I know. Can't be too mad, if it came back. Maybe the thing's lonely."

Leila made a soft chirping noise and was relieved when Mistrock answered her with a rumbly trill. It was not angry or displeased. She repeated the chirp, and a moment later she felt Mistrock's knobby body bump against her shoulder.

"What is wrong, Mistrock?" She petted it and crooned. "Did you not find your own kind to spend the night with? Were you cold? Hungry? Is there aught we can do to please you? Stay with us for as long as you desire. We welcome you again, as a companion."

The irritated rumbling continued. "Jack, I think something is wrong. Its sound. I do not think it anger, for no *grucheek* will stay where it does not wish to be. But the sound it makes is not pleased."

"Mistrock, what's got you riled?" Jack asked with affection.

Just then, Mistrock moved. Not away, but onto her shoulder, then down her arm to her wrist which was resting across Jack's shoulder. Using her as a bridge, the *grucheek* moved to Jack. The rough grumble changed into a relaxed purr as Mistrock settled atop the Scientist's talisman.

"He sounds better, but I think something is wrong," she fretted.

"Whatever the problem, it's gone." Jack stroked her back. "You're fussing. You'd make a good mother, Leila."

His hand stilled, and Leila froze as they both realized what he'd said. And what they'd been doing.

Jack cleared his throat. "I never thought . . . I never took the time . . . Leila, are you using any form of birth control?"

"Birth control?"

"Something to prevent pregnancy. That is, if djinn procreation is the same as human."

"I believe it to be." The fatigued muscles in her stomach cramped. Tonight she had not thought of her original desire for a child, she realized. For her, this past night had only been about her desire for Jack.

"Are you on birth control?" he persisted.

"No djinni tries to control the birth of a child. We have no need."

Jack gave a short curse. "Because you use *ma-at*?"

And you don't have any. He didn't have to add the corollary.

"Because djinn rarely have children." She laid a hand on his arm. "We are not a very fertile people."

"Still, if we do this again, we're using the condoms in my wallet."

He'd said "if," not "when." Casually, as though their lovemaking were a moment finished and an event to be dismissed. As though he could make a rational choice, when she had been driven by a frantic need.

Her throat felt suddenly tight. Did he mean this night had not been special for him as it had been for her? Why should it, when they had known each other so short a time, and had opposed each other so often? The tightness swelled into her chest.

His fingers stroked through her hair, smoothing it.

"I'm sorry. That wasn't a very romantic ending. But . . . Leila, you are so very special, warm and giving and—"

Even the sweet words could not banish the pain. She felt him shake his head.

"But we're from two different worlds, and I mean that in the most literal sense of all. The idea of a child of mine growing up here, so far away . . ."

"I understand," she answered, barely able to find her voice. Her chest ached with a sadness all the more keen in the wake of such joy. Carefully she drew in a single breath. Then another, quelling the threat of tears. She had not cried in more cycles than she could count. She had gone into this relationship with her eyes wide open, and she would not shed tears now just because her feelings had changed.

"Some day, would you want a child?" she ventured at last.

"Yes, I would," he answered promptly. "Several, as a matter of fact."

"Several? Humans can have more than one?"

"Of course."

"Solomon has never blessed any djinni with more than one."

"That's too bad." He gave a small chuckle. "I told you about my brothers and sister. Sometimes we fight, but I can't imagine life without them. Especially Beau."

"Because he is your twin? You are close?"

"Yes, we have always understood each other, although we're opposites in everything but looks. Isis says Beau could charm a vampire into the sun."

"Charm? He has the scientific magic as well?"

Jack laughed. "No. He's got charisma."

"What do you have?"

"Damned if I know." He shrugged. "Bluntness, maybe. I'm not one for beating around the bush."

Why would he want to beat a bush? Sometimes Jack's words were too confusing.

He was silent a moment, then said, "Of all my family, I understand Isis the least, but I still hate that I can't even phone her. That her child is growing up in a world I can't even visit."

"You are here now."

"I'm not staying."

"I know." She didn't have the courage to ask if he would ever come back, for in her heart she knew the answer.

He toyed with her hair, then let out a breath of air. "Actually, all five of us are different, but I would give my life for any one of them."

"That is very brave."

"No, it's what I would do for someone I love."

What I would do for someone I love. What he would have done for their child. She laid a hand on his cheek, feeling the golden bristle of the growing beard. Her fingers tangled in the shag of his hair. There was enough light now to see just a smudge of his intriguing blond hair, but she could feel the thick strands.

She thought of his patience and kindness, and knew he would have been a good father. Her hand froze, and her insides shriveled.

She still wanted a child, wanted it desperately, and more than ever, she wanted *his* child. But there were so many complications she had brushed aside and too many doubts she could no longer evade.

Did she have the right to have his child and not let him know? Did she have the right to deprive him of that joy? As he said, there was no future for a Scientist and a djinni.

Could she separate father and child? A djinn child knew many fathers and mothers who participated in his nurturing. But the birth parents had special bonds, special joys unshared by the others. One ritual in particular bonded sire and child: the naming ceremony. A father chose the name—the true, full name, not the name of common use. The name of lineage and of talent and identity. The name that could be used to bind a djinni with the hated bands of servitude; the name that was closely kept from all but parents and *zani* or *zaniya*.

Jack would not have been given the privilege of naming his firstborn. How could she have so foolishly thought to deprive her child of that sacred rite?

She laid a hand on her stomach. It was too early to tell whether this loving had brought her the child she had wanted, and too late to change what had been done already. And if she were pregnant? What would she do? She and the child could not live in his world. Djinn must renew their bonds to Kaf every fortnight or wither and die. And Jack refused to stay on Kaf.

"Why do you hate this world?" she asked abruptly.

He curled a hand around her shoulder, and she felt

191

the tension in him. All of a sudden, she was sorry she'd raised the subject. Instinctively she knew the answer, and the voiced question had destroyed their relaxed closeness. She stroked his temple soothingly. "Never mind. It does not matter."

"I don't hate the land." His hand moved up and down her arm. "Just the *ma-at*. I don't like being subject to someone else's whims. I don't like being controlled. I can't accept that."

Her stomach knotted as she heard the harsh, unyielding note in his voice, and suddenly she understood. The only reason he was with her now was because she was powerless. He would never have made love to her otherwise. When she got her *ma-at* back, he would want to have nothing to do with her.

The fact was a sharp stab to her gut—and her heart—but pain made it no less true. And the ironic thing was, she understood how he felt. She understood how it was to stand helpless beneath the power of superior *ma-at*, no matter how well-meaning the wielder.

Tears welled again, and she fought them back. She drew in a shuddering breath, refusing to give in to weakness.

Just as she refused to give in to the sudden knowledge that somehow during these few short days, she had fallen in love with Jack Montgomery.

She closed her eyes, squeezing them hard against the pain, even as her lover burrowed closer. The scent of him was a temptation. His hand roved across her body with the familiarity he now took as his due. His talisman glowed like white ice, foreign and cold. Abruptly she turned away.

She could not make love when her heart was giving all and he wanted none.

"I'm tired. I must sleep." Inwardly she winced at the abruptness of her voice, but she could not temper it.

His hand stopped; and he gathered her in close. "All right; I understand. You're probably sore, too. We'll both get some sleep." A moment later she felt his muscles slacken and his breath grow even as he fell asleep.

He did not understand, but she could not explain. Nor could she move from his embrace. Cradled by her lover's arms, she lay in silence and sadness.

Suddenly Mistrock broke the silence with a discontented rumble. And then she felt it—a touch of *ma-at*. *Ma-at* seeking a home, a connection. She sucked in a breath and rolled away from Jack, extracting herself from his embrace. Was her soul healed and the *ma-at* returning? She held herself very still, straining to gather in the *ma-at*, to heal.

Ma-at, sweet and strong. *Ma-at* with a siren's call of power. *Ma-at* more powerful than she had ever felt. Oh, by Solomon, she could gather this *ma-at* and be stronger than she had ever been before.

Ma-at, yes. But not hers. She opened her eyes and realized the darkness had faded further, replaced by a purple mist so dark and thin that if she had not heard Mistrock she would have thought she'd imagined it.

The mist surrounded her like the tender embrace of a lover. Fascinated by the touch of the power, Leila

193

inhaled deeply, as though she could make the *ma-at* hers by the simple act of breathing.

Mistrock's renewed growl pierced the spell, warning her that something was wrong. The *grucheek* still sat atop Jack's shoulder, beside the glowing talisman, quivering with a rocky tumbling sound that reverberated around the cave. The talisman's crystal gleamed brighter, a single focused beam piercing the mist.

Purple, a beautiful rich shade, surrounded her. She was a well empty of *ma-at*, and the color enticed her to drink deep and fill the emptiness. The mist swirled and gathered about her, drawn to her as though she were the lodestone and it the filings of metal. With each moment, it strengthened. Though she held it at bay for now, she knew she could not long resist the relentless temptation.

The mist, she noticed, avoided the Scientist. It eddied around his sleeping body on its path toward her. Even in sleep, somehow the Scientist conquered *ma-at*.

"Scientist," she whispered, her voice hoarse under the strain of resisting the lure of the mist. "Mistrock. Wake him."

The mist pulsed around her. Oh, how she wanted that power again, better and stronger than she'd ever known. But some instinct told her that she must not accept it, must not use it to reconnect to Kaf. The mist reached her throat. It filtered into her, even as she held her breath. So sweet it was, even as it stole the voice from her.

"Jack," she croaked one last time. Then she drew in a long, needed breath.

And she was filled with *ma-at*.

The *ma-at* of a stranger.

Chapter Twelve

"Jack!"

The single cry penetrated Jack's sleep. He awoke to Mistrock tugging the hairs on his arm as the *grucheek* scraped its rocky body across his chest, abrading the skin. "Ouch. What are you—" Jack sat upright, then froze.

A purple mist filled the chamber. Everywhere except where he sat.

The crystal on his chest shone with a white nova brilliance. As he took in the scene, electricity shot from the crystal through his arms, then spread throughout his body. It surrounded him with a sharp current. The mist retreated and thickened around Leila, where it pulsed with an entrancing purple iridescence. A tendril snaked out and curled around his ankle.

He felt the enticing need to draw the mist in. *Ma-*

at, he realized, as the wires charged with power—from the battery, from him—and the crystal glowed silver. The mist retreated again, to coagulate around Leila. Yet the purple mist did not emanate from her, he knew. It was taking her over.

Fury shot through him. The wires sparked. The mist roiled and curled about Leila. She cried out, part agony, part ecstasy.

Emotions. He remembered his earlier suppositions, his small experiments. The bands responded to his emotions as well as to the *ma-at*. He had to be very careful, very controlled, or he would hurt Leila.

Jack forced a breath into his lungs. He was a scientist and a doctor. Detachment was necessary to do his work effectively. Now he sought that cool logic and that honed focus. Study each step; do what needed to be done.

Except he wasn't detached. Couldn't be. Not with Leila at risk.

Focus. Focus. For her sake, focus. He repeated the mantra until he had regained some small measure of control. Until he contained the roiling fury and commanded the power radiating inside. Only then did he stand, Mistrock clinging to the wires at his neck.

With a deliberate stride, he penetrated the mist, which parted before him. *Moses and the Purple Sea*, he thought with sudden irreverence. A moment later he was at Leila's side. He sat behind her and wrapped his arms and legs around her, surrounding her with his body. He draped the chain of wires over her shoulder.

Where he touched her, the mist retreated. Yet still

it swirled about her ankles and across her nose and eyes. He leaned his face against hers. Still not enough. Wherever he wasn't, the mist was.

He remembered the wall he'd touched, the thin line of gray around his hand. Drawing in a deep breath, he concentrated. Not on the mist. Not on Leila. Not on his anger or his fear. He concentrated on the mesh of wires and the glow of crystal.

He stilled and focused on the power coursing through him. Slowly, methodically, calmly, without emotion, he focused on increasing the power. On multiplying the current as it sped through wire and sinew. On expanding it beyond his skin to the solid rock of Kaf. To the soil and to the drip of water. Outward, negating the mist.

The opposition was working. The mist retreated, sliding off Leila like a satin cover. It hovered in the cave, waiting. Waiting for weakness. Waiting for resolve to fail.

Drawing on years of practice in the lab, during internship and residency, he kept his focus. Kept his mind alert. Did what needed to be done. Though his muscles quivered from the strain of stillness and his body ached with the relentless tension, he focused on the power he generated and shoved the mist back, away from him, Mistrock, and Leila.

The mist retreated, but still it did not vanish. He drew deep into his core, concentrated, then shoved the power outward, in an unstoppable flood of resistance. The mist exploded and disappeared. There was not a droplet left, as though it had never existed except in his imagination.

Yet his imagination had not conjured up the malevolent mist. He remained unmoving, still holding Leila while she breathed, but he did not stir or speak. He leaned over, kissed the corner of her lips, teased them open with his tongue, and then added his gentle breath to hers.

A shudder coursed through her; then she leaned over and coughed, a wrenching spasm that racked her body. She coughed until she was hoarse; then she hung in his arms, gasping and trembling. He held her, rubbing his cheek against her hair in a soothing motion. At last she straightened and drew in a long, deep breath.

Jack released her then, moving away and dropping the circle of his arms.

The mist did not return.

Leila turned to him, her eyes bleak. "What did you do? What happened?"

He stared at the crystal and the pattern of wires. "I don't know," he whispered.

Xerxes jerked backward, falling onto the sands of Kaf. The fire before him flared upward in a brilliant purple column, and the searing heat scorched his naked flesh. Then, as quickly as it burst, the flame collapsed, burned out in a rush of returning *ma-at*.

He blinked to clear his vision, then stared into the cooling embers. Elation mixed with confusion and anticipation. He had found the strange force. Oh, not precisely. The touch had been too fleeting and the method too imprecise for that. But he had found the direction the force had taken from the *Kaliamahru* to the isolated regions near the Tower Lands.

Still, there was too much he did not yet understand. Xerxes slowly pushed to his feet, feeling the aches in muscles unmoved throughout the night. He began a series of *chi-zhao* movements and chanted the mantras of focus. He loosened the stiffness and returned suppleness to his body. Only a body at its peak could withstand the rigors of the upper levels of *ma-at*. Only a clear, focused mind could interpret and use such a foreign power.

When he finished the rituals of *chi-zhao*, he stood still and let the arid winds of Kaf dry his sweat, while he sorted through the revelations of his seeking. The power that had repelled his was alien, unlike anything in his vast experience. First there had been a hole, a break in the mist. Then . . . what? The power became directed, he realized. It actively repelled him.

And succeeded.

He was sure now that the wellspring of this negating force was not a natural phenomenon. It was not an undiscovered quirk of Kaf or an aberration from the sinister forces. It was under the direction of someone.

Such a power could not be allowed to counter him. He must rule it. The power, and the one who wielded it, *must* yield to him.

He stood motionless, waiting, until the wary insects emerged, until a small desert mouse peeked its nose out of its hole, testing whether it was safe to nibble the grass.

Xerxes waited, watching the mouse, touching the pitiful creature with a drop of his *ma-at* to allay instinctive fears. The brown mouse emerged, sat on its haunches to sniff the air, then, reassured, scampered to a small patch of green at Xerxes's feet and began to nibble.

He knelt and petted the mouse's head. The creature continued to eat, unperturbed by the unthreatening touch. Xerxes stroked its throat, lingered on the soft fur; then with a touch of the sinister forces woven delicately into his *ma-at*, he closed the throat and collapsed the lungs.

The mouse looked up with wild panic, unable to breathe, unable to escape the black bonds. Xerxes crooned softly, soothing the mouse even as its chest heaved in fruitless endeavor. A moment later it convulsed, then dropped. Dead.

So, that was killing. Xerxes submerged the instinctive, ingrained horror beneath fascination and thrill. It would be easier the next time.

With a wave of his hand, he buried the mouse beneath a mound of sand. He glanced at his hand—the wrinkled mottling had spread. His use of the other forces could no longer be denied, but it could still be concealed. Holding his hands before him, he chanted an incantation. The skin smoothed, and the discoloring disappeared; all traces of the poisons there were hidden. Then he stroked a hand across his tablet. The turquoise had turned to onyx, but this, too, he hid. He must be cautious; each drawing of the killing forces would unravel the spell, and it would not do to reveal his purpose with so minor a slip.

He shrugged on his robe, then strode back to his home. He had a journey to prepare for. Unfortunately, the foreign sorcerer was in a remote area he had never visited, so he could not transport directly to the area. No djinni could transport to a spot he could not visualize at the moment of transport.

If this were an ordinary need, he would find someone who had been there to take him. Xerxes immediately discarded the notion; no one could know of his plans. Instead, he could go back to the *Kaliamahru* or to a nearby village he had once visited. He chose the village. From there, he would find the sorcerer.

Or wait for the wielder to come to him.

Either way, he must have absolute control over the wielder and the power.

Or he must destroy both.

What had he done? *How* had he done it? What was happening to him? Was it this place of magic, or was it something else? The questions roiled through Jack as slippery as quicksilver while he pulled his pants on.

"Leila, are you okay?" That one question overrode all the others.

"Yes. I am fine." She slipped her robe back on, then bent her head as she knotted the belt. Her hair hid her face, but not her trembling hands. "Will you excuse me? I need a moment's privacy." Without another word or glance, she hurried from the cave into the graying morning.

Jack sat back down at the edge of their rocky outcropping and held the crystal in his palm, while his eyes traced the runes in the mesh of wires leading to the heart of the device. Prismatic colors danced deep within the crystal, and he felt a matching electricity spread through him.

There *had* to be a logic to this whole situation, and his scientific mind demanded the explanation. No longer was the device he'd created merely a passive shield—he had begun to suspect that already. Either his chemistry reacted with it, or . . . Had the crystal awakened powers dormant within him in some strange, electric symbiosis? Scientific magic, Leila had called it.

No matter how fascinating and horrifying the facts were, he couldn't ignore them. When the facts didn't fit the hypothesis, then the hypothesis had to be modified, a basic principle of scientific method. So, what were the facts?

Tonight that power had flowed across him and in him, and then he had controlled and directed and spread the power by the force of his will and mind. He had met the mist's power and not only stopped it, but stopped its effect on Leila, too, and then had sent the mist packing. Much as he must have done instinctively when he'd first met Leila.

So the effect wasn't Kaf working on him. His reaction to Leila had happened before they got here.

The power was created by the device and him, a hypothesis both satisfying and unsettling.

Leila returned and sat beside him with her knees drawn up and her arms wrapped around her legs. Her chin rested on her knees, and she stared straight ahead. In front of her was the brilliant red of the sunrise. Mistrock skittered from the cave to perch on her painted toenails, its rocky gills vibrating with a happy purr.

At least one of them was content. Leila seemed withdrawn, and he . . . he didn't know how the hell he felt. He only knew that last night, before the purple mist invaded, had been . . . incredible. She had roused and awakened him, not just sexually but emotionally. Since he'd come here and met her, he'd *felt*. Deeper, more passionately, than ever before.

In his life on Earth, had he wrapped himself in some protective cocoon, never letting himself feel too much? A cocoon that Leila had torn apart with her humor and her complaints and her passion?

What was she thinking this morning? He couldn't tell, couldn't penetrate the cool mask that had fallen over her.

He raked a hand through his hair. Emotions were too confusing. He didn't understand his reactions to her, nor did he know how to handle her silent withdrawal. All in all, it was best to avoid the quicksand of emotions. Focus instead on the crystal and the mist.

He watched the sun rise and felt the warmth of day return. "The Night of No Moon is over."

"Yes."

"Have you ever seen a mist like that?"

"I have not seen one, but I've heard of a seeking mist." She kept her gaze straight ahead.

"Seeking mist. What was it seeking?"

"Whatever the conjurer wants." She frowned, as though considering the matter more deeply. "This mist was intense and wide-ranging. I felt its seeking even without my *ma-at*. Whoever created it was powerful."

"It seemed attracted to you."

She drew in a shuddering breath. "I felt the *ma-at* inside me; I wanted it there. It filled me, like water fills an empty vessel."

"Leila, your *ma-at* . . . I didn't take it again, did I?"

She shook her head. "That was not my *ma-at* you repelled." She tilted her head to look at him. "The mist avoided you, and then you banished it."

Jack laid a hand on the hard rocks. A beam of sun finally reached their shadowed perch and caught in the crystal. A prism spread across the back of his hand. "Could it have been drawn to you because you are without *ma-at*? Could that be what it was seeking?"

Leila didn't answer. Instead, she straightened as the sun touched her face and glowed on the sheen of her hair.

"Leila?" He gave her a curious glance.

"What? Oh, um, that does not seem likely." She touched the turquoise tablet at her throat. "Why would a mist on Kaf seek someone without *ma-at*?"

Another disturbing question he couldn't answer.

She shot to her feet, still looking toward the sun.

Mistrock tumbled off her feet, emitting a rumble of surprise. She picked it up and handed Jack the rock. "I think we should continue our journey."

Without another word, she set off down the hill.

They had not traveled for more than a couple of hours when they reached the far edge of a stand of trees and discovered, on the other side, a gentle slope with a village at the base. Surrounding the village were more trees, the most he'd seen so far. From the concealment of the grove, Jack paused to study the details.

The village was larger and more settled than the temporary encampment of yesterday, but still small by Earth standards. Mostly, he saw a central square with a pulsing fountain, which changed color and rhythm randomly. The residences were hidden in the trees, mere spots of color spread through the greenery. Leila had indicated that her land was sparsely populated, and he gathered that the djinn did not like crowding, a sentiment he could appreciate.

As he watched the scene, he was struck by the sensations of color and fluid motion, with one stunning exception. A man sat in the center of the square, absolutely still except for his strumming on a guitar-like instrument and his singing. Unlike the colorful townsfolk, the singer wore dark clothing, but whether midnight blue or black, Jack couldn't tell. His single spot of color was the rich auburn of his waist-length hair, which concealed his face as he sang.

A few people lounged at his feet or around the square; others listened from a distance. Above them, the air sparkled and glinted with fleeting sparks of color.

As compelling as the man was, it was his singing that held them still. Jack slowly sat, as did Leila, drawn into the spell of the music. No, not just a spell. He caught wisps of sensation that the singer's *ma-at* wove into his performance—a taste of grape, a scent of jasmine—before the crystal negated the effect. But the power of the crystal did not lessen the impact. Nor did the fact that Jack could translate only a few of the lyrics. Words and sensations were window dressing to the poignant tug of the music.

The sun was a scorching warmth, the air shimmering clear, the sky a cloudless blue. Beside him Leila rested her chin on her knees, also listening to the song. A perfect day for being outside, for enjoying life. Yet as he listened to the mournful song, sadness and a yearning for lost opportunity washed over him. He was such an idiot to have wasted his time in this land fearing chaos. Kaf was no different from strange lands of Earth; the people were like people everywhere with their hopes and dreams and weaknesses. He should have been studying, learning, enjoying life to the fullest.

At last the final note faded into the hot morning. For a moment there was utter quiet. Not a birdsong or a djinn voice or an insect chirp broke the silence. Even the wind died, and Mistrock's rocky purr ceased.

The silence ended when the singer spoke with a merry lilt, followed by the sounds of the appreciative audience. Another song followed, a cheerful frolic that brought only a smile.

"That singer has an incredible voice," Jack commented.

"That would be Zayne," she said with a soft smile. "Our minstrel."

"You know him?"

"Yes." She offered no further explanation. Instead, she abruptly rose to her feet, then smoothed her fingers through her hair. She brushed the dirt off her wrinkled robe and straightened her turquoise tablet in the V of her lapels. Her chin lifted and her lips tilted in a self-confident smile. She was the picture of a woman without a care or a doubt in the world. What had changed her from the withdrawn woman of the sunrise?

Jack got to his feet.

"Stay here." She pointed to a flat rock hidden behind a clump of trees.

His eyes narrowed. "I'm going with you."

"Please do not be stubborn, Scientist. Wait where you can be hidden. I will return very quickly."

"Why should we separate?"

She fisted her hands at her waist. "Because you have such fair hair. And bristles."

Jack rubbed a hand across his chin. "What does that have to do with you going in there alone?"

"You do not look like a djinni and are difficult to disguise. You have learned much of our language, but you are not fluent. And you have Terran magic, not *ma-at*."

"None of that stopped us before."

"But I should like to refresh myself, eat something I have not just plucked from the earth, feast on spiced cake and steeped tea. Your differences cannot be concealed that long. Soon they will know you are human."

"Sooner or later. What's the difference?"

"My people generally welcome strangers into their midst. Now that the Night of No Moon is past, they will be more accepting, less wary. Give me a short time to discover if there are any of those who actively dislike humans, ones who would cause you problems. If not, we can enter. If so, we will find another plan."

He hesitated. Something didn't seem quite right about her plan, but he couldn't put his finger on what it was.

"Please." She laid a hand on his arm. "Let me do this."

It was her world. He gave in to her knowledge and settled down on the rock she'd pointed to. "How long will you be gone?"

"Before the shadows reach that tree."

Half an hour, he guessed. "If you're not back by then, I'll come looking for you."

"Very well." Without another word, she pivoted and started down the trail.

He watched her leave, watched the sway of her hips and the swish of her scarlet robe. Her step was eager, and this time he saw no reluctance to enter the town. In fact there was something different about her. Ever since they'd left the cave this morning, she'd had a glow about her, an excitement, that he wasn't egotistical enough to attribute to his skill at sex. Maybe she was excited that their journey seemed to be nearing an end.

The sun glinted off the smooth pearl of her skin; she seemed more alive and vital than he had ever seen. Just before she rounded a curve, she glanced over her shoulder, gave him a saucy smile, blew him a kiss, and then disappeared from sight behind the trees.

Would he ever understand her?

Jack sat in the heat and the silence. Faint scents of mint, orange, cedar, and olive wafted to him. A bee buzzed past his ear, and he heard the sides of a silky tent snap in the wind. Through the veil of leaves, he saw rainbow colors shift in the distance.

This should be a moment of contentment and joy. Yet he could not relax and enjoy it. A lingering sense of melancholy and fear urged him not to let Leila go. His heart whispered that he was making a mistake, even as his throat closed around a yearning need he couldn't identify.

Logic told him they should rest and provision themselves here, just as Leila suggested. Emotion told him to skirt the village and continue their solitary journey with Leila at his side, safe and warm and loving. Instinct told him he would lose her here.

Logic told him she was never his to lose.

His hands were trembling, and he rubbed them together, stilling the telltale motion. Mistrock chirruped in his ear, as though sympathizing. Jack gripped the chain of his device, the wires shining beneath the sun. Leila was djinn; he was human. She relied on her powers of *ma-at* and her emotions. He respected logic and science. There could be no future between them.

Logic and science, not sorcery, had banished the mist last night.

It was time he started thinking, and acting, like a scientist. Jack laid one hand on the rock and began to experiment.

•

Chapter Thirteen

Her *ma-at* was back!

Leila could scarcely contain her dance of joy as she sped along the path to the village.

Such a faint touch had come to her with the rising sun that she had at first thought it was a remnant of the purple mist. But, no, the *ma-at* was hers, sweet and familiar, yet so thin and fragile that she had not risked even the smallest of rituals. She had yet to test her strength and taste the richness of the power. What if she strained her *ma-at* and lost it again? What if the return wasn't permanent or was a mere illusion?

No, she refused to believe that Solomon would be so cruel.

Throughout the morn, though, the reestablished connection to Kaf had strengthened, and she savored each moment with her revitalized *ma-at*. Each passing moment assured her the return was real. Now she ached to try out her power.

She had promised Jack she would tell him that her *ma-at* had returned before she used it. Used it in his presence, she amended. Before she said anything to him, she wanted to make sure her *ma-at* was back, and that she was at her full, if meager, talent. She wanted to rejoice and revel.

At the edge of the square, she gave in to delight and danced in a circle of celebration, then turned her face and arms to the blessed sun. On this day, she did not care that her *ma-at* was weak. It was back, and it was hers.

Zayne looked up from strumming his oud. *Leila, love. Is disheveled your new look?*

His amused voice sounded inside her head as he switched from singing to strumming. Oh, she had missed this, this intimate conversation with another djinni. Her people weren't telepathic; they could not read each other's thoughts, but they could send their own thoughts to another willing to receive them. She grinned a response, too excited to take the slightest offense. Not when elation beat against her chest.

Ignoring me, sweet bit? Zayne asked.

Finish. She tried out the single word, then risked another. *Alone.*

Are you all right?

Yes. She gave him a reassuring smile even as her body knotted. How weak she must have sounded. Indeed, she felt like a youngling trying out the first exercise.

Accepting her choice, Zayne bent back to his music, his unique auburn hair flowing over his shoulder.

She had always liked the musician. Zayne knew of her weakness in *ma-at*, but he had never coddled her or shown her pity or condescension or felt the need to demonstrate his superiority. He had too much confidence in himself to worry about someone else's power, and little could compete with the lure of his music and the power of his *ma-at*.

She suspected there was much about Zayne that he chose not to reveal. One had only to listen to his music to know the charming surface hid a darker soul. But she trusted him as much as she trusted anyone; he knew how to keep a secret.

Zayne finished his song, then stood. Ignoring the pleas for more, he insisted he needed rest, but hinted that a small bit of refreshment would not be amiss. From the warm smile he gave the woman at his side, Leila guessed that food was not his only needed refreshment.

Not surprising. Zayne was one of the most sensual men she'd ever met.

Can you spare a few moments first? She tested her returning power and found it came easily, like the comfort of a favorite garment. Oh, it was such bliss to wield her *ma-at* again.

For you, always.

He touched the cheek of the woman beside him. At first she pouted prettily, but her face relaxed as he continued to stare at her. Whatever their private conversation, apparently Zayne was persuasive, for the woman kissed his cheek in acquiescence, then left with a sway to her hips. A moment later he was at Leila's side, his oud slung on his back. He drew her into his arms and gave her an expert kiss, the kiss of a former lover who was still a treasured friend. The kiss of a man who enjoys kissing.

She was glad Jack was not here to see that kiss.

Gently she extricated herself from his embrace. His kiss, seductive as it was, no longer stirred her, and it was not his dulcet voice she craved, but the husky voice of the human.

Zayne murmured his disappointment, then held out his hand. A sesame-honey cake rested in his palm. He touched the cake to her lips. "Can I tempt you?"

"Always." Trust Zayne to remember her fondness for sweets. She plucked the treat from his hand and took a big bite of cake and honey. Oh, bliss, she had missed this. "But there's someone I want you to meet."

"Who is he?" Zayne crossed his arms.

"What makes you think the someone is a he?"

"Because it is you I'm talking to, Leila. So . . . ?"

"The story is long, and I have a favor to ask, but we'll need some privacy."

A group affair? he asked with amusement, even as he produced another honey cake. *Not my preference, love.*

She gave him an annoyed nudge, deftly retrieving the cake in the process. "Not mine either, and you know that. Just meet him."

"The indigo tent there is mine. I will wait for you."

"Your 'refreshment' won't mind?"

"She won't, not in the least."

She probably wouldn't; Zayne had a way of making even the most outrageous acts seem acceptable. Leila reached on tiptoe to kiss him on the cheek. "Thank you." A moment later she risked one more use of her *ma-at*. She transported a short distance from Jack, then walked the rest of the way.

The shadow had not reached the tree; she had returned early. She watched Jack, for he was so intently focused, he had not yet realized she had returned. He was staring at his hands, which were pressed against the rock. The air around him seemed to shimmer with heat, and a small breeze stuck his white shirt to his damp chest.

Only two snippets of fear marred her happiness, two other reasons why she had not told Jack of her *ma-at*. One was the heartbreaking fear that he might want nothing more to do with her once she got her *ma-at* back. Much as she detested the discomforts of camping, she liked being with Jack more.

The other was the terror of losing her *ma-at* again. Her word in the bargain and her love for him kept her near him, and she believed him when he promised he would not willingly take it from her. Yet she also believed his claim that the choice was not always his to make. Jack was a powerful Terran Scientist wizard, but she suspected there were forces at his command that even he did not fully understand.

Perhaps her silence would guard her.

A popping sound circled the grove of trees, coming straight at her. She jumped back, startled, until she realized almonds were dropping from the trees, as though the spell that held them there had ended, and she gave a long sigh.

Jack must have heard her, for his head snapped up and his blue eyes swept over the trees before him. He saw her at once; his shoulders relaxed, and he smiled. "Sorry, I didn't see you."

"You were concentrating. On what?"

"Power." Jack sneezed and rubbed his nose. "Damn, the *adamana* ashes are back."

Leila glanced around, noting for the first time the glittery ashes carried on the wind. "The Tower Lands must have been active last night for the ash to drift this far. Let us go into the village. I want you to meet Zayne."

"Why?"

"He could transfer you to Terra," she suggested, then held her breath, not ready to lose him yet.

His refusal was swift and adamant. "No, I'll go back only with Isis." Then his voice softened. "Besides, we have a bargain, do we not? To Tepe-ma-adaktu?"

She smiled back. "Yes, we do. We will be approaching more settlements; I believe you need better command of our language than I can teach." She glanced around. "Where is Mistrock?"

The *grucheek*, as if understanding her question, grated a greeting from a rock. She picked it up, and for once it was content to stay on her shoulder.

As they skirted the edge of the village, she saw Jack

looking around him with an eager interest that she hadn't seen in him before. Something had happened that had eased his reluctance, as if he'd loosened a barrier that had held him back and muted his power. She had never seen him look so vital, confident, or strong.

Or so alien. Here in the company of the dark djinn, his whitened-blond hair stood out like a beacon of sunlight in the night. His bristly beard appeared a strange fashion statement. His height and rugged muscles and blunt hands all branded him different. The air fairly crackled with his curiosity. While the djinn tended to glide with a smooth motion, or flit from place to place, Jack strode with purpose. Her people exhibited a graceful pace, a leisurely enjoyment of their world, while in Jack she could almost see his rapid processing of thoughts and his leashed energy. The only thing he had in common with the djinn was the air of absolute confidence and command.

She imitated it. Jack embodied it.

Leila drew in a deep breath, loosening the tightness in her chest. If she had any doubts about her feelings, they were quelled—she loved him.

But to believe they could ever fit into each other's world was a futile dream. That realization struck her anew. He was human. She was djinn. He might appreciate her mind, but her *ma-at* was anathema to him. She had not much power, but she clung to what she possessed, and unless he also accepted her *ma-at*, there could be no future for them.

*   *   *

Leila led Jack to the small indigo tent set at the furthest reaches of the village. Mistrock rumbled loudly in her ear, and she set it on the ground outside the tent. The *grucheek* promptly slid away.

"Guess it's going exploring." Jack touched her shoulder. "It will come back."

The interior was sparse, yet sybaritic. The silk, the finest that Kaf and *ma-at* could provide, made a soothing whish as it rippled in the breezes. A small fire crackled in the center of the room, filling the air with the fresh, pleasant scents of sandalwood and cinnamon. Yet there was no smoke to irritate the eyes and lungs or to mute the brilliant colors, like the fires of a lesser-skilled djinni. Beside the fire was a small pot of heated tea—she could smell the green aroma— while a palm frond held more sesame-honey cakes.

She expected the luxury, but she could see that Jack was surprised. "It is Zayne's," she explained. "He travels and chooses to take little with him. He desires nothing to root him to a single city or dwelling."

"But he does enjoy his comforts." Jack punctuated the observation with another sneeze.

"Who does not?" Zayne spoke from a lush mound of pillows in one corner.

"You speak English?" Jack observed.

"I had occasion to learn it once."

Zayne's green eyes narrowed, revealing briefly the hardened man behind the charismatic exterior, and his disapproving voice sounded inside her. *This is the man you travel with? He is not djinn.* With an invisible move, he shifted from his pillows to her side, then drew her into his arms. He nuzzled her ear and kissed her, again.

Troublemaker, she accused.

You belong with no human.

Not your choice to make.

Jack's warm hand rested on her shoulder even as she extricated herself from Zayne's embrace. "Introduce me to your friend, Leila." Impatience, possessiveness, curiosity all tinted Jack's hoarse voice. He settled her into his embrace, a hand around her waist keeping her close.

Zayne gave the two of them a speculative look, and she was relieved to see his suspicion and mistrust lighten.

So that is the way it is? Amusement tinted his voice again.

Yes, and you were simply trying to find that out.

Guilty. He didn't sound the least repentant.

She touched Jack's hand, and his fingers curled around hers. "Jack, this is Zayne, Minstrel of Kaf. He is one I trust with my life, although he can be a pest sometimes."

"Like that kiss?"

"Yes."

Jack gave her a searching look, then nodded. He turned to Zayne. Still holding her with his left hand, he held out his right. "Jack Montgomery. Your singing is a rare pleasure."

Zayne hesitated, then took the proffered hand. "Thank you, Jack Montgomery."

For a moment the two men stared at each other.

She saw the crystals in Jack's talisman flare and saw Zayne's green eyes narrow again. Their hands released.

He is no ordinary human, for he blocks my voice. By Solomon's toes, what are you up to?

"He's a Scientist. You feel his Terran magic." *Do not anger him.*

"Leila, I would talk to you. Alone." Zayne took her by the wrist and began to mutter the words to transport them.

"No, Zayne."

Jack's hand clamped around their wrists. "The lady said no."

The men stared at each other. Beside her was Jack's hard body, each muscle tight. The crystal at his chest glowed with piercing brightness and emitted a low hum. Energy swept past her to envelop Zayne.

The hum stopped and the singer jerked backward. "What in Solomon's name . . ." The air glinted and crackled with his angry *ma-at*.

The talisman glowed white. "No one will force Leila, not if I can stop them," Jack said with low determination.

"Don't, Jack. Stop, Zayne!" *Are you still connected to Kaf?*

Of course, he answered, the surprising question halting his retaliation.

Relief flooded her. The Scientist had not stolen Zayne's *ma-at*. Only negated the unwanted transport. Leila gripped Zayne's forearm. *Forget your pride and help me.*

For a moment she thought anger would win. "You protect her?" Zayne asked Jack.

"Yes."

At last the Minstrel relaxed. "Then I will overlook your arrogance. This time."

Wisely, Jack did not respond. Sometimes her Scientist showed remarkable restraint. "I warned you, Zayne."

"Not about that." He rubbed his arm. "What are you scheming? I am Minstrel; I will not risk upsetting the harmonies of Kaf."

"Her concern is for me, actually," Jack interrupted. "She seems to think I could be in danger in the village."

Zayne made a sound of disbelief.

"Does anyone here nurture a hatred for humans?" asked Leila.

Zayne ran one long finger along his chin. "The Adept was Simon's friend. He hated Simon's servitude; hated it more that Simon chose Terra."

"Who's Simon?" Jack asked, then coughed and sneezed.

"A djinni who spent too many years bound with the copper bands, compelled to grant the wishes of humans," Leila explained. "Yet when he was freed, he chose the magic of Terra over the *ma-at* of Kaf."

"The only djinni in history who switched the source of his power and lived," added Zayne.

"Could the Adept pose a danger to Jack?"

Zayne shrugged. "He recites prophesies no one ever heard of; most pay no attention to his warnings."

"Still, I want you to give Jack our language. He has learned much, but not enough to allay suspicions of the Adept."

"Why do you not give him the words?"

"I cannot," she said simply, hating that Zayne would assume it was her weak powers that prevented her, though she had once possessed at least that much skill. She was not yet ready to put her newly regained *ma-at* to the test. And if Jack knew about it, if he insisted she simply transport him home or to his sister, then their time together would be finished.

Not yet, she thought, her fists tight, careful not to send the thought to Zayne. *I am not ready to lose him.*

Why should I agree? Zayne's question broke into her thoughts.

Because I ask it as a friend.

Zayne eyed Jack with more curiosity, his glance lingering on the arm still about Leila's waist; then he smiled. "Okay, sweet bit, I'll give you your favor. But you're going to have to persuade him to let me. I can't touch him."

The electricity—he refused to call it magic—tingled at the tips of Jack's fingers. His chest felt warm beneath the crystal, but it was a satisfying heat, not one that scorched.

He had used the energy of the crystal to defend the woman he held close. He had not only used the energy, but he had controlled it. No sharp explosions or wild *ma-at* stealing. The force had flowed at his direction while the crystal glowed with a satisfying steadiness.

No one would force her to do anything she did not want. His fierce feeling of protectiveness surprised Jack, but he didn't bother to analyze the emotion. Leila was under his protection. The matter was as simple, and as complex, as that.

Leila touched the back of his neck, her fingers kneading lightly. "Scientist," she said with a throaty purr, "will you allow Zayne to give you our language?"

He crossed his arms and eyed the singer, who returned the look with a hard stare. "What would this transfer of language entail?" Jack asked.

"He will touch you on the temples like so." Her hands gently bracketed his head. "And you will have to allow him access to your thoughts."

"He could read my mind?" he asked, horrified.

"No, no. But he needs freedom to give you the words. Do not block or stop him. Do not resist."

In other words, he'd have to turn off his device and let a djinni muck about in his mind. "No."

"Jack, please trust me. Allow Zayne in. An exchange of language is all that will transpire."

Jack leaned against her cool fingers, cursing the pounding in his head. The *adamana* ashes were bringing on a full-fledged allergy attack.

Her voice lowered. "I would like to spend a few hours in comfort here with you. I cannot do that if we fear the Adept may try to banish you to Fire Streams."

Despite the allergy pain, Jack chuckled. "Ah, Leila,

how can I resist that plea?" And the truth was, he was intrigued—by the process, by the idea of fluency. He gave a short nod, then surreptitiously turned off the crystal. "All right. Will it hurt?"

"Not when Zayne does it, although you may be disoriented a short time."

"Sit there." Zayne gestured toward the corner.

Jack sat awkwardly on the pile of pillows, and Zayne knelt in front of him. Just as Leila explained, the djinni rested his fingertips against Jack's temples. The pressure was firmer than Leila's demonstration, and the man's hands were stronger, less delicate, but the touch was not uncomfortable.

"Open to me, Jack Montgomery. Receive the boon I grant to thee."

Jack felt something, a touch of something alien. A touch of *ma-at*. Denial welled inside him, with a spurt of resistance that startled him. *You don't want this*, his instincts whispered. *Don't let him mess with you.*

His intellect must control his instinct. He cooled his rising panic with long breaths.

"Chant with me," Zayne commanded. "This I do seek."

"This I do seek."

"The knowledge."

"The knowledge."

"This I do seek."

"This I do seek."

"The words."

"The words."

Jack concentrated on the soothing rhythm of the

chant and tried to ignore the rising tide of panic that roiled inside him. He had always craved learning. This was just a different way of acquiring it. He could do this. His rational ego could overcome the irrational id. Intellect controls emotion.

No, don't let him inside. Don't give in. Do not be controlled. His fists clenched; his chest heaved as the instincts clamored to be heard above the force of reason.

"Hear the words of Kaf, Jack Montgomery."

Suddenly he felt the rush. Words, images, sentences all jumbled together in an almost painful surfeit. So many at once, too many to control and catalogue.

No! Primal instincts flared to life. Invasion became threat. His chest squeezed until breathing hurt. He could not stop the onrush or the pain.

Terror erupted. Stop, stop! the child of five screamed. The irrational id took over.

"No!" he shouted. "Get out!"

He flung himself backward, breaking the contact. Fumbling, he turned on the talisman, and the sweet repelling energy coursed through him. The words stopped, severed by a crystalline blade.

Zayne jerked backward, cursing.

Lightning faded to a whisper of sparks. Terror receded to a whimper.

"Zayne, are you all right?" Jack rubbed his chest, easing his pounding heart and dousing the heat. Gradually, his panting breath slowed.

"Yes, I am fine." The singer sounded a bit dazed as he clenched his hands together. A second later he levitated, cross-legged, beside Jack, then leaned forward with a hard-edged glare. "Do not think to practice your magic on me, human."

Jack gave a sigh of relief. Without the crystal on, his instinctive resistance to *ma-at* was powerless to do any damage to Zayne. "I'm sorry; I didn't expect that. I thought I could talk myself into accepting it, but I can't."

His apology seemed to mollify the djinni. "We will not attempt this again."

"No, we won't."

"What happened?" demanded Leila. "You touched and chanted, then Jack shouted and Zayne recoiled."

"I can't do it, Leila. I can't allow him into my thoughts. Everything about me shouts that it's wrong." Jack rubbed the aching muscles in his neck.

"You didn't take—"

"Does it look like I did?" He nodded at Zayne, who floated a honey cake to his hand and began to eat. Jack fingered his crystal, uneasy with the thought that if he'd turned it on before breaking contact, he might have taken the *ma-at* from Zayne.

"Did you get any of our language before the connection was severed?" Zayne asked.

He sought through his mind. "Yes, I did," he answered slowly in *Fahrisa*. Apparently, what had gotten through before his barriers slammed down remained.

"Good." Zayne closed the subject.

Jack could not so easily dismiss the experience. He had enjoyed the rush of knowledge. For a brief moment, the seduction of learning and the tingling of the power of *ma-at* had been a pleasure he had not expected. Then instincts he couldn't control had risen and he'd broken it off. The worst terror, however, had not come from *ma-at*. It had come from his memories. Was it *ma-at* that he feared or his own nightmares?

Zayne offered them the cakes and tea. "How long will you be staying?"

"Until tomorrow," Leila answered. Like Zayne, she appreciated her comforts. "I should like a meal of something other than mango, a soft pillow for my head, and another bath."

"Is there a djinn equivalent to an inn?" Jack asked.

She hesitated; she had not thought about where they would stay. Accommodations were never an issue when her people traveled. They could be home in a blink or could provide their own pillows.

"Enjoy the hospitality of my tent until tomorrow," Zayne offered, rising to his feet.

Jack shook his head. "We don't want to put you out."

"I have been invited to share another pillow. Now I am going to sing."

"Thank you."

Silence followed his departure. Leila nibbled the sesame-honey cake she held, embarrassed because the truth behind Zayne's offer was that he knew she had not sufficient powers to conjure shelter for them. It had taken her years—through her minor talents, the generosity of others, and a lot of hard work—to assemble her small, comfortable home.

"When we reach the city, before you leave, I should

like you to see my home," she said abruptly, then was sorry she had. She didn't need reminders of their dwindling time together.

"I would like that, too." He wrapped his arms tightly around her, as though the thought of his leaving made him want to hold her close. At least that was what she hoped.

"Is your home also a tent?" he asked.

She shook her head, unable to speak for a moment because of the lump in her throat. "The walls are made of cedar and gossamer linen. I have a large garden and a stream."

"It sounds beautiful." He kissed the top of her head. "Like the owner." Then he took a deep breath. "I'm sorry the experiment with Zayne failed."

She shrugged. "We will find a way to explain, should it be needed. You will avoid the Adept, and we will stay but a single night."

"Always practical."

"When there is no other choice." She popped the last bite of cake in her mouth, then lifted her finger to her mouth to lick off the drops of honey.

"Let me." Jack took her hand, his eyes suddenly scorching.

Mutely she held still while his tongue slowly licked her finger and his lips closed around the tip. Leisurely he pulled her finger deeper inside, then grazed her skin with his teeth as he let her go. With deliberation he turned to her next finger. By the fires of Kaf, his mouth was warm. Wet. Inviting. She softened and moistened in response.

"You always smell of clover to me," he said in that low, seductive voice. "And the best honey comes from bees fed the nectar of clover. I want to taste." He kissed her between her fingers, a place she could never remember being kissed, his breath warm against her skin. From a distance she heard Zayne's song, not the words, only the melody. A love song to stir the soul and fire the blood. Brilliant shades of green, orange, red, gold, and silver sparkled around them.

She had turned away from Jack last night in the cave and the darkness. Now she found she could not. She could not resist this playful Jack, this man who looked at her in the sunlight with such heated desire. Love could make you strong, but sometimes it could make you oh, so weak.

With her *ma-at* she set the stones of privacy outside the tent aglow; then her free hand tunneled through the soft, fair strands of his hair, holding him to her. For this day, he was hers and she was his. She kissed his throat, his shoulder at the band of his shirt. Too much cloth lay between them.

"Take off your shirt," she commanded.

He complied, then pushed her robe off her shoulders until it formed a crimson pool about her hips. "Don't move." He issued his own command.

With a finger he scooped a dab of honey from the puddle on the frond. Deliberately, his intense focus unwaveringly on her, he painted it on the tip of her nipple. For a moment he studied it, and her breasts swelled from just the heat of his gaze. Her nipples tightened until the anticipation was nearly more than she could tolerate. Then, with the tip of his tongue, in a touch so fleeting she barely had time to feel it, he licked off the honey.

He sat back on his heels. And waited.

"Again," she demanded, her body primed, her breath coming in short pants.

He daubed the other breast, but again the touch and lick were too fast to satisfy her growing hunger. Then he sat back again, waiting, his gaze intent upon her, so hot, so focused.

"Jack!" she cried, eager for what he promised.

He grinned. "I read once that sexual fulfillment is possible just by looking in your partner's eyes. Wanna try it?"

She straddled his hips, blatantly opening her lower body to him. "I have heard that satisfaction comes from filling the deepest corners of the body," she countered. "Wanna try it?"

"This same book said a month of preparation and anticipation, of brief rubs and small pressures"—he pressed a thumb at the V where her legs spread, no movement, just a point of pressure—"ends in the perfect sexual experience."

She leaned forward, her gaze locked with his, honeyed breath commingling. "More perfect than last night?" she whispered.

"Impossible."

"Are you sure?" She undid the fastening of his jeans, lifted her hips enough to slide the garment down, felt him kick it off the remaining way. He was hard beneath her, as ready for her as she was for him. Instead of taking him inside her, however, she reached for a dab of honey. She held it up for him.

"The book said—"

"You read too much," she countered.

"You wouldn't," he challenged.

She just lifted one brow. After last night, they both knew she would. She teased him as he had teased her. A dab and a lick, a dab and a quicker lick.

Together they laughed and they played. They caressed and took longer, slower tastes. Her heart pounded; her skin grew slick. The only momentary imperfection came when he paused to slip on a condom.

But when he came into her, when she held him tight, she knew this was different, better. This was making love.

"*Janam*," she whispered as they lay together in the glow of afterward. *My soul*. But she didn't think he heard her. *T'dost mi dara*. You have my love. She was careful not to send her thoughts. *Frasho*. Forever.

Chapter Fourteen

An hour later a sneeze woke Jack. His sneeze. He rubbed his itchy nose, sneezed again, then pushed himself upright from the pillows and raked a hand through his shaggy hair.

"Oh, you are awake."

Jack squinted in the direction of Leila's voice and saw she was standing at the doorway. She looked radiant with her robe a shimmering crimson and her hair a lustrous black, and he'd never seen her skin glow like that or her lips look so invitingly lush. Never had she looked so beautiful. Or so inaccessible.

"Where are you going?" he asked, his voice raspy.

"To look around. I thought you would prefer more sleep."

He'd prefer her beside him or around him. He sneezed again and cleared his dry throat. "You took a bath?"

She nodded toward a large brass saucer off to one side. "Stand on that and say the words, '*Allat vasha punya mia*.'"

Water come to me, his mind translated.

"To turn it off, say, '*Valait vasha punyaba mia*.'"

Water be gone from me. "Doesn't that saucer fill up fast?"

She looked puzzled a moment, then shook her head. "*Ma-at* will . . . dissolve it." She waved her hand. "I found soap and shampoo for our use. And clothes for you to wear while you wash your garments."

In other words, he'd gotten ripe again. He raked his hand through his hair. A cold shower sounded damn good right now. "Thank you." Sneeze. Cough. Swear. "Leila . . ."

She turned expectantly. "Yes?"

Jack hesitated, unsure what to say. *I want you, come back to the pillows. Don't leave me. I need you; you make me feel so damn good.*

It was all true. When he was with her he felt . . . alive. She was bright, funny, curious, uninhibited, courageous—all qualities he prized. Yet they were of two alien worlds, and all he had done for her was to take away her treasured *ma-at*.

"I'll join you when I'm finished," was all he could say in the end.

He didn't imagine the flash of disappointment that crossed her face. "All right." A moment later the tent opening dropped and she was gone from his sight.

All right, he'd blown that in a major way. But what could he have said? Thank you? Let's do last night again? Live with me and be my lover? Marry me?

Oh, hell, where had that one come from?

He could never live with someone who used *ma-at*. And Leila was a woman of Kaf and of *ma-at*.

He rose stiffly from the pillows and stretched. Sneezed. Did a regimen of sit-ups. Coughed. Sneezed. Decided to try out the brass saucer.

He stood on the metal and spoke aloud. "*Allat vasha punya mia.*"

Nothing happened.

"*Allat vasha punya mia,*" he repeated with the same result. Then he noticed the glow of the crystal. Of course, Zayne's shower would be driven by *ma-at*. He took off the chain, turned off the crystal, then stepped back into the saucer and repeated the incantation. Water flowed in a gentle rain.

The warm, vanilla-scented shower felt good. Good enough that he was able to quell the instinctive murmurs of unease at the actions of *ma-at*. It wasn't trying to get inside him, wasn't trying to control his thoughts or his actions. He could end it whenever he wanted.

Just to make sure, he whispered, "*Valait vasha punyaba mia.*" The water stopped, and some of his reluctance also dissipated. This was something he controlled, not the other way around. It felt good, as good as when he wore the chain and felt the comforting surges of power.

Getting clean felt good, too, once he figured out that "shampoo" meant running a glowing green wand through his hair. The wand was effective, for when he finished his hair was squeaky-clean and smelled like melon. He never did determine how to use the blue stone that must be the soap, so he settled for a thorough rinse.

Not seeing a towel to dry with, he stood in the tent, allowing the water to evaporate into the warm, arid air. He rubbed his itchy nose and blinked scratchy eyes, knowing they were an unappealing red, then picked up the chain. He flicked the switch, turning the crystal back on, and slipped it over his neck. Electricity hummed through it, through him with a warm vibration. Power. Curiosity rose again.

He'd designed the device as a passive, personal shield, but it seemed to be reacting to him as well as the *ma-at*. The incident in the cave—where he expanded the power and directed it along the mist—wasn't a fluke, brought on by his emotion. He'd shown that today, when he stopped Zayne transporting Leila. How much control did he have over it? How much could he direct it?

Perhaps another experiment? Speculatively, he eyed the saucer shower.

"Allat vasha punya mia." The shower turned on. It would not work if he stepped under it; the crystal would interfere with the *ma-at*. Could he do the same thing from outside the shower?

He concentrated, not on the water, but on the crystal. The colors of the rainbow within it sparkled to life. The vibrations and the soothing hum spread outward and inward, becoming part of his muscles and nerves. He drew on the power more, trying to spread it beyond him, while keeping its force reined and under his bidding. Slowly, slowly, he focused on the shower.

Nothing happened. The water still flowed.

The crystal heated against his chest. More lightning sparked through him, deeper into sinew and axon. He ignored the pounding headache in his skull, the ache at the back of his neck. The crystal, the shower—bit by bit he connected them.

The water flow lessened, became a trickle, stopped.

He stared, unable to believe. He had directed the power of the crystal.

Experimentally he tried it again with the same results. And a third time. At last, however, he stopped and turned the water off with the incantation. His body ached as though he had slammed it repeatedly against a brick wall, and pain throbbed inside his head. Whatever the hell he was doing, it was not easy on him.

Nor did the concept sit easy on his mind. The idea of controlling the crystal with his mind seemed too close to magic.

Was he losing himself in this provocative, enchanting world?

Or was he finding himself?

Scientific magic, Leila had called it, and he uneasily wondered how close to the truth she was.

He rubbed the bridge of his nose. No more experiments, at least not right now. Instead, he suddenly found himself eager to see Leila again. He glanced around, looking for the clothes she'd left, and spied them laid out on a pillow. Not the style he would have chosen. The navy pants were made of some unstructured fabric that gathered at the waist and ankles, and the deep-V-neck shirt reminded him of the gay poets who performed their art in the French Quarter. When he picked up his T-shirt and jeans, however, he couldn't bring himself to put on the dusty, sweaty clothes.

Instead he rinsed them in the saucer, laid them out to dry, and put on the clothes Leila had chosen. They fit surprisingly well, and he was amazed at how comfortable they felt in the hot climate.

He rubbed a hand over his bristly beard. If only he had a razor. He sneezed. And a Claritin. But those were small nuisances when he had the chance to spend time with Leila.

Outside, he waited a moment, and, sure enough, Mistrock skittered out from beneath the underbrush. "Hey, how've you been doing? Finding any fellow *grucheek* to pal around with? Or some nice gravel to munch on?"

Mistrock's answer was to butt against his feet and begin the shimmy upward. Jack lifted it to his shoulder, and a moment later he felt the wet glue as Mistrock fastened its body to his new shirt. Man and *grucheek* turned their faces to the village.

As he headed out, he remembered the words Leila had whispered earlier to him. *Janam*. It was a word he was able to translate. *My soul*. His heart twisted in his chest, and his blood throbbed. *My soul*.

Special words he could not repeat. Words—he could hear, analyze, study them, yet when it came to the simple, and profound, act of saying them, he failed. Maybe, when he had mastered the power of the crystal, he would find the courage.

Leila reveled in the return of her *ma-at*. Her favorite robe repaired. Her hair rid of dust. Her hands buffed and smooth.

Feeling the nip of hunger, she plucked a date from a tree. She was tired of fruit; a cucumber would be nicer. She held the date between her palms and began to mutter the words of transformation.

Her *ma-at* fluttered and faded. Quickly she stopped and pressed her lips together in frustration. She had never mastered creation; only the strongest djinn could create out of nothing but air and fire. Transformation was easier, but for her it had always been an unreliable skill. Apparently, that had not changed. She gave a fatalistic shrug, denying the weight of disappointment.

Instead she passed her hand across the date, and made it two. Smiling, she popped one in her mouth. Duplication, one incantation she had always been able to master. At least her hunger would be assuaged, and exercising even that small power again was refreshing.

Waiting for Jack to join her, she wandered around the village, talking idly to some of the djinn she encountered. Travelers were common on Kaf, and since most provided for their own comforts, they were a welcome source of entertainment rather than a burden. Her vague story of completing a Night of No

Moon pilgrimage was readily accepted. After all, what would be her purpose in lying?

She spoke with a young woman who was stirring a pot of stew over a small flame. They spoke of life distant from the city, of a male the woman eyed with pleasure, of the beauties of a fire bloom. The woman—she gave her spoken name as Kala—tasted the stew, then grimaced. "I wish I had greater skill in seasoning."

"Let me taste," Leila suggested, and after a single sample, she agreed. The stew was unappealingly bland. "If I show you how to add spice, will you share two bowls? One for me, one for my friend?"

There was more than enough to share, and Kala readily agreed.

"I'll be right back." Her stomach rumbling, Leila hurried into the surrounding trees and found the patches of sage and sorrel she had noticed earlier. She plucked some leaves, then returned to Kala.

"These grow in the trees over there. Note the shape of them, so you can select them yourself." Leila crumbled the leaves in her hands until they were no more than tiny flakes. She sprinkled them into the stew, stirred gently, tasted, added a bit more sage, and then sat back and motioned for Kala to taste.

Kala stared at her. "I thought you were going to teach me an incantation for seasoning and spicing. Who wishes to dig dirt?" she added with scorn.

Inside, Leila shriveled, and a hard knot formed in her throat. Outside, she lifted her chin and gave Kala her practiced haughty look which said: *Would you re-*

nege on a bargain? It is not I who lacks, but you.

"Did I say I would teach you my *ma-at*? Taste the stew," she commanded, her stomach roiling. What if the woman refused?

Reluctantly Kala did taste, and reluctantly she admitted the seasoning superior to her efforts. In silence, she handed Leila two bowls filled with stew, then said with stiff formality, "Thank you for your assistance."

"You are welcome." Leila rose gracefully to her feet, then walked away, biting her lip, biting back old feelings of inadequacy.

Dammit, she thought bitterly, using one of Jack's words, *that stew was good*. She glanced around at the village. Could anyone here season like that? Her jaw tensed. Could anyone climb a rock face with bare hands?

She could do something they could not.

And that was an empowering feeling.

She carried the stew carefully to the square and discovered that Jack had finished his cleansing. He wore the clothes she had gotten him, and her breath caught as he strode forward. The fabric and the muscle beneath flowed as smoothly as the waters of Kaf. Her heart did a little fillip; he was such a fine figure, even if his nose was a trifle red. She smiled, noticing the covert looks the other djinn gave him. She recognized curiosity about the blond stranger, interest in the muscled man, confusion about the sneezes, hesitance to approach one who had such an air of intensity.

She had no such hesitancy. She neared him, and her

body warmed when he noticed her and joined her with a big, welcoming smile.

She handed him the bowl of stew. "You smell better," she commented, then petted Mistrock, once again glued to Jack's shoulder.

"I imagine I do. Thank you for the clothes."

"Do you like them?"

"I wasn't sure," he admitted, sitting down on a tree stump. "But they are very comfortable." He took a mouthful of stew, then rolled his eyes in appreciation. "This is good. Did you make it?"

"Partly." She settled beside him, tucking her robe beneath her so the winds could not catch it. She had known the seasoning was good, even without *ma-at*. Foolish Kala, who didn't even know when to appreciate something fine. The other woman didn't know how to attract the male she fancied either, Leila couldn't resist adding with a touch of smug superiority.

They ate the stew slowly, glancing around the square as they did. The djinn did not approach while they ate, but she knew it was only a matter of time before curiosity overcame caution and manners.

Zayne began to sing again. The lively song set her foot tapping in time with the rhythm. The song begged for motion, and soon another man appeared and started to dance. While Zayne was dressed in the colors of darkness, this man was all in white, a white that hurt the eyes with its brilliance.

This dancer's moves were just right for such a song. He was sinuous and sensuous and in perfect harmony

with the tune. His long black hair swung around him
as though it, too, danced for the sheer joy of the music. It covered his face, and she strained to see who he
was. Something about him was familiar, but she didn't
remember seeing him on her tour of the village.

Oh, by Solomon, he was good. Truly a worthy in-
terpretor of Zayne's music. The crowd stilled in awe
as singer and dancer created a slice of beauty before
their eyes.

At last the song ended. The dancer made a final
twirl and flung his hair back, refusing to bow. He
looked straight at Leila and gave her a knowing, inviting, familiar smile.

Her throat tightened, and her heart did a somersault
in her chest.

"Xerxes," she whispered.

What was Leila doing in this town at the beginning
of nowhere? Xerxes hid his astonishment behind a
practiced smile.

At the song's end, he made his way steadily toward
her, acknowledging the accolades that were his due,
charming the onlookers even as he extricated himself
from their clinging touches until at last he stood before her.

"Leila," he said with affection, taking her hand in
his. She always had stirred him, though he scorned her
lack of talent.

He had first met her in school, when the Adept,
despairing of Leila's inability to master any but the
easiest skills, had asked him to instruct the younger

student. Even so many cycles later, his blood burned at the insult. The Adept had mistakenly believed that because he, Xerxes, had also started slowly, the two would have something in common, and he would be able to help the inept girl.

He had hated the reminder of his slow start. He had fought long, still fought, to overcome the stigma, ill content until he amassed the knowledge and power he craved.

He was nothing like Leila.

He had power.

Still, she did have her attractions. He had found, in their studies together, that he genuinely liked her. She had a quick mind for anything but *ma-at*, and a willingness to learn. She had a zest for life that was rare.

"It has been too many cycles, my friend." He kissed her wrist, touching it lightly with his tongue, then pulled her gently into his embrace. He had never made love to her; he had worried at the time that her weakness might taint him.

He no longer had that toothless fear. He had even discovered ways she might increase her power, if she were willing to pay the price. Would she not be grateful?

To his annoyance, however, she pulled away when he urged her flush against him. Her companion stiffened. The Scientist, Leila had introduced him; his spoken name was Jack.

Xerxes gave the minimal bow, mouthed the routine greetings. The stranger was of little interest—ragged hair, sturdy hands, unappealing red eyes and nose. He could not even keep his cheeks smooth.

Most important, no power emanated from him.

Poor Leila, that she was reduced to this. Xerxes smiled to himself; she would welcome his attention. Welcome what he could do for her.

He gave the powerless blond Scientist a final glance, then dismissed him.

Jack was not given to snap judgments, but in this case he was willing to make an exception. He did not like the man Leila called Xerxes.

He seemed to be the only one of that opinion, however, judging by the town's greeting. He couldn't pinpoint his dislike. Maybe he disliked the eyes that never ceased to scan the area. Or the white, gauzy clothes, multiple layers that didn't seem to conceal Xerxes's anatomy. Or the dry unpleasant touch of the man's hand.

Or maybe he disliked the welcoming look Leila wore and the embrace Xerxes gave her.

Or maybe it was Xerxes's subtle snub. Jack crossed his arms, biting back the urge to test whether he could spread the *ma-at*-negating field of the crystal. He wasn't confident of his ability to control it, or of the wisdom of trying when no harm was directed toward him. The crystal was designed for personal protection, although he now included Leila under the protective mantle. Jack shifted closer to her, swallowing back a sneeze.

"What are you doing here, Leila?" Xerxes brushed

back the hair the winds blew across his face, then waved his hand. The hair stayed clear of his face.

Jack pressed a finger to his nose, forcing back another sneeze. His eyes watered, and the wind dried his throat.

"We are completing a Night of No Moon pilgrimage. This is not where I would expect to find you either."

"I am searching for a rare stone. A *berlianum*."

Bloodstone.

"I have heard that those hills are a possible source," the djinni added.

"Nobody's found one of those in five hundred cycles," Leila protested.

Xerxes shrugged. "The possibility is worth a few days' search."

Leila's face softened. "The fluid that drips from the stone is said to be a potent source of power."

"I am merely curious about it." Xerxes's gaze flitted toward Jack, then narrowed as he noticed Mistrock glued to his shirt. "Legend says a *grucheek* can find any stone desired. Perhaps yours will find my bloodstone."

"Ask it," Jack answered with a raspy voice.

"Mistrock is independent; it makes its own choices," added Leila.

Xerxes held out a hand to stroke the rock, and Jack heard Mistrock's harsh grating. Xerxes crooned under his breath words that Jack could not translate. The crystal beneath his shirt tingled, awakening to the touch of *ma-at*. He concentrated, trying to keep the electricity quiescent, if not dormant, unwilling to reveal the power to Xerxes. For the moment, he held the force in check, probably because the enchantment was directed toward Mistrock, not him. The touch of *ma-at* became stronger, and Mistrock's grating grew rougher. The wires warmed, the charge flowed through him. Tension sparked between the two men.

"Guess Mistrock's not interested." Jack's sneeze punctuated the challenge.

"I am disappointed." Xerxes gave him a pleasant smile, and his outstretched hand fisted against Jack's shoulder.

Leila laid her hand over it, returning her friend's smile. "I'm sorry, Mistrock can be temperamental. Perhaps later I can ask."

Xerxes bowed his head. "That would be kind of you."

Jack, however, fighting the urge to wipe his itchy eye, felt a tendril of *ma-at* curl around his chest. The air-diffusing alveoli in his lungs clogged. Dry air pulled moisture from the mucous membranes in his throat. He fought to breathe against the twin threats of *ma-at* and histamine.

As swiftly as it had come, the *ma-at* withdrew. Simultaneously the crystal flared and a gust of wind whirled irritating ash around Jack. The allergen released a storm of IgE and histamine, and Jack doubled over, coughing and sneezing and breaking contact with Xerxes's outstretched hand. He squeezed shut his itchy eyes and pulled in a wheezing breath. Unable to see, he felt more than saw Xerxes's instinctive withdrawal from the strange illness.

Dammit. Damn this allergy. Unable to spare the breath, Jack mentally cursed while the dust settled and his lungs relaxed. Damn the weakness and his help-lessness. Jack straightened and wiped his tearing eyes.

Mistrock gave a settling rumble in his ear. *Thank you*, it seemed to say as it rubbed against Jack's neck.

Xerxes seemed to lose interest in both man and *gru-cheek*. Instead he turned his hand over, laced his fingers through Leila's, and then lifted their entwined hands to his lips. "If you speak with the *grucheek*, I will be content. For only you understand the importance of the bloodstone."

Only you understand me. Apparently the pickup line wasn't confined to human use, and judging from Leila's soft smile, it was just as effective on Kaf.

"Can you join me for a repast?" Xerxes asked, his gaze locked with Leila's.

Leila shook her head. "Thank you, but we just ate."

"Tonight, then? I have settled for a few days over there." He made a vague gesture toward the far side of the square.

She glanced quickly at Jack, then nodded. "We would be delighted."

Jack was pretty sure the invitation hadn't included him, but he warmed to the fact that Leila had auto-matically assumed it did. "Yes, thank you." He ce-mented his inclusion.

Xerxes was astute enough not to offer argument. "When the sun sets, then. Now I must be going." He kissed Leila's hand, gave Jack a nod, and left, making his way through a variety of conversations. Apparently,

Xerxes was a popular man. It seemed Jack was the only one whose skin crawled at the djinni's touch. He sneezed again.

"You are drawing attention." She nodded toward the square where a number of djinn stared at him. "They do not know *al-ar-gee*."

Jack rubbed a finger against his burgeoning headache. So much for keeping a low profile. "How long have you known Xerxes, Leila?"

"Many cycles. We were at school together. He was assigned as my tutor, for he had surpassed anything I could do. Nonetheless, he was always patient with me, and he taught me much."

"Do you like him?"

"Of course! He was very kind to me at a time when I needed kindness." She laid a hand on his shoulder, her fingers tangling intimately in his hair. "He is a friend, and I want nothing more than friendship from him."

Jack heard the tone of affection. Childhood bonds were strong ones, and he'd have to be careful what he said about Xerxes. He didn't want his animosity to force Leila to defend her mentor, maybe even drive her into the djinni's arms.

For Leila might only want friendship, but as a male he'd recognized the djinni's moves. Xerxes was after a hell of a lot more than friendship. Jack chose his words carefully. "He seems sociable."

"He can be. His home is in the remotest regions of Kaf, very isolated. But when he is not there, he chooses the city entertainments. Or so I've heard; I haven't seen him in some cycles. Strange to find him here," she added thoughtfully. "He must be anxious to find that bloodstone."

Xerxes wanted something here, Jack guessed, but he'd bet a year's pay that it wasn't bloodstone. The question was, what did he want?

Chapter Fifteen

The center of the village was the heart of its activity. Jack watched as a man pulled out a brazier and snapped his fingers. Blue flames shot upward, and the man began heating a glass on them. As it heated, the glass melted, not to a soft malleable material but to different shapes—a long-necked bird, a colored sphere, a rippled bowl, a bell, a leafy tree. A child came skipping through, the only child Jack had seen in the village, chattering to what looked like an animated mop with emerald eyes. Two women disappeared, then reappeared at a distance downstream. A young man strutted through the square, scattering incense before him with a lazy wave of his hand.

Jack closed his eyes, overwhelmed for the moment by the strangeness, the utter foreignness of such random acts. He didn't belong here. He shouldn't be a part of this scene.

He opened his eyes. Yet he was part of it. He could taste the metallic ash, smell the chunks of meat cooking on a fire, hear the hum of strings, feel the hot winds. And each sensation, familiar in its own way, grounded him firmly to Kaf. He had come to appreciate the beauty of this world, he realized.

A woman, a shock of white in her hair, her dress of multicolored scarves flapping in the wind, appeared at Jack's side.

"One of the elders," Leila murmured in explanation.

"Not the human-bashing Adept, I hope?"

"No," she answered with a grin.

The elder poked his arm as she fired questions at him, ending with: What exactly did a Scientist do?

Or at least that was what he thought she asked, as he picked words from the stream of verbiage. Explaining to her what a biomedical engineer did, and why there would be a need for artificial limbs, remained beyond him, however. He settled for "I solve problems. And keep people healthy." That was all his limited *Fahrisa* vocabulary and dry, scratchy throat could manage.

She flung three of her scarves—one white, one purple, one that shifted between bronze and silver— around her neck. The ends stood out, waving in the rising wind like a pennant. She said something, then looked at him expectantly.

" 'Ah, a wizard of the special arts. Is that how you got that hair color?' " Leila translated under her breath.

The explanation was as good as any, and Jack nodded.

A second later she was levitating, cross-legged, beside the tree stump where he'd eaten the stew. Her pointed chin twitched, and her fingers gripped his wrist as she pulled his device from beneath his shirt. She spoke rapidly, beyond his ability to interpet.

"She says," Leila explained in an undertone, "only one skilled in the rare metals could make this. She would hear more about this science *ma-at*."

Leila said something to the woman, and the elder nodded her head sagely and patted Jack on the knee. "We will go slow," she said, very deliberately.

"What did you tell her?" Jack asked Leila.

"That you were attempting to interpret ancient texts from the lost languages, but the spell you did has mixed up the words in your mind. So you speak a little of the current, a little of the old, until the two become sorted out."

In other words, he was the village idiot again. Jack sighed, running a hand through his hair. Still, they seemed to accept the creative answer. Between the elder's slow, simplified speech and Leila's occasional low-voiced interpretation, he managed the conversation, picking up proficiency and ease as he spoke. In some ways, it was like talking to his Aunt Tildy back home.

Jack tilted his head and asked the elder, "Do you practice the special arts?"

She gave a high-pitched chuckle and lifted his hand. As she did, her scarves fell back, revealing an intricate weaving of metal threads from her wrist to her elbow. He recognized gold and silver and glass tubes of mercury, but there were others he'd never seen.

"I am a Forger. I would learn how you formed the talisman you wear."

"If you are not careful, Elder Sholeh will keep you for hours, Scientist." A laughing female voice interrupted them.

Jack turned to find a dark-haired woman—he'd guess she was in her thirties if they were on Earth—standing next to them. She greeted them with a wide smile on her pixie face. She was holding an infant, the first baby he'd seen since he'd arrived.

Sholeh gave a cackle. "As would you, Cyra." She gave Jack another bird-like look. "Cyra has a talent for the enchantments of the metal and the voice of the gems."

The newcomer was dripping with jewelry. She wore rings on all ten fingers and thumbs. A line of bracelets went up her arm. A pair of earrings dangled not from her lobes but from a ring that surrounded her ear. The jewelry glistened and swirled and transformed in both shape and color. Even the infant sported a pair of smaller, matching earrings and a ring on each thumb.

"Oh, you have a child," Leila breathed in awe. "May I hold her while you talk with the Scientist?"

Cyra hesitated, then handed Leila the baby. Jack watched as Leila cooed to the baby, who wrapped a tiny fist around her silky hair. The gems on the infant's thumbs twinkled.

"She likes you," Cyra said with a touch of relief, levitating beside Sholeh.

"What is her name?" Leila asked.

"Roanna."

"A beautiful name for a beautiful child."

Jack was reminded of the children he fashioned limbs for. What if they had had a chance to be exposed to *ma-at*? What if the bartender's daughter could have had her diabetes arrested? She wouldn't have lost her leg. What if the boy he'd seen last week had never succumbed to the osteosarcoma that took his arm? He remembered Leila telling him that *ma-at* could not be used for global purposes or to thwart the natural cycles. The potential for devastating damage was too high. *Ma-at* was a personal power, a personal choice.

But what if someone could treat those children, one at a time? How often he had wished there were such things as miracles. What if those children were helped by *ma-at*? Wouldn't its use be a good thing then?

He watched, his insides softening, while Leila sang to the baby. The child patted her face and hair. Leila laughed, bringing a happy gurgle in response. For a moment, she was not looking at them, not thinking of anything except the baby, and he was surprised by the naked longing revealed in her face.

She had told him djinn children were rare, and he believed her, yet in that moment he could see how much she hoped against hope for one. He stared at her, something inside him struggling for acknowledgment, some key to understanding this enigmatic woman.

She told a story to the baby, and the small child who had skipped by earlier stopped to listen. Leila wove a tale of *ma-at* and wonder, enchanting them both. She was a natural with children. He couldn't imagine her pregnant, with belly rounding and breasts swelling with milk, but he could easily see her with a child.

And the child he saw was blond.

Jack dropped to the stump, stunned by the idea. What if she had his child? The idea was instantly appealing, infinitely right. Leila. Him. A child. Together.

What if she were pregnant? They hadn't used any protection last night.

He and she were of two different worlds, but if she carried his child, they would have to find a way to work things out. *Even if it meant a life amongst the* ma-at-*wielding djinn?* He couldn't answer the question. He just knew he could no more abandon a child than he could abandon Leila in the Tower Lands or cut off his right arm.

"Perhaps we should talk another day?" Sholeh's dry voice interrupted his thoughts.

He turned to find the two levitating women staring at him with amusement.

"I think his mind is on other things," Cyra agreed. "Like his woman."

His woman. A politically incorrect expression that, he suddenly realized, exactly described how he felt about Leila. His, and he'd fight anyone who doubted it. Leila. A desirable, stunning, complex woman.

256

A woman who had deceived him with her seductive act?

No, that was not the woman he knew.

"No, um, we can talk." Jack ran a hand across his chest, confused by the buffeting emotions. The woven chain tingled and glowed, stimulated by the emotions coursing through him, though no *ma-at* worked against him. "Talk about hot metals and, um, welding. Fusing."

Try as he would, every word, every syllable brought heated images of Leila. He'd think he was enchanted, if he didn't know that no *ma-at* love spell was at work. Only his lonely, foolish heart, which wanted to believe her when she called him *janam*. My soul.

Cyra gave a tinkling laugh. "We will talk, then, to allow your woman time with the children." She arched her brow. "Perhaps she will be in need of that experience one day."

"I . . . I don't know."

"True, it is in Solomon's benevolent hands. Still, you will be first to know. All djinn males do. My *zani* could tell long before I knew."

His heart contracted to a lump in his chest, and the racing emotions froze. *All djinn males are the first to know.* But he wouldn't be. For he would be gone. And he wasn't djinn. Had Leila counted on that?

Leila was humming a song to the two children, her face alight with laughter.

Why had she come to him on Earth? She'd never answered that question. Curiosity and dread gnawed at him.

Djinn children are rare.

Unlike humans, we are not a fertile lot.

I have waited long for this pleasure, Scientist.

Facts clicked into place. A child. My God, was *that* why she had first come to him? Was that why she had first tried to seduce him? All this time, had she been manipulating him, toying with him? Last night . . . was last night part of her scheme?

A sour taste rose in his throat, followed quickly by anger.

"So," said Sholeh, "do you use the Enchantment of Valishayara to meld your metal, or do you chant the Circles of Unity?"

"Personally, I prefer an enchantment over a mantra any day," observed Cyra. "Although I like Valishy-muria rather than Valishayara."

"I'm partial to a soldering iron myself," answered Jack.

But as he talked, part of him watched Leila with the baby. His conviction grew: She had come to him de-liberately; she had come to seduce the hapless Terran sperm donor.

And as his conviction grew, so did his anger.

The rising sirocco whistled around the indigo tent, seeking holes invisible to the eye and unprotected by *ma-at*. Though the wind was hot, Leila shivered.

I want to speak with you, Leila. In the tent. Now.

They were the only words Jack had said to her since she'd returned the baby to its mother. Confused by the terse command, she had nonetheless followed him back to Zayne's tent.

But he said nothing. He stood, his back to her, his fists clenched. She waited behind him, then laid a hand on his tense shoulder. Not in desire, but in simple comfort. How to comfort when she did not know what was wrong? When she couldn't recite any of the words of ease? She slid her hand to the back of his neck and gently rubbed the tense muscles.

His fingers clamped around her wrist, stopping her, and he pivoted to face her. His eyes were hard, expressionless. He flung down her arm, then removed himself from her touch. Slowly she backed away from him; he was a dreadful shadow over her.

He spoke without preamble. "The night we met, the night I got stranded here, why did you pick me for your game of seduction? Why me? Or was I just a random sap?"

For a moment she was tempted to lie, to cajole, to distract—her frequent weapons. Then she looked at him, looked into his unflinching eyes, and her chin lifted. No, not again. He wanted truth, and she would give him truth. What she felt for Jack, even if he didn't reciprocate, deserved that.

"I chose you. I saw your picture and thought your looks pleasing."

"But why come to me in the first place? To manipulate me? To play some amusing game with a human?"

"No, it wasn't like that." By Solomon, the truth could be difficult.

"To seduce me into being a sperm donor?"

"A sperm donor?" She shook her head, confused. "I don't—"

"Did you hope I would give you a baby?"

Leila flinched at the bald accusation, yet that was exactly what she had done. She stopped delaying, though her insides roiled with nausea, and swallowed hard. "Yes."

"Because my looks were pleasing? Leila, your whole damn race is pleasing to look at."

"That, and Isis said you were a genius."

"Ah, yes, let's not forget the 170 IQ. And the fertility. You figured a man of your world couldn't give you a child."

"I would have given you pleasure," she added desperately, her stomach a hard knot.

"Oh, yes, I got pleasure out of it. Last night. Several times."

She refused to apologize or feel shame for what she had done with him. Last night had been one of the few fully honest moments in her life. "I got caught in my own spell. Seduction is a trap that springs both ways. Last night was not about a child. Last night was for us."

His disbelieving snort offered no hope that he accepted her words. "Are you pregnant?" he asked.

"I do not know."

He raked a hand through his hair. "God, Leila, didn't you think I'd care? Did you think I could just up and leave you and my child?"

"I didn't think you'd ever know."

"Helluva plan." Derision dripped from each word. "Thanks a lot."

"It wasn't a plan. I was feeling, not thinking. I didn't know you then. Not like I do now." Desperately she gripped his arm, sought forgiveness for the unforgivable. Tears streamed down her cheeks until she could barely see. "If you want, we can find an answer."

"You deceived me." He shook her off. "Last night you used me."

She stared at him, wiping back tears. She gazed at his beautiful, bristly face. At the appealing shock of blond hair. At the uncompromising jaw and the hard eyes. Unformed hopes, unspoken dreams, vanished like the last star of morning winking out before the power of the sun. He might make love—no, call it what it was. He might have sex with her, but she had fooled herself into thinking he cared about her.

"Yes, I deceived you, but you deceived me, too," she returned quietly.

He threw her a challenging stare.

"For a while," she said, meeting his gaze head-on, "I thought I had both a man of power and a man of genius. But I don't, do I?"

His hard eyes turned wary. "What do you mean?"

"You have no magic. You have only this." She touched the neck talisman, feeling the hum of its power through her skin. Quickly she withdrew her hand. "This sits outside you. Inside, you have no power to create beauty or comfort or to satisfy needs."

"I have these." He held out his hands, then touched

261

his temple. "And this, my brain. It's what you wanted me for, isn't it?" he added bitterly.

"Yes." He gave a slight flinch, as though she'd struck him. She pointed to his talisman. "But this has only the power to destroy. You do not use the power of the positive. You are a negative to everything here."

"Do you know what it's like to be powerless before *ma-at*, Leila?"

"Yes. You took mine away."

"So you had the discomfort of sleeping on a rock instead of a pillow? Of having to walk instead of flit? Big deal."

How dare he dismiss what she had gone through? He had a right to be angry at her deceptions, but he did not have the right to minimize what he had done. Anger replaced sorrow and pleading and desperation. Good, clean anger.

He battled on without stopping. "Do you know what it's like to have someone put a Truthspeak spell on you and not be able to stop it? To be held down while someone else beats you up because you didn't give him your lunch money? To be five years old and have someone draw a knife down your cheek and threaten to kill you?"

He was dredging up more than his antipathy to *ma-at*, she realized, but at the moment she didn't care. She refused to look at the scar line on his cheek, refused to acknowledge the empathy she felt, refused to let his horrors negate her anger.

"Do you know what it is like to be the slowest one in your class? Unable to master more than the simplest of incantations?" she spat back. She didn't pause for an answer. "Have you ever gone with people you thought were friends, only to be abandoned in the sightless bowels of a Tower cave? Have you listened to them *flit* away, laughing and telling you to use your *ma-at*? When you don't have the power to undo their stasis spell? Do you know what it is to be so powerless that you do not have the means to provide for your basic needs? To want someone to love, and all anyone who looks at you can see is a seductress or an idiot?"

Her head felt ready to burst from her rising fury. So much she had bottled inside, like a bound djinni, and now that the pain was released and free, it demanded retribution.

"And then you see a picture. A man who looks different from the men you've known. A man who looks kind and gentle. And you learn he is a genius, a man whose wisdom is renowned."

"Isis exaggerated," he muttered.

She didn't bother with his response. "And you think maybe you can have a child, a person in your life to love, and who will love you. A child of *ma-at* and of science, a child of beauty and of intelligence, who will grow up to be a person with perhaps enough power and enough genius to be happy." She looked away, unable to watch him anymore. "Instead of gentleness, though, you find a man who reviles the essence of your soul, who takes away the small store of power that you have nurtured over cycles." She hooked her fingers through the wires at his throat. "A man who does naught but destroy," she whispered, the fury finally

263

leaving her. She dropped onto a pillow, then sat back, utterly drained, utterly embarrassed at what she had revealed.

Total silence filled the tent. She glanced once at Jack, then looked away. She didn't want to see the softening in his eyes, the sympathy or, worse, the pity.

"God, Leila," he whispered back. "I didn't know."

Stiffly she got to her feet, still refusing to look at him. If she did, she might blurt out something stupid, like the fact that she still loved him. "I wanted you to like me without knowing. For me. I wanted you to like my people, my land. My *ma-at*, my soul." She brushed her hands down her robe, smoothing the wrinkles. "For a while, I wanted too much, forgetting that it is foolish to want what you cannot have." She straightened her sleeve. "Now I think the sun has set. I shall go to the evening meal with Xerxes."

Jack made to go to her, but she held up her hand. "No. I would like to dine with my friend without you tonight." She cast him a quick glance. "Besides, you are quite ill looking from the al-ar-gee. You should rest. Tomorrow we leave."

They would reach the city, the bargain would be ended.

"Leila—"

"Stay there," she said sharply. If he touched her, she would shatter.

He stayed. "All right, if that's what you want. But, Leila, don't trust Xerxes."

"He has given me no reason to doubt him."

"Because he tried to kill me today. Or at least showed me he could."

"Imagination," she scoffed. "Djinn do not kill." She shivered at the mere thought.

"Nonetheless, when I had that coughing spell, I felt a tendril of *ma-at* squeezing my lungs."

"Still afraid, Jack?" she said with disdain, moving to the entrance. "I think you were mistaken. Xerxes has neither the power nor the desire."

"Then he's stronger than you realize. Think what you will about me, but don't trust him," Jack warned.

"But I do trust him." She paused at the tent flap, ready to leave. "Remember that cave I just told you about? It was Xerxes who rescued me."

Leila had a way with exit lines. Jack flopped down to the pillows, feeling about as low as the rug. He hadn't known, hadn't even bothered to speculate, what she had endured in her life. No, he'd been too wrapped in his own fears to even notice hers.

He still didn't like what she had done, but he could understand it.

And he had to believe that last night was real, not a calculated seduction.

He rubbed his itching eyes. Damn, but he hated letting her go to Xerxes. He hated wondering what Xerxes might do to draw her into his web. But to have insisted on going with her would have been worse. He would have lost any chance at reversing her loathing. Not that he had much of a chance, since most of what she'd said was true.

"The way you two were yelling, it is fortunate I have a mantle of silence around this tent."

Jack opened his eyes to see Zayne sitting beside him on the pillows. The djinni wasn't smiling this time, but at least he wasn't spitting fire. "If there's a mantle of silence, how did you know what we said?"

"My tent. My mantle."

Of course. "How much did you hear?"

"Oh, most of it, I expect." Zayne traced a finger along the wires. "Is this the talisman?"

"Yes."

"What does your talisman do?"

Wearily Jack sat up. Apparently, Zayne wanted to talk, and he couldn't evict the man from his own tent. "Creates an energy that negates any *ma-at* directed at me."

"Does it draw on the forces of earth and water from Terra?"

"Not that I know of. I think it draws from me," he added reluctantly.

"You *think*?" Zayne's astonishment wasn't hidden. "You mean you made this without knowing what it could do?"

This was not the time for prevarication or avoidance, Jack decided. "Apparently. The more I've worn it, the more it becomes . . . attuned to me, I guess."

"Well, of course. Isn't that the way of a talisman?" Zayne gave him a sharp look. "Which is in control? You or the crystal?"

Jack gave a rueful half laugh. "I'm not always sure."

"You must be sure. With an object as powerful as

that which you wear, you must be sure it is you who is the master. You wear it close to your heart; the magic feels the pulse of your blood. You have a power flowing through you."

"I can't do magic. Or *ma-at*," he insisted.

"No? Maybe not. But everyone has power. Take Leila. She survived not with the power of her *ma-at* but with the powers of mind and heart." Zayne tapped Jack in the middle of his forehead. "You have the power here. Untapped power, not yet loosened to the crystal. Which one will be in control?"

Jack didn't have an answer.

"You should talk to Darius," Zayne said abruptly, sitting back.

Automatically, Jack shook his head; then he stopped. "Perhaps I should."

"Do not expect compassion for your dilemma because he is united with your sister. His first duty is to protect the *ma-at*."

"I won't."

Suddenly Zayne was not sitting but standing beside Jack. "Ah, but I must be going. I only came back for my oud, but stayed for the entertainment. I, too, am dining with Xerxes tonight. You," he added drily, "I understand are not."

"So it seems." Jack stood beside him. "Zayne, could you . . . I don't trust Xerxes. And Leila—"

The musician tilted his head as he picked up his instrument. "So you are not as uncaring as you sounded."

"No."

267

"I will see her safe. I, too, have entertained a doubt or two about Xerxes. In school he started out as weak as Leila. He did not end that way."

"Perhaps his quest for power didn't end with graduation?"

Zayne shrugged. "Perhaps. Do not worry; I will guard her. Give her some time; our Leila is quick to temper, but keeps little ill will. Go to her. Tonight, at least, she will share the tent with you." He gave Jack a masculine grin. "What happens after that depends upon you."

Chapter Sixteen

Leila paused outside Xerxes's tent, taking a moment to compose herself. She would not greet him with her face blotchy with tears, her cheeks red with humiliation.

Why had she said all that? The words had tumbled out, beyond her will. Anger and hurt and humiliation she had never revealed. Once loosed, they were like a wall of sand before the great winds, unstoppable, filling every bit of air between them.

But, by Solomon's wisdom, it had felt so good to let the anger out. The anger at the loss of her *ma-at*, the anger of so many cycles of pretending not to care or pretending she was more than she was, the anger when she'd finally realized that Jack was not the powerful wizard who could solve all her problems, but only a simple man with a single talisman that could be turned on or off. A man who did not love her, could not love her.

She wiped a hand across her face, drying the tears. No, that was not right. Jack was not a simple man, and that was why her love for him did not die.

She pressed her fingers to her eyes, erasing the telltale redness she knew would be there with the outline of dark kohl.

Nothing about Jack was simple, from the energy that exploded from him, to his tender fuss over her feet, to his willingness to laugh at himself, to his encouragement when she climbed the rock. His quick mind saw much, knew much, learned much.

And at one time he had admired her, not for her beauty or her small store of *ma-at*, but for what he saw inside her—her mind and her feelings.

For that, she would always love him.

The last remnants of anger slid away behind resignation and acceptance. What could not be changed must be endured, and she could not change Jack's opinions about her *ma-at*. Only he could do that.

She drew in a deep breath, though the tightness felt as though a circle of *grucheeks* sat upon her chest. She brushed from her robe a small wrinkle and a smudge of dirt accumulated on the short walk over. With a muttered chant and the symbols she drew in the air with her hand, she painted a glittery rainbow of color on her feet and hands.

The hard part was, she actually understood a little of his distrust of *ma-at*. She didn't like his distrust, but she understood it, for in some ways their experiences were so similar. They both had suffered at the hands of others.

Ma-at was not the villain, though; cruelty could be in the nature of man or djinn. Many were good; some were not.

She ran a hand over her hair, smoothing the strands to a glossy sheen, then dabbed a small amount of perfume on her wrists. She lifted her chin, as ready as she would ever be.

This was her world, where she belonged and where Jack had no place. Tomorrow, before they left, she would tell him about the return of her *ma-at* and let him go on alone if he wished. She would talk to him about the child, if there was one.

This was her home. Kaf was where a djinn child must be raised. Except the child would have a human father, and she could no longer deny Jack his paternity. She did not know yet what the answer to that dilemma was.

She stepped forward, and the tent flap opened as if in response to her readiness to enter. Inside, she was surprised to find that Xerxes had invited others to his dinner. At least twenty djinn were enjoying the appetizers, which floated around the room on bronze platters and in silver bowls. Music came from the top of the tent, although she could see no source in the dim lighting. Intricate, lilting, barely audible melodies surrounded the guests with a background of beauty that touched the heart and the soul. Small braziers burned with a pleasing scent of sandalwood.

A surprising feeling of relief passed across her that

271

she would not be dining alone with him. *Bah*, she scolded herself, she had never worried about being alone with her friend, had enjoyed their times together, but now Jack's warning spoiled her delight. She gave herself a mental shake. The Scientist's mistrust would not color her world.

Xerxes removed himself from a small group as soon as he spied her, and a moment later was at her side. He gave her a charming smile, and Leila relaxed and returned the greeting. This was her friend, her mentor.

He took her hand in his and kissed the palm. "Leila, at last. I feared you might have decided against my invitation, but my wait is rewarded. You are absolutely stunning." There was no mistaking his warm admiration.

"Thank you." She eased her hand from his even as she basked in his praise. "I would never fail to accept an invitation of yours."

"Never?" He raised one sculpted brow.

"Never without telling you."

"Ah. But where is your companion?"

She thought hurriedly. Jack's discomfort from *al-argee* was not a reason Xerxes would understand. Nor did she wish to relay the fact that she had asked Jack not to come. "Other matters arose that required his attention. He bade me extend his apologies."

Xerxes inclined his head. "Apologies accepted." He didn't seem too upset. "May I offer you a drink?"

"What are you having?" She nodded toward the

crystal goblet he held. A swirling cloud of blue within the glass hid the contents.

"Nothing more exciting than water, with a small sparkle I've added." He held it to her. "Here, take this, I have only just poured it."

"I don't want—"

"I shall get another. I decided I prefer my drink warmed." She blinked, and a moment later she found the goblet in her hand, while Xerxes held another, this time with a brilliant blue flame embedded in the glass.

She sipped the drink. Water, yes, but icier than she'd ever tasted and with an effervescence that tingled on her tongue. It was delicious.

"Now, can I tempt you with something?" He paused as a tray appeared in his hands. "A sweetmeat? A portion of sesame bread? Cucumber and yoghurt? Melon slice?"

"An impressive array." She dipped the cucumber into a spicy yoghurt dip, enjoying the hum of conversation and the fragrance of incense. "I imagine you shall figure in the village tales for some time."

He seemed pleased by her admiration as he rested a hand at her waist and guided her to a knot of people. "Have you met the local Adept?"

The Adept, a djinni of many cycles who affected a long thin mustache and curls in his hair, stood in the center of the group. After the introductions, he frowned at them. "I have heard disturbing news."

"Oh, and what is that?" Xerxes asked casually, but Leila noticed his fingers tighten around the goblet.

"Humans have come to Kaf." The Adept nodded at the buzz he'd created.

Leila's insides turned to dust. "Of course they have." Casually she bit into a date. "The Protector has taken one as *zaniya*."

"Not Isis," the Adept retorted. "A wizard."

"How have you heard this?" Xerxes asked. His polished fingers stroked the goblet.

The Adept leaned forward. "I lit the divination fires and was led to a parchment found last cycle at the Towers. The prophecy was most clear. 'Fires cease in dark. Air dies to cold. Rock walks and rainbow glows. Then look to the heart of lava, for runes of water rule.'" He glanced around.

Xerxes lifted one brow, looking faintly amused. "How does this foretell humans here?"

"Fires cease and air cold—the Night of No Moon. Last night. Heart of lava must be the rocks. Put that with runes of water—" He spread his hands. "A human wizard."

Leila glanced around, her tension easing slightly. His audience doubted the reasoning of the Adept, and she remembered that Zayne had mentioned the old man's obsession. Apparently, this was not the first prophecy he had quoted.

"What about that middle part?" someone asked. "Rainbows?"

"I have not figured that out, but 'rock walks,' I saw a *grucheek* today." A satisfied nod punctuated the statement. "Everyone knows they stay near the Towers."

"They are said to bring luck."

"I hope so. It rubbed against my palm, then scurried away among the brush."

"Leila's companion carried a *grucheek* on his shoulder today." Xerxes gave her a speculative glance.

"The *grucheek* has chosen to travel with us."

"Must be more to that odd Scientist than I thought," muttered one of the group. Then he flushed and cast a quick glance at Leila, searching for her reaction to his words.

She gave him a cool glance.

"If a human is on Kaf, I think we have little to fear." Xerxes, however, was eyeing her with renewed interest. "Perhaps, Leila, you have seen other oddities on your pilgrimage?"

"No," she lied. "Our journey has been quite dull."

As the night progressed, Leila found she met a good portion of the village leaders and respected talents. Xerxes hovered at her side, making her feel like an honored guest. He had a smooth style, an ability to set the nervous at ease and encourage conversation between strangers. Not that she ever needed much aid in conversing; she'd developed that skill long ago, and she enjoyed the talk of *ma-at*, the Night of No Moon, the oddities observed in life, and the latest gossip. As for questions about her recent activities, she kept to vague truths and quickly changed the subject with an amusing story or a question for the other person.

Conversations flowed as endless as the river that nourished the village, as sweet as the honey in the tea. Laughter and confidences came as readily as the food replenishing the trays. The passage of time blurred, until she suddenly realized that a good portion of the night had advanced and few individuals remained. She found a quiet corner of the room, while Xerxes spoke with the Adept about bloodstone. Zayne remained, too, sitting alone with his oud, playing softly along with the music of the tent. She sipped the effervescent water, trying to clear a head that spun with the mix of drink and incense, music and voice.

I should be going. She sent Xerxes the thought during a lull in his conversation.

Please do not. His voice, low and mesmerizing, filled her.

We travel tomorrow.

Since when do you find that travel requires a night's rest? he asked with amusement, his words suffusing and lulling her.

Since I travel with Jack. She could not stop the retort.

He keeps you that . . . busy? A definite edge shaded his words. He transported to her side and took her hands. "Stay with me tonight. I would speak with you of the bloodstone and of power." He turned her hands over and kissed the palms. The heated look he gave her was lustful admiration. "Stay. Please."

"You never say please." Was it beseeching or was it commanding?

"For you, I do." His lips touched the pulse at her wrist.

She hesitated, her mind filled with the sweet incense and the compelling plea, with the glow of long friendship and admiration. Perhaps he wanted her aid, a fresh pair of eyes in his search for the bloodstone?

She looked again at him. He wanted much more than to search for bloodstone.

Gently she tried to pull her hands from his. She did not want to hurt the feelings of a good friend, but she could not give him what he asked. She wanted no man on her pillows except Jack.

For a moment, he did not release her.

The tent flap pushed open. There, as if her thoughts had the power to transport him to her side, stood Jack. His gaze swept the room until it lit upon her; then he stepped inside and strode straight toward her.

He looked awful. His eyes were blinking; his shaggy blond hair stood on end as though he'd run a hand many times through the strands; his nose was a faint pink; his bristly cheeks lent him a fierce look; his sneeze punctuated the air.

He looked wonderful.

Had he come for her? Why? Had his hot anger died? Did he desire confrontation or release from the bargain? She quickly withdrew from Xerxes's grip, murmured an excuse, and met Jack halfway, at the center of the tent. At once he gathered her into his arms.

He laid his cheek on the top of her head. "I'm sorry," he whispered, too low for anyone else to hear. "I was an ass, and I had no right to judge you."

"I regret deceiving you."

"Come back to me, and we'll talk."

Why had she spent so much time angry and at the party alone? They had so little time, and she belonged with him. She wrapped her arms around his waist, resting her cheek against his chest. All of a sudden she was warm and happy and even more light-headed. "Talk, talk, talk. All you do is talk."

He gave a brief laugh, then pulled back and frowned. "Are you all right? You look glassy-eyed."

"I am fine now. Fine and happy."

His arm around her waist tightened. "I like to see you happy. Are you ready to go?"

"Must you?" Xerxes had rejoined them, and he interrupted, sounding irritated. He rubbed a hand along his jaw. "And when your friend just arrived."

She flushed; for a moment, she had forgotten about her host and friend.

Stay, he added, speaking only to her. His voice held the promise of more, the reminder of friendship.

But beneath her cheek was the strong beat of her lover's heart, and she knew where she wanted to be. "I am sorry, but I'm tired." As she spoke, she realized the words were true. The day had been long and filled with many changes and emotions after a night of little sleep.

Xerxes's jaw tightened; then he must have heard the weariness in her voice, for he relaxed and lifted one shoulder in acquiescence. "I would like to see you before you leave tomorrow. As an old friend?"

"Of course." She bowed. "We thank you for your generous hospitality. May Solomon bless the winds at your back and the sand at your feet as you complete your journey."

"Your words are most kind for my simple repast. May the benevolent fires of Kaf burn bright for you."

They completed the ritual departure by kissing each other's cheeks, and a moment later Leila found herself outside. She drew in a deep breath of sweet, fresh air, clearing the fog from her brain, then pointed upward. "Look, I can see a star. The first I remember seeing this evening."

He rested a hand at the curve of her waist. "We have a custom on Earth of wishing on the first star you see at night."

"A wish fulfilled by a djinni?"

He shook his head. "Just a wish."

"Do they always come true?"

"Rarely. But sometimes it's necessary to dream impossible dreams."

"Do you have an impossible dream, Jack Montgomery?"

"For my world," he said after a moment. "No more war or poverty or disease."

"I meant for yourself. *Ma-at* is personal; we do not attempt to use it on such a wide scale—the results are chaotic. What is your impossible dream?"

He didn't answer, but instead looked skyward. "There's a poem you have to say: 'Star light, star bright, first star I see tonight. I wish I may and I wish I might have the wish I wish tonight.' Then you say, or think, your wish."

"Wishes are more powerful when spoken."

"And more revealing."

"True. And sometimes wishes granted turn out to be bad." She had wished for a human to sire a child. Had her wish come true? She did not know, but the wish had brought her both sorrow and a precious love.

He nodded. "We have another saying. 'Be careful what you wish for.' "

They fell silent; apparently, he was as reluctant as she to invoke the power of the star.

"Will you tell me if there's a child?" he asked at last, his face still raised to the star, his arm still about her waist.

"I will."

He let out a sigh. "Thank you."

Leila curled the belt of her robe around her finger. "Tonight I was told there is a *hamad-el-halad* that visits here."

"What is that?"

"A large beast."

"Does it scare the people in town?"

She laughed at the idea of being frightened by the placid animal. "No, the beast moves too slowly and is too lacking in cleverness to be of concern. What it can do, however, is carry us to the city. The *hamad-el-halad* is very enduring. We could make the city by nightfall if we start early."

She turned in his arms to look up at him. With his free hand he brushed a strand of hair behind her ear. She could not read his blue eyes in the dark shadows, but perhaps it was not her imagination that his hand trembled as he cupped the back of her neck. "It would be easier to ride than to walk," he said.

"I have never much appreciated the camping."

His thumb traced the line of her lips. It was a sturdy thumb, the skin less than smooth, but he touched her so delicately and gently that it felt as if the air kissed her. "You have done well on this trek; I think I owe you that small amount of comfort."

A portion of her rejoiced in the compliment even as another portion knew disappointment that their moments together were almost at an end. The practical portion knew that using the beast was the right choice. She blinked, forcing back tears, but a single one trickled from the corner of her eye. "Tonight will be our last night."

Jack caught the tear with his thumb. "Then let's not waste it with argument or anger."

She nodded, unable to speak around the tightness in her throat.

In answer, he gathered her closer and she wrapped her arms about his waist, holding him so near that she could feel the pulse in his neck. He molded her body to his, holding her as though she were the most cherished person in his life. The air about her sparkled with rose, emerald, and turquoise, the colors of happiness.

The truth. Only the truth tonight. It was time to be brave. "I have something to tell you," she whispered.

"What?" His hand stroked down her hair.

She took a deep breath. "My *ma-at*. It has returned."

His strokes stopped. The night, her breathing, indeed her blood stopped while she awaited his response. He was silent, unmoving. Oh, by Solomon, why had she told him?

"The bargain is completed." She waited, chest tight, for his answer.

"No, it is not," he said softly. "We travel to the city together."

"Then—" Hope flared.

He tilted her face to look at him, and his palm cupped her cheek. "I wondered what was different about you."

She gave a small *tsk*. "Because I was groomed and tidied. Prettier."

He shook his head. "You are always beautiful to me. Because you were happy. And I'm happy for you, Leila."

Then he picked her up in his arms, the swish of motion making her dizzy, and he laughed. "Welcome back, my Leila."

He was, she realized with joy, happy for her. They kissed, deeply and passionately enough to last a lifetime of separation. His lips never left hers as he strode surefooted through the quiet night. She clung to him in desperate need, and when he found the tent and lowered her to the pillows, she knew that she would carry these memories forever.

Chapter Seventeen

The day dawned clear and hot, with no wind and no fluttering ash. Jack took a deep breath, grateful for that small blessing. His allergy had disappeared with the ash, leaving only a slight scratchiness in his throat as a reminder. Leila snuggled closer to him, and he smiled as he drew in her familiar clover scent. He smoothed a hand through her silky hair, enjoying the way the strands clung to him as though they were electrostatically charged.

Last night had been . . . special. He'd used a condom again, and he'd seen the flash of disappointment on her face, felt the short-lived withdrawal before she returned enthusiastically to his arms. In that moment of her willing acceptance of him, he knew.

He was in love with Leila.

His fingers curled around the curve of her hip, and he snuggled closer, craving the touch of her skin. A quiet, sure elation filled him, accompanied by satisfaction.

Love hadn't come as a blinding *aha* moment but more as if a veil had been slowly lifted, allowing him to see what had been part of him for a while. He couldn't pinpoint the moment, nor could he vocalize what it was he loved about her. He just knew the awareness of love sat in his heart like a glowing ember.

And he didn't know what the hell to do next. Telling her seemed the logical first step, but he hesitated. Would she welcome a declaration of love right before they were preparing to part? Despite her whispered *janam*, she was still, in many ways, an enigma to him. How did she feel? Did she love him, too?

He had never held the optimistic belief that love conquered all. Some things could not be solved with a simple "I love you." Problems like living in two different worlds and the fact that she was a woman of *ma-at* while he mistrusted the powers of her world.

But did he mistrust Leila?

Jack pondered the question as he pulled her closer to him, burrowing deeper into the mound of pillows that formed their bed. He rested a cheek against the top of her silky head and hugged her close, his arms crossing beneath her generous breasts.

He trusted Leila, he realized. Despite the way they'd started, despite her initial schemes, he trusted the woman he had come to know. He trusted her with his heart, with his secrets, with his shame, with his hope.

Even if there was no child to bind them, with love

and trust was there a way to span two worlds?

For when he thought of leaving her today and never seeing her again, a huge, yawning chasm opened inside him. In it was only emptiness and solitude and darkness. An emotional darkness that he feared even more than the physical dark had once terrified him. A terror now conquered because of Leila.

Maybe she would consent to live on Earth with him. Could he live on Kaf with her? He shied away from answering the question, reluctant to face the consequences of either a yes or a no answer.

His arms tightened around her, and he kissed the top of her head, feeling desperation engulf him. There had to be a way. On the way to the city, when it was once again just the two of them, he would tell her he loved her and raise the subject.

His kiss lowered to her ear and his tongue traced its smooth rim. He stirred, blood heading south in a rush, although he wouldn't have thought getting hard was a possibility after the repeats of last night.

He knew the instant she awoke by the change in her breathing, the tightening of her skin, and the first colored sparks of desire.

"Good morning," he growled in her ear, his voice still a little hoarse.

She turned in his arms and smiled up at him, her dark eyes gleaming. "Good morning to you, too." She trailed the back of her hand down his cheek. "Your bristles are almost soft now, the beginnings of a true beard."

"Which means I can do this without scratching

you." He bent his head and rubbed his cheek against the clover-petal softness of her neck and chin.

"That is good, because I like that," she purred back.

His heart contracted, then dilated with the influx of emotion. He leaned back, looking at her. Her lips were full and moist, and in her eyes brimmed emotions he couldn't fathom. *Tell her. Tell her now. Tell her you love her.* The words pounded in his thoughts, as strong as the beat in his chest.

"Leila, I—"

"Jack, I—"

They spoke at the same time, both sounding serious.

Then her eyes shifted away, as though something had caught her attention. She put a finger to his mouth, hushing him. "Wait."

Jack pushed up, biting back the words. "What is it?"

"Zayne says he is outside with breakfast."

He shut his eyes in frustration. Telling Leila his feelings was hard enough already; he wouldn't do it in front of an audience. "We're busy," he called, rolling to his back.

"Then you should have lit the privacy stones," Zayne answered with amusement. "The tea will get bitter if it steeps much longer. How fast can you be?"

"Not that fast," he muttered.

Leila laughed, then whispered. "After he lent us his tent, it would be inhospitable to forbid him entrance."

"He probably wouldn't pay any attention to our strictures anyway."

"True."

Reluctantly Jack rolled away from Leila and shoved to his feet. His unrelieved erection throbbed with the withdrawal, and inside he ached with frustration. "I'll take a quick shower, then." A quick *icy* shower.

"Very quick," suggested Leila. "I think I hear the—"

A bovine-looking face with curly-fry horns pushed back the tent flap.

"—*hamad-el-halad* sniffing at our door."

"The creature is anxious to meet those who will ride on its broad back this day," said Zayne from outside.

Leila said something in her language to the animal, then made a shooing motion with her hands. The *hamad* whatsit backed out the door. "We have not long before it comes back in."

"The *grucheek* is rumbling away out here," added Zayne.

Jack ran a hand through his hair. Hell, how had they acquired a menagerie? "Give us five minutes."

"Minutes?"

"Count to three hundred slowly," he explained, heading for the shower. So much for the mood of the moment. So much for revelations of the heart.

Well, they would have the trek to talk in. That would please Leila. For once he would be talking and not thinking.

Xerxes was not pleased. He was no closer to locating the strange power than he had been when he'd first found it. The divination fire remained without answers, as blank as an unwritten scroll. No one in this useless village had the strength of will to muster such talent, no one had felt the power's alien touch. The only strangers were Zayne, Leila, and Jack. Zayne was the essence of Kaf; Leila was weak, and her companion bordered on idiocy. That she was leaving this morning, after having spent the night with her buffoon instead of him, was another drop to fill the poisonous well of his fury.

Leila's companion. Xerxes shook his head, tasting the bitterness of a rivalry that should never have been. What had Leila found of interest in such a one? She was smart; he had always recognized that in her, even if others had not. So what was it about her silent companion that kept her satisfied?

Her companion. His eyes narrowed, and he passed a hand over the divination fires, extinguishing them. Leila rarely did anything without purpose and benefit to herself. So why was she consorting with the odd stranger?

Xerxes closed his eyes, feeling the cold lick of discovery. Had he, had everyone, been played for a fool?

He glanced at his bed and the woman, Kala, who sprawled there. Last night she had shared his pillows and his wine and his potions. She had been eager and he had used her thoroughly and often, but she had been a pale substitute for the woman he really wanted. Leila. With a flick of his wrist, he returned the woman to her own tent, moving her so expertly that she did not waken from her sleep. He dressed, renewed the concealment spells over his hands and tablet, flung on clothes and cape, and strode from the tent. Outside, he squinted against the bright, newly risen sun.

With one thought, he transported near the indigo tent. A *hamad-el-halad* grazed on a patch of grass nearby. Xerxes stayed within the trees, careful not to send a whiff of his presence or his thoughts to any who might be near. For he wanted to watch, to see the man in the clear light of the Kafian sun, without artifice or ash to hide him.

A few moments later his patience, and his caution, were rewarded. Leila and Jack stepped out with Zayne. Jack bent down, picked up something, and set it on his shoulder. The *grucheek*.

The three of them were talking softly, but Xerxes had trained himself to listen to the whisper of an insect, and their conversation was audible to him.

English. A language of Terra. He gritted his teeth against rising anger.

Zayne bowed good-bye, then, on his departure, made a comment that set Jack tilting his head back with laughter while the musician disappeared.

The laughter stilled, and only Jack and Leila remained. The Scientist's hands lingered on her waist as he leaned forward and gave her a possessive kiss.

This was not the man of last night. That man had been silent with dull eyes, labored breathing, and reddened nose. This man stood tall with power in his muscles. His eyes shone clear, and his face spoke of strength.

Fire raged through Xerxes. The wizard's disguise had been a clever one, so clever it had fooled even him. His fingers dug into his palms, the concealed black onyx at his throat burned him with cold. Only one test remained.

Carefully he slowed his breath, drawing in his anger. Not a hint of emotion could escape. This had to be delicate, innocuous-seeming. He sent a single thought. Something common, without threat. *Do you leave now?* He sent the question to Jack, a tight, narrow beam for one person.

And he ran into a wall as solid as the *hamad-el-halad*.

His thought curled back upon him, driven away by a strange, repelling force.

His control loosened and the fury rose, coursing through him with the heat of a river of lava. *This* was the man who wielded the strange power. This was the man who had disrupted his Circles. This was the man he must control. Or destroy.

Xerxes raised a hand—chanting the words, feeling the strength swirling through him—then lowered his fist. With his rage came a keen analysis, a sharp eye, a willingness to employ whatever methods were needed. He watched Jack touch a hand to the small of Leila's back. Watched her smile in return. Watched them laugh over the beast that deigned to carry them. Watched Jack lift Leila easily to the beast's back.

It was always good to have a second plan.

Jared, Apprentice to Darius, Protector of the *ma-at*, was bored. He sat in a workroom filled with scrolls, spices, amulets, feathers, scented oils, crystals, arcane books, candles, and other relics just begging to be put to use, and what was his assignment? Memorize the seventeen Mantras for Assimilation of Air Transference. Boring!

Cupping his hands, he muttered the words of creation, and a fireball materialized between his palms—brilliant red and scorching to anything it touched other than himself. He tossed the fireball on the tip of his finger and spun it around. Once, when he'd visited Terra, he'd seen a human do that with a soccer ball. He'd never managed the feat without the use of *ma-at*, but then the human couldn't do it with fire, so he figured they were even.

The fireball rose like a whirling top and spun around the room, singeing the civet moss and releasing a foul odor. "Yuck!" Jared snapped his fingers and extinguished the fireball. He set up a cleansing wind, but not even his skills could get rid of all remnants of the odor.

A green message sphere suddenly winked into place, chiming softly for attention. The message was for Darius, he knew, but Darius was still asleep this morning, having guarded Kaf throughout the Night of No Moon and having dealt with the aftermath during the following day.

If the sphere wasn't keyed to open only for Darius, Jared could listen to the news it brought. The green shade said the information it carried was of no great urgency. No harm in listening to the message. Maybe he could handle the request of the Protector. Anything was more interesting than memorizing mantras.

Jared glanced around, then held out his hands. "Come to me." The green orb settled onto his palms.

"I, Jared, Apprentice to the Protector of Kaf, do bid thee speak."

"This is Zayne," recited the sphere in a tinny voice. Jared remembered having met the Minstrel and having envied him his freedom. The sphere continued, "I'm at Bak-ar-Legandermal. We have some interesting visitors. Xerxes is here, Leila too, with a human named Jack. They leave anon. And, just for your pleasure, here is a new song." The sphere ended with a snippet of a sweet, heartrending tune. Then it winked out of existence.

A human? On Kaf? Jared's heart beat faster. He'd been to Terra several times and he enjoyed that world, enjoyed the respite from his duties. He had a special friend there, Mary Calderone, a friend he sorely missed, for recently Darius had forbidden him to return to Terra. He'd said that as Jared's *ma-at* strengthened, Terran magic would pull too hard at him, a conflict he wasn't ready to handle.

Maybe this human knew Mary and could take her a message.

What Leila was doing with a human, though, he couldn't fathom. As his voice had deepened, and his number of cycles grew, he had grown to appreciate Leila's charms, even if she did not fare well with Isis, Darius's *zaniya*. He suspected they disliked one another because Leila had once thought Darius would be hers, although it was obvious to all now, even Leila, that Isis was the only one for Darius.

Trust females to hold a grudge.

So the message held nothing of danger. But much

of interest, and they would be leaving very soon. Jared drew in a deep breath, choking on the odor of civet moss. Luckily, he'd been to Bak-ar-Legandermal before. He might even get back before Darius awoke. Just in case, however, he waved his fingers and left a fire message.

Then he lifted his arms and, in a whirlwind of parchments and moss, disappeared, just as the door to the workroom opened.

Isis Montgomery, perfumer and *zaniya* to the Protector, opened the door to the workroom and spoke to the two-year-old daughter she carried on her hip. "Now, Jessamine, I'm going to teach you about the scents of orris and jasmine, your namesake. The root for orris . . . Whew, what is that smell?"

The stench of burnt civet moss halted her, and she wrinkled her nose. Jessamine put a hand over her face and said, "Yuck."

Isis grimaced. Two years old and the child's vocabulary consisted of "mommy" and "daddy," in both English and *Fahrisa*, "smell," "Jared," and, thanks to Jared, "yuck."

"Jared, what have you been doing?" She glanced around the empty room, then muttered, "And where have you gone?"

Playing hookey again. She knew that her *zani* and his apprentice were increasingly at odds over Jared's training. Darius loved the boy and worried that his fast-burgeoning skills surpassed his ability to control them, while Jared chafed at the restrictions Darius imposed. Mostly she tried not to interfere, but every once in a while . . .

She spied the fire-note Jared had left, along with the gleaming message orb. "At least he had the sense to tell us where he went," she told Jessamine. "If you ever get like this, remember that."

As she listened to the orb, however, her heart squeezed.

Jack? Could it possibly be her brother Jack? Here? Who else could Zayne have expected them to recognize by first name only?

But . . . Jack? Practical, no-nonsense, logical, scientific Jack on Kaf? And with Leila? How the hell did that happen?

Isis glanced toward the door, thought about waking her *zani*, decided against it. The message indicated no urgency, no danger. If the visitor was Jack, she wanted to talk to him herself. And get Jared back here before Darius came looking for him. Luckily, Darius had taken her once to Bak-ar-Legandermal when he'd shown her the Tower Lands. And, luckily, Darius had once gifted her with the ability to transport.

She hitched Jessamine more firmly to her hip. "C'mon, sweetie, let's go for a little trip." She visualized the town, said the necessary words, and a moment later disappeared in a whirlwind of parchment and moss, just as the door opened.

Darius rubbed sleepy eyes as he opened the door to the workroom. He had missed Isis in their pillows when he'd awoken, had missed her warm body and the fragrant scent of jasmine. Perhaps he could persuade her back? Had he seen her slip in here, probably to keep company with his rebellious apprentice?

The room was empty. No Jared. No mantras. No Isis. His eyes narrowed as he spied the message orb and the fire-words and he strode over to them, his robe swirling about his bare feet. He held out his hand, and the orb settled onto his palm.

"Speak," he commanded the orb. "I, Darius, Protector of *Ma-at*, do command you."

When the message was finished, he cupped his hands and the orb disappeared. Jack? Could Zayne mean Jack Montgomery? Isis's brother? What, by the love of Solomon, could he be doing on Kaf? And with Leila?

In the Night of No Moon, and during the days before, he had caught strange ripples in the *ma-at*. Disturbances he could not pinpoint or identify. He had attributed them to the workings of the Night, but . . . Xerxes, Leila, Jack. They formed a strange triangle, which his apprentice had seen fit to step in the middle of.

And he would guess that Isis had reached the same conclusions about Jack as he had, and followed. Beyond his duty to protect the *ma-at*, though, his heart squeezed in fear. His greatest loves—his *zaniya*, his daughter, and his apprentice—were all gone to Bak-ar-Legandermal.

Swiftly he muttered the words of transport and disappeared in a whirlwind.

* * *

The chain at his neck tingled so faintly that Jack wondered if he had imagined the touch of *ma-at*. He glanced around, then groaned when he saw Xerxes emerging from the trees. He had hoped that the previous night was the last he would ever see of that particular djinni, but Kaf's benevolent Solomon was up to more tricks of fate this morning.

Mistrock wasn't too happy either. Its rumbling grated with irritation.

At least this time the man wasn't undressing Leila with his eyes. He was staring at Jack, but he called out to both, "You are getting an early start?"

"Yes," answered Leila. "We have a ways to travel. You came to say good-bye?"

"I said I would." His eyes widened with innocence. "Why do you not simply transport?"

"Part of our pilgrimage experience," she explained glibly.

"Good-bye," Jack announced. He rested a hand on the back of the *hamad-el-halad* and prepared to mount behind Leila.

"I want you to stay," Xerxes said mildly. "Both of you. Join me at my tent."

Leila hesitated; Jack shook his head.

"Leila," entreated Xerxes. "I think I've found the bloodstone, but I need your help, both of you. You know how much I've wanted this, how important it is. For an old friend, can you not spare a morning?"

Leila slid off the *hamad-el-halad*, then went to Xerxes. "Jack, please. A short delay?"

"No," he said shortly, every protective instinct

clamoring a warning. He could not let Leila step into that lair. "No, we have to leave now."

"Does Leila not have a choice?" Xerxes asked, his hand resting on her hip.

"Not in this."

The wires at Jack's throat flared to life; electricity coursed through him. He tried to step forward, but the resistance felt like pushing together two norths on a magnet. What the hell? *Ma-at* shoved him back. The power inside him heated, allowing him to stand straight, but barely. Mistrock leaped from his shoulder, grating and scurrying to the bushes in fear.

This *ma-at* was stronger than any he'd ever felt. Mightier and more unpleasant. Where it penetrated his defenses, his blood chilled to sludge.

Nerves rioting with electric discharges, sweat breaking out, he faced his enemy. The djinni continued to persuade Leila, drawing her away with honeyed words and earnest entreaty, as amiable as though he hadn't a care in the world. Or hadn't just had a blow of *ma-at* forcibly rejected.

Jack ignored their conversation; he was too busy focusing. On the *ma-at* that curled around his ankles and fingers and throat. On the man who wielded the *ma-at* while looking as innocent as a child. On the crystal that glowed diamond white. On the forces gathering within him.

Bands of *ma-at* circled his throat and head. Trying to knock him out or trying to bend him to the wielder's will? He couldn't be sure. He fought back, concentrating the river of power wherever the *ma-at* touched him. Sweat ran into his eyes, and his vision blurred, but he didn't need sight to counter. Under the force of necessity he learned to repel a choking hold and reverse an arrhythmia.

Xerxes was unrelenting. The djinni didn't stop the pressure, gave no space for breath. His *ma-at* was sour and dark. It left a grimy feel, a bitter taste, a black veil. It was endless and unstoppable.

Jack could only meet and counter. Could only watch and wait and feel and react.

Did Xerxes tire as well? Despite his relaxed pace with Leila and his easy manner? A ribbon of hope slid into Jack. He spotted clues: sweat at the top of the djinni's brow, and his hand clutching harder at the tablet beneath his shirt.

Jack focused on the hope and, under the trial of fire, grew stronger. Power shifted, from the crystal to him. From external to a core inside him. For himself, for Leila, he had to endure. Not endure. Triumph.

The repelling force he commanded spread, from a point of contact to an aura. He shook with the effort. Pain shot up his side. His breath came in sharp pants. Muscles shifted to anaerobic fuel. Not much more strain possible.

Xerxes seemed to tremble. Yet his *ma-at* grew stronger and more forceful.

Could he last against his seasoned opponent?

Leila felt the touch of power, the power that stole *ma-at*. Twice she had experienced that wrenching force, and she recognized it now. It was aimed at Xerxes, not her, but she felt it raveling the edges of her new connections. She broke off her conversation with Xerxes to turn stunned eyes on the Scientist.

The crystal glowed as brilliant as she'd ever seen, so bright her eyes hurt to look at it. Instead she looked at Jack's eyes. They were hard, emotionless, locked on Xerxes.

Her throat burned with the betrayal. The Scientist was attacking her friend. Stealing his *ma-at*, spreading his power to steal hers again. Why? *Why?* Terror seized her. She felt long talons of horror at being powerless again, at bringing such a fate to a man who had been kind to her. Tears swelled in her eyes and overflowed down her cheeks.

"Do not, Scientist!"

He didn't listen.

"Cease. Please, stop," she begged, sobbing. "Why are you taking our *ma-at*?"

He did not stop. She felt the force spread around her, through her wrist, to Xerxes.

"Leila, what is he doing?" Xerxes sounded so weak. "Why does he attack me?"

Oh, by Solomon, why was Jack doing this? "Turn off your talisman!"

"Turn off?" Xerxes echoed, his face suddenly not so innocent as he glanced sharply at the gleaming crystal.

The Scientist did nothing, so intent was he on his quest.

Xerxes gave a strangled cry and staggered backward. "Leila! Help me!"

She had to do something. "Stop, Jack, or I will stop you."

Jack's gaze shot away from Xerxes. For one moment she looked at him, seeing his disbelief, his anger. Then she held out her hands and chanted the words she needed. The words that would separate him from her forever. Chanted the words to the Ritual of Telemotion.

Tears streamed down her face and blinded her. Her *ma-at*, directed not at him but at his talisman, found its mark. The switch turned off. The brilliant glow from the crystal faded.

The power no longer stole her *ma-at*.

His crystal was off. The field was broken. Alone, he had not the strength to resist.

Jack staggered backward under the force of the blow from Xerxes. The *ma-at* curled around his chest until he could no longer feel his hand for the fire whip touch, until it brought him to his knees in pain. Invisible, incandescent flames seared his skin.

But no pain was as devastating as the bitter flood of betrayal. Leila had used her *ma-at* against him. She had saved Xerxes and condemned him.

Bent over in pain, unable to breathe, he raised a disbelieving gaze to her. She was crying. God, even when she cried she was beautiful.

"I am sorry; I am so sorry, *janam*. I could not let you take his *ma-at*. Or mine."

"He attacked first," he croaked out.

"What?" Leila looked from one to the other, confusion stamped across her face.

"I do not lie, *janam*."

Xerxes wrapped a hand around her waist. She struggled against him, but he held her fast and lifted his hand.

"Xerxes, no!" Jack saw Leila grab Xerxes's arm, then heard her piercing scream.

She gave him the distraction he needed. The necessary second to snap on the lifeless crystal.

Mistrock growled a split-second warning.

Ma-at seared across Jack.

His reaction was immediate, swift, reflexive, powerful. Lightning shot through him, looped between man and crystal, between mind and instinct in a single explosive burst.

He blocked the ruthless, murderous blow of *ma-at*.

The force of the backfire slammed against him and he collapsed.

Xerxes and Leila disappeared, leaving only the *hamad-el-halad* placidly chomping grass. In their place, a figure materialized in front of Jack, a boy of about fifteen. He saw another figure. His sister? Then Darius?

The pain overwhelmed him, and he passed out.

Chapter Eighteen

Isis knelt beside her unconscious brother and clutched his hand. Why hadn't he woken up? They'd moved him to Zayne's tent and it must have hurt him, for his skin had turned bone white, but he'd remained unconscious. What had happened?

"Do something," she demanded of her *zani*, running a hand through her cropped black hair.

"I cannot," Darius answered, setting down a squirming Jessamine. The baby toddled over to Jared, who levitated nearby, and the young djinni picked her up.

"What do you mean, you cannot?" Isis demanded. "Can't you just fix what's wrong? Or zap him awake."

"Something in him resists the *ma-at*. I must wait until he wakes up. And I do not 'zap,' " he added with irritation.

"Then can you find me something for this nasty

burn? Soap and water and a bandage." A moment later she had what she needed.

When she opened Jack's shirt, she bit her lip against nausea. A line of red blisters ran from shoulder to waist, as though he'd been struck with a lash of fire. The strange necklace he wore was in the way, but when she tried to remove it, he tossed and moaned, so she left it in place.

Although she tried to be careful while she tended him, Jack's occasional unconscious flinch of pain told her that her efforts were clumsy. Isis sniffed back a tear. In her family of overachieving brothers, Jack was the cerebral one, the strong, neat, logical one. He wasn't supposed to be shaggy and pale, covered in sweat and unconscious with a burned chest. He could have wrapped the gauze without fumbling and causing pain. When she finished, she brushed his hair off his forehead, cringing at the jagged slash above his brows. Would he gain another scar to match the one on his cheek? "This isn't the way it's supposed to be," she whispered.

He wasn't supposed to be on Kaf.

"Maybe he's under a somnolence spell," suggested Jared. The young djinni stopped entertaining Jessamine and leaned forward. "I read about one once, although I don't know anyone who can do one. Can you, Protector? Is it true that such a spell can be drawn out for years?"

"I would know if *ma-at* worked against him." Darius threw Jared a disapproving glance.

"What if he doesn't wake up?" Isis swallowed hard.

"Your brother is too strong-willed to let this defeat him." Darius's answer was dry, but his hand on her shoulder offered comfort.

True. Jack could be infuriatingly tenacious and stubborn.

"I heard some people of Bak-ar-Legandermal talking," Jared said, still bouncing a bit on his perch. "They said there was an explosion and a vanishing. That the stranger commands a strange *ma-at*."

"He does," Zayne said quietly as he heated water over a small fire.

Isis made a disbelieving noise. "Jack? Do magic?"

"Everyone has innate strengths, Isis," said her *zani*. "Even humans. Strengths many do not tap."

Before she could answer, an odd grating noise from the mound of pillows caught her attention. "What's that?"

"I believe it is"—Darius fished around in the pillows, coming up with a small rock—"a *grucheek*."

"*Grucheek*," echoed Jessamine, delighted with the new word.

"What's a *grucheek*?" Isis asked.

"It has become attached to your brother," Zayne added.

"That thing's sentient?" she asked, staring. The rock's sides were moving, as though it breathed through gill-like fissures.

"Of course."

The creature slid down Darius's arm to Jack's shoulder. Isis thought she saw tiny claws attach it to a remnant of her brother's shirt. The rumbling and grating grew louder, but more content.

"Strange. *Grucheeks* are notoriously elusive and selective." Darius sounded thoroughly surprised at the rock's choice.

Suddenly Jack groaned and stirred on the mound of pillows. "He's coming around." Hope stirred as she stared down at her beloved, irritating, puzzling brother.

"Jared, go and investigate those rumors you heard. Take Jessamine with you; she's getting restless." Darius handed him the toddler and pointed to the tent exit. "Find out exactly what transpired. Who saw it. What led up to it."

"But I wanted to stay here and talk to him!"

"Your duty is to the *ma-at* and the people."

"And to do what you say," Jared muttered, lingering at the entrance to the tent and idly giving Jessamine a water-scented cloud to bat at.

"Yes," Darius answered with calm. "Now go."

Complaining under his breath, Jared disappeared from the tent, Jessamine in tow.

"I shall go with them," Zayne murmured, heading toward the door. "There is tea if you desire it."

"Thank you." Darius returned to Isis's side and again laid a warm hand on her shoulder. "Is he fully awake?"

"Not yet, but he's stirring." She looked up. "He's my brother, and he's hurt. Don't go badgering him with questions."

"I need to know what happened here. How your brother resists my *ma-at*. Why he lies injured. I be-

305

lieve, Isis, the answers are vital to the well-being of my people."

"You don't know that Jack is involved in anything." Darius gave her an incredulous look. "Okay, just give him a chance to recover."

"If I can."

Jack groaned again, and Isis spun back to watch him. His eyelids fluttered open, and he glanced around, the confusion in his eyes rapidly turning to comprehension.

Isis leaned over him. "Andrew Jackson Montgomery, what the hell are you doing on Kaf?"

"Hello to you, too, sis."

"Hello. Now, what is going on? What happened to you? Are you all right?"

"Leila?" he asked, struggling to sit upright amongst the pile of pillows. His pale face whitened with the effort, and he pressed his lips together, probably against nausea. The *grucheek* clutched and swayed with the motion.

Isis dropped her questions and braced Jack with an arm around his shoulders, helping him to sit upright. The *grucheek* sounded like a distant landslide next to her ear. Sweat dotted Jack's face from the effort of sitting. His breath came in slow pants, as though he still fought the nausea of pain. At last he exhaled cautiously.

"Leila," he repeated. "Where is she?"

Leila? What connection was there between her brother and that seductress?

"She's not here." Isis easily dismissed the woman.

Leila was not one of her favorite people.

"Then Xerxes did take her."

The anguish that ripped across him surprised Jack.

Shouldn't he be glad she wasn't here? Shouldn't he be bitter about her betrayal? She'd turned off his device and left him helpless under Xerxes's attack. Leila had made no secret of her affection for Xerxes. She was where she wanted to be.

She was gone, and it was better that way.

"And good riddance," muttered Isis.

Except it wasn't better. Her loss hurt, as bad as the burn across his chest.

He raked his hand through his hair. Why had she done it? As always, he needed to understand why.

The answer came with blinding clarity. Because Xerxes was her friend, or so she thought. Because Jack had taken her *ma-at* and had made no secret of his distaste for the power. Hell, she hadn't betrayed him; she'd been loyal to a friend.

None of that mattered, he realized. It didn't matter whether she still thought Xerxes was a friend or whether she still thought Jack was a heartless bastard. It didn't matter whether she had betrayed him, been loyal to a friend, or, in the end, tried to help him against Xerxes.

What mattered was that Xerxes had taken her. The djinni was unstable and dangerous, and would not hesitate to hurt Leila to get whatever it was he wanted.

Jack knew he had to rescue the woman he loved as quickly as possible. He tried to push to his feet. "I have to find her."

With both hands on his shoulders, Isis pushed him back down. It was a measure of how injured he was that she succeeded. She laid a hand on his cheek. "Jack, you shouldn't go anywhere until that burn heals."

He gripped her fingers. "I can manage."

"For someone so smart, sometimes you can be so dense. You can't even move without a hell of a lot of pain."

"I have to find Leila. I don't care what she did."

"Add delirium to your list of injuries."

"Let us share some tea." Darius interrupted their burgeoning argument. "And sustenance for strength." He snapped his fingers and a table appeared. On it were plates of bread triangles spread with bean paste, melon slices, cucumber rounds, and cinnamon shortbread. "And answers for understanding."

Kaf must have unhinged Jack, Isis decided. He was logical in the extreme, but today he seemed to be operating on sheer emotion and adrenaline. Sort of like her. She handed her brother a bread slice. "Wherever you think you need to be, it can't be so important that you can't get well first."

"It is that important," he said quietly, although he collapsed back on the pillows, pain contorting his face.

"Why?"

He ate the bread in a single gulp, and Isis handed him another. "Because Xerxes has Leila."

Well, that cleared things up. "Who is this Xerxes?"

"He is a djinni you will never meet, my sweet," Darius answered.

308

"You know about him?" Jack asked.

"Recently I have questioned what forces he has made part of his studies."

"Some nasty ones." Jack grimaced and rubbed the gash on his forehead. The rock on his shoulder gave an angry-sounding chirp. He gave it a soothing pat before choosing a melon slice and proceeding to eat steadily, as though he knew he needed to garner strength. Isis poured him a cup of tea.

"So, why is it important that he has Leila?" she demanded. She could not face the thought that her brother might have been hurt because of that woman. "How do you know her?"

He looked at her, steady and determined. "Because if I can get her back, I'm going to ask her to marry me."

Isis felt her jaw drop. There was no clouding of his eyes, no confusion in his voice. He meant it!

She shook her head. "Oh, no, Jack. Don't. Don't even think that. I don't like the woman. I don't trust her. She tried to take my husband from me."

"Once I saw you, my love, she knew there could be no other for me," Darius interjected mildly.

"The hell she did," Isis muttered back. "She flirted with you. She . . ." She broke off and turned to Jack. "She must have enchanted you. A spell or something."

"It's no spell. Leila has had no *ma-at* while I've known her."

That surprised her, and she noticed Darius lean forward in interest. But surprise silenced her for only a second. "Then what happens when she gets her *ma-at* back?"

"He is immune," answered Darius.

"You stay out of this," she snapped. "Jack, Leila is tricky and devious. She—"

"Not the woman I know."

"How long have you known her?"

"Four days."

"Four days!" she screeched.

"If you get to know her—"

"No way. Never!"

Jack's face hardened. Isis had seen her brother when he was annoyed by her, when he was confused by her, when he was teasing her, but she had never seen this cold anger directed toward her. "I love her, Isis."

Isis let go of his arm, stunned.

"I don't know that we can survive Xerxes," he continued, "or that we can work things out, but if she becomes my wife, you will either accept her or you will not be welcome at our house."

Isis stumbled back, shaking her head. "You would pick *her* over your family? A woman you barely know?"

"Yes. Just as you chose Darius over all our objections."

She stared at him, unable to believe this was Jack. Had Beau, his twin, slipped in here to play a practical joke? No; even though the twins were identical, she had always been able to tell them apart. This was Jack. Practical, think-things-through Jack proposing to marry a woman he'd known for only four days. And a djinni at that!

Darius cupped the back of her neck, his finger rubbing against her hairline, an action that always mellowed her and replaced anger with desire. She gritted her teeth. Not this time.

She would not appreciate me telling you this, for Leila has her pride, but there are reasons she has acted the way she does. Darius's voice sounded in her thoughts. *Reasons you might even sympathize with.*

Isis shook her head. She refused to entertain the idea that she might have something in common with that woman.

Can you not imagine what it would be like to be born here and discover you have very little power to command?

Isis gave him a startled glance.

Would it not be like being unable to read and do sums in your world?

Damn him. He had found the one thing she couldn't ignore, the one thing guaranteed to touch a chord of sympathy. She'd struggled all her life with dyslexia, embarrassed by her lack of scholarship in a family of overachievers. Had Leila felt that way, too? So much of life on Kaf revolved around *ma-at*, as much as reading commanded center stage on Earth.

She glanced back at Jack. Determined, intent, he waited for her answer. He might have no people skills, but he didn't tolerate meanness or spitefulness in others. If he had found someone to love in Leila, then there must be something more to the woman than she had imagined. For Jack's sake, for her own sake because she could not tolerate estrangement from him, she would try to find out what it was.

Isis fisted her hands on her hips and stabbed him with a fierce look. "Before she and I have this little buddy-buddy heart-to-heart, we have to get her back. Right? So who is this Xerxes, and what the hell do you mean by 'if we survive'?"

Jack winced, sorry that he'd let that part slip in front of her. He'd hoped she had not heard or had forgotten, but no such luck. He took a gulp of his tea and forced another bite of food down his throat, knowing he needed to regain strength before he faced Xerxes.

At least Isis was willing to mend fences. Family was important. An estrangement from his sister was something he would have given almost anything to avoid. Anything but Leila.

A sudden whoosh sounded in the tent and the door blew open, then closed. A tornado of light spun inside, and pain shot across his chest. He couldn't bite back an involuntary moan. The streaking light careened around the inside perimeter of the tent before coagulating in a far corner. Letters. The light formed into letters, then imploded.

"It seems," Darius said, "you have a message."

Xerxes. Immersed in pain and nausea, Jack squinted at the lettering in the air. The message was a dull black, reflecting no light. He struggled to read the lines, to assemble their meaning. The letters were straight-angled cuneiform, with no flourishes to soften them, or their content. His heart thudded horribly, and he prayed he'd misread.

"What does it say?" he asked Darius.

"Come now and alone or she suffers."

Jack clenched his fists, welcoming the wave of pain that engulfed him. It kept him alert. Kept him focused on what he had to do. The gravity of Darius's voice was no match for the weight inside him. He'd had a taste of Xerxes's torments, and the thought of Leila with that monster brought a rush of bile to his throat.

"Then I'll go alone."

Isis gasped. "What? This guy sounds bad, Jack. Look what's happened already."

"I'm going," he repeated. "Will you go and collect some supplies for me?"

Isis refused to move, glaring at him. Then her eyes relaxed, and she glanced at Darius. Apparently, he had said something to her thoughts, for she nodded.

"Supplies. Fine. I'll give the two of you exactly fifteen minutes." She pointed to Darius. "And I expect you to talk him out of this idiocy."

"What did you say to her?" Jack asked after she'd gone.

"That you would probably speak more freely with her gone. And I would tell her all later."

"Will you?"

"I keep few secrets from Isis."

Which meant he'd tell her exactly what he decided she should know. Knowing Isis, though, Jack thought with a spurt of amusement, she'd piece together the entire story in no time.

"Why does he want you?" Darius asked quietly.

Jack remembered Zayne's advice to speak with Darius and decided it was a good idea. He dangled the chain and crystal over his fingers. "I think it has to do with this . . . talisman."

Darius touched the wires, and Jack felt the surge of energy. The djinni jerked back as though shocked, and he raised a questioning brow.

"It's a device I made. Designed to negate the effects of *ma-at*."

"So that is why I could not heal you while you slept?"

Jack nodded. "Tell me about Xerxes. So I know what to expect."

"I do not know as much about him as I should." Darius outlined Xerxes's slow start, his craving for power, his rapid advancement by sheer determination; then Jack explained how the fight had erupted. "He has grown strong, far stronger than I realized, and has touched forces best left untapped. I have felt their workings, but until today I could not be sure it was he who called on them. He has hidden his activities well."

"If he's into power, he'll be threatened by anything that negates that power," Jack mused. "He'll want to control it."

"Or destroy it." Darius studied the wires.

Before Darius could ask another question, Jared bounced into the tent with rapid gestures and even more rapid speech.

"English," Darius commanded. "So Jack may understand more easily."

Jared broke off and grinned. "Cool! You never let

me speak English. Here's your supplies." He tossed a leather pouch toward Darius, who deftly caught it in one hand. "There's a clean shirt, bread, and cheese in there. Would you believe someone actually had a map? Isis sent it back with me. Zayne was singing and Jessamine was listening, so I asked if I could bring it and she agreed."

Jared dropped onto a pile of pillows and turned excited eyes toward Jack. "Rumors in town are that you stopped Xerxes from destroying the *grucheek*; that you are a human wizard come to either destroy or to steal our *ma-at*; or that you're angry because Xerxes and Leila went off together. Which rumor is true?"

"None," he answered. "He attacked me; I repelled him."

"How? Did you use a Breaker Demonic?"

Jack explained: about the way the power was attuned to him, about learning to direct it, about the effect his emotions had in exploding it outward.

"You've awakened the power within," Darius commented. "It is as much a part of you now as *ma-at* is to me. Do you no longer require the talisman to focus it?"

Jack shook his head. "Alone, I'm powerless."

"Are you?" Darius murmured, eyeing the device. "You should stay here and heal. This is a djinn matter for the Protector's attention. Leave Xerxes to me."

"Do you care what happens to Leila?" Jack demanded.

"Of course I care," snapped Darius.

"You heard what he said, and you know I have to

go alone." Mistrock butted up against his ear with a demanding growl. "Well, almost alone." Awkwardly, Jack stood, swaying slightly as he conquered his dizziness. "Test me."

"Oh?" Darius lifted a brow in challenge.

A second later Jack felt the touch of *ma-at* at his feet, grounding him in an effort to keep him from moving. Calmly he turned it away, and the sensation disappeared, no longer affecting him. Another touch, another repulsion. He felt the power flow as the crystal worked, felt the vitalizing energy fill him. The game of feint and counter continued, a test of the mind, until suddenly . . .

Wham! His feet were encased in ice, unable to move as the ice spread to his knees. Blindsided. Jack cursed. Damn, he hated that *ma-at*. The crystal flared with his emotion, and the encasing ice melted away. He stepped forward.

Darius started at the severing of his *ma-at*; then his eyes narrowed. "You are a dangerous man, Jack Montgomery."

Isis rejoined them. "Zayne is playing with Jessamine . . ." She broke off, eyeing them both. "You didn't talk him out of it, Darius?"

"Your brother is annoyingly stubborn."

"Sort of like someone else I know."

Darius looked back at him. "If you fail, think of what Xerxes can do with that power."

"True, but I don't plan on giving it to him."

Darius fingered the turquoise tablet at his neck. "Ah, I see. You will give the talisman to Leila?"

He nodded. "She can come back here and get help."

"You love her, so you're going to go there and sacrifice yourself to save her? And she's going to act all cool and logical and leave you there?" Isis grabbed his wrist and tugged him to face her. "Come up with another plan, Jack."

"There's more." He took a deep breath. He had never sought *ma-at*, never wanted it, but to save Leila he would do anything. "Darius, is there a spell or incantation or something that could protect me while Leila wears the talisman?"

Darius stared at him, then shook his head. "There is none—"

"Why don't you try the curse of Abregaza?" interrupted Jared.

"The what?" asked Jack.

Darius flushed. " 'Tis not a curse, 'tis an ancient charm, Apprentice."

"I've heard you mutter 'that cursed Abregaza' often enough."

"What is it?" Jack demanded.

Isis scratched her cheek, a faint smile crossing her lips. "It's this little innate talent I've got, Jack. What you've been trying to do with your crystal thingy. Any *ma-at* I don't like doesn't work on me."

"What?" He turned to Darius. "Is this true?"

"Yes," muttered the djinni with annoyance.

"Why don't I have it?"

"Because it came to me from the line of my mother," answered Isis.

And Isis was his half-sister—same father, different

317

mothers. So he had not inherited her family gift.

"The charm that Abregaza used to gift her descendants with immunity has been lost to the ages," Darius said.

Jared studied his fingernails. "Ah, not really. I asked Isis about it once, after I'd heard you, um, complaining, and she explained it all to me. So I went looking. Here and on Terra, when I got a chance. I think I've found it. Wait, I'll get it." He disappeared in a whirlwind of transport, then a moment later reappeared with a parchment in his hand.

Jack held his breath as Darius read it over. At last he set it down and shook his head. "It is the charm of Abregaza, but I cannot do this. It is a Terran ritual. *Ma-at* will not call the proper forces."

Silence followed his announcement, and Jack clenched his jaw in frustration. If he had to sacrifice himself for Leila, he would; if he had to submit to Xerxes, he would; but he wasn't ready to give up. There had to be another way.

"What about Simon?" asked Isis. "He's of Earth now."

Jack remembered being told about Simon, the only djinni to create bonds to Terra.

"Yes, it might be possible. I shall ask him." A moment later Darius disappeared into that whirlwind vortex.

Asking Simon took longer than finding the parchment. Jack, Isis, and Jared waited in silence. Isis held her brother's hand, while Jack went over his plan in his mind. If this spell of Abregaza worked, he'd have to conceal the protection until he could get the talisman to Leila. Otherwise, Xerxes would turn on Leila in retribution while she was still vulnerable.

At last Darius returned with another man at his side. This was Simon? Jack stared in astonishment. Simon—dressed in jeans and a Sierra Club T-shirt—was taller and more broad-shouldered than Darius, but he had the dark eyes, black hair, and sleek, easy motion of a djinni. He was also Simon James, a noted woodworker in New Orleans. His prized furniture graced many mansions of the city.

"I know you," Jack blurted out. "I bought a rocker for my Aunt Tildy from you."

"I remember. My wife, Zoe, speaks well of you."

Jack ran a hand through his hair. "She consulted on a computer project at Tulane that I was in charge of."

"She said you were a gentleman and a pleasure to work with." Jack got the distinct impression that if Zoe had disapproved of him, Simon would not be here now.

"You're a djinni?"

"Yes. Now, where is the charm of Abregaza?"

While Simon read through it, Jack tried to wrap his mind around the idea that a man he had known for over a year was a djinni. There was more to this magic than he realized.

At last Simon returned the parchment to Darius, who snapped his fingers. The parchment disappeared.

"Hey, that's mine!" Jared protested.

"We will discuss *that* matter later. Can you do the ritual, my friend?" asked Darius.

319

"That depends upon Jack." Simon sat cross-legged on the pillows beside Jack. The djinni's steady gaze took his measure. "For this to work, you must desire the protection. You cannot have doubts; this is not something I can force upon you despite your reservations or resistance. If you cannot accept this, it could be dangerous for us both."

"I have trouble with *ma-at*."

"So I gathered." He waited.

This was the only way to save Leila. For her sake, Jack had no choice. He took a deep breath, then removed the chain from around his neck and turned it off. "All right. Let's do it."

"I will withdraw if any resistance persists."

"Understood."

Simon waved his hand, and a myriad of candles, all blue and green, sprang up in a circle around them, the wicks lit with a white-blue flame.

Jared handed him a small vial of oil. "You'll need this. And this." He handed Simon a leather satchel, then stepped out of the circle, as did Darius and Isis.

"Thank you." Simon sprinkled the oil on the fire, and the room filled with the scent of a sea breeze. He dipped his hand into the satchel and came out with a handful of sparkling sand. This he sprinkled around them, just inside the ring of candles.

"To the ages we begin." He laid one hand on Jack's heart, the other hand on his temple. The pressure was so light, Jack could barely feel it, but coolness stole across him. A cool breeze stoked by magic.

"Do so bring to this man of Terra sweet water and pure earth," Simon intoned.

The chill spread, seeping deeper inside Jack. He felt a power from outside, seeking a place to settle and call its own.

"Water and earth ascendant. Water and earth conjunction. Water and earth free."

Magic flowed through Jack, bubbling like a stream over rock. It thickened, took on substance, spread. Instincts arose: the instinct to resist this invader, the instinct of self-preservation sharpened by the past days, the instinct of fear carved by past years. They welled inside him as they had when Zayne had tried to give him the language. He felt an urge to fight back.

Simon gave him a sharp look. "Do you resist?"

"No, I do not." He turned inward. Breathe in. Slowly. Breathe out. Slowly.

"Accept or deny, the choice is thine. Accept or deny, for a step is a journey."

The magic continued, relentless, unceasing as the ocean tide, unstoppable as an avalanche. He could see nothing, hear nothing. Blackness overcame him, the blackness that once more contained terror. His cheek burned, blood dripped to his neck. The man stood above him, knife ready.

"Do you accept?"

The voice was hard, demanding. Simon? The kidnapper?

"Do you accept willingly?"

The five-year-old inside screamed in denial.

He was no longer five, no longer had to bow to his own nightmares.

For Leila—this was for Leila. He called her face to mind, remembered her throaty laugh. Don't resist. Leila. Indomitable spirit. Allow the magic. No, don't stop it. He fought years of training, years of logic, which denied the power of magic. Let the cool water and the solid sand work. Leila. Beautiful eyes alight with curiosity; the dark held no terror. He thrust back the darkness and the screams, relegated his nightmare to the past. Leila had replaced fear with desire.

Sweat dripped into his eyes, his muscles ached for release. He fought the battle with love.

"Earth and water to meet. Water end fire or earth doth fuel it. Earth smother air or water doth raise it."

To accept the magic, he must accept the *ma-at*. *Ma-at* held no terror for him. Leila had replaced it with understanding. He drew in long, slow breaths, forcing his mind and his power to his bidding.

"Do you accept now willingly?" Simon asked again.

Magic stopped; the water was dammed for the instant of decision.

"I accept," Jack answered, letting down all barriers, all resistance, letting in love.

The magic resumed its flow. It filled him, every sinew, every axon, every cell, mitochondrion and nucleus. Filled him with the power of choice. Filled his unresisting soul.

"By the will of Abregaza, this spell is complete."

Jack slumped on the pillows as the pressure of

Simon's hands was removed. Slowly he opened his eyes to find them all staring at him.

"Thank you." He inclined his head toward Simon. "I am in your debt." Then he got to his feet, surprised that he wasn't more tired.

Darius laid a hand on his shoulder. "I will give you until sunrise; then I will do what I must."

"Agreed."

"Then Solomon bless your journey and your courage and bring you and your love back to us."

Jack bowed, slipped the talisman over his head, picked up his supplies, kissed his sister, and left.

Chapter Nineteen

The garden contained a sample of every plant on Kaf. Or so Xerxes claimed, and Leila was inclined to believe him, in this at least. She wandered the sinuous paths, forcing the appearance of calm pleasure as she examined the multitude of specimens.

She knew not why Xerxes kept her, but he did, and she was not strong enough to fight his power. He was not weak, as she had thought, but held a might nearly as strong as the Protector's. When she had tried to leave, the forces around his house prevented her from either transporting or walking beyond the confines of his grounds. The more she had tried, the stronger and more painful the opposition had become. Now her single, faint hope of release was to convince him she was of little consequence, harbored no ill will, and could bring him no harm.

She had to convince him she was the woman she had been before she'd met Jack.

Jack. She pressed her lips together, fighting the agony of loss. For an aching moment she closed her eyes, fists clenched, until she could once more assume her role. At last she let out her pent-up breath and continued her walk.

Worry—over Jack and over what Xerxes planned—gnawed at her, but she let none of it show on her face. Instead she examined the gardens. She saw all that was in her plot at home, and much she did not recognize. Some of the plants were set in carefully manicured beds, some seemed to grow wild. All were well cared for and arranged with an eye for harmony and beauty.

In another time, another place, another person's garden, she would have delighted in recognizing her favorites and learning about the strangers. However, she could not rid herself of the notion that Xerxes surrounded himself with this profusion of beauty to make up for the ugliness in his soul. That he lived surrounded by harmony to silence the clamor of sinister voices in his mind.

She sat on a bench placed within a tangle of blooming gardenias. Their sweet scent perfumed the air, and she felt her eyelids droop, her body grow soft and warm. The scent curled around her nostrils, inviting her to sprawl on the cushions and to take a lover in the bower. So vivid was the image, she could almost feel a man's cheek caressing her breast, a man's lips touching hers in a gentle kiss.

Her insides knotted in resistance and denial. The cheek was too smooth and the lips too cold. She wanted only one man, and he had bristled cheeks and incredible warmth.

Abruptly she stood and strolled away, feigning a casualness she could not feel. Her ruby robe swirled about her feet, and she snugged the tie at her waist, lessening the V at her neck. She would issue no invitation. For she knew Xerxes watched her, knew he had designed the bower to lull and seduce her.

Once, many cycles ago, she would have been thrilled. Now the thought nauseated her, for she saw him through eyes no longer dazzled by his *ma-at* or his charm. Beneath both she saw the need for superiority, for power and control. It was a need she recognized because she, too, had longed to rise above her weakness. His ambition, and his success, however, had taken him on a different path.

She paused and rubbed a hand against the rough bark of a juniper, releasing a small amount of resin. Holding her hand to her nose, she sniffed the fir scent, banishing the last lingering remnant of gardenia. This was a clean scent, an honest scent.

Two men. Each claimed that the other had attacked him. Only one could speak the truth, and in the end, she had had no doubt that man was Jack Montgomery. She had seen through Xerxes at last, but too late.

The damage had been done. She had betrayed Jack and used her *ma-at* against him, the one thing he'd asked her not to do.

She struggled to keep her face calm and placid despite the grief swelling in her throat, despite the roil of anger at her stupidity and the devastating hollowness of lost hope. What she had done, she had thought was right at the moment. She had thought to help a friend, to save him from the loss of *ma-at* that had so devastated her.

Good intentions, but her action was one Jack could never forgive. She had left him vulnerable to a dangerous man.

Her one consolation was that Xerxes had been unable to destroy Jack. Her hope was that Jack would leave Kaf, get far away from Xerxes, and forget the whole episode. She wanted him safe and well and happy. For her love would be with him always, wherever he was, even if he loved her not.

A rush of air stirred the strands of her hair and the fabric of her robe. Xerxes had materialized behind her, his scent of frankincense as clear a herald as his voice.

Before she turned to face him, she took a moment to compose her appearance. She took a deep breath, ready for her performance, and then turned and smiled at him. "Xerxes."

"Are you enjoying my garden, my enchantress?" He delicately smoothed a strand of her hair down her chest, but she could feel no warmth from his hand.

"Oh, yes, very much." She shifted away. "What is that one? I have never seen it."

"It comes from the far side of the Tower Lands. I named it sun blossom. Do not touch it," he added mildly as she reached toward the beckoning yellow bloom, "for its brilliant flare will blind you for days."

Leila jerked her hand back. "Thank you for the warning."

He wrapped a hand around her waist. "I would not have you hurt, Leila. It would be a shame to mar such beauty."

She fought back a shudder at the threat hidden in the solicitous words and melodious voice. Her body pressed against the rock of his arm, which kept her close to his side.

"Do I make you nervous?" he asked.

"A little," she admitted. "You were a youth when I last knew you well. Now you are a man, and a changed one."

"A changed one? How?"

"Confidence. Power. Beauty. All radiate from you."

"And do you like those qualities in a man?"

"Yes, I do." However, her definition of beauty now included sun-kissed hair and strong working hands. Her admiration was for a man with the confidence and power to also be kind and gentle.

"So why did you try to leave?" he asked. "Is my hospitality so lacking?"

"Of course not! You are most generous, and all this is so beautiful. But I have been gone for several days; I had things I needed to do. My garden needs tending."

By Solomon, what a feeble excuse, but she could think of nothing else in the pressure of the moment.

"It was not necessary to steal away."

She flushed and covered it with a pretty smile. "I

had thought to return before you discovered my absence. But why could I not go?"

His fingers played with the sash at her waist. " 'Twas for your own protection."

"My protection?" They had reached the edge of the garden, and she swung to face him, sliding out of his embrace and away from his touch.

Xerxes smiled and clasped her hand with his. He lifted it and kissed the underside of her wrist, right at the point where her blood beat. "Your companion, your Scientist. He is a dangerous man. I fear he will seek you out again." He kissed her wrist again and then the center of her palm.

She swallowed against a tide of nausea at his touch. He thought Jack would come after her. And when the Scientist did not? "Ah, I am in no danger. He cares not about me; he will not chase after me."

Xerxes laid his smooth, cool cheek in her palm, holding her hand so it cradled him. "My enchanting Leila, I think you underestimate your charm and desirability."

Then he laced his fingers through hers and lowered their joined hands, bringing her once more in contact with his muscled body. "But while we wait, until I am sure you are safe, we must have a way to pass the time. I have something in mind."

There was desire in his eye, the brightness of excitement in his smile. Oh, by Solomon's benevolence, she did not know if she could do this. She had once thought she could do anything to survive, but to accept the invitation he extended? Her stomach burned at the mere thought.

She saw the edges of his lips curl into a smile. *He knows*, she thought. *Knows of my feelings toward Jack, and he does not care*. If anything, the challenge excited him.

"What?" she asked, outwardly still playing the game.

He leaned forward, his body flush against hers, his lips but a breath away. "Something you always wanted," he whispered. The tip of his tongue licked the lobe of her ear; then he nipped it with his teeth. "Something you longed for all your life."

She wanted to run, to vomit, but she was held motionless. His *ma-at* wove around her, as soft as a cobweb, as unbreakable as the threads of a diamond robe. He pressed closer for a moment, stirring against her, then pulled away. "Ah, but your enchantments divert me from my purpose. Let me show you."

The whirlwind of transport spun around her, and a moment later she found herself standing outside on a rock ledge high in Xerxes's abode. She stood in a circle of stones; behind her was a bedroom carved out of the mountain. Xerxes's bedroom, she guessed from the spaciousness and the sheer decadence of it.

"You cannot do this clothed," he whispered. A moment later her robe disappeared, and she stood beside him naked. Still he held her hand with his, still he held her captive with his spell, but she would not grovel or plead. If she could not fight, if she had no choice but

330

to endure this *rape*, then she would endure with her pride.

"I do not go to you willingly," she told him.

"You will. And do not worry about losing your favorite robe. Soon it will be replaced by one finer and more suited to your beauty." He waved his free hand, and his sandals and robes disappeared, leaving him dressed in loose white pants and a shirt as thin and soft as a fern. "This, Leila, is power."

"What do you want?" she demanded.

"To give you something."

"How can I enthusiastically receive anything when you bind me with this stasis spell? Release me."

"Not until we begin. I fear I detect a measure of suspicion in you. My spell will melt under your entrancement." He waved a hand, and a blue fire blazed in the circle of stones surrounding her.

A divination fire?

"What?" She gave him a puzzled look, feeling the clutch of fear.

He moved closer, pressing his body against hers. Smooth skin to smooth skin, and still she could not move away. His sex hardened against her thigh. He cupped his hand around the back of her head, then leaned forward and kissed her mouth. A hard, sensual, sucking kiss that drained vitality and will.

A glass appeared in his hand. It held two liquids, the right one fire red, the left one clear. Two liquids met but did not mix in the glass. "Drink this," he commanded and held it to her lips.

No, no, no! Her mind screamed against the invasion.

Her heart pumped the blood to fight, her nerves readied the muscles to flee or to resist. But her body refused the call. Only her lips moved, drawing in the liquid against her will.

Salty. The glass tasted salty. The liquids had no taste, however, only temperature. The red was so hot it burned her tongue, the clear so cool it freshened like a night wind. Fire and air, the souls of Kaf.

Confusion and fear shifted. Could she have been so wrong about Xerxes? This was not the sexual attack she had anticipated. This was not the sinister force she had feared. This was the power of Kaf. She drank now of her own will, eagerly gulping the sustenance of her soul. Drank until the glass was empty.

Abruptly he released her, and she blinked, startled at the sudden shift.

"Go," he said. "Go to the divination fire."

"What?" She could move now? She took an experimental step. Not toward the exit but toward the beckoning fire.

"Put your hands in the fire," he said.

"I cannot—"

"You can. It will not burn."

"I do not understand." Yet, even as she protested, she knelt at the fire. Something in it drew her, something sweet and compelling. Hope.

"Your gift, enchanting Leila." He had moved to the opposite side of the fire, and now he smiled at her. Alluring and strong. The friend she had once known. "Power."

Power. The word sang inside her, beckoning with

irresistible sweetness. To no longer be the weak one? To no longer scramble for what she needed? She gave Xerxes a startled glance.

"Yes, it's true," he answered her silent question. "Now the power must be sealed with the fires of divination."

Dazed, Leila held out her hands to the fire. Though the flames blazed with a great heat, her skin did not char. She felt her bonds to Kaf deepen and widen until she was carried on the wind and shared in the ageless flow of lava. Never in her life had she felt the *ma-at* of Kaf so intimately. This was not the sinister force she had feared when Xerxes first foisted his potion upon her, but the true *ma-at*, the heart of Kaf.

Slowly she pulled back into herself, and the bonds to Kaf still flowed strong. She stared into the divination fire, and it flared up. Reflected within it, she saw her own face with a single tear, diamond bright, trickling down her cheek. Behind her was Jack, his face slowly fading as the glow about her grew stronger.

Leila swallowed hard against the reflected sadness, feeling again the hollow ache of loss. Jack was lost to her. Hard as it was, painful as it was, she had to accept that truth. She had known it all along, but knowing did not make the heart any less sorrowful. One question remained. Did she carry the child of their union?

She pressed her lips together, and then her body began to tremble as a second tear slid down the face in the fire. A second tear, a second loss. The glow about the reflected face flared, as bright as the midday sun on Kaf, and the vision of Jack disappeared behind it. With her newfound awareness, she knew at once what it told her.

She did not carry the child she craved. She would not have even that connection to her love. Abruptly she pulled back her hands and squeezed her eyes shut. She didn't want to see any more, to know of any more losses. Her chest heaved as she drew in a shuddering breath, even as her throat tightened around the sorrow. Grief racked her; every part of her ached with emptiness. Jack gone. Love gone. Her hopes of a child destroyed. All gone.

All she had left was Kaf and her strengthened *ma-at*, and at this moment it seemed a cold consolation.

She opened her eyes and discovered that Xerxes had shifted to her side and the fire had settled to bright coals. Her body shook with fatigue, and her head throbbed with unvoiced sobs. Yet, beneath it, in a bittersweet harmony as poignant as the melody of the *Kaliamahru*, was her renewed *ma-at*.

She needed time: to grieve, to ponder, to absorb both learned sorrow and achieved joy. However, not even this small boon was she granted. Xerxes put an arm around her, and instinctively she recoiled from his touch.

"Please. My skin is too sensitive."

"It will fade soon."

Why did she flinch, when it was he who had given her her first heart's desire? She should be grateful, but instead she was more wary than ever. Why? What did he want? For she did not doubt there would be a cost. There was always a cost.

"Try out your *ma-at*," he urged. "What could you never do before?"

She shivered slightly as she watched·his gaze shift from her face to her body, as he examined her too intimately. "A diamond-thread robe," she suggested, wanting only to clothe herself. But Xerxes would expect her to seek some luxury.

"I doubt you are strong enough to create one. You'll have to transform." He shrugged off his linen shirt and handed it to her. "Try this."

Leila held the shirt with two fingers, not liking the faint scent of incense and man it held. Yet she dared not protest, for Xerxes would wonder why.

For a moment, she could not think of the needed words, then suddenly they came to her in a rush. Hesitantly she chanted the spell, growing more confident as the *ma-at* flowed through her, more swift and more powerful than she had ever felt it before. The fabric beneath her hands shifted, from green linen to brilliant silver. The transformation spread, slowly to be sure, but as smooth and inevitable as sunrise.

She was doing it! She stared at the transforming cloth, still chanting, the flow of power new and strange and exciting. Oh, it felt so good. No longer would she struggle to provide. No longer must she manipulate to hide her powerlessness. Eagerly she donned the garment, reveling in the soft feel of the gossamer fabric and the way the diamond threads caught the sunlight and sparkled about her. Joy and excitement topped grief and fear.

"You did it!" Xerxes clapped his hands. "The fit

must be a little tighter, with a scoop at the neck . . ." He made a small motion, and the fabric shifted, cinching at the waist, growing snug at the hips, smoothing at the neck, until the fit was as sleek and perfect as anything she'd ever worn. With effortless ease he snapped his fingers, and the linen of his pants changed to a soft, woven gold. "Now we match in brilliance," he said gaily.

She gave him the expected smile, but his actions tempered her pleasure in her newfound gifts. For the message was not lost on her. She might have more power, but she still was no match for him. It was a message she would do well to remember.

He touched the corner of her lips. "I like to see you smile again, Leila. What did you see in the divination fire that upset you so?"

"Loss."

He nodded. "You feared the loss of your newly acquired *ma-at*."

She didn't correct his assumption. Though loss of *ma-at* was not what had been revealed, it was a fear nonetheless.

"Do not worry, my enchantress. The power is yours. I cannot take back my gift, even if I should want to. No one on Kaf can."

Her blood chilled. No one on Kaf can. But she knew one person who could.

Jack Montgomery.

Xerxes's touch shifted to her cheek; then he stroked her neck, the caress intimate. "Stay with me, Leila. I can show you so much more than this taste of power.

I can give you more, make you one of the strongest women on Kaf."

He was offering much, but his generosity came with a price. A price she was not willing to pay. She could be with no other man but Jack.

Especially not one who had touched the darker forces.

"Why are you willing to do this?" she asked, shifting away from his touch, stalling as she sought the best way to extricate herself.

"Because you are so very beautiful, my enchantress."

"So this is to be the price I would pay for your gift?"

He frowned. "Do I ask so much in return for more? Your beauty. Your presence. Your warmth."

She understood that he wanted a beautiful, adoring shadow. Jack had cared about her mind and her accomplishments and her feet. Even in the unlikely event that Xerxes was willing to have her stay without intimacy, she could not agree. Giving in to Xerxes would be a betrayal of the man she loved and of the woman she had become. Xerxes, she feared, would suck the very heat from her soul.

She had lost Jack; she had lost hope of a child. The only thing she had left was herself, and that she would not lose. She wanted to be done with delay and prevaricating. Best to tell him directly and let the consequences begin.

"Xerxes," she began, shaking her head. "I cannot—"

Abruptly he tensed, not listening to her. "Hush." He released her and turned away.

She waited, breathless.

A moment later he turned back to her with a cold smile of triumph. "He walks through my defenses as easily as a finger through honey, but they fold behind him stronger than ever."

Leila froze. No, it could not be. "He?"

Xerxes's smile widened, grew even more satisfied. "I told you that you underestimated your charms, my dear Leila. Your Scientist has come for you."

Stunned, she staggered backward, bracing herself against the cedar tree on the rim of the ledge. The scent of fir resin wafted around her as her grip broke through the bark. "You are mistaken."

Xerxes's face hardened. "I do not make mistakes."

"Then he has come for you, not for me."

Xerxes smiled again and clasped her wrist. "Has he? Make your choice right now, Leila, before you know his intent. Stay with me. What I gave today is but a small taste of the immense power you can enjoy with me. Can you not feel it? That beautiful bond to Kaf. Do you not want more? Share my home, my body, our years of friendship and understanding, all the gifts I can offer." For a brief second he allowed her to see and feel the sweet song of power, the racing energy and the deep connection, and then all faded, leaving in their wake a longing for their return.

"And my other choice?"

"Leave. Alone, if the Scientist shuns you. With a powerless man if he does not. But let me warn you, Leila. If you leave, what you have now is all the power you will ever touch. But you have seen the possibilities. You will always have an emptiness inside, an unfulfilled craving for what you have abandoned. Leave, and you will always regret your choice."

Leila lifted her chin and shook her head. "No, Xerxes. For our past friendship, I would not see you hurt, but I would always regret the decision to stay. My path is different. At last I have accepted what *ma-at* can and cannot give me, and I have learned other ways. My choice is to leave."

She spoke confidently although she knew he would never allow her to leave and had no intention of releasing Jack.

He was silent a moment, his lips pressed tightly together; then he shrugged. "You have made your choice." A searching look was followed by a cruel smile. "I do not think I would have believed you, or trusted you, even if you had decided to stay. Let us go."

A moment later she found herself inside Xerxes's house, the warmth of the interior startling after the coolness atop the mountain. They stood in the entryway to his home, just beyond the courtyard. It was an impressive room, but unsettling, for it tricked the senses. The ceiling appeared to be one with the sky, the walls held the beauty of a misty rainbow, and beneath a clear floor was lush green an indeterminate distance below. In the center flowed a fire stream. Random flares of blue-hot flame burst from the stones beneath the water, while a red fire topped the green water, the two flowing together through the room. With a serpent's hiss, the walls shifted, erasing the doorways and sealing everyone in the room.

Her eyes were only for the man who waited on the opposite side of the fire stream.

Jack.

Her heart beat faster, and eagerly she drank in the sight of him. Oh, thank Solomon, he looked well. There was no lasting damages from her perfidy and Xerxes's *ma-at* that she could see. He looked well and healthy, despite his solemn demeanor.

None would mistake him for one of the djinn. He looked like a human. Blue-eyed, fair, rugged. His arms hung easily at his sides, and the crystal lay on his chest, glowing with a soft, steady yellow she'd never seen.

Powerful. The image was so undeniable that her breath stopped in her mouth. He stood so still, mastering his space with an air of confidence that had her almost believing there was a way out of this trap.

He looked not at Xerxes but at her. "Are you all right, Leila?"

"Yes." She held out her hands, a silent entreaty for understanding. "Jack, I am so sorry I did not believe you. I was wrong."

"You thought you were helping a friend. Can I blame you for having a generous heart?"

She stared at him, startled. He had forgiven the unforgivable?

"I hope you will always tell me when you think I'm wrong." He laid a hand on his chest, and his lips lifted in a faint grin. "Although in the future, you could choose a less painful method." Mistrock, perched on Jack's shoulder, added a scolding chirp as well.

"You brought Mistrock?" she asked, stunned that he would speak of the future.

"I tried to leave it behind, but the stubborn cuss wouldn't stay." Jack reached up and gave the *grucheek* an affectionate pat.

"You should not have come here. I love you. Revenge against him is not worth the danger to yourself."

"I did not come for Xerxes," he said softly. "I came for you."

She stared at him, her blood rushing so loud against her ears that she thought she had misheard. He had come for her?

And in that instant she knew he loved her. She might never hear the words from him; Jack Montgomery did not speak with flowery phrases. But his love was there in his actions.

"Enough." Xerxes interrupted their brief exchange with a wave. A comfortable chair appeared, and he stood adorned in robes of deep purple. He sat, throwing the ends of the robe back with a graceful swish. "The Scientist and I have other matters to discuss now. Matters of *ma-at* and magic. Come, my enchantress, sit beside me. I think this will interest you, as well."

Xerxes waved a hand again, and the chair elongated, undulating like a snake uncoiling from sleep. Leila tried to resist, but his stronger *ma-at* pulled her onto the chair beside him. With a warm, deceiving smile, he brushed her hair off her shoulder, then caressed the length of it in an intimate gesture.

341

"Let go of her," Jack said. He didn't raise his voice; he didn't need to.

"I have no desire to do so." Xerxes stroked her again.

Leila fought against his hold, her increased power strengthening the flow from Kaf. She drew on reserves she'd never tapped, never knew existed, and then—

She did it! She broke the invisible bond that held her! Oh, the surprised look on Xerxes's face as she scrambled to her feet, free of him.

His surprise changed to anger. A moment later his *ma-at* slapped against her, stronger than she had ever felt before. Though nothing changed in her body, her bones felt as though they had turned to mud, too soft to hold her weight, and she dropped limply back to the chair.

Bitterness coated her throat. She was strong, but not strong enough to defeat Xerxes. He had made sure of that.

"That's better, my pet." Xerxes stroked her cheek, then gave her a kiss. She could stop neither.

"Let her go." Jack rushed forward.

"Stop!" she shouted. "The fire stream!"

He paused, one foot poised to enter the river of fire and water. "It won't hurt me. I can repel his *ma-at*. You know that. He knows it, too."

"The fire stream is not *ma-at*. It is natural on Kaf." Fear for him made her words abrupt. "Move back before a spurting flame catches your foot. Please."

He set his foot down on the clear floor. As if to punctuate her warning, a flame shot up just where he had been ready to step. Had the eruption hit him, it would have charred his leg.

"And to think that, because a fire stream is not of *ma-at*, I almost omitted it from the decor," Xerxes said cheerfully. "How fortunate I admired the juxtaposition of water and fire enough to overcome my reluctance."

His hand stroked down her back, and she saw Jack's jaw tighten.

This was why Xerxes had brought her and kept her, she realized. She was to be used as a pawn to force Jack to cooperate with whatever schemes the djinni had planned. Xerxes could not use Jack directly; his *ma-at* could not force the Scientist to do anything. But she did not have the same defenses.

Through her, Xerxes would control Jack.

Leila set her jaw. She would not allow such an abomination to happen. Somehow, whatever she must do, she would stop Xerxes from using her like that. Jack would not be forced to submit to the *ma-at*.

Chapter Twenty

Jack burned hotter than the fire stream scorching his skin. Somehow, regardless of the danger, he would cross that inferno. To stop Xerxes's touch on Leila. To protect, to claim. To hear again the words *I love you*.

When she struggled against the power of the djinni, almost succeeded, then failed, his heart swelled with pride at her spirit and he began a covert study of the stream, gauging its width, the timing of its explosions. Only the sure knowledge that he couldn't reach her in time, that he couldn't envelop her in his protection before Xerxes would retaliate, kept him on the other side. Until Leila was protected by the talisman, he would have to bide his time.

Xerxes leaned forward. "Leila has been well occupied while we waited for you, Scientist."

Fury licked deep with the sordid insinuation. Jack

clenched his fists, forcing himself to wait.

"It is not as he intimates," Leila interjected.

"No?" Xerxes smiled and fingered the dress she wore. "I have given her what her heart desires most. Power."

"My heart's desire lies elsewhere now," she answered softly.

"Ah, Leila, you used to be fun. Now you grow tiresome." He looked at Jack. "You will find her much more talented. Does that bother you?"

"No. Her *ma-at* is part of her." Jack turned a questioning eye toward Leila, ignoring the taunting djinni. When he'd first come in, his concern was for her well-being and safety. He'd been so relieved to see her that he'd looked no deeper.

Now he did. There was a radiance about her, a radiance he'd seen when they'd first entered the djinn village. The radiance that came with the return of her *ma-at*. It shone from her skin and in the deep dark of her eyes. It gleamed in her hair and the arch of her manicured brows.

"You have your *ma-at* still?" he asked her, his heart swelling.

"Yes."

At least he had not taken that from her again. "Stronger?"

"Yes."

Although she could speak, her body seemed unnaturally still. Xerxes, he suspected, kept her under some kind of spell. He forced back the anger again; retribution would come later.

"Now, Scientist, I would talk of your talisman." Xerxes leaned back in his chair. "This is the source of your strange power? The power to negate *ma-at*?"

So the game began. Even as his gut clenched with fear, Jack's mind raced, sorting through various plans to get the talisman to Leila. "Yes."

"Jack, you don't have to answer him. Don't tell him."

"Silence." Xerxes held out his hand. Yellow light glowed from his palm, and a heartbeat later Leila stiffened, breath stopped, eyes rolled back.

"Don't!" Jack demanded. "Ask me what you want to know."

The yellow glow faded, and Leila drew in a shuddering breath. He saw the misery in her eyes, the heart-wrenching knowledge of how she was used.

Jack clenched his fists. *Don't, Leila. Don't blame yourself. Only Xerxes.*

Xerxes settled back on his chair. "How does it work?"

"I designed it as a personal protection against the power of *ma-at*." He answered the question easily, shortly.

"Personal protection? Do the wires work only for you?"

"No. They should disrupt the *ma-at* for anyone who wears them."

"Then it occurs to me, I do not need you. Give me the wires."

Jack hesitated and glanced at Leila. She was utterly still, but her eyes gave her away. She was looking, thinking, seeking a way to escape. Would she think of what he could offer—the protection of science? Would she be able to get it?

It would not do, however, to seem so ready to toss away his only power. He gave Leila one last look, telling her as best he could of his love, trying to relay his plan.

Xerxes stood. "Toss the talisman over the fire stream."

"No." Jack braced himself, his gut knotting. He had never been a convincing liar, never showed any talent for the stage, but now he had to convince Xerxes that the talisman was his only protection.

"I am not accustomed to refusal, human." Xerxes held out a hand, palm up.

"I cannot give it up," Jack answered with gritted teeth. *Oh, Leila, forgive me for this.*

"Perhaps I can convince you." Xerxes closed his fist with a snap.

Leila jerked backward with a sharp cry. Her chest heaved as she sought to find the air denied her.

"Stop!" Jack shouted hoarsely, barely able to speak for fear. Iron bands squeezed his stomach. "Don't. Let her go. I'll give you the chain."

Xerxes smiled, then flicked his wrist. Leila slumped back, drawing gulping breaths.

"Deny him, Jack." Her words were faint. "You will be free."

"The talisman," Xerxes repeated, glaring at Leila, his hand uplifted.

With a show of reluctance, Jack removed the chain.

His fingers clutched tight the familiar metal; then, with a determined set to his chin, he threw the talisman across the fire stream, directly toward Leila.

Damn! Xerxes deftly intercepted the toss.

"Power courses through it," he mused.

"It's called electricity. Like lightning."

"In time, you will tell me all about this Terran magic." Eagerly the djinni slipped the chain over his head. At once he screamed in agony, clawing at his chest.

Jack stared, rooted in astonishment. The talisman was attacking Xerxes?

No, it attacked Xerxes's *ma-at*. External or internal, the crystal couldn't distinguish between the two. Like an antibody-antigen reaction in a human, he realized. Helpful in fighting an outside invader, like a virus or bacteria, but devastating when misdirected. On a djinni, the device acted like an autoimmune disease, which turned the body's defenses on itself.

"It disrupts *ma-at*," Jack repeated softly. "Protects the wearer against any *ma-at*, even his own."

It would do the same to Leila. Especially with her increased *ma-at*.

She could not wear the talisman.

Defeat pounded against him, in his chest and in his throat. He could not protect her. And if he could not protect her, he would not stand against Xerxes.

With a string of curses, Xerxes grabbed the loop of wires from his throat and flung it down. His arm shot forward, and a heart-stopping blow of pain slammed toward Jack.

348

Slammed against the Charm of Abregaza and stopped.

Xerxes's eyes narrowed. "You are protected by *ma-at*?"

"By Earth magic." Damn, he hadn't wanted Xerxes to know, but the retaliation happened so fast, he hadn't had time to prepare and the charm had acted automatically.

"Untouchable, hmm? But she is not." Xerxes spun toward Leila, hand upraised.

"No!" shouted Jack. "Use me!"

Xerxes stared at him, hand poised. "How?"

His insides churned with fear for Leila even as his mind sought options. He had to bring Xerxes's attention back to him and give the djinni a reason to keep them alive. "The Charm of Abregaza. I can choose to let *ma-at* work on me. Let her go, and I will let you do whatever you want with me."

"I do not think this is a bargain you will keep." He turned back to Leila.

"The talisman offers power," Jack shot back.

"Useless personal protection."

"No, the talisman contains more. Ask Leila. I took her *ma-at* from her when we first met."

"Is this true?"

Leila glanced at Jack, then back at Xerxes. "It is."

"But only I can wield it. Do not hurt Leila, and I will do whatever you ask of me." He held his breath. All his life, Xerxes had craved power. Would he be able to turn from the temptation of this offer?

"I need proof that you submit to my will." He

rubbed a finger against his chin, then said casually, "Take away the *ma-at* from Leila."

Jack shook his head.

Xerxes raised a hand toward Leila. "You defy me already?"

"Leila's not part of the equation. I won't hurt her. This is between you and me. Test me." Jack held his breath, hoping Xerxes would turn away from Leila, that he would prefer the human as the current vent for his revenge.

"Yes, this matter is between us." Xerxes's upraised hand pointed toward Jack as he accepted the challenge. "This is my command, and if you want Leila to live, you have had your single moment of defiance. Accept my *ma-at* and what it can do. Accept this."

Ma-at slammed against Jack, bringing a searing pain, and he forced himself to accept it. He collapsed to the floor, curled in agony as hot needles scraped every nerve.

Don't resist, he told himself. *Let* ma-at *work on you. Accept.* His heart slowed, too slow. Each pulse resounded in his ears, accompanied by throbs of pain. A beat. A beat. A beat. Pain and pulse. Mistrock rumbled, not loud but so close it overlaid all. Rumble, rumble to the timing of the heartbeat, the *grucheek* kept him aware.

He heard Leila shout, felt her work against Xerxes, for the killing pain lessened. His blood raced, his heart pounded, replenishing the oxygen. For a few precious moments until Xerxes repelled Leila's counterspell.

A beat. Pain. Pause. Pain. A beat. Every survival

instinct screamed for release. Unresisting, he submitted and allowed *ma-at* entrance. *Ma-at* was not evil, only this one who wielded it.

"Now stop me with the Charm." Xerxes increased the power and the pain. "If you can."

He couldn't respond, not at first. Couldn't get his mind to move from endure to resist. At last he gasped out the words. "I do not want this."

As abruptly as it came, the deadly agony withdrew. He pulled to his knees, head bowed, gasping for breath. Irregular pulse straightened to an even, rapid beat. His whole body ached as though he'd been battered with a cudgel, and nerves and muscles shook like a terrified puppy. He braced his hands against the clear, cold floor.

Endure. Jack fought the mind-numbing exhaustion. *Bide your time.* Xerxes *would* be stopped.

He heard Xerxes chuckle. "So, human, she means that much to you."

Agony swept over Leila as she watched the man she loved kneeling and suffering. Because of her.

"You will disrupt whatever *ma-at* I ask," Xerxes demanded of Jack.

"Yes, if it works against me, I can," Jack answered.

"I'm sure we can arrange that."

Her gut knotted; her body felt numb with denial. No! He could not. He could not allow himself to be used like this. The cursed demands would be a slow death for the Scientist.

She looked around frantically. It was because of her.

If she were gone, Xerxes would have no hold over Jack.

So far, she had been unable to extricate herself. She had been unable to directly attack Xerxes. She had been unable to open one of the doors and flee for help.

The fire stream? Jump in? Her death would take her beyond Xerxes's power. And beyond Jack's love. Everything in her recoiled at the thought of killing herself. She wanted life. She wanted Jack. She was not ready for death, not until all hope was removed.

She swallowed back sheer terror. If her death was the only way for Jack to live, then so be it, but there had to be another way. She was not ready to concede defeat to Xerxes.

The talisman. She looked at it again, lying on the floor at her feet. The crystal still glowed within the mesh of wires.

Her gaze spun to Jack. Xerxes had lifted him and was bringing him across the fire stream. The talisman was their one hope. Jack had intended it for her; that was why he had accepted the Charm of Abregaza, she realized. He had thought to protect her with science, while magic guarded him.

Then Xerxes had worn the talisman. What had Jack said about the power in it? That it would repel the *ma-at* of whoever wore it? If she put it on, it would repel her own new sweet power, drive it away. She would be without *ma-at* once again, perhaps forever. But the power would also negate Xerxes's vile threats against her, freeing Jack.

The choice was easy.

If only she could reach the wires. But her bones still felt like mud. She struggled, sliding down the edge of the chair. It was still out of reach. She couldn't move away from the chair.

A low, grating chirrup sounded. Mistrock? Jack was on this side of the fire stream now, swaying before Xerxes. Mistrock must have dropped from its perch on Jack's shoulder.

She tried to shift closer to the talisman, hoping Mistrock would see what she needed before Xerxes's attention returned to her. The little *grucheek* skittered out from beneath the chair. Its rocky body hit against the crystal and shoved it forward. Slowly the creature nudged the chain against her waist.

Now how to get the chain on? Mistrock slid across her arm, its rocky body a comforting roughness in the smooth room. Small talons appeared, and it pulled the chain up, scraped across her arm, and settled the chain into its proper place.

At once she felt its power. Xerxes's stasis spell thinned. She could move her hands. Ignoring the crawling sensation as the electricity moved across her, she reached for the chain and slipped it over her head.

The crystal glowed, bright red.

Xerxes's *ma-at* disappeared.

Leila bent over in agony. Snakes. A multitude of snakes writhed inside and attacked her soul. The electricity slithered over her. Each thread severed was an agonizing, wrenching loss. Pain shot up her muscles. Her nerves burned. Every sinew felt shredded. Everything in her, every survival instinct, screamed at her. Rip off the crystal.

Her jaw clenched. *Solomon, give me strength.*

Mistrock settled on her shoulder, and its comforting grate sounded in her ear. She raised tortured eyes to her love. For Jack's sake. For Jack, she would endure. Endure. She pushed to her feet, no longer held in place by Xerxes.

I have the talisman.

Jack spun at the voice in his head. Leila! Her face was contorted in agony as she allowed the crystal to rip away her *ma-at.* "Leila, no!"

"It is the only way. Do what you must." She gave a strangled laugh. "With haste, my love."

Jack spun back to Xerxes, throwing off the band of fire the djinni had wrapped around his throat. He grabbed Xerxes's wrists. "No, you bastard."

"What?" Xerxes cried, astonished. The djinni tried to pull away, but Jack, honed by years of physical challenge, was stronger.

Desperately the djinni called on darker forces. Forces of destruction and shadow and death. Overwhelming forces. Forces that hit against the Charm of Abregaza and died.

But the Charm was passive, a mere shield. He couldn't draw on it, expand on it. Sweat coated his hands, but he gripped harder. Only the Charm and the contact kept Xerxes from transporting away, but the impasse could not last much longer.

"If *ma-at* does not work, then let the power of Kaf destroy you," Xerxes snarled.

From the corner of his eye, Jack saw the fire stream divert and edge toward him and Leila. No charm would protect them against those natural, scorching flames.

Suddenly he felt sweet heat at his back, and he inhaled the scent of clover. The crystal, still around Leila's neck, was draped over his shoulder. Rejuvenated power shot through him. He blinked and cleared his vision. Leila's hands were above his, helping him grip Xerxes. The crystal throbbed a bright red in time with his pulse, like the arterial blood of his heart.

Leila. Leila stood at his back, surrounded him with her arms and her love, shared with him the strength of the crystal even as it ripped the *ma-at* from her.

Mind to mind, power to power. The crystal drew the primal forces from deep within him, while Jack shaped and directed them. Repel. Negate. Spread. Sever. Sweat coated him, dripped in his eyes, blinded him. His muscles shook, but he kept his grip on Xerxes. The djinni struggled, drawing the fire stream closer with his *ma-at*, spewing poison for his release.

Lightning shot through Jack, racing along nerve and sinew. The crystal grabbed mind and will to defeat his enemy. Cut the *ma-at*. Do not give in.

"For us, my love," whispered Leila.

Grumble, grumble, the rock on her shoulder grated.

"For us." The sweet scent of clover surrounded Jack.

With mind and soul and love, he pulled it all in. The power, the force. With a mighty roar, he blasted outward all he had. The negating power careened through the crystal and through the hands that connected him to Xerxes.

Negate evil. Destroy *ma-at*.

Wind whipped around him so hard he staggered to keep upright. Wild, whistling, hot wind spun upward in a tornado, then blasted outward. The doors of the room were flung open. With a howl of release, the wind exploded out, escaping to the freedom of Kaf.

Screams. From Leila. From Xerxes. Sweat-slicked hands could hold on no longer. Xerxes stumbled back from his grip. Leila dropped to the floor.

A deadly silence settled in the room, and utter stillness filled the air.

Chapter Twenty-one

Slowly Jack's vision cleared, and he looked around, dazed. The walls, the floor, the ceiling had all vanished. All that was left was the fire stream and the rocks. His ears once more picked up the vibrations of sound, and for a moment he wished the deafness had continued.

"What have you done, human?" Xerxes's voice shouted venomously. "Die. You will die after a thousand torments leave you begging." His hands shot out.

Nothing happened.

"Suffer, Leila."

Nothing again. He spun around, chanting wildly, then stared in horror at his hands. They were shriveled and mottled, as though a veneer had been stripped off to reveal the poison beneath. He ripped open the gaudy shirt. The tablet at his throat was colorless.

Xerxes crumpled. He dropped to his knees, sobbing and rocking blindly. "Gone. Gone. Gone," he whispered in a mindless chant. "Gone, gone, gone, gone."

Xerxes no longer concerned Jack. Instead, he knelt and tenderly lifted Leila into his arms. He felt for a carotid pulse, and a cleansing relief washed over him. Strong, steady. She lived. But at what cost?

She stirred with a soft sigh; and her eyelids fluttered open. Her gaze darted around. "Xerxes? Is he—?"

"There."

Leila studied him a moment; then her chin lifted. "He is not handling the loss of his *ma-at* as well as I did."

Jack chuckled, her resiliency astounding him as always; then the smile faded. "Your *ma-at*?"

"Gone," she answered simply.

He hugged her tightly, tears rolling down his cheeks for the first time. "Oh, Leila, I am so sorry. Can you forgive me for taking it again?"

She pulled back a little to lay a hand on his cheek. "You did not take; I gave willingly, my love. For I have found something better."

"It's temporary. Like the last time." Desperately he ignored the shake of her head. "There might be something in the scrolls of Xerxes. Or Darius—"

She cut him off with a finger to his lips. "I think the severing is permanent."

Slowly, as though movement pained her, she took the chain off and slipped it over his head. The red of the crystals sparkled with rainbow hues. There was a red mark on her throat, as if the wires had burned her.

What convinced him, however, was the infinite sadess in her voice.

Still, he resolved, he would not stop trying to find a way to restore what she'd lost. Holding her close, he kissed her neck. "I love you, Leila. With or without your *ma-at*, I love you."

"And after I brought you such troubles."

"Maybe, but you have filled my life with a joy I've never known and never expected." His arms tightened. "As soon as you are strong enough, we'll get married."

To his surprise, she drew back. "No."

No? He swore. "Because I took your *ma-at*. I know that's pretty damn unforgivable."

"No, you have forgiven me, too. I do not want you to marry me out of duty, Jack, because I know I do not carry your child. Nor do I want you to marry me out of pity or guilt." Her chin lifted. "I have survived with little and with no *ma-at*. I shall again."

"Pity?" he exclaimed. "Hell, no. I want to marry you, or unite with you, or become your *zani*, whatever you call it, because you've got me so tied up in knots that I'll never get free."

Her eyes narrowed. "That is not a very romantic declaration, Scientist."

For the umpteenth time since he'd met Leila, he wished he had the gift of words. He eyed her, trying to judge what to say. Damn, she was so beautiful, inside and out. To hell with words. He worked better with actions anyway.

He drew her closer and kissed her. At first the kiss was gentle, seeking her acceptance. When at last she gave a soft sigh and settled in his arms, when she opened her mouth to his probing tongue, a primitive joy leaped through him.

She was his.

He deepened the kiss, pulled her body flush against him, curve to hollow, soft to hard. Her fingers tunneled through his hair, and desire sparked between them, rising with a hot healing that burned away sorrow and pain, left only pleasure and love.

There were no colors dancing in the air, no visible sparkle of djinn emotions. He didn't need that. His heart, her response, told him all he needed to know.

Need demanded release, but he refused the enchanting temptation. "No," he whispered. "Not here. Not in this place."

She gave a soft sigh, leaning her forehead against his chest. "Later," she agreed.

Mistrock sidled over to them. Jack gave the *grucheek* a pet under its fissure-gills, then set it on his shoulder. It rumbled happily between the two of them.

Jack stroked Leila's hair, allowing his blood to cool. "This is why I want to marry you, Leila. Because I love you. *T'dost mi dara. Frasho.* I love your mind, your soul, your laughter, your concern, your generosity, your curiosity. You. Will you marry me? But say yes only if you love me like that, too."

She raised her dark-eyed gaze to his. A whirlwind blew her hair about her, but Jack paid it no mind. He had eyes only for Leila, for the joy he saw reflected in her face.

"Who said you did not have words?" she teased.

"Answer, Leila."

"Yes."

Jack let out a pent-up breath, suddenly so light-headed he thought he might be able to transport all by himself. "Good."

"Good? That's all you can say?"

He laughed, laying his cheek on her sleek head. "Good. Great. Tremendous. Stupendous. Mind-boggling. Magical."

"All right, you have convinced me."

"Excellent." He kissed her temple. "You've given up so much; I won't ask you to give up your home."

She touched his cheek. "You would do that? Live in a world of *ma-at*? For me?"

He swallowed hard. "Yes." And the answer wasn't as difficult as it would have been yesterday.

"No." The melodious male voice came from behind him.

Leila's eyes widened. "Darius?"

He twisted to see his brother-in-law standing with crossed arms, a frown on his face. Jack's sister was beside him, glaring at her *zani*. He got to his feet, wincing at the ache in his muscles.

"Darius, what do you mean, he can't live on Kaf?" Isis demanded. "He's my brother."

"He may be family, but he's also a dangerous man." Darius glanced around at Xerxes and the emptiness surrounding them.

"You might want to take steps to contain him," Jack said, nodding toward Xerxes.

"I already have."

"I don't know if the reversal is permanent, and when the shock wears off—"

"He will not practice his dangerous craft again," Darius said. With a wave of his hand, Xerxes disappeared, taken someplace known only to the Protector.

Jack felt Leila shiver and he, too, stepped back from the cold, implacable note in Darius's voice. For a moment, he was heartily glad he had never truly angered the djinni.

Darius's glance swept back to the two of them. "As Protector, Jack, I cannot allow you to stay. Leila may."

"Darius, no," Isis protested.

Jack faced the djinni. "I understand, but you have to understand something, too. I will not leave Leila."

Leila laced her fingers through his. "I will live on Terra."

He turned a startled glance to her. "Are you sure?"

She nodded. "There's nothing to keep me here. And everything there. All I ask is that you love me and find me a place where I can garden."

"My home has a riotous garden."

Before Jack could blink, Darius was beside them. He laid a hand on Leila's shoulder. "Can you do this? I feel no *ma-at* in you. You cannot transport. You know that djinn must renew their bonds to Kaf frequently. We cannot survive on another world without that renewal. How will you get back?"

"I don't think I need to, Darius. I have no bonds to renew."

Jack saw the Protector's hand tighten on Leila's shoulder. "If you are sure," Darius said.

"I am."

"Still, I will return to you until we know there is no danger."

"Thank you."

Darius stepped back and turned a fierce look on Jack. "Take care of her, Jack. Or you will have me to answer to."

Jack wrapped an arm around his *zaniya*-to-be. "I don't need threats to do that." He stared at Darius until at last the djinni stepped back.

Jack turned his attention to his sister.

With a deep breath, Isis took Darius's place. She held out a hand to Leila. "Welcome to the Montgomery family."

Leila hesitated only a moment, then took the proffered hand. "Thank you."

"I have to warn you about Montgomery men. They tend to be an overprotective lot. Without me, my brothers are going to transfer all those macho instincts onto you."

Leila gave her a quick grin. "I believe I can manage."

Isis laughed. "Oh, are you going to be a surprise for them."

Jack relaxed. Isis had made the initial gesture of friendship, and Leila had accepted.

Isis gave him a hug and a kiss. "Don't you ever do anything to scare me like that again, Jack Montgomery. I have to get Jessamine now, but I'll come visit you soon."

A moment later she disappeared in the whirlwind of transport.

"Are you ready to go?" he asked Leila.

She nodded, then glanced at his shoulder. She tickled Mistrock. "I shall miss you."

The *grucheek* gave a grating noise, and Jack felt the talons of its feet tangle in his shirt as it glued itself firmly in place.

"Mistrock," said Jack. "We're going to Terra."

Grumble-purr. More glue.

"You can't come with us."

Grumble-purr. More glue.

"It is not a creature of *ma-at*, so it can survive in Terra," Darius observed. "And it seems quite taken with travel."

"Then I guess we've got a pet." Jack smiled and gave the rock an affectionate tickle.

"Where would you go?" asked Darius, gripping them by the arm.

"To Leila's home."

"No," she corrected. "To *our* new home. I'll get my belongings later."

A moment later the whirlwind of transport descended on Jack, and he felt the slide of movement. He'd felt it only once before, but it was a sensation never forgotten. A sensation he now accepted without fear. With a stomach-whirling twist, the motion stopped, and they all three stood in the hot, humid night air of New Orleans.

For a moment, disorientation shook Jack. The sounds, the humidity, the lights, the air—all seemed so foreign. Then he recognized the garden of his Aunt Tildy's house, a place Darius had been before.

"Are you close to your home?" the djinni asked.

"Yes. We can walk from here."

Darius gave Leila a kiss on the cheek. "I shall be back." Then he left.

Leila looked around the place where she stood. It was noisier than she'd expected. There was much moisture in the air. Yet she smelled a sweet flower blooming in the night, and the heat was a welcome companion. And when Jack wrapped his arm around her and kissed her, she knew all was well. Things would be different, but they would still be good.

Mistrock gave a loud, excited rumble, slid down Jack's shirt, and disappeared into the lush under-growth.

They two of them stared in amazement, then burst out laughing. "It appears your Aunt Tildy has a new companion," said Leila.

They had a short walk to Jack's house. Nondescript outside with a profusion of plants and ivy covering the exterior, it was a joy on the inside. During the brief moments she'd spent here when they had first met, she had noticed little but him. Now she delighted in the smooth wooden floors and open spaces. There were soft fabrics on the walls, all kinds of interesting artifacts, a clean scent of citrus.

"I have always liked lemons," she said.

"Does that mean you like my house?"

She smiled at him. "I love it."

"Do you want a tour? It will be brief."

She leaned forward and gave him a kiss. "Not brief enough."

"You could use some aloe on your neck."

"No, what I could use most is a pillow. Tend to those needs first, my Scientist."

Jack laughed, picked her up, and carried her into the bedroom.

She wrapped her arms around his shoulders, drawing him with her as he laid her on the soft down of his bed. "Ah, Jack, I do love you."

"*T'dost mi dara*," Jack whispered in return.

"I have another request," she said, playing with the neck of his shirt.

"Demanding woman."

"I still want a child."

He kissed her, delicately and with promise. "So do I. With you." Then his lips tilted up in a playful smile. "I suggest we get started on the project right away."

"Djinn are not very fertile."

"If no child comes, then it doesn't, Leila. I will still love you."

"It may take a lot of trying," she warned, grinning.

"Most definitely."

Only moments later, her diamond-thread robe lay on the floor beside his pants and shirt. As Jack kissed her, she sank into the down covering.

There were no sparks in the air, only sparks in her heart and body. And when he came into her, it was like the first time, new and fresh. Jack Montgomery enchanted her with his own touch of magic upon her.

Afterward, her skin still tingling, her body relaxed

and sated, Jack snuggled up at her back. Soon she heard the even tempo of his breathing as he slept.

She was unable to find sleep so quickly. Though her body was satisfied, her mind sought all the wonders of her new home. She opened her eyes. Moonlight filtered into the open window, and outside she could see thick leaves and vines. He had said he had a garden.

Suddenly she needed to see this riot of plants in her new home, to feel the soil beneath her bare feet. She slipped from the bed and found the door to the garden. The night was warm, as hot as it was on Kaf, but the moisture gave the night air a strange feel. She liked it, she decided. Liked the idea that water was all around her.

The garden was beautiful, thick, and lush. She drew in a deep breath and smelled flowers. It would be fun to learn their names and nurture this patch of beauty. And there in the center—was that a fountain? Oh, it could not be more perfect.

She went to the fountain and sat in the soft grass beside the stone basin. It was decorated, she realized, with waves and runes like the ones Jack had incorporated into the wires of his talisman. The water rose in a graceful central column, then flowed down from level to level in a soothing song.

"My Aunt Tildy helped me design this," Jack said, coming up behind her.

"The fountain or the garden?"

"The garden. The fountain she found. She insisted I needed to put it smack in the center." He settled down beside her and wrapped his arms around her.

"I'm sorry, I didn't mean to wake you."

"You didn't."

She reached out to the fountain, curious about it, drawn to it. Her hand hovered above it for a moment.

"Go ahead," Jack urged. "Put your hand in the water. I always do."

She did, and at once she felt the flow, the connection, the power. Different, very different, but . . . oh, it was clean and sweet.

Startled, Leila gasped and jerked her hand out of the water.

"What?" demanded Jack. "What is it?"

Leila shook her head, then stuck her finger in the water again. Again it came, that faint flow of energy, like the course of a sweet stream emerging from the fresh scent of earth. It touched inside her with beautiful harmony, then settled into her heart and mind. So perfect, so . . . right.

"Magic," she whispered.

Jack sat up. "*Ma-at?* Your *ma-at* is back?"

She shook her head, almost too awed to speak. "Not *ma-at*. Magic. The connections of water and earth. The connections of Terra. I felt them." She raised awestruck eyes to him. "I felt the magic. And it's strong, Jack, it's strong in me. I can *feel* it." She swished her hand through the water. "With each touch it grows stronger. Jack, my bonds are to water and earth, not fire and air. That's why I was weak on Kaf. My connections are here. I have magic." Suddenly she tensed and threw him a worried glance. "If I have magic—"

His arms tightened around her with fierce protectiveness. "I will still love you. I can accept your magic, Leila, and I can rejoice in it because you do. Show me your magic, Leila. Enchant me."

"Oh, Jack, I love you." She leaned over, and as she did a moonbeam played across the surface of the water. Her breath drew in with sharp surprise.

A cloud passed across, and then left, leaving only the silvery moonbeam and the still water's surface. And the image reflected within.

There, in the divination water, she saw a child. A blond boy with dark eyes.

Her hand fluttered to her belly. "I see him," she whispered.

"Who?" Jack glanced around. "Where?"

She pointed to the water. "Our child. In the waters of divination. Tonight, Jack, we have conceived our child. A child of Terra. A child of science and magic."

He kissed her temple. "A child of love."

More Than Magic

Kathleen Nance

Darius is as beautiful, as mesmerizing, as dangerous as a man can be. His dark, star-kissed eyes promise exquisite joys, yet it is common knowledge he has no intention of taking a wife. Ever. Sex and sensuality will never ensnare Darius, for he is their master. But magic can. Knowledge of his true name will give a mortal woman power over the arrogant djinni, and an age-old enemy has carefully baited the trap. Alluring yet innocent, Isis Montgomery will snare his attention, and the spell she's been given will bind him to her. But who can control a force that is even more than magic?

__52299-3 $5.99 US/$6.99 CAN

KATHLEEN NANCE

THE WARRIOR

Callie Gabriel, a fiercely independent vegetarian chef, manages her own restaurant and stars in a cooking show with a devoted following. Though she knows men only lead to heartache, she can't help wanting to break through Armond Marceux's veneer of casual elegance to the primal desires that lurk beneath.

Armond returns from an undercover FBI assignment a broken man, his memories stolen by the criminal he sought to bring in. His mind can't remember Callie or their night of wild lovemaking, but his body can never forget the feel of her curves against him. And even though Callie insists she doesn't need him, Armond needs her—for she is the key to stirring not only his memories, but also his passions.

___52417-1 $5.99 US/$6.99 CAN

THE TRICKSTER
KATHLEEN NANCE

Long after she's given up on his return, Matthew Mark Hennessy strolls back into Joy Taylor's life, bolder than Hermes when he stole Apollo's cattle. But Joy is no longer the girl who had so easily trusted him with her heart. An aspiring chef, she has no intention of being distracted by the fireworks the magician sparks in her. But with a kiss silkier than her custard cream, he melts away her defenses. And she knows the master showman has performed the greatest trick of all: setting her heart afire.

Mark has traveled to Louisiana to uncover the truth, not to rekindle an old passion. But Joy sets him sizzling. It is not her cooking that has him salivating, but the sway of her hips. And though magicians never divulge their secrets, Joy tempts him to confide his innermost desires. In a flash Mark realizes their passion is no illusion, but the magic of true love.

VIRTUAL WARRIOR

ANN LAWRENCE

Where does reality end and fantasy begin? With a computerized game that leads to another world? At the fingertips of a bedraggled old man who claims he can perform magic? Or in the amber gaze of an ice princess in dire need of rescuing? As the four moons of Tolemac rise upon a harsh land vastly different from his own, hard-headed pragmatist Neil Scott discovers a life worth struggling for, principles worth fighting for. But only one woman can convince him that love is worth dying for, that he must make the leap of faith to become a virtual warrior.
